WITHDRAWN

Cover by **Michael**

Acknowledgments

PACM respect always to the brothers, sisters and elders. To the creator known by many names and all of those who fight against injustice. To the organisations and community groups. Let freedom reign.

Rest in peace Baba John Henrik Clarke
Rest in peace Baba Amos Wilson
Rest in peace Baba Kwame Ture
Rest in peace Endugu Tony Francis.
This is for you. Let your spirit live for ever.

Preface

This book is dedicated to the reader, may you leave this world in a better state than you found it.

'All that is necessary for evil to flourish is for good people to do nothing' (MLK).

About the Author

Onyeka is one of the foremost, controversial Black writers to have been born in the U.K. Controversial, because he tells it how it is. "Stories," Onyeka, says, "are the foundation of a culture. We have forgotten to tell stories and tell them well and because we have, they will be lost in time. But a people like a history are strong by their memories. We can quote the Book of Coming Forth by Day and Night, but we don't know what happened on our street five, or ten, or fifty years ago. If we are unable to connect to recent history, how can we connect to the ancients."

Onyeka born and lived most of his life in a small island in the Atlantic ocean known as England, spent the early part in institutions of intellectual indoctrination - producing severe psychological strain on himself and fellow sufferers. The consequence from his contemporaries was to assimilate as quickly as possible, white women, white drugs, or to react, and by that reaction, to end up institutionalised again, i.e. prison, borstal.

He calls himself the most eligible, illegible bachelor in the country. People ask him: why aren't you married yet, you know children, happy families and he answers in riddles, almost evading the question - as he does, "this is no competition, I've got more to achieve before I bring children into this world." Perhaps he just wishes to distance himself from being stereo-typed as a good black man. But he is and I believe - he knows he is.

Writing what he likes comes easy to him since he studies his subject well. By study he examines, and cuts through the image presented to reveal the inside - though the guts are stinking and foul. He says, "writing, should not be an exercise in masturbation, it should create something, so I write because of my activism, because I believe that black people must do for self."

Training within the law equips him to cut deep through the rhetoric, he is not one to be treated or taken lightly, beware imitators. As a literary activist, a writing pugilist, Onyeka doesn't mess about. I remember once in an interview he was asked, "do you think the world is really like how you paint it, is it really like this?" All Onyeka said, was, "are you calling me a liar?" The commentator looked at him with surprise, "what do you mean," she replied. "I mean," Onyeka said, "ignore me, hate me, or love me, but don't ever call me a liar!"

So there he is. It was about as much as I could get out of him, certainly more than he ever likes to reveal, perhaps he has secrets, then again perhaps he wants his work to stand for itself without embellishment. Make up your own mind. Enjoy.

Pepukyai

Introduction

So why read, why write? Hell why live!

Because we must.

They used to say if you want to hide something from a black man put it in a book, true or not the cliché is far too close to reality to be utterly ignored. Very strange it is that the people who founded some of the earliest learning institutions at Karnak, Alexandria, and Timbuktu, should now be **afraid** of books.

Yet the definition and the legacy of the times will be kept for whom can package reality. Even if in the future it is downloaded on to computers. Those who have been unable to master and record the history of a times, their history will be lost, or worst regurgitated by their oppressors. How can such a people deliver to the youth and following generations the story to inspire them to go forth and conquer the world? How shall they be equipped with the framework, the background through which to put the world in to context?

Perhaps we are afraid to tell a story, or our story, for fear that it will not show the world as the cosy place we were told it was by those who claim to be our leaders, as they look through their rose tinted spectacles.

No doubt they are afraid that fairy stories are better than the truth, even if it means living a lie. When everyone knows without truth, that life is not worth living anyway.

It has been a year now, since **Waiting to Explode**. To say I was surprised by the response would be an understatement. Some accused me of being a racist, an extremist, ill conceived, illiterate, unimaginative, stereotypical.

I have been told "you have so much to say, why don't you conform to the standards of novel writing which are expected." But I already told you last year, I write what I like.

The fact that the majority of Africans in this country still believe the nonsense, the simplistic nonsense, that is taught to children, that colour does not matter and race is not an issue. When quite plainly it is and it will remain, until we as a people change it.

More often than not the novels we write and the history we tell our people, is the disconnected foolishness, written in an abstract and vacuum. We seem oblivious to what other people think of us.

So the challenge was on, I did not produce a book for the scholars to look over and say, "Oh what an amazing book, Onyeka, you really are an up and coming talent." So I can be the endorsed radical alternative. If they do, that is their choice. I wrote so that everyone from the youth on the street can read, understand and visualise, picture themselves overcoming obstacles and succeeding. Winning against a bunch of corrupt locals in a pub in Waiting to Explode, or the whole world in the Black Prince.

So as I said before, read, understand, but above all do not forget. For it is the doom of mankind that we forget.

Onyeka

Farewell to innocence

When I was young everything was so beautiful, innocent....then they took me away and showed me a world that was ignorant, ridiculous, violent, cynical....

Welcome to the real World.

Welcome to your life. Come inside......

The Black Prince

The London Cat

The ghetto was an open, festering, maggot infested wound, on the fabric of respectable Britain. A black reality with a white framework, beautiful yet ugly. Honourable, noble and full of so many possibilities, yet cowardly and hopeless. Just and unjust, the great mingling with the small. There were more deceivers, dissemblers, liars, cheats, thieves, frauds, freaks, fakes, than a Government party conference. Muslims, Christians, escapists, realists, policemen, armchair revolutionaries, walked side by side, as if they were all the same. The living dead ruled, whilst the wide awake pretended to sleep, sharing each other's dreams.

Filth, filth, filth, heaped on the decaying, urban, city streets. Concrete filth, human filth, animal filth, filthy people with filthy minds living their filthy lives. Crisp packets, coke cans, biscuit wrappers, KFC boxes full of half consumed chicken pieces, the skin hanging rotten to the mouldy bones, dead flies laying maggots in the meat. Vomit, sick and urine still wet decorating the pavements. Puddles of blood like claret staining the grey concrete red like some huge Roman Amphitheatre after a fight, and preparing for another.

Fascists, Marxists, prudes, pimps and prostitutes jostled with each other for respectability. Virtuoso virgins sang for their supper. Musicians rich and poor busked, prostituting themselves. The well dressed, badly dressed, no dress, ramped and fronted. The back teeth, front teeth, gold teeth, fraudulently faked their way along the streets, what a shame they were in love with every colour under the rainbow except the one they were born with. Able disable bodied, disabled able bodies, the wrong people with the guns, in the wrong place, at the wrong time. The wrong people smiling, the wrong people dying, the wrong people crying, the wrong people lying to themselves, that what they see is not wrong, when it is. Cool Britannia so called multicultural Britain was all and none of these things.

A stray cat bounced across the road, its black tale in the air, fur shining through the grey blandness of South London. Black, sleek shining like he had been dipped in gloss paint, its vibrant body bristling. He bounced, the pads of his feet not even touching the grey concrete of the city streets. His claws gleaming white, retracted for a while, only to dart out again after each bounce like little pointed knives.

The cat bounced, over the filth, past the death, like he owned the world, like a leopard for the day and this was his jungle. His black pupils shining like burning coals in the furnace of his agile body. Prancing, until he pranced the streets of London into the shade. The light shone on his black, black, black-within-black fur.

A leopard for the day indeed!

Johnny the Vic

Johnny the Vic was smoking a cigarette like a SS nazi and stamping out the fag ends on his latest edition of Bulldog magazine entitled, "Rights for whites, keep Britain white, all right." In his beat up white Volvo he looked the ordinary everyday Fascist on his way back from murdering little children, raping women and torturing men. He rubbed his hands together like an ogre from a fairy story that has just eaten his fill of human flesh for the morning and is looking for an evening meal. "Cooar look at that!" he said, in a cockney accent, looking out of the window of his car at Jennifer walking down the street who from that distance looked completely naked.

"Cooar, that's a bit of all right, a bit of Ebony next to my Ivory. I could jam that bitch all day. You know what they say about coons," he said, turning his neck round to look at his mate Dave. "Those black bitches love white meat," he said, rubbing his white hands together yet again. "I never told you mate," he said, turning to Dave, "I shagged one before, outside the Rose and Crown on Old Kent Road, it was like shagging a black pig. Boy that cow was fat." Dave laughed, and giggled like a delinquent child, even Toni who had been sleeping woke up.

Dave looked out of the window at Jennifer who was wobbling in all the right places, at the wrong time - into a red brick building on their right, with a sign over the top reading, 'Polytechnic.'

"What's it like then?" Dave asked, inquiringly, "I mean with one of them."

"I tell you what son," Johnny said, rubbing the dandruff out of his hair and feeling his groin again, "give mea' an English rose any day, blacks, you know spades, is all right for the experience, but like Adolf said, he was right you know, he was bloody right, though he was a stinking kraut, he was right, when you mix with them, you're diluting your race. You see that's why you see so many of their men with our women, cause they know their lots finished and they want to take us down with them."

"You never said a true thing bud," Toni said, fully waking up and rubbing the sleep from his eyes, "I am sick and tired of seeing those niggers with our women."

"Phawwat, (farting) that's better," Johnny said, smiling, "I needed that."

"You dirty bastard," Dave mumbled, covering his mouth and nose with his hands.

"It must h've been that vindaloo from the dirty Indians." Johnny blabbered, wafting the air in front of his face, "Cooar it does sting though, I think I stained my pants."

"You smelly git," Dave shouted, "if this weren't your motor I'd have you like a coolie running by the side." They all laughed again, Johnny wiped the saliva from his mouth like a dog.

Between the insane ramblings, sexual innuendoes and flatulence you would have thought the three distinguished gentleman, loyal supporters of the flag and English patriots, would have remembered that they were in a car on a Monday morning in the middle of Elephant and Castle. It was only when Mr. Patel and family in his blue Austin Metro, newly washed and newly brought from Mad Mike's used car mart, beeped his horn. He had been waiting behind Johnny's Volvo for the last seven minutes hoping that he would notice the gap that had now occurred in front of his vehicle in the cue. How was Mr. Patel to know that these fine up standing men and servants of the crown were busy exercising there rights to abuse and ridicule at will.

So Mr. Patel in his best blue ironed suit and white shirt, newly trimmed mustache was not looking for trouble. He wanted to get his two darling daughters to school on time and get his wife to work in the hospital. (Ironic isn't it, hospital).

Mr. Patel beeped his horn again, and smiled back at his children with a fatherly expression. He saw for the last time without glasses the delicate familiar faces that he had worked so hard to protect and defend.

Johnny stopped in the midst of the laughter and scowled, "who the hells' that? You what," he said "you see that," pointing behind him for Dave to see. "There's a cheeky paki beeping his horn, Fucking hell," he shouted, working himself into a frenzy and clenching his fists like a mad man. "A curry eating Punjabi, a paki's beeping his horn at me. What the bloody hell is happening to this country. This is England. Fucking England."

"Calm down, calm down," Dave interrupted, "if you're going to do 'somefink' then do it, stop talking about it."

"As I was saying," Johnny said, "This is England, is it India, is it

Pakistan, is it what's that place called," scratching his head, "bloody, bloody".

"Sri laanka," Toni said.

"Yeah Sri 'Laanka,' is this bloody Sri Lanka. Na ....this is England," Johnny said with pride.

The Sun was trickling through the smog and concrete buildings, illuminating everything unnaturally. Johnny's precious Volvo car with the number plate smolded on, his coarse white face, unkempt, unclean, his yellow broken teeth and those deathly pale blue eyes, they all gleamed like a scene from a horror story.

Johnny wrenched the hand break on with the ferocity of an axe murderer putting in the last cut to his victim.

"Go on Johnny, do him," Toni shrieked, "kick his ass."

"Ja patti boy," Johnny muttered, under his breath, as he opened the door and stepped on to the road. A long line of traffic was now building up behind him of bleeping horns and irritated drivers. He brushed his brown hair from his face like a designer thug and strode confidently towards Mr. Patel's car. Mr. Patel looked at his wife's cheeks, large bosom and stubby brown fingers and wished that he had some young agile fighter with him instead of a fat wife that ate and spent too much.

Mr. Patel turned to his children hoping that one of them would turn into a road warrior to fight his battles for him. But they just smiled a serene smile, completely content that Daddy was going to rescue them. But Daddy was wondering how he was going to get out of this situation. When people threatened him before he paid for protection. Paying was not an issue, it was fighting he did not like. There was the cliché, Patel remembered it when he first came to England in the 1970's. It was said Asians cannot fight, they are good at making money but no good at fighting.

He remembered as a boy the skinheads coming waving sticks and shouting, "Ding Dong the bells are clapping, were goin' Paki bashing." The only thing he was thinking was to run away, but blacks would come, violence and some arrests. He would never forget the blacks. How they fought.

From that day on it had put an indelible mark in his mind. So the first time he got the chance he hired one to work in his shop.

'Jamaican Bob', as Patel called him had worked for him for over fifteen years and since the day he started, there had never been any trouble there, not one theft, robbery or violent incident in his shop. Despite the fact that it was on Peckham front line. Perhaps it was 'Jamaican Bob's' propensity for violence and complete hatred for anything that looked like him, which was the deterrent. After all Bob would have scarred the average maniac, with just his appearance, one eye, scars all over his face and hands like shovels, as ignorant as an ox and twice as coarse.

Jamaican Bob alias Robert Delroy Constantine protected Patel's untidy, smelly, little shop as if it was a palace. It did not matter that Patel sold cigarettes and alcohol to under age youth, so long as they paid in cash and did not cause any trouble. It did not matter that drug dealers used to sell cocaine, heroin and women under his very nose. So long as they did not affect his business. Mr. Patel's open till late shop in the heart of Peckham front line was a beacon for every sexual, drug dealing, deviant in the whole community.

In the morning Patel would have to step over some accomatised tramp, lying in his own urine and sick. Singing something in Jamaican patwa. The evening would come and yet another would be there, in the same condition, bleary eyed, motley skinned, stinking, with no self respect and no pride.

It was not that Patel disliked black people, though he underpaid Bob for all the work he did, told his children that if they ever married a black person he would kill them, and continued to operate business in an unscrupulous fashion poisoning the future youth of the community. No Patel was not a racist, even though the local community centre hoped that one day the shop would close down and stay closed for ever. Though the conscious youth whispered to each other that they wished it was his shop that had been fire bombed by the BNP and not the African Bookshop next door which had been educating black people for over thirty five years.

No Patel had friends in the local community, well he had one, that was Bob. Bob liked his boss. He liked the money he got any way. Though he knew Patel under paid him, he was grateful. Where else was a Black Ex British solider who had served 15 years for murder going to find work. There were young black graduates who had never been convicted of a criminal offence who had to wait in the unemployment line. Bob knew it.

So whilst he saw Patel bend the law, cheat, deceive, and exploit the local community, he just did his job. Sometimes he would go home just a little ashamed as he washed the blood of yet another black youth off his hands. He rubbed the soap in until his hands were raw and yet he still felt they were not clean. The sound of the blood trickling down the sink and the silent drop of the water in the basin, echoed in his empty flat. There were no other sounds, no wife to mop the blood and sweat from his tired forehead. No children to ask if, 'Daddy was okay.' Just the sound of the water. But Bob was not unhappy to be alone. After all he had whisky to drink and work in the morning.

But Bob was not in Patel's car that Monday morning in Elephant and Castle. It was just Mr. Patel, his fat wife and his two spoilt - but 'sweet' children. For once he was going to have to fight his own battles.

Johnny was already by the side of Patel's new Austin metro, when the shop keeper decided to step out. Perhaps he thought he could talk his way out of the situation, or pay him a few dollars, or it was some terrible nightmare he had imagined and he would wake up. He opened the latch of the door, pushing it open and placed his right foot gingerly on the road out side. He felt it almost slide on the tarmac beneath, like his small shiny brown shoes had been swallowed up by the road below. He felt dizzy, unstable, trying to stand up, the adrenaline running through his veins as fast as a deer being stalked by a hyena.

Patel could feel Johnny's, heat, the alcohol on his breath. Closer and closer like a steam train speeding down the track, his brown hair flying in the air and his eyes flashing demonically.

Patel was only half out of his car when Johnny reached him, "you cocky little coolie," Johnny shrieked, standing over him, "who the fu.....(the word got lost in his rage) do you think you are? Who do you think you are ! Eh, eh, what,... what.....what,.. do you think this is," staring down at him, his face scarlet with rage and sweat dripping from his head in beads.

Mr. Patel tried to get the energy to stand, but failed.

By now the line of traffic behind them had become a river of dis-contented drivers, all honking their horns and screaming abuse out of their windows, as the sun beamed down on their gleaming windscreens.

Johnny's head was glistening in the sun and his red cheeks seemed illuminated, almost excited by the event of stomping this little insect before him. He looked at Patel's chubby little round head, the soft, brown cheeks almost feminine, the pencil mustache and the unbroken row of white teeth.

Johnny looked up and down at the pudgy delicate frame, the short stubby fingers, he had talked enough, he walked over to him and grabbed him by the scruff of the neck, as one would a small child. Patel helpless, his legs wobbly like jelly, feeling himself passing out, he did not hear the screams of his children, or his wife, as Johnny began to beat him unmercifully, but the blood that ran from the punches to Patel's head did not satisfy Johnny, only to spur him on to future endeavours.

He grabbed Patel's little neck and then he stopped, like he was looking for a convenient place to put the shopkeeper's head. He smiled a sinister smile as he saw Patel's new blue bonnet on his new blue car. Lifting the little man almost off the ground he began to pound Patel's head into his car bonnet, until the blood ran down his arms in pools. Patel's body was like a rag doll, when Johnny decided to give his hysterical family the piece'd la resistance. Lifting the small motionless body, he picked him off the ground and smashed him into the windscreen, shattering glass on his wife and small children.

Johnny smirked to himself, with his arm still blood soaked and looked inside Patel's battered car. He walked over to the passenger door and saw for the first time Patel's two children. With a Reggie Kray smile he went over to the car door and went to open it. It was only the shouts of his mates in the car who had turned from one of adulation and praise for his 'workmanship,' to one of concern at the increasingly astonished and astounded audience which now surrounded them behind and on both sides of the pavement.

The cars had stopped honking their horns and some drivers had stepped out of their vehicles to see what all the shouting and screams from the women 'spectators' were all about. Johnny saw his 'fan club', 'I'd better get out of here,' he thought, stepping unremorsefully over the slumped body of Mr. Patel lying in a pool of his own blood. He strode arrogantly away from the scene of the crime, with a smirk on his face and calmly opened his car door and sat down.

"You did alright," Toni said, looking at him through his brown eyes, like he had just been looking at a theatrical performance.

"But you took your bloody time," Dave blurted out, "that's your problem, you love all the attention, just quietly and silently that's how it's supposed to be done. I'll show you one day, the master at work; but it was alright for an old fat bastard."

"Who are ya calling old," Johnny said, as he slipped the car into first gear, put his foot down on the accelerator and sped down the road, almost knocking down an old African lady who had crossed the road to see if she could help. "You always were a cheeky bastard," Johnny added, glancing at Dave, as he beat the red lights and disappeared down the motorway.

William Lynch

William Lynch was shuffling along the payment in his beat up, old rain coat, trying to avoid the obvious glare that it brought on a sunny September day. He dragged his feet like a tramp and tried in vain to pick them up. It must have been all that drill he did. His feet like the rest of him felt quite deformed, old, fed up, worn out. He took out a cigarette, lit it. Slowly inhaling the toxins, he coughed slightly and relaxed. William shuffled in his coat pocket and pulled out a weather beaten piece of paper a rough map had been crudely drawn on it. 'The Polytechnic,' he thought, 'where is it.'

The scene was almost comical, William stood at the base of the building, like Mr. Maghoo with the sign he was looking for right over his head. He rummaged inside his bag for his personal stereo. His fingers searched through the pile of papers until at last he found the cool black little box. He slipped the tape he had in his pocket into it and switched the volume to high. "Well it's one for the money, two for the show, three to get ready and go cat go, but don't you, step on my blue suede shoes," reverberated from the speakers inserted in his ears. William tapped his fingers to the beat (or lack of it).

In fact he was so absorbed in Elvis Presley, he forgot what he was supposed to be looking for. It was already 9.35 am. He was late. The course he applied for was in sociology, or that is how the story went.

William was swinging his head to the beat like a geriatric train spotter at a heavy metal dance. Just as he got to the climax he noticed the crowd that had built up by the side of the road opposite. He took the plugs out of his ears very slowly, though the ends were by now yellow with ear wax. Slowly he walked towards them, they seemed to be gathered by a beaten up blue Austin Metro.

A young pregnant woman ran past him in the opposite direction screaming, her blonde hair flying all over the place and tears rolling down her cheeks. An old woman with her curlers still in her hair was by the side of the road, talking to what must have been her husband.

William went over to eavesdrop, dodging the traffic which had all but ground to a halt because of the commotion. "All makes you ashamed to be English," the woman said fiddling with her rollers and her double chin wobbling like a sucking pig. "Poor little geezer," she muttered, "I don't usually have much truck (Patience) for their kind, but I really felt sorry for him I think they might have killed him."

William peered over the crowds, many of whom seemed more curious than really upset. The ambulance men cleared a path pushing a black youth who was standing there a little to hard, he kissed his teeth and muttered something like, "there're all racists in it together." Then kissing his teeth again, he walked over to the other side of the road and almost bumped into another youth going in the opposite direction.

William stopped to look, the first youth apologised, but the latter held him in the spot. William watched, 'there's going to be a punch up. Cooar I've seen some things, some of these black geezers really go to town on each other. It's terrible, yet sometimes so funny,' he thought sadistically, 'see them beating each other up. Sometimes I have to confess I've just stood around watching until there soaked in blood, only arresting them afterwards. After all in my line of work its par for the course.'

William watched intently, then he noticed, 'they're not arguing, but talking, earnestly, what's all this about then, what are they up to, what's all this?' The first youth seemed to relax and the second to be instructing him. At intervals he would just nod in approval, or smile. In fact as the conversation progressed, the later was telling the first what to do and what was more, he was doing it.

'I've never seen anything like it,' William thought, 'there certainly not like the so called bad men from the street. I know they keep their power in their community by just being violent to their own lot. I don't know one single black man whose supposed to be bad whose not a pussy cat, when some good white men got hold of him.'

In fact William had been so engrossed in watching the youth he did not notice them putting what was left of Patel's broken and bloody body on a stretcher. He did not see Patel's two daughters scarred for life by glass from the windscreen, or see their mother in shock being led to the ambulance. All William was interested in were these two young black men. He left the crowd now beginning to melt away their curiosity satisfied and wondered within ear shot of their conversation.

The first youth seemed to have an awkward disposition, untidy and erratic, with a short afro and almost feminine features. A pair of thick rimmed glasses perched on top of what looked like an inquisitive, some would say nosy little face. His build was slight and apart from a Timberland shirt tucked into a pair of baggy, scruffy, faded jeans, he had no distinguishing characteristics.

'But this second youth is different. Almost a 'different breed,' thought William. William stared, he was tall, slim, yet having a build which concealed power, hidden strength. There was something about the arrogant way he rotated his hips and raised and lowered his shoulders simultaneously, that made William look in awe. He had a defiant air about his whole demeanour, as if the earth was too ugly a place for him to walk, like he should be in a palace. His complexion, was black, like ebony, his features chiselled like on a statute. 'A prince, a **Black Prince**,' William thought.

The youth's head was bald, but for the funky dread locks on top. Each of which seemed perfectly formed and hung down just over his forehead. He had a black T-shirt on, not remarkable for itself, except the black leather pouch that was strapped on it. 'What's in that pouch,' William thought, 'I bet it's not the rent money for his little old mum.' The pouch did up at the back, with a silver stud. With at least two straps across his middle like some kind of leather armour. But the really remarkable piece of clothing he was wearing was a pair of what looked like red baggy pantaloons. They were lose at the waist, tapering only by the ankles, to be tucked into a pair of black combat style suede boots. The trousers looked foreign, African, eastern or something and had gold lettering embroidered up the side. On another man they would have looked extreme, or ridiculous, but this youth seemed to carry himself with such poise and grace. He could have worn a clown's outfit and he still would have been cool. 'He moves with such ease. When one part of his body moves, it is like the whole of him.'

William looked again, 'I've been wrong after all,' he thought, 'I thought the most remarkable thing about him was his trousers, but it's not what he's wearing at all, it's his eyes. The pupils are black like ebony and rest of the eye so white. The shape is perfectly elliptical and there around the entire circumference like eye liner a thin black line marks the shape.' William was obsessed.

He never thought he would feel something like envy for another man. But he felt it when he saw this youth, this was how a man was supposed to look and he did not look that way. His bland washed out complexion, pale, thin lips and lank hair were no comparison. William would have given all the money in the world to be him. In the middle of that thought the youth looked up and stared William straight in his eye. William looked away, there was too much power there. William had read about the days of slavery, how a slave was not allowed to look his master in the eye. As he remembered, the explanation was they might realise they were both equals. 'But then,' William thought, looking at this young man, 'I think it's in case the slave sees he's not merely equal, but superior.' He tried, to get that thought out of his mind, but he failed.

The youth had long since finished the conversation with what had become his friend and was about to turn and walk away. William saw his chance, 'after all was he not lost,' he thought, as he scampered after him. "Excuse me, excuse me," he said irritatingly. The youth pretended not to hear.

"Please excuse me," William said again, this time a little irate, more like a command, than a request.

The young man turned swiftly, effortlessly - William took a step back surprised, as the youth stared at him. He fidgeted with his stereo still hanging from his bag. "I'm sorry," he mumbled, "....I seem to have got lost. Do you know the way to the Poly?"

The youth smiled a sublime, intelligent smile, the kind of smile that one gives to a small creature. It was then William noticed, 'what's that on his forehead, a scar, I wonder how he got that, bloody thug,.....doesn't affect his looks though, arrogant little bastard.'

The youth looked at William and raised his finger in the air, "Look," he said politely, with no trace of accent and pointing above his head.

William looked and then tried not to look embarrassed. In large letters the sign read Polytechnic.

"It's all right," the youth said, still staring at him, "policemen always ask me for directions." With that he laughed a deep heavy laugh like a much bigger, heavier, man and bounced and I do mean bounced, up a flight of stairs and into the Poly. William stood dumb, trying to gather his senses, trying to get his wits together, to regain some pride. 'Good looking is one thing, but he thinks he's smarter than me. At least,' he thought, consoling himself, 'I know were this place is.' After fidgeting a little, he managed to get the ear plugs in his bag, brushed his straggly hair back and trundled up the stairs were the youth had disappeared.

William should have been worrying about trying to find out what crime had taken place just five minutes before under his very nose. The flicker of remorse should have passed through his mind for the family now hysterical and scarred for life, tears streaming down their eyes, blood stains down their best new frocks. William as a good policeman could have phoned his station after interviewing the crowd and reported a possible racial incident.

If William was quick he may have been able to get the police to hunt them down, after all they had only gone thirty five miles down the road to a local pub for an early morning drink to hear Johnny the vic tell his story over and over again. About how he single handily and heroically, "Kicked that filthy paki's ass." It would not have taken William too much investigation to have located and apprehended them, that is if he really wanted too. But the irony is that even if William wanted to arrest the criminals and do not get me wrong, he didn't, but even if he did, for every Johnny that is arrested their is another to take their place.

But William did not care less about the violent incident which had just taken place, he was thinking, 'what are those black youths saying, what are they up to, insurrection, kill the bill or something I bet, that arrogant one's a ring leader of some secret, covert gang. If I can find it,...I'll smash it! And get policeman of the year.'

Of course William came from a cultural background where he had been indoctrinated as a child with little gollywogs on fruit jars, with the black and white minstrel show. He laughed at Mike Davidson as he told racist jokes and Bernhard Banning as he insulted black people. He laughed even louder when black comics came later and did the same thing. But besides all that cultural indoctrination of every history class that he had ever had, which taught him European history was the best, that England was great and would be great again, and part of that greatness meant an understanding of what was important.

'What is important,' William thought, 'is law and order, justice is for those who deserve it, 'he had seen his colleagues after the Tottenham riots, after all had he not attended PC Blakelock's funeral. Comforted his grieving family. Then to see the murderers paraded in some of the press as if they were the victims, to see that 'smiling, that smiling thug's face,' it was too much for him.

It was not that William was a racist, it was just that he could not help being other than what he was. What made it worse, was that he was from a generation of Lynchs. He had researched the family name.

As he tottered up the stairs one at a time he thought, 'it's lucky that most of these liberals don't know their stuff. But everyone should be proud of their history - but sometimes I feel just a bit ashamed of being a sixth generation descendant of William Lynch. That same William Lynch I've read the books, who owned slaves in the eighteenth century. What was it .. I remember reading it , that's right...... perfected the 'breaking system' like one would break, 'his horses.'

'I've done enough research on genetics to know that you can't escape from your genes. It's been proved scientifically that alcoholics had 50% propensity of delivering that tendency to their children, or something like that. I'm sure I read it. Why then can't other characteristics be transmitted psychologically. Sometimes,' he thought, as he cleared the last steps and opened the door of the Poly, 'I have an uncontrollable desire to kill one of them, to open his stomach and see the colour of his black guts hanging swinging form his broken prone body.' He pushed that thought out of his mind, as he stepped into a shabby walk way badly decorated in peeling red paint, the bits of which flitted from the ceiling like red confetti at a wedding, as soon as he opened the door to enter.

William was still trying to control that savage, brutal murdering mind of his, when a black youth pushed passed him, only to be followed by another, each one seeming to knock him in the shoulder in the same place. He hurriedly adjusted his coat in an attempt to compose himself, but he failed. He saw them bouncing down the corridor as if they owned the place. 'Who the hell do they think they are?' he thought so loudly he almost said it. He looked enviously at their slim, handsome, muscular frames, their effortless stride and way that even blue jeans seemed to fit them like a second skin.

William watched them walk all the way down to the end of the corridor, he only stopped when he heard, "Tayo!"

He looked around for the source of the shouting and the person it was aimed at.

"Tayo."

William heard the name shouted again. He looked up to an adjoining staircase, the apparent source of the sound. William heard hurried footsteps descending a nearby staircase. The click, clack of very high heels on a wooden floor. The sound was familiar. He waited expectantly for the approaching female looking past the entrance, past the walls littered with posters advertising extremist societies, raves, and music contests. Noticing the small crowd that had built up at the other end of the corridor.

Finally she arrived. William watched and smelt the perfume in the air, sweet and strong like the sexual urge in his pants. She was wearing the most delicate black shoes, made from some sought of lace material. At least three inch heels and holding up the most elegant shapely legs he had ever seen, even on a cat walk. Black leggings so tight they looked like she had poured them on. Firm thighs leading to pronounced firm buttocks, obscured by a short waist length green jacket. 'A firm upright posture, like a ballet dancer, with the kind of rounded breasts that I wish my wife has, but doesn't,' William thought. A noble upright neck 'How sweet,' he contemplated, 'she's ssso sweet. She's good enough to eat, I could eat that.'

He stared at her pronounced brown chin, the full pouting lips adorned with a little too much red lipstick. The nose round and proud, the eyes as black as ebony set in white pools, the pencil thin eyebrows underneath the straight forehead. The hair frizzy in cascading ringlets, some falling to the side of her face, the rest gently bouncing behind her.

William was staring like a rapist, as the sister walked towards him. She saw him from the corner of her eye and stared at his quivering mouth, a dribble of saliva on his lips like a rabid dog.

'Uhhhh....he's nasty,' she thought. Then she noticed, the dirty old rain coat, the tardy old shoes. She saw that yes, there was something malevolent, evil in those eyes. She looked at him as someone would look at their shoe if they stepped in 'doodo.' It was a look of disdain and absolute disgust. William saw the young woman scowling at him and quickly averted his eyes attempting to look at a nearby poster for a black event entitled, "*Black talent contest, find out whose the sexist black man in college,* (subtitled) *watch them strut their stuff and reveal more than just their personal lives.*'

William genuinely became distracted with the poster, only remembering her as she whisked passed him, her pungent perfume hitting him again as she swung her hips, in the most seductive fashion. "Swwoo," he said, under his breath, as she sauntered past him, to the small crowd which had gathered at the other end of the concourse.

William for at least the third time that day was curiously excited.
He scurried after her, trying to stop himself from taking her down
one of those corridors and committing an indecent act. He watched
her hips swinging, the tautness of her entire frame and he sneered
just like his ancestor William Lynch.

The small crowd of what appeared to him, black youths of
unsavoury dispositions. Some looking like rejects from those
American rap videos he had seen on Top of the Pops mixed with
Bob Marley. The whole gathering looked disconcerting and a more
than a little foreign.

The young sister skipped into the crowd and they seemed to part
like the red sea, "Let the sister, through," "Go'w 'on," some of
them called out.

'But how can they all be her sister?' William thought, ignorantly.
The gathering opened to reveal a young African man with a slightly arrogant, handsome dark face, a black T- shirt with a leather
pouch strapped to him and red pantaloons. This was the same
youth whom he had seen outside. 'So his name is Tayo,' William
thought, 'I'll remember that.'

The young woman kissed Tayo a little too fervently. Tayo looked at
her, "if you're going to kiss me, you should take this stuff off first,"
he said, wiping the lipstick off his cheek. You know I' don't like all
that stuff, do ya know what they put in lipstick."

"I just couldn't help it," she said, "you're just so handsome. I swear
in the space of one year you've got more handsome, a little too
confident, but your definitely gorgeous."

Tayo was going to say something else, when he caught sight of
William staring at him for the third time that day. He laughed, a
deep booming laugh. "That guys a fool," he mumbled.

"What's the matter?" the sister said, looking up at him, he pulled
her closer by the waist and whispered in her ear.

She looked up and they both smiled sarcastically. William could
feel his cover disappearing. 'Before long all these black radicals, will
be looking at me, probably thinking, its Brixton all over again,' he
thought. He picked up the ear phones which had fallen out of his
bag yet again, adjusting his rain coat and shuffling off like a train

spotter, just finished for the day, down an adjoining stairway and away from prying eyes.

Tayo kissed his teeth so hard they hurt, 'what the hell's wrong with this country,' he thought, 'I haven't been in this nasty little Poly for more than three minutes and I've got this pig following me around like he's my dog, or something. If he was my dog at least I could send him away, worse thing still,' Tayo contemplated, 'I think he's got a real problem with us, he followed my sister here, like he owned her and would have probably arrested us all for loitering with intent, if he could have. But they must have real fools working in there, if they send idiots like him.'

"What's up," Melanie said looking at him, "Tayo, you should be looking at me, what's more important than me?"

Tayo looked at her and gave a half smile, "nuthing, really nothing."

"You mean nothing you want to tell me, tha's what you mean, isn't it. I bet it's more of that black stuff you brother's talk and feel it's too high for the sisters to deal with. Isn't that the truth."

Tayo just looked at her and the small crowd that had gathered around him. He looked for some empathy, understanding, familiarity and he found none. Some wearing their locks like fashion accessories, ask them if they had read Marcus Garvey, and they would say, "me nah deal with nah ism schism, just pure levity, through the father." Others in black, with boots, Ankhs and African symbols, like extras from a X clan or Public Enemy video. But ask any of them if they had read Malcom X 'or Destruction of Black Civilisation, see the reply 'destruction of who,... what, I could never get into that reading thing, I h've to read enough on this course, you must be joking.' But if it was a joke, it was a **sick joke** and the punch line was yet to come.

Tayo stared at the crowd as they looked at their Swatch watches, scratched their bald heads, puzzles and locks. 'They have lost interest in me, why do they bother, I don't know. Just to past the time of day I guess. After all,' he thought, 'I'm two to three years younger than most of them, but seen a lot. Served my time here. Sounds like prison, you know whose done most time, well perhaps...... it is sort of. Any way....besides that, the fiasco of the previous year and the disbanding of the society..... we're probably cult status now, the seven of us. You know famous, part of a society that's been banned. I could tolerate all the double dealing and foolishness that went on, but for what. Meetings with the director of

the Poly to discuss how we would pay back the money, Police inter-
views, etc, etc.... It's like we're public enemy number one, when all
we did was defend ourselves.'

'How much this is like white society,' Tayo thought, kissing his
teeth again, 'to blame the victims, whilst the perpetrators walked
free. After all today had a white man not almost beaten an Asian
man to death for simply bleeping his horn at him and was this
criminal in jail. No. He was probably getting drunk in some pub
(and he was) and then go home and beat his wife (and he did) and
now,' Tayo was getting crosser the more he thought about it, 'this
pig is watching me like I committed a crime today, when a would
be murderer, a real criminal was sitting with a pint of beer in his
hands in a pub down in Greenwich.'

"Your really are miles away," Melanie said, staring at him with
wonder and a strong sexual urge she had felt from the beginning
but was trying to suppress, because she had a boyfriend (on paper
at least). "I was just joking before, y'know," she said, softly taking
his hand in hers and feeling that sexual urge all over again, an
impulse to just jump on him and hold him close to her.

'It's not like I'm man hungry,' she contemplated, 'but Tayo has
something honourable, virtuous about him, apart from being one
of the handsomest men in the college. Beauty and intelligence are
hard to come by,' she was posing like she was on a catwalk.

'How much more of a man he is than my boyfriend, look my man
can't even make up his mind whether he's black or white,' she
thought. She had started going out with him when her friends had
egged her on, after all they said, "he looks so cute, and he's got
coolie hair." So she dated him, 'it was not just because of his hair
and light eyes,' she tried to convince herself it was not. But her
mother had always said she had good hair and she wanted to make
sure her children had it. 'After all,' she thought, 'mixed parentage
or mixed race people were black after all. What else could they be.
They got stopped by the police just like other black people, suf-
fered, abuse from the legal system, disproportionate sentences, and
figured heavily in the mental institutions.' Melanie knew all this
but if she examined her own motives she liked the idea his mother
was white, that his skin was not too dark, that all the other woman
looked enviously at her when they went to dances. She liked it for
all the wrong reasons.

Then Melanie came to college, all these dark skinned brothers, all
those dark bodies, taut muscles, she looked at the brothers at first

like a slave owner might look at specimens he might choose to buy. Then the physical desires gave way to the spiritual wants. She began to notice an air of superiority that her boyfriend had to other men. A tendency to avoid anything too black. This was when she was moving closer to it.

She concluded in her mind, 'he could be light, or dark, it did not matter, what was important was the state of his mind, his soul, where he was going. All he wanted to do was make money, drive fast cars, and pose with his coolie hair. She felt, 'I want to cut that hair of and see how he get's on then.....'

'But with Tayo there is no wavy hair, wavy consciousness or wavy anything,' she thought, looking at him, 'well perhaps one thing,' she giggled. 'But it's not just sexual, I like his arrogance, though he vexes me still, correction, I love his arrogance,' she thought and smiled.

"What you smiling about?" Tayo said, emphatically reading her mind, "don't forget you've got a man."

Melanie grinned, "you know I've got a man, but that doesn't stop you from holding my hand, or fancying me, does it."

"I didn't say you weren't attractive," Tayo said, "but you have a man and there is too much of that kind of slackness going on." Tayo was trying to convince himself. He looked at the curved firm body, that beautiful elegant face, a part of him wanted to go straight to bed with her now!

Melanie smiled, "Yeah, right!" she said, releasing his hand and walking away seductively swaying her hips. Tayo watched her go and bit his bottom lip. 'One day she is going to ask me with come to bed eyes and I don't know whether I'm going to be able to say no. A nineteen year old can only be so virtuous. The thought of pulling those fine black leggings down to see those finer black legs, the idea of wiping that lipstick off to kiss those firm broad lips and hold that fine brown frame, has crossed my mind more than once.'

After all he had spent most of his life deprived of the love of African women, exiled to the wilderness of the bush, he remembered looking at those straggly haired blonde bimbos who were supposed to be the epitome of beauty. Their flat backsides, red lipstick smeared all over the face, foundation to obscure the red puss and dead skin of acne.

Tayo used to wonder as a boy what that faint smell of fish was which wafted from the naughty girls in the class who used to sit in the back row. Was it a natural smell, or was it because they had not washed between their legs for two weeks.

Tayo remembered going on a school trip with a girl called Julie Thomas, nick named the dog. He did not know why such an unassuming girl would have such a cruel nick name. Tayo looked at the slightly plump girl, with her brown hair and blue eyes, her little pony tail which bounced behind a round and rather too well proportioned body for a fourteen year old. Tayo still had not understood.

It was not until the 15th of July in the Summer of 1985. The day of the trip to Ironbridge. It was an uneventful annual event that Tayo's school took every year. It consisted of a very tedious journey to South Wales, the Severn River and a bridge built by Isambard Kingdom Brunel known as Ironbridge, literally a bridge made of iron over the Severn river.

The entire outing consisted of a long coach ride to Wales, a stay in a hostel, a field trip the next day, including the drawing of such interesting things as trees. A visit to a black smiths and metal works and the study of bridge building.

For a fourteen year old boy in the early eighties it was not the kind of event to get the testosterone active. But Tayo decided to make the best of the entire event. It was not as if he was trying to impress anyone, there was no one to impress, but if he was going he might as well look his best.

So Tayo got himself ready, white socks, loafing shoes, stay press burgundy trousers, and a La' Coste T-shirt. He was the height of fashion, a real 'rude boy' English style. But no one was really interested in his fashion, they were interested in what Julie was wearing (or not wearing).

Tayo remembered stepping onto the coach packed back to back with children, their white faces all staring at him and his La Coste T-shirt. There was a look of admiration, envy, after all not only was he the only black child in the entire school, but he was the best dressed, and certainly the best looking. He was still enjoying the attention and jealous stares, when Julie stepped behind him and bounced up the stairs pushing her breasts into his back giggling like the virgin she was not, Tayo was caught off guard.

He did not appreciate the jeers and, "go on mate, she likes a bit of black, a bit of rough trade, go on mate have some of that. Cooar she's gagging for it." 'I don't want some of her,' he thought, looking with disdain at her and kissing his teeth though she batted her eyelids and smiled, trying to look sweet. He felt he had been violated. It was as if all those staring, jeering white faces wanted a show.

'Was I supposed to put on a show for them? The only black guy in the school and they want me to perform.' The boys at the back stared goggle eyed like they watching a porn show. 'It's as if,' Tayo thought, 'they want to see if it's true. Is it really true that black men have huge cocks. By the stupid look on Julie's face she certainly wants to find out. I feel abused, ridiculous, violated.' He pushed himself gingerly to a seat at the back of the coach, pushing a salt and vinegar crisp packet and a cocoa cola can out of the way, the latter spilling its black, sticky contents over the coach's carpet.

Julie had not finished her entertainment. Tayo was the first and only man to have refused her advances, though she was only fourteen. She was annoyed that Tayo had totally ignored her, now she was looking for attention to confirm she was still desirable. Deep down she had very low self esteem. The attention she got from the men of the school even if it was just for sex made her feel wanted, attractive. She wiggled her curvaceous hips past Tayo to sit on the back seat between Chop and Kev. short for Kevin. Chop a.k.a. Charles Worthington nicknamed after he reportedly chopped a local boy in the head with a butcher's knife. They were the two rudest, ugliest, toughest and most popular boys in the school.

An over worked and badly dressed female school teacher, with a grey jacket done up to her chin to hide the body she did not have, rushed forward, down the aisle to do a head count, not noticing as she was a little short sighted, wearing broad rimmed National Health glasses, Julie sitting on Chop's lap and rubbing her buttocks on his thighs. Nor did she notice her undoing Kev's flies - and she sat down, before she could catch the little professional, as she tried to please Chop and Kev. at the same time! Kev. had a smile all over his face like a clown, though his skinny, pale, penis was out for all to see- dribbling from his mouth like a dog urinating in the park.

Tayo did not notice the pornographic act, or the sequel, as Julie proceeded to hitch up her skirt, pull down her pants. Even as Chop undid his trousers and proceeded to enter her from behind. Tayo was too busy trying to hide the embarrassment of all those faces who had been looking at him before.

It was only when she began to moan with excitement and giggle like an insane prostitute that Tayo turned round to see the finale, as she dropped the top of her dress to reveal two large bulbous, white, flabby breasts. Tayo looked away with shock and shame, peering to the front to see why the teacher had not seen. But she was preoccupied with looking at the shabby map which she had retrieved from her duffel bag. The coach jerked forward, as the engine started, but this had not bothered the back seat who were doing their own jerking.

Tayo would never forget the smell of fish and sweat, the grunts, groans and the leering children, the movement of the coach, the swaying of his seat not properly fixed on its metal hinges, the filth which lay scattered around his seat. Tayo felt the nausea rising in his stomach. He felt sick, violently sick.

'They probably wanted me to be part of the act, so they could see if their fantasies were true.' Tayo kissed his teeth, for the second, but certainly not for the last. 'Was I supposed to drop my trousers and please them, to give them pleasure?'

Tayo was later to see black men with their white friends indulging their friends every fantasy as if they were their own. Tayo just looking at them as they told jokes about the size of black men's dicks, or their supposed sexual potency. He stood in wonder, not understanding why so many black men could run around splashing their sexual prowess as if their were all professional porn stars.

'I'm not a pimp, I'm not a prostitute, I don't have sex with people to fulfil somebody else's sexual fantasy, I am a man, I have the right to be respected as a man, and you had better respect me as a man, or I shall have teach you to,' Tayo thought, so loudly it almost burst a blood vessel in his angry mind.

The last waft of Melanie's perfume hit his nose, though he tried to clear it with a youthful finger. The perfume woke him from his memory and he stared at her. 'I'm a man starving all my life and then released into the biggest supermarket in the world,' he thought, looking at Melanie's ample everything. 'Was such a man going to behave cautiously, with discretion, no. He would try and taste everything he had been missing all his life. Every time I see a sister like Melanie, instinct, well it takes over from reason,' he thought, 'I simply can't risk being alone with her. It's not that I don't have control, it's that I don't want to control myself. I want to feel that Africaness next to me. So Melanie with all her melanin, had better be careful,' he thought, 'brother's have been played before. Two black men fighting over the one woman. Breaking each other to pieces whilst the sister stood their and laughed, just to see who the was last man standing. I don't need to prove I'm the best man to anyone. But my God,' he thought, remembering, 'Melanie is fit. Man she's nice, I mean she's really nice. Worse still,' Tayo thought, still trying to get her perfume scent out of his nose, 'she knows she is.'

It seemed like Tayo was the only one taking time to think for himself, no one else was giving themselves any time at all. Tayo watched the other students scurrying around like little rabbits to their warrens, clutching their bags and paperwork as if they were winter stores for hibernation. Adjusting their spectacles and weave on hairstyles, trying to appear composed and yet not excited as well. After all for some, it was their first time living away from home. For all it was an opportunity, a make or break time in their careers. Either they made it here, got their degrees and qualifications, started earning cash, or they would be left behind.

Tayo watched the Africans hustling and bustling, to get into the corridors leading to the lecture theatres. Seeing them fighting, to get into the classrooms, watching grown men and women behaving like little school children late for class.

'Do they not understand they are here by choice,' Tayo thought. Then he realised looking at them combing their hair and doing up their top buttons, this is their only chance to be more than the average 'Joe Bloggs'. 'Society has been teaching us,' he thought, 'that we are less than nothing. This time we could take on the system and beat it at it's own game.'

'But what is the reality,' Tayo contemplated looking at the corridor becoming increasingly empty. 'Did a few Africans getting degrees alter the status quo, are we not tokens, pawns in a much bigger game, could not a few people's success be used to justify the continuation of an inhuman and evil system. After all they could say you made it didn't you, so things can't be that bad after all.'

Tayo kissed his teeth so hard he felt the reverberation throughout his whole mouth. His brain was racing faster and faster, 'what the hell am I doing here? I don't want a fifty thousand pound job. I don't want to be a pencil neck, a suit and tie boy, in a starched white shirt and nice short back and sides. What the hell am I doing here ! I ain't never going to be like them, I swear, I would rather die, do you here me, I swear never, never,... never..'

Tayo bopped down the now empty corridor, grown quiet, still, just the rustle of the posters on the wall advertising an event' *Black talent contest ....'* the words caught his eye. He reached out a youthful hand and read it, at the bottom were written the words *Afro Caribbean Society in conjunction with the Black British club.* 'What the hell is that,' Tayo thought, forgetting all about Melanie, Ironbridge the students running to their lessons and just about everything else.

"What the hell is that!!!" this time he said out loud. 'Black British Club, what the... .is the Black British Club. 'It sounds like British National Party. Is this for black people, for African people?'

If it was possible his mind was working, quicker than before. 'Where are the AS posters.' Looking around irritated, 'is this what the AS is, a hair style (Afro) a cannibal (literal translation of Caribbean) and a coloured version of the BNP.' 'No wonder,' he thought, tearing the poster from the wall, 'black people look like they're on eze. Have I been away for one year from this place only to see our voice degenerate into a hair style. We are an African people, not Afro's. The African experience is a statement of reality,' he thought.

He scanned the torn poster in his hands, still shaking with anger, *"come to a planning meeting on Wednesday the 26th of September - be there or be square. In Room 7 London Road site,"* Tayo read.

'Well,' he thought, tearing the paper into little pieces and scattering them on the floor. 'If this is an open call, if anyone can attend, since I am anyone, I'll be there,' trying to stop himself from kissing his teeth for a fourth time.

He tried to put all his thoughts into a logical pattern and he almost succeeded, until he realised that he was the only one standing there and had been for several minutes, looking at the battered clock face of his watch and then suddenly remembering, 'wasn't I supposed to be somewhere.'

'All returned students are supposed to report to the auditorium for the welcome talk and registration at nine thirty a.m. He looked at his watch again, it was already ten past ten. The thought would have made lesser men forget all their previous notions of self respect, black power and rush off like a naughty school boy to be told off and receive punishment, especially as if he did not register, then he could not claim his student grant.

The one thing Tayo needed right now was his grant. But he was determined to take the whole day in his stride. 'What a day!' Tayo thought, bouncing down the corridor and, 'it is not even lunch time.' 'Why I'm master of everything,' he thought, looking at the empty corridors, walking through the empty canteen, 'it's just me and the ancestors.'

Tayo bounced down the stairs, following a sign that read, 'Auditorium.' He looked at his watch one last time, fifteen minutes past ten, 'what!' he exclaimed, 'I might as well not bother.' 'Oh well, I need that cheque,' he thought, 'the big wide world is not ready for me yet.'

He skipped down the stairs two at a time, avoiding the old Coca-Cola cans and sweet wrappers stuck to the stairs. The walls did not have the look about them of an institution looking to make a clean start. 'Is this place ready for us, or just ready for the money we will bring,' Tayo thought, 'where are the new facilities, they haven't even been bothered to redecorate, paint is failing from the ceiling at the entrance, and coming off the hand rails,' examining the flecks of Dulux on his hands. 'This is really an inner city institution, forgotten by the establishment. No wonder so many Africans are here. I think they call this a Ghetto Poly, but,' Tayo smiled, to himself, 'let's see if we can make it a Ghetto heaven.'

'Auditorium,' the sign read, its' faded lettering just visible under the gloom of the passage-way. Tayo was going to try and slip in, catch the end of the meeting, sign the forms and then get out. 'I don't relish the idea of all those servile faces bowed in front of a selection of pompous lecturers, as they walk to and fro trying to count heads, like slave masters at an auction. That's funny, why not call it auction, not auditorium,' he thought, and laughed, 'it serves the same function.'

Tayo tip toed forward, if his calculations were correct then he would be directly opposite the fire exit.

Tayo was calculating in his youthful mind, for the fire exit doors to be faulty. He remembered four years ago how they had been forced open and broken. It was the kind of humourous event which made you laugh out loud when you were sitting on a train full of complete strangers, only to see everyone look at you as if you were insane. Tayo scratched his head and twisted his locks - it helped him think. The story went something like this......

Tav

It was 1986, two years before Tayo even set foot in the Poly, it was the middle of a decade which had seen economic depression, right wing extremism and self interest become the main political force. The fascists had lost control of the streets, most had gone underground and become respectable racists in suits and ties, making money, working for a big corporation, after all the 1980's was about individual self development. If everyone else was making money so could they.

But a few of the die hard kept to the original script, refused to grow their hair, or put on slacks. They kept their jeans rolled up and the boots long shiny and black, with red laces. Being a racist was not a fashion accessory for them, it was a way of life. This was true for Paul, and David as much as any other of the knife wielding-baby-eating thugs, who thought that their colour was a badge of honour, and their blood a privilege.

So Paul and David kept true to their convictions, right down to the swastika that Paul would play with in an irritating manner whilst he talked to complete strangers as if it would have the same affect as a cross on a vampire. In fact Paul liked the image a little more than the substance.

David would discern a little too much reservation as they put in the boot to 'a local paki' that 'caused some bother.' And he became positively worried as a ' bunch of local coloureds, started givin' it the big'un,' and instead of getting his knuckle-dusters out for a fight, he had just wanted to walk away.

David was worried, he was thinking, if 'I could get Paul out, if we could beat up a proper paki, ...,'. he thought, scowling at a Sikh as they sat on the train on the way to Elephant and castle; 'you know one of them with a turban.' I know my mate will be alright, he just needs to get his blood up, poor bloke, all these niggers in this area,' looking around and frowning at an African woman plump from eating too much eba, plantain and fresh fish, who seemed completely and absolutely oblivious to his intentions. Even though as he looked at her two very small, sweet twin girls, with pony tails, braids and best white dresses on, he was thinking, 'I 'haven't beaten up a nigger for over a month.' But the woman just had a smile on her face, because she was thinking about what she was going to be cooking for dinner tonight, her favourite, 'eba with stewed fresh fish.'

Paul seemed a million miles away, not even noticing the Rasta with the biggest, thickest, blackest locks this side of South London get on the train, arm in arm with a little scrawny white girl, who did not seem to have reached the age of puberty

David looked at his boots and wondered, 'if I kick that filthy coon in his head, from here, it's going to get a blood stain on my new DM boots. I don't fancy explaining that to the DHSS,' (they were going to sign on) 'the last time I went in there with just a bit on me it was like I was the bloody foreigner, a bloody criminal, I had to go home and look in the mirror to make sure I was white. Of course I did and thank God I was!'

His train of thought was interrupted by the jerking motion of the tube train as it ground to a halt at the station.

"Last stop, everybody change," the announcer said over the loud speaker in a broad west country Jamaican accent. Paul heard the announcement and spat on the floor some phlegm that he had kept in the back of his throat. 'What kind of country is this? ' he thought , 'Blacks breeding, every where, pakis making all the money and even our national services are bloody ran by foreigners, I'm bloody fed up with this shit, I can tell you,' he thought loudly.

He skipped out of the open doors of the train with Paul trailing behind him. In fact Paul was so busy that he almost bounced into a tall Sikh who was walking along the platform. The Sikh looked down at him like he was a bit of dirt and strode away. Paul shock his head,' just a minute, did that paki, just give me a dirty look,' he thought.

"David," he said, "did that lanky paki just give me a dirty look."

"I can't tell you mate," David replied, looking at his swastika under the tube lights, "but since when did you need an excuse to do one of them."

"Na, you're right son. Let's do him."

The two skinheads followed the Sikh, who was disappearing up a flight of stairs. They raced after him. Paul was breathing a little too heavily for a man supposed to be a tough, white, racist. At last they reached the top, only to see him disappear into a lift.

 He was moving so fast that Paul was almost running to catch up, with David trundling on behind.

"We'll take the stairs," Paul gasped, trying to catch his breath, "or will miss him."

When they did reach the top of the stairs Paul was sweating and panting like a dog at a race track, 'where is he,' he thought. 'He's bloody disappeared, gone back to India or something.' He walked past the ticket booth, ignoring the collector's question for his ticket. And out on to the street. He looked left and then right, only to see the same Sikh bouncing energetically towards a red brick building with the words, '*Polytechnic*,' written on it.

"I'll have him," Paul muttered under his breath, "where's David, he's bloody useless." He kicked his boot on the pavement in agitation as the Sikh got further and further away.

'Where is he ?' he thought, looking behind. 'If you won't a job done properly, then I guess you've got to do it yourself.' There was a slow thud of heavy boots as David finally emerged at the top of the stairs, almost tripping over the last step and stumbling into the ticket booth, "come on Dave," Paul shouted, as he ran out of the tube station and almost into an old pensioner that got in his way.

David just managing to collect his thoughts together between the shouts of the ticket collector now coming out of his booth and the exhaustion which had come over him from climbing the stairs. He moped the sweat from his face and tried to look up, only to see Paul disappear down the road. Paul collected his thoughts together and staggered out of the station, pushing the ticket collector who had now come, out of his way.

Paul was running as fast as his little legs would take him. His red braces flapping around his waist, his black bomber jacket open and fluttering in the morning summer breeze, his bald head glistening with sweat.

He pushed at least five people out of his way, until he almost stumbled into the brick work of the Poly like a drunkard. He shoved an Indian girl in a sari who was in his path against the wall, her glasses fell off and broke on the concrete and she dropped her new brown duffel bag on the floor, scattering the contents all over the pavement. Paul jumped over the spewing papers and leapt up the stairs.

It was 9am, the concourse was empty. He peered down the hall, littered with posters for African events, Punjabi festivals, Hindu religious ceremonies, Africana talks and PACM debates.

Paul thundered down after the Sikh, as he caught sight of his turban disappear down an adjoining tunnel. He looked up at the sign reading "Auditorium" in black letters.

'Where the hell's he going?' Paul thought, floundering after him. Through a doorway and down metal stairs. He almost tripped, as he came bursting through the rear entrance of the auditorium and tripped on a nearby chair.

Paul looked up and realised he was in a very large hall with seats arranged for a lecture. In the hurry to follow the Asian man he had not even realised that he was in a college. He tried to rationalise his mind. A sudden throbbing began in his knee and spread to his leg, he had banged it coming in, he reached down to feel it, "paki," he mumbled under his breath irately, rubbing his leg. In the midst of his own race hating, and feeling sorry for himself, he felt the presence of someone else.

He looked up to see the Sikh standing, staring at him. Paul brushed himself off, 'where's Dave, my mate Dave,' he thought, trying to stand up. The Sikh stepped forward, closer and looked Paul deep in the bluest part of his eye.

Paul stared back, there was something in this Asian man's face which did not look like the comfortable stereotype of a passive Indian, he was tall at least six foot, his beard black and thick like a rastas and his mustache shaped like the Maharajah of Sashpoor. His build was slim, but their was something lean and smooth about the muscle tone. Paul had not seen it before in an Indian, 'he's got a body like a middle weight boxer, where's Dave?' he thought, gritting his teeth.

The Sikh bounced right up to Paul and stared down at him, Paul fumbled backwards slightly against the door he had just come through. The Sikh stood over him, he saw a small skinhead, with jeans so tight they looked like they had been poured on, stupid red braces dangling down at his waist and wearing an old black bomber jacket ragged and worn. But the thing he noticed which stood out most of all, was not the bare head glistening with sweat, or the tattoos on his neck written '**Made in England**,' it was the simple badge on his jacket with the letters NF on them.

The Sikh frowned and raised his chin like he was expecting a knock on it, Paul just looked up at him dumfounded.

"Do you know who I am," the Sikh said, calmly smiling.

"You what?" Paul said.

"I said," the Sikh replied, this time a little less calmer, "do you.... know who I am?"

Paul tried to gather his senses for the third time that day and failed. He clenched his fists, but too slow, for the Sikh had already slapped him across his face and sent him flying back against the door. Paul tried to take a swing, but the Sikh blocked his arm from the inside with his left hand and slapped him again harder if possible than the first time with his right hand. Paul fell back against the door, on this occasion against the latch, partly wrenching it out of it's sockets.

The Sikh leapt forward and slapped Paul again with the back of his hand, as if he was the hero of some 1940's detective movie beating up the villain.

"I said, do you know who I am," he shouted, as Paul fell, blood all over his mouth..

"My name is Tav, Tavinder Kaur Khalsa Singh, you will remember my name, because I am a living leg...end," the Sikh said, calmly slapping him for the fourth time as he fell.

Tav had seen them following him from the Tube Station, he was the President of the Sikh society, an Ex middle weight boxer and Wing Chung expert. He had grown up in Stockwell sparring in gyms with Africans, picked up the method and style from them and then taught his own people. He loved his own people and if anyone ever dare disrespect his religion, his identity or race, they had better have a Government health card.

'I don't care,' Tav thought, looking down at this very little man, 'whether you're black, white, Hindu or Muslim, anyone who disrespects me, is either insane or a fool.'

Tav had been training from the time he could walk, conflict was as natural to him as taking a bath, it was as much a part of his religion to be a warrior, as it was part of his nature to be unafraid of anyone.

David at last came sweating into the Poly, he heard the commotion and ran down the stairs like a stampeding elephant, two at a time, stumbled over Paul's unconscious body and saw Tav standing their smiling.

David hesitated, 'in truth,' he thought, 'I'm fed up with all this shit, half the time we fight this lot, they fight back, it's not like the past, there's a surprise round every corner.'

Tav smiled at him, "do you know who I am?" he said, striding towards him, looking at David's stomach hanging over his trousers and his clumsy manner. "You're friend didn't know, so I had to teach him," Tav told him, "now do you need a lesson?"

But David was already stepping backwards over his friends body, he stumbled, his back hitting the remnants of the door. Tav smiled, bounced closer, wrenching the door off it's hinges, like the Incredible Hulk and hurling it. It seemed to rise from the ground - striking Paul in his head, cutting his forehead and sending him tottering backwards. He fell, blood trickling from the open gash, somehow managing, blood still all over his face, to scramble to his feet. Trundling as fast as his legs would carry him up the stairs and as far away from this mad Sikh, as possible.

Meanwhile Tav stood their laughing, hands on hips, his bangles hanging around his wrists and looking down at the devastation he had caused.

Ever after, no matter how they tried to fix the Auditorium back door it would never quite close. Tav had broken it forever.

Tayo never forget the story, the lesson or the line, "do you know who I am?" But most of all he learned that discipline and not non-violence were the key. They were still talking about 'Tav the living legend' when Tayo came to the Poly. 'Hell,' Tayo thought, 'the Sikhs are still talking about him now. Every Sikh in this place wants to be a Tav. That's how it is with role models, for good or bad, the youth need someone to follow, emulate. I watch the Sikhs training, fasting, studying their history, I listen to their exploits and wish my people have better stories to tell. But what did most of us want to do, rave, pose and pretend. Where is the resistance in the African culture, my culture, where is it,' he thought, pushing the door of the Auditorium open, 'well I will resurrect that spirit, even if I have to do it myself, the African youth are goin' to have **stories** to tell their children I swear it.'

Tayo put his hands around the make shift door looking like it had not been repaired since Tav had used it for a missile. Tayo felt around the edge and moved it carefully towards him. The space opened up and he could hear the meeting was in full swing by the sound of the lecturers as they gave their instruction. Then there was silence, 'perhaps they are having a break, let me get in there quick,' he thought, stepping gingerly through the open space.

Mr. Thomas

There was silence.

Tayo stood at the top of the Auditorium, looking down at the multitude of students all looking back at him. Even the teachers at the front, were staring from beneath there broad rimmed spectacles and their lecturers podiums. Shuffling their tweed jackets, attempting to gain an element of middle class, liberal composure.

White students trying to be trendy with Hillfiger sports jackets on, African students probably asleep until Tayo made his entrance. Even two Asian students who were sat at the back reading the Koran not listening to a word being said, or the proceedings, but they stopped reading their holy book and looked at Tayo. Even an African couple who had been looking into each others eyes since the time they had been going out, which was all of one week, stopped fantasising about moonlight walks along the beach, Champagne and red roses, they stopped and stared dumfounded at Tayo. A white couple who looked like they were having sex on the very last row in the corner and were both about to reach their climax, simultaneously stopped in mid orgasm and looked at this angry, arrogant, African youth.

"Who, and," said a wry looking Lecturer from the front of the hall, "I pray, who are you supposed to be?"

Tayo looked arrogantly down at the little white man with his tweed jacket, white shirt and blue tie. 'Blue tie,' Tayo thought, 'with a tweed jacket, that just doesn't go.' He saw the national health glasses and thin pouting lips - like a underfed porn star, the irritated little face, with his features contorted by frustration. Frustration for what,' Tayo looked at him again, 'frustration for being born, an under-paid-nasty-little white lecturer, who can't even get his dick hard when he wants,' Tayo thought, sniggering to himself.

"My name is Tayo," he shouted down to him, "T...A..Y..O" (spelling it to the lecturer who by now was scribbling his name on a piece of paper). "So you know who I am, now. So who are you supposed to be ?" Tayo said, with a smirk on his face.

There was a roar of laughter from the hall, which did not die down despite shouts of, "order, order, we will have quiet, or we will all go home!"

"Suit's me fine," Tayo said, through the uproar, at which the crowd began laughing all over again.

"Order, Order, do you hear me," the lecturer shouted.

"I'll talk to you later," he shrieked, like a wife to her adulterous husband.

"Not if I talk to you first," Tayo blurted out, grinning like a cat. This time the crowd erupted into uncontrollable laughter, the Muslims reading the Koran giggled so much they dropped their holy book. The white lovers even forgot they were supposed to be having sex.

The African couple just looked in awe, they had never seen an African act so fearlessly in front of white authority before. A sudden streak of fear gripped them, in case their laughter grew so loud it drew attention to them, after all the lecturers might think they were in league with him. They looked nervously around, she brushed her dyed brown hair away from her face and fidgeted in her bag for a college prospectus. Even while the laughter roared around them. But beneath the calmness which she tried to create, a faint smile emerged on her face, though she tried to suppress it. The smile turned into a snigger, made worse because Tayo was standing with his arms folded, looking calmly down at the irate lecturer, getting redder and redder in the face - as the audience descended into whoops of laughter.

Tayo's spirit may have skipped a generation, after all his father was a Christian love everybody, that is why it had been so easy for him to give away his children to white people.

'Okay,' Tayo thought, still smiling at the lecturer, 'excluding my father, I'm a fourth generation African nationalist. My Grandfather was an officer in the first world war, he killed so many Germans they had to move him from the front - in case it became fashionable for Africans to kill Europeans. Tayo had seen the pictures, dressed all in white, with a fourteen inch bayonet in his hand. My great grandfather was a chief in Benin, fought against European colonisation. What they call an unmixed brunt negro. My great, great grandfather was a High Priest, not only black as ebony - but a pagan as well! They used to say he could kill with words. How the hell with such a pedigree, was I going to be an uncle tom, footshuffling Negro. Nurture is one thing, but nature is another. It is not in my nature to be a slave. I wouldn't know how to do it,' Tayo thought.

'This is absolute anarchy,' Thomas thought, looking at the students, as some in the back row began to throw make shift missiles at the front. He watched them like an owner might his bad dog as it tore up toilet paper or worried next door's cat. He fidgeted with his glasses, finally resorting to wiping them clean with a starched white handkerchief from his jacket pocket, (his mother had given it to him that morning). Mr. Thomas looked up with the newly cleaned articles at the students giggling and playing around, he looked around for someone to provide a level of control, he stared at the other teachers, but all they could do was shrug their shoulders dumfounded.

Then Thomas realised seeing the auditorium in anarchy that they could not control them. They were adults, they had chosen to come here. The local authorities, or the students from their own pockets had paid to be there. It was not as if they could suspend the entire year.

Thomas felt redundant, insecure. It was then that he realised, 'I must look really stupid.' He stopped in mid thought; and looked down at his badly polished shoes, his blue tie and tweed jacket. The white shirt ironed by his mother this morning.

'This jacket and tie don't go together,' he thought, 'they just don't fit. I just don't fit. Well not here any way. Well! Fit in, or not, one thing is certain,' Thomas thought, 'we don't have to watch this rabble descend into beasts. After all if I had a first class honours degree and not an upper second, I could have taught at a proper University, like Oxford, Cambridge or the School of Economics, not a Poly,' he thought, folding his handkerchief and putting it back in his pocket. 'This place is full of absolute riff , raff, rif raff. I'm sick of this third rate, shabby little hovel and I don't see why I should stay here any longer', he contemplated, walking over to an adjacent table, quietly folding up his papers in preparation, to walk out.

Tayo's was smiling like a Cheshire cat as he saw Thomas fumbling, like a red faced school boy with his papers. 'I think I've upset him,' Tayo thought, humourously to himself, 'oh well he should learn some manners, who am I supposed to be, he's lucky I didn't go down there and teach him who I am. Who am I supposed to be in deed, feisty little pencil neck. I guess,' he contemplated, looking around the hall at the near riot which was developing and the lecturers agitated red faces, 'we'd better hold it down. Exercise some restraint, I don't won't to be here any longer than I have to.'

Tayo raised his index finger, "Shoooo," he whispered loud enough for the back row to hear. 'I don't know what good it's going to do,' he thought, playing with his leather pouch.

He looked on surprised, as his action started a chain reaction. Throughout the hall there were cries of, 'shoo' and 'shush,' 'shut up,' and 'man I won't to get out of this place today, not tonight,' 'hold it down alright.' At last there was silence. The African couple went back to staring in each others eyes, the Muslims picked up their Koran and feverishly began reading it and the white couple started on round two of how to have sex in a packed hall on the first day of college.

Mr. Thomas looked up like a rabbit who had just been saved from Rabbit pie - only to be eaten by the next door neighbour's cat. The silence was stunning cold.

'I preferred the shouting and noise, I don't like them quiet,' Thomas thought. Then he realised how odd he looked shuffling all those papers and trying to leave, when now there was no reason to. He looked up at Tayo's grin, he could feel his eyes almost burning a whole in his head.

'Who do you think you are,' Thomas contemplated, staring at Tayo, 'so he can start a riot and stop it, can he,' looking at the now well behaved students, 'he's been reading too much Malcom, what did they say about him,' Thomas thought, ordering his papers and walking into the centre of the hall. 'That's it, Malcolm X was the only man in Harlem who could start, or stop a riot. Well,' he thought, playing with his glasses yet again, 'we will have none of that, none of that, none of that sort of thing here, we will have no black radicals, heroes, martyrs or anything of the sort. This is not Harlem it's **England**. So long as I am head of the Humanities faculty and a deputy principal, there will be no Malcom X's here, the cheek of it, how dare he!'

Mrs Lawson the lecturer for politics in society waddled forward like a duck, peering forward at the now quiet crowd. She looked like one of those double ice cream Sundays with a red cherry on top, a pair of black rimmed spectacles perched somewhere near the summit. She was at least four stone over weight and should have gone on a diet, especially as her local doctor said she would probably have a heart attack within the month. In all of her time as a teacher she had never witnessed such a disgraceful spectacle.

Mrs Lawson was a nasty little bad tempered teacher, as ignorant and short sighted as she was fat. She taught politics like she lived her life, everything was done to give maximum pleasure to herself. Her early career had been marked by no intervening period of excellence, on the contrary, she had begun as a primary school teacher, teaching little girls their ABC. She ran her classroom like a army drill square, not because she felt that they would learn more, but purely because it gave her pleasure to see the little girls jump to her voice. When she had been 'promoted' to the Poly she had tried to function in the same manner, only to be met with abuse and even threats of violence, that was just from the teachers.

She had resigned herself after a few years to a kind of overweight complacency. She spouted irrelevant information, she did not care what the students learned. But one thing she did care about was anything affecting her safe comfortable career. If there had been inspectors here that would be another bad report for the institution, perhaps even for her directly, she could not bear that.

Tayo looked down at Mr. Thomas, Mrs Lawson and the rest of the lecturers shuffling papers at the front of the hall trying to collect their thoughts together - like pieces of a jigsaw that just did not fit. They wanted to complete their induction session for the Humanities department.

 "Right," Mr. Thomas said, trying to be assertive, but only managing to spit at the front row. He held up a long list on a white sheet of paper, almost as white and ashen as the expression on his face. "When I call out your name, please come to the front, so I can cross your name off the list," he mumbled. "Abe Michael, Abifarin Dayo, Ade David, Adetunji Rotimi."

'There are more Yorubas here than Lagos,' Tayo thought, listening to the names and looking around, 'I wonder what there here for, Africa, or the Dead Presidents.'

 "Akinjo Tayo."

Tayo heard his name, like a boxer hears the bell to start round two. 'Should I go down there and play the game, or not,' Tayo thought, staring at Thomas who half read his mind and smiled. "Alright, I'll do it," Tayo muttered, under his breath, "he probably knows who I am anyway."

Bouncing down the steps of the auditorium two at a time and pushing past a white student who was coming up the opposite way.

"When you have finished, get your name ticked off here and exit this way," Mr. Thomas said, pointing to an exit to his rear.

"Did you hear that," Tayo said, to the white student who was still in his face, "that's the way out."

"Piss off!" the student spat, looking Tayo in his eyes.

Tayo hesitated, looked around and smiled, "I will remember you," he said, looking at the blueness of his eyes, the strained-coarse-white expression, a brooding troubled face, with a slight strain of authority, like an Aryan version of Adolf Hitler and "I want you to remember me." Tayo pushed past him, 'I don't have the time or patience to find out why young Adolf acted like that. It could be all these black faces and then him, he probably 'feels swamped'. Now he knows how I feel every morning in rush hour getting pushed in the back and the face by all those city gents in their pin-strip suits, staring at me like I'm a criminal. Well..... But see now when the tables get reversed just a little, you'll see enough of them, even the most liberal white sign up for a copy of British Bulldog and buy a pair of jack boots.' But Tayo did not have the inclination or patience to query the cause. 'The BNP are as active in this college as they are in Bexley,' he thought, as he looked at young Adolf push past a group of black people and out the fire exit. 'But I don't really care,' Tayo contemplated, ' I will beat him up, feisty little nazi, he's lucky that I want to finish this course, or he'd be hanging from the ceiling with SS cut into his forehead - cocky little cracker.'

Tayo was still thinking about retribution as he cleared the steps and stood dazed at a small cue formed leading to the lecturers in front.

'In African society,' Tayo thought, 'boys and girls go through a rights of passage, tests to turn them into men and women, it was not something to be left to chance. This college for most would be their test. But the question is will they understand the true nature of their challenge. It's not just to get a degree, assimilate as quickly as possible, it's to understand the world and play a functioning role within it. That's the challenge. I'm not going to be one of those people, who reach fifty five and then say to themselves what the hell was that (Life) all about. '

An African woman with a small child no more than four years old stood at the back. She looked agitated at her watch and then turned to Tayo, "I'm going to be late," she said, in a hurried tone, "for my child care."

She smiled a serene smile and fastened up her jacket to conceal a large bosom. Tayo was trying not to look, but he could not help himself. Her locks tied into a pony tail, with a few for effect hanging over a dignified forehead. The eyes calm, relaxed but forceful. There was something strong, yet powerful about her entire expression. Tayo wondered why he noticed her bosom first, when there was so much else about her, so spiritual, 'they say that men think of sex every six seconds,' he thought, still trying not to look at her body.

"Come on Simone," the woman said, pulling her forward. But Simone was to busy smiling at Tayo behind her, to pay the least bit of attention to her mother. "Oh hell, I'm really going to be late if this lot don't hurry up," she said frowning. She smiled at Tayo for the second time, who was wondering what he had done to deserve such treatment from mother and daughter.

"Just look after her for a minute, brother," she said, looking at Tayo, "I've got to make a phone call to the nursery."

He was about to protest and suggest that she take her with her and then his fatherly instincts took over. He saw the sweet delicate little face, the inquisitive, alert expression.

"Take his hand Simone, and be good, I won't be long," the woman said, with that she disappeared out of the exit to her front.

Simone looked up at Tayo like a daughter to her father and took his hand in hers. "Mumme says that I'm an African, are you an African," she said, confidently staring at Tayo.

Tayo looked down at her in a surprised manner. He had met children like this before, one's who put adults to shame with their intelligence and wisdom. In an ancient African society they would have been trained to become chiefs, Obas, but in modern times parents saw their wisdom as a burden and tried to force it out of them. Either by a constant injection of Mc Donalds, kiddies shows on TV and hair damaging clinics. Any latent African spirit would be spoilt and damaged. She was a returned ancestor. In the past she might have been an ancient mystic, or a princess.

"Yes I am an African too," Tayo said, looking down at her, "all black people are Africans, but some don't know it yet! But we do."

"Yes," Simone said, looking up at him," and Mummie says though her Grandpa and Mama were born in the Caribbean - she's still proud of who she is, but why Uncle do so many black people not want to be African."

Tayo bit his lip. He did not feel this was the right time to be explaining to her five hundred years of Black people's destruction. 'Nah,' Tayo thought, 'this is not the time.'

"Well Simone," he said, looking at her expectant face, "it's like this......"

Fortunately, Simone's mother appeared at the entrance to the Auditorium, adjusting her bag with a smile all over her face.

"I see you have acquainted yourselves then," she said, looking at Tayo and her.

"Simone here is very smart," Tayo replied, "old before her time. She was teaching me."

"She does do that," her mother said, "I hope she wasn't a bother."

"No not at all," Tayo stated, adjusting his leather pouch, "I got more sense from her today, than from all the adults I have spoken to this week."

"I know what you mean," the mother said, doing up her top button, which had come undone again. "By the way what's your name? That's terrible don't you think I left my daughter with you and I don't even know your name. Mine is Susan."

"Tayo," Tayo replied, looking at her.

"It's strange," Susan said, "I felt comfortable enough to leave Simone with you. I just felt you were, well honest."

"I am. Did you not see me honestly cuss that cracker over there," he said, pointing to Thomas at the front of the Auditorium ticking off names on a sheet of paper and trying to look important.

"Oh that was you," Susan said, pretending not to know. In fact she had observed him from the outset, she had never seen a brother handle himself with such dignity.

"Akinjo Tayo," Mr. Thomas said again, "is there a Mr. Akinjo here."

"I've got to go sister," Tayo said to Susan, "take care, and you too

Simone be good."

"Good bye uncle Tayo," Simone said, as Tayo bounced towards Mr. Thomas. Susan watched him go past her, 'he doesn't walk, he bounces, like a cat,' she thought, and smiled to herself.

Tayo stood and looked Mr. Thomas straight in his eyes, "ummmh" he said, "Mr. Tayo Akinjo, I presume."

"Let's not start that business again," Tayo snarled.

"But your name is Tayo Akinjo, isn't it."

"Yeah that's right," Tayo replied, "I thought we established that an hour ago, I thought you were supposed to be the teacher and me the student."

"Tayo Akinjo," Thomas muttered under his breath, "obviously you are Yoruba, probably from Ondo state, that's right, Ondo state, definitely from some where like there. Probably from a little village like Idanre or somewhere like that."

Tayo stared at Thomas emotionless. He had been absolutely correct right down to the village that his parents came from. Tayo smiled, "Nah mate I'm English, born in Clapham, but thanks for the geography lesson. I thought you taught Law."

"But seriously young man, your antics really intrigued me," Thomas said, "such command, such poise, have you ever thought about the Debating Society, whilst your here."

Tayo gazed at the lecturer, 'it's strange when I was at the Poly two years ago I don't remember him at all. Where did he come from and why is he so much in my face,' he thought.

"Haven't I got to sign something or other, you've got other students to see. Besides I thought you were going to put me on a charge or something," Tayo said.

"Charge, young man, a charge, (he giggled like a baby) no your behaviour was impertinent, but this is not a school as you well know. No Tayo if I may call you Tayo, my name is Michael and I am one of the deputy principals," he said, "we shall definitely be seeing each other again, "because as I understand from the paperwork you are a second year law student, you took a year out. Well, getting in touch with your roots were you," laughing to himself,

"you've been here longer than me. How does it feel being a nine‑
teen year old geriatric (laughing again)."

"Hah, hah (fake laughter)," Tayo muttered, "is this where I sign,"
pointing to the piece of paper. But Tayo really felt like grabbing
him by the scuff of the neck, and shouting 'do you think what you
said was funny, it wasn't you know, but I will show you something
funny and then giving him a good hard slap and shouting, now
that was funny. Who the hell does he think I am?'

Tayo unzipped his pouch and took a pen out signing the paper that
Thomas had in front of him. "Is that okay, Michael," he said sarcastically, "cause I've got to be going."

Mr. Thomas peered at the scribbling, "oh what interesting hand
writing you've got, have you ever had it looked at," he chuffed. But
Tayo had already disappeared through the exit.

'What an arrogant youth, I will know the content of his mind,'
Thomas thought to himself as he watched Tayo bounce towards the
exit, 'this is the only interesting specimen in this good forsaken little ghetto. Perhaps this year would not be as unstimulating as I
thought.'

Smoke gets in your eyes

It was three p.m. when Tayo walked into the canteen. A sign above him read, 'Closed until 6pm.' Tayo was hoping to see a group of black revolutionaries sitting huddled together, the familiar faces Carl, Fred or Tony, but there was only a tired worn out old Dinner lady, with her apron smothered in grease and a blank expression. With chubby brown fingers and the energy of a snail, she was mopping up some spilt milk on a nearby table.

When she saw Tayo skipping in she called out, "you know we're closed love," in a Jamaican accent and under her breath, "can't they read, (looking him up and down) we open at six p.m."

Tayo just smiled, as if he was a sweet boy, (and he wasn't), he could not be bothered to reply. Tayo bounced the door of the canteen open and bounced up the stairs two at a time, 'there are no familiar spirits here,' he thought to himself, 'no brothers here, who I have seen with an ounce of anything except front.'

Some people may look for friends on their first day who are wearing the same jeans as them, who come from the same village, who where the same baseball cap, or have the same liking for Atlantic Starr or Luther Vandross. Or more often than not the same amount of money in Daddy's bank account. Tayo could here the conversation and he was dreading the first lunch time, when all the brothers and sisters whose mothers and fathers were diplomats and generals came out and compared notes. Preparing for the day that they would go to the country of their parents and exploit them, live life high whilst the majority of the people starved. How ? Because after all, 'Daddy was this and daddy was that and I am going to grow up and be just like my Daddy.'

Tayo had seen it all before. But he did not choose his companions because they wore the same jeans as him, he did not wear jeans. He was not going to call someone a brother because they were simply from the same village. And he had never worn a baseball cap, not even to play baseball. As for Luther Vandross, 'no disrespect,' he thought, 'I can't stand that middle of the road, sluggish, sellout, excuse for black music. What happened to soul singers who could sing with their heart in their mouth and their soul on their sleeve. What happened to Otis Redding, and Sam Cooke, Luther Vandross, and Atlantic Starr indeed,' as he bounced up his third flight of steps without breaking into a sweat, 'I can't stand them.'

On walking across the corridor, 'how quiet it is up here,' he thought, looking down at the concourse now three floors beneath him. The students were milling about like little insects, trying to gather information, or check the notice boards, so eager to start the life that would lead them to, 'riches and success. Glory and gravy, nothing but glory and gravy,' Tayo contemplated. He looked down at them, like an avenging angel, watching the dammed running to hell.

Tayo was in the midst of this thought when a smell caught his nose. A sweet aromatic smell which would not come out of his nose though he tried to close his nostrils, "that is weed," he said, out loud, but to himself. 'Who the hell, would be brave, or stupid enough to smoke here in the college,' Tayo thought, to himself, adjusting his leather pouch and walking through a pair of red double doors and closer to the smell. The corridor when he reached it was hazy with smoke, Tayo coughed a little, finally deciding to hold his breath, 'I want to know who this person is, with out them knowing who I am,' he thought, bouncing towards the centre of the bellowing smoke. 'This guy must be crazy,' he looked up, 'this is a classroom too,' observing the vacant sign outside the door on the wall.

Tayo waited there for a second, hoping to hear a sign, or a murmur from within, but there was nothing, 'well let's see then,' he said, to himself, pushing the classroom door open and standing in the middle of the smoke filled room. He coughed slightly and waved the smoke away. Finally his eyes became accustomed to the surroundings and he picked out three figures sitting down the other end of the room who seemed completely undisturbed, or even interested that Tayo had just burst into the room. He walked forward and stared at them. The central figure was a young man no more then twenty, wearing timberland suede boots. Tayo noticed the boots, because he had his legs stretched out on the table like he was on holiday lying at a beach.

The young man like a modern day Buni Wailer blowing smoke rings with the largest spliff Tayo had ever seen, whilst his yellow shoe laces dangled around his ankles and baggy jeans were flapping in the veritable cloud of smoke he had summoned. A white T shirt was obscured by a leather jacket which appeared to stretch all the way to the ground. Tayo had not seen a jacket like it before. It reminded him of one of those first world war coats, that flying aces would wear as they went off to 'fight the Huns(Germans) and fight for good old Blighty (England).'

'No doubt,' Tayo thought, 'this brother probably thinks his coat is so black, original and stylish, that it makes him so correct, but the former owner was probably a slave owning fascist. How ironic,' Tayo contemplated in his mind still trying to figure the guy out, 'we think these things are so black, we talk patwa, what is that feisty, and fit, 'renk', 'maagre,' we use them all the time, but they're old English, seventeenth century swear words. The words the slave master gave us on the plantation, forced on the threat of starvation to give up our own languages and use theirs. We got so used to it we believe they're are own. But....Is it possible that they could have become our own. Culture after all is not a static thing, surely.. it transforms grows and develops, it is constantiy expanding. I know it is.'

The young 'Buni Wailer' was taking a deep drag on the illegal substance between his fingers, and flicking the ash with the dexterity of a Rasta in St. Thomas. His young almost feminine face adorned only by a small tuft of hair on the chin. The eyes opal shaped and serene like a cat, the pupil full and rounded, gave a different expression of youth, vitality and there was something else, fearlessness. 'Yes,' Tayo thought, 'I have seen others react when they read it in my face, to look at my reflection is not what I expect, I am not looking for a twin brother, especially one whose sat smoking weed in a classroom with two sisters, when he should be doing something more positive. What, I don't know exactly, but definitely something progressive.'

A grey Kangol hat lay up turned on the table and appeared to be used to cover the young man's funki dreads which adorned an other wise bald head. But these were dreads with a difference. Thick and long, perhaps three feet long and tied at the top like a Cherokee, 'how does he get the hat on,' Tayo thought, 'or does he have it purely for show, a Kangol hat to impress his girlfriends or his spars.'

The brother leaned over to the chubby girl on the left who looked like she was about as irritated with Tayo as one could be without committing murder, he had interrupted their 'menage a trois.' She brushed her straight, brown, (dyed) hair away from her rather too spotty face and frowned at him with a look of disgust. Doing up her shirt top and buttoning up her jacket.

"Did I interrupt something," Tayo said, sarcastically looking at the girl who in an embarrassed way and rather clumsily was struggling with her buttons. The brother stared at him and the girl with her head in her hands seemed asleep and motionless.

"Obviously I am talking to myself," Tayo said. The brother glared back, flicking ash in all directions with his index finger, the girl was still frowning.

"Listen brother, you will do me the respect of replying when I talk to you," Tayo said, pretending to be angry, "you're sitting here smoking your life away, wasting time, what's your plan."

"Do I know you," the brother eventually replied, looking Tayo up and down and finding none of the familiarity that he had found in his spirit. Tayo noticed the slight country accent, the lack of real venom in the reply. 'Perhaps he's got something else in him apart from smoke and ragga,' he thought.

"The question is do you know yourself?" Tayo continued, staring at the brother and then the girl who by now was beside herself with agitation.

"What the hell do you want," she spat out, "we we're just having a quiet smoke and sit in here and you come and disturb us, what's your problem," brushing the hair from her face.

"My problem," Tayo said, "is you. Whilst are people, Africans are dying, and suffering through out the world, you feel you have the luxury to sit here and smoke your life away."

"What's that got to do with me," the chubby girl said, "I don't care what they do, I ain't no boobo African with a bone through my nose and a tutu."

"Shut up!" the brother said, raising his voice and looking at her, "you're an African, shut up your foolishness."

"Alright," the brother continued, he turned to Tayo, paused for affect, "don't go on ignorant, if you want to fight, I don't business, who ever you are, we can fight."

"Go and kick his arse, Michael," the girl shrieked, as the young man stood up.

"If that's the way you want it," Tayo said, looking at his adversary who had now put down his spliff with the dexterity of a Western gunslinger, and was bounding towards him.

'How quick he is to come and fight me,' Tayo thought ,'I wonder if he would be so eager if I was not the same colour as him, well at least I know his name.'

But Michael was already in his face, "So what you're 'sayin," he said, with his arms in the air like he was in South central L.A. (but he wasn't).

"Alright out here," Tayo said, opening the door and he turned and walked out of the classroom and into the corridor, still empty but for them.

Michael followed, "So what you sayin," he said.

"I'm saying," Tayo replied, looking at the brother's eyes, "if you want two black man to fight and kill each other over foolishness we can. But it's not going to prove anything. I would rather bust up a skinhead or any other cracker. But if you got something to prove then that's alright. But what I said still stands, you should not be in there with your two little friends smoking weed whilst are people are suffering."

Michael looked at Tayo and eventually he recognised him. It was not that they had met before. No they were complete strangers. But there was something about the shape of the nose, the roundness of the pupil that reminded him, of him, or a version of him, at least. 'But it's not really physical, it's his spirit,' Michael thought, 'he's fearless, totally fearless. He seemed so arrogant, but when he went on about the race, that went and 'wah' there's 'nothink but truth.' Michael took his hand out of his pocket, but left the knife that he was carrying there. He had been ready to stab Tayo to death if necessary, 'I don't business,' he would always say to his friends, 'it's better that I do it to them, before they do it to me.'

Tayo heard the click of the blade as it clipped back into it's sheath and he smiled, "so you were going to be a perpetrator, a perpetrator of black on black violence," he said looking at him.

"I don't care what colour you are, I don't business (for the third time), remember it was you who asked me out," Michael said, nonchalantly.

"Okay," Tayo replied, "you should put those skills to better use. You know only this morning, (thinking on his feet) a group of whites were out hunting black people. Just outside this college. They almost beat an Asian guy to death. You know they would not have done less to us."

"So what," Michael said, insolently.

"So we can change it, not by sitting in their hiding from the world, but organising. The Sikhs do it, the Muslims you will find out do it. In fact everybody does it but us."

"Organising, I'm not in it," Michael said sighing, "I don't do it. You see whilst all of you are in there bowing to those greyback teachers writing reports on you and smiling, when they would rather cut your heart out."

"I agree," Tayo said leaning against the wall and looking in both directions of the corridor, "but I'm telling you, just between you and I that I'm goin cause so much chaos in this place. You wait and see, I'm goin expose it for the nasty little racist place it is and Michael, that's your name isn't it, you are goin ' to help me."

"Good luck," Michael said, "having a smart memory and a smart mouth is not goin' to be enough. Black people aren't ready," with that, before Tayo could speak any more he disappeared down the corridor and back into the smokers room.

But as Tayo disappeared down the corridor smiling to himself at his days work, Michael sat down in his seat a little less easy than he had done before. There was something which Tayo had said which made him think. 'There's truth to it, an undeniable, indefatigable, (he smiled to himself that he remembered such long words) truth. Black people are dying, too often, too much still, like at-a-nothing, turn on the news and you see black people on TV starving, some where, or going on bad against one another. Why is it that we go on so with each other, cut up another black man for stepping on my shoe, or giving us a bad look, being too stush, too dark, or too light, for being from South London, or North London, or in the wrong place at the wrong time still - any excuse. How's that? Even me eager still; too eager, to take this brother's life so quickly, without really checking where he was coming from.'

'Besides talking the most sense,' Michael thought, 'that brother was good looking, almost as good looking as me,' as he took out the rizla paper to roll another spliff. 'But then nah, no body can be as good looking as me. Still, there's something else,' he thought, 'his spirit's familiar, it's like staring at me. That's how' it is, you can meet someone for the first time and there more familiar than people you've known your whole life,' he thought looking at Debbie the plump girl next to him.

They had grown up in the same street in Northampton and been together since childhood, even born in the same hospital, but her spirit was alien. 'I'm not an African, she said,' Michael thought, 'and all that foolishness like one of those brother's from the street on crack.

He looked at her chubby face and the third chocolate bar she was cramming in her mouth, whilst spluttering, "did you bust that fool's sledge?"

He stared at her, 'if there's anyone's sledge that I should be busting, it should be yours. Bust his sledge indeed,' he thought.

BMW's and chicken

Tayo bounced down the corridor looking at his watch, it was almost six pm, where had the day gone. He pushed the door open skipping down the stairs winding to the ground floor two at a time. He could see the sun setting in the sky, sending an orange glow across the stratosphere. The sky illuminated, broken up only by the occasional puffy cloud like white candy floss. Tayo sprang towards the exit and pushed the door open, skipping down the stairs of the Poly and on to the streets of south London.

The blur of the speeding cars flitting to and fro down the nearby road, new, old, borrowed and stolen cars, all in such a hurry to reach their destinations. Top executives who had bought houses in the slums to avoid the house boom, in new pinstripe suits, smoking £25 cigars and talking to their wives on their new mobile phones. Even though their mistresses were sat next to them, thumbing through the pages of Vogue.

Workmen in transit vans on their way home to the wife and two point four children, ogling and staring at young women old enough to be their daughters. All the while their mates studied the latest offering on page 3, "She's got big tits, get a load of that, mate."

Meanwhile Busta Manley with gold chops, (except no imitation) and three inch silver chain bouncing up and down on his steroid induced chest. The silver and gold in his teeth and chain gleamed unnaturally. 'Solid silver chain, honest mate, would I lie to you,' the seller Alf had told him. He remembered looking at it and grabbing the little white trader by the scruff of his neck and spitting in his face, "if I find out 'dis' fake I'll come back and chop you in the head, understand?"

The trader gave a half nod, it was not that he was genuinely afraid. He had black mates bigger and harder than him, besides he had been a member of the BNP since he was twenty, if anything happened to him 'they would burn this geezer like it was 1830's Mississippi.' His mate Toni and Johnny loved beating his kind, just for the hell of it. Anyway no market trader in Camden Town Market was without protection. He carried a 9mm pistol in his bag under his stall table and was not afraid to use it.

So why did Alf with such a background allow himself to be abused in public? Because Alf that's what his name was, new that the chain was stolen, and the foolish man (black man) who had stolen it, had battered his victim to death. The police were looking for a, 'large black man with a silver chain.' The person responsible was his mate, he called him, 'Black Charlie,' 'he was alright you know,' Alf thought, looking at Busta, 'unlike this spade who thinks he's in bloody Jamaica, this is England mate, bloody England,' he thought, as he handed over the chain for a crisp twenty pound, which he quickly tucked in his pocket like a hamster.

But Busta in his Black BMW and his silver shining chain, did not know or care that he was wearing something that could mean him increasing the black British prison population by one. No Busta did not care. All he cared about was looking the part and being a real black man, with his white girlfriend sitting next to him. Even though she kept moaning just a little bit too much that he, 'never took her out enough.'

He loved her, after all she had partaken in at least three affairs with his best friends and even the child she was about to abort was not his. But Busta was in seventh heaven, speeding down Elephant and Castle with his beautiful (is in the eye of the beholder) girlfriend, nagging him like a fisher wife at Sunday market. She had not washed her stinking lank hair in three days and stank true to her trade of fish, but Busta loved her because, she gave him status. He had been out with black girls before, but he wanted loyalty, beauty and trustworthiness from his wife, that is why in his stupidity, he had married a selfish, ignorant, adulterous woman, bad tempered rude and down right ugly.

He was typical of many first generation brothers who had come via the Caribbean with a gun in one pocket and a crack in another, who came to England to make as much money as possible, any way possible and go back to 'Jam' and live like a king and Busta did not care how many black people he had to kill, or beat, to achieve his goal. He was the epitome of all the stereotypes of the big, ignorant, black woman beating brother. He was the kind of brother that had been raised in the ghetto of Kingston dodging bullets until he had robbed and stole enough to buy a gun, now he did the shooting. England for him was an easy ride. 'Black people are soft, unorganised.' If this was Africa the whole village would have turned out to beat him to death for selling death to their children, but here people just behaved as if he did not exist, waving his gold chops and grinning through his fake silver and gold teeth.

His black BMW paused at the lights, he could see the blur of the Poly in his right window and just caught sight of Tayo bouncing down the street.

"Wa who dat?" Busta said out loud, when he saw the tall dark skinned brother skipping down the road without a care in the world. "Like he's a don, or something."

"Are ya talking shit always wanting to start trouble," his girlfriend said, pushing her hair away from her face and brushing cake crumbs from the meal she had eaten an hour ago from her lips.

"It's alright love," Busta said to her, "me na start no trouble, that bwoy jus goin on like he big though, ma feel to jus box him two time."

But it was not alright. Because Busta in his twenty thousand pound Black sporty BMW was not watching were he was driving. The lights in front had changed from yellow to red. A yellow mini was crossing from the adjacent road and Busta went straight into the side of it.

Tayo was oblivious to Busta, his silver chain, girlfriend, the work-men, or the unfaithful businessmen, they were just a blur of lights and flashes. He did not even see or hear the crash of Busta's car as it hit the yellow mini full of three Oxbridge students on their way to University for their first week.

Tayo was oblivious to the damage he had caused by simply being an upright dignified African in a country that did not respect or honour such pride.

He bounced passed the Tube station, a little too packed with over-paid businessmen on their way home to suburbia for their supper and disappeared down the subway.

Elephant and Castle had not changed much in a year, there were still the drunkards, the alcohol, the faint smell of sick and filth. It was enough certainly to put a brother off his appetite, but his drive was stronger than that.

An African man, arm in arm with his wife almost bumped into him as he turned the corner, "sorry brother," Tayo said, "I did not look where I was going, you know how brothers are these days."

"No problem," the brother said doing up the top button of his rain coat and hardly stopping to look at his woman's big brown eyes. They smiled so sweetly and so serenely like a king and queen on some ancient stone statue in Memphis (and I don't mean Memphis Tennessee). Her noble chin and proud upright posture like a model and his effortless bouncing gait seemed to compliment each other. Oblivious to the whole world as if their African love could blot out the world. Tayo stopped for a while just to stare. 'How much I've forgotten what it is to hold a sister, how long has it been, two years. Oh well,' he thought, 'monks go for years without, and discipline is the key to success,' he said, almost convincing himself.

He was so busy in thought that the hunger which had begun as a tingling in his stomach now became a grown spreading to the whole of his body. Then the smell hit him. A sweet smell of fried chicken. Not the kind you find in KFC but the type cooked back home, the type where you could taste the smell. Tayo rubbed his nose, and liked his lips like a cat. 'Where's that smell coming from? It's like Africa just came to Elephant and Castle. Man where is that food.'

Tayo was allowing his nose to lead him. The smell was getting stronger, he felt like a thirsty man looking for an oasis. Then he saw it surrounded by all the concrete jungles. "SUYA" the sign read. Large black lettering over a red sign board. Tayo peered a little closer, it looked like a mobile cafeteria, but the twist was instead of hot dogs, and beefburgers, they sold spicy chicken, rice and peas, plantain (dudu) fried fish and dumpling, stewed vegetables and okra.

The owners were two brothers from Nigeria who on seeing Tayo bouncing towards them greeted him with a "Ba wo ni, nkan (how are you)?"

Tayo replied, "K'ob'ade, (fine) Kil' ode (What's up)," coming up close to the canteen and inhaling the full smell of frying chicken and spices.

"Ko'si (not much)," the brother behind the till replied, adjusting his glasses which were becoming steamed up and wiping a little to much grease from his hands on his apron.

Tayo was looking to change the conversation from Yourba, he was not as fluent in the language as he would have liked. Some day he was going to learn, he felt so envious seeing Africans speaking to each another in a language he could not understand, he wanted to be able to giggle and laugh along with them, tell jokes and chat up women, cuss and most of all educate, in a language other than English.

"We weren't sure you were Yourba," the brother in glasses said, cleaning his glasses and looking at Tayo's strange dress sense, "you dress like a West Indian."

"Like a what," Tayo said, forgetting about the food for a moment, "a West Indian, what is a West Indian?"

"You know one of those Jamaicans!" the other cook said, turning to look at Tayo and staring a bit to long at his funki dreads. Tayo could feel the rage rising inside himself. 'Where am I going to start with these brothers,' Tayo thought, 'how am I going to explain the so called Caribbean is only another name for Cannibals, what the Europeans called the people there. That those islands are not west of India, they are not the west Indies. They only got that name because Christopher Columbus (not his real name) in 1492 went west looking for Asia and instead of admitting he was lost and had landed in a new continent had the arrogance to say that he was west of India, hence West Indies.'

Tayo looked at the little brother and took a sigh as he examined his small insular face. "Giveme some chicken and rice and peas, please," Tayo said, trying to change the subject and avoid losing his temper. The little brother read his emotion and scurried off to fry the meat, Tayo could feel the steam rising.

"No but seriously, where are you from?" the taller brother said, staring at his locks.

"Where do you think I'm from," Tayo stated looking at him. The brother look dumfounded for a moment.

"No seriously," he interjected, "are you West Indian or Nigerian. You know some Yoruba but you don't look Nigerian. Or just oyibo (white)."

Tayo's anger was rising to a breaking point, some how he managed to gain control of himself.

"How exactly is a Nigerian supposed to look," Tayo said, staring at them.

"Well...., you know," the taller brother said.

"No I don't know," Tayo said, emphatically, "you're an expert tell me."

"Well...." the brother said obviously lost for words and beginning to stutter. The smaller one by now had resigned himself to cooking

Tayo's chicken, he did not relish going back into the conversation.

"Oh but you must be born here," the taller brother continued, hoping to win the argument with the statement.

"You what," Tayo said, "what the hell has that got to do with anything, and besides you don't know where I was born, why are you presuming?"

The brother looked completely confused. For him the world was made up of safe little boxes there were Jamaicans who were Rastas, listened to reggae music and were known for their violence. There were Nigerians, industrious, hard working but divided, badly led and prone to corruption. Asians hard working and competitive and white people who ran the world, and that was it. But Tayo was not going to allow these brother's stereotypes about the world to be so comfortable. 'What is certain unless we as Black/ African people do not get ourselves out of them we are finished,' Tayo thought, thinking of a reply.

"I tell you what," Tayo said, "I'll put you out of your misery." Both brothers stopped what they were doing and stared at Tayo like two children waiting for a father. "I'm from....." he paused for affect, "........Africa, just like you," he said, "every black person is an African I'm telling you that now. There is no such thing as a West Indian, they are **African** people who were taken to slave ships by force in chains by white men and unfortunately some of us. Something which it would have been impossible to do without our help. How was that possible, because of that tribalism you are demonstrating right now. West Indian indeed, west Indian, we are an African people. That's just about the end of it, read a book," he said, reaching inside in his pocket and pulling out a five pound note.

The short brother was still so mesmerised by Tayo's words he forgot what he was supposed to be doing.

"The food," Tayo said, "look man it's burning."

"Oh sorry," the brother said, hurriedly putting it all together.

"That'll be three pounds fifty," the other brother said, "five pound okay, one pound fifty change, there you are." But the short brother still had a look of confusion on his face.

"So where are you from?" he asked again.

"Didn't you hear what he said," his friend replied, "about Africa and all that."

Tayo took his change pushed it in his pouch and wrapped up his food in the carry bag it was in. He shock his head as he walked away from them. 'I really don't have the patience right now. This day feels like a whole week,' he thought kicking a nearby stone across the court yard.

Tayo did not even notice the change in atmosphere as the wind picked up and the evening drew on to night. Even as he boarded his bus to Brixton crowded as it was, he did not notice the life on board, another day he would have revelled in it, but now all he wanted to do was go home, sleep and eat, and as he reached his bus stop and walked along his own street. He did not notice the crack dealers, pimps, prostitutes, the liberal white students going to buy their weed. As he walked along the landing that led to his flat, unlocked the latch and stepped inside, he wanted to shut Johnny the vic and his mate Toni, Tav, the skinheads, Michael, Alf, Busta, Melanie, even Susan, he wanted to close himself off from the world just for tonight, tomorrow he would put his armour on, go to battle, but tonight. Then he thought, like a shadow passing over his spirit, 'I have died a thousand times and been reborn a thousand times, in a thousand places, with unfamiliar faces, but I've never found me, how can this be? So we struggle with our minds, against the tide of times, to become what we would be. Like a stray cat, or a dog howling at the moon, as if my howls could bring the moon down, but it can't, so why do it? Because howling is all I know what to do,' and he rummaged inside his pockets for his keys, hoping the shadow would pass, but it just hung there.

Wednesday the 27th

Thomas Mensah was walking rather briskly down Elephant and Castle road in one of his smartest grey suits. His shoes were as black and shiny as an officer on parade. His shirt white, starched, his tie done up tight, to his neck like a student off for his first interview in a city firm. His jaw was firm, resolute, without a touch of compassion, austere and pedantic and there was something in his face, his expression, that conveyed a man who was used to bossing others around and having his way. Thomas Mensah or uncle Tom as he liked to be called, was a retired army officer from Ghana, who after serving four years in the Ghanaian Parliament had become disillusioned with the status quo, especially the rise in Marxism and the dropping of standards in Public life.

He had an overriding hatred for communism and being a follower of the famous JB Danquah one time Pan Africanist/ Cultural nationalist. Thomas Mensah believed in individual excellence and yet there was something in his jaded, faded eyes, a discolouration in the pupils, a lack of focus in the retina, that conveyed a lack of clarity of mind, mixed with ruthlessness, even cruelty.

As he walked along the faded streets of South London on the way to the Polytehnic he cut a dignified approach. People would stop to see what a dignified well dressed man was doing in the area. But Mr Mensah did not care what ordinary people thought of him, all he cared for was power, money and wealth. He had sold out members of his own family in his ruthless rise to the top and he would sell out you (and I do men you) just for the fun of it, he liked to see people squeal.

Being an Asante and tracing his origin back to Premph the first, he revelled in the idea of having power, exploiting others and making decisions and if he could not, he would want to know why.

Bouncing along the road like a much younger man, encountering a black youth dressed ragged and definitely the worst for wear. The youth had worn out combat trousers, wholes all over and stinking. His hair was matted and consisted of four or five locks grown together, definitely not for fashion. A worn out combat jacket in a pattern of olive green and khaki. The zip busted and torn, tied round his waist with string. He saw Thomas coming and hailed him, "yes Pappah, gives us some change please, so I can buy some coffee."

Thomas looked at him, as if he was looking at a piece of filth,

"Ge...t out of my (he had an affected very English way of talking)..
fucking way you filthy little bastard. You ...don't do do this. All of
you West Indian filth are the same, get a job, you are a disgrace, "
he said, looking at him. With that Thomas who was carrying an
umbrella, pushed the young man aside with the point of it, as one
would a dog that walked across his path and strolled past him.

The ragged youth was still trying to work out what he had done to
deserve this, when he saw a young man no more than nineteen
years old coming in his direction. He half thought that his begging
might produce a similar response. But he bit his lip and looking at
the youth (Tayo) he saw despite the arrogant disposition, something which was kind.

"Brother can you give us some change, please, brother," the young
man said to Tayo.

Tayo pushed past a white business man who had crossed his path
and made his way straight to the youth who had his hand outstretched. Tayo reached inside his pocket, he only had a pound for
his dinner but 'he needs it more,' he thought. 'There you go brother, just don't spend it on drink, or foolishness,' he said, handing
him the pound.

"May the ancestors bless you," the young man said.

Tayo turned back to look at him on hearing the word ancestors and
stared, "what do you mean?" Tayo asked inquisitively.

"I mean," the brother replied, "let your ancestors watch over you. I
used to be in the SAS, ..do you believe me.. it's true, ...do you
believe me." Tayo nodded, it was not just the combats that made
him think it was true, but part of the brother's general attitude,
even with his hair stinking and matted and his trousers torn and
hanging around his waist. The young man continued, "I've killed
people, lot's of people, lots of them all over the place for this country, loads of people, do you believe me.? (He hesitated). I was
meant to be dead. I should be dead. Do you know what saved me,
do ya, do you know, do ya." Tayo shock his head.

"What saved me was my ancestors," the young man said, "I'm
telling you my **ancestors** saved me.. even when I thought wa' this
is me for dead. Now I give that to you."

Tayo looked at him puzzled.

"I mean, I give you the protection," the young man said, "do you believe me.. do you believe me....," looking into Tayo 's eyes desperately. "I'm goin to die soon and I need someone to pass it over to. I give it to you." With that he turned and disappeared quicker than Tayo thought his legs could carry him.

"Tayo sweetie, who are you looking at, another girl, don't you know you are mine." Tayo turned around to see Melanie's familiar features. Too preoccupied to notice her sneaking up behind him.

Her figure was more voluptuous than ever. The ruby red lipstick the jacket open at the top, to just conceal a figure hugging bra.

"How are you Melanie," Tayo asked.

"So who is she then," Melanie said, "the girl of your dreams, and I know what kind of one's you have."

"Why do you presume it was a girl," he said ,"see," he said pointing, (in the direction where the young man had gone.) But there was nobody there, almost if he had imagined the whole thing.

"Yeah right," Melanie said, looking in the direction and batting her eyelids at him.

"You know what," Tayo said ignoring her advances, "this country has so many secrets, you know the brother that was just here said, it's really strange, he said he'd been in the army, more than that in the SAS." He looked at her blank expression, "you know the SAS, the army special forces and that. But d'you know what, the funny thing is I actually believe him."

Melanie noticed the serious expression on his face and stopped batting her eyelids.

"We don't know half of what goes on here, why would he be begging on the streets on London if he has done service for this country," Tayo said, "you see, even when you serve, when you are no longer useful, like a machine you are replaced and thrown away. There was something else he said to, it was really strange, really strange, I don't expect you'd understand, something about protection, giving me his protection, though why he should think I need it, I don't know." Melanie was just looking into Tayo's eyes. "I wonder," Tayo continued, "if he was a man at all, or whether I just imagined him, or was he one of those spirits."

Melanie looked at him, "my you are sexy when you talk like this," she said, "why don't you come round later to my bedroom and talk to me again, you can talk to me all night, or whatever else you want to do."

"Why is it?" Tayo said, looking at her, "that you only think about one thing." Trying not to look at her open jacket revealing her ample bosom imprisoned in her bra, he checked himself, 'I am supposed to be an upright, righteous brother, remember, I am supposed to be one of the good guys.'

"What are you looking at," Melanie said again.

"I told you, that brother, " Tayo said, rather irately.

"No I mean what are you looking at now!" She could feel Tayo's eyes burning their way down her body.

"Nothing," he said remembering that they were on a busy street and that people were beginning to look.

"Yeah right," she said, "anytime and I do mean anytime you want to see me properly, you don't have to be bashful, just let me know. You can come and see me tonight if you like, then you won't have to imagine anymore. Do you fancy that. I mean me do you?"

"Haven't we been over this already," Tayo said, pulling his eyes off her fine brown frame.

"Anyway," Melanie said, changing the subject, "are you going to the meeting."

"What meeting?" he asked, puzzled.

"Come on now, you being one of the organisers in the past for it and you're asking me now, what meeting," she said. Tayo still looked puzzled. "Why the black student's society meeting of course."

"You mean," remembering the poster he had seen two days ago, "that Afro- Caribbean society, and what is it Black... British Club (he emphasised the last word so it reverberated in his mouth). "

"Yeah that's it," She said, "are you comin' with me, 'I'll make it worth you're while, you can sit next to me and cuss them and I'll listen and laugh, come on I know you want to," she said, taking his arm in hers. Tayo felt himself being led not necessarily against his will, 'besides,' he thought, 'I have no lessons today, I might as well go, and see what it's like.'

Thomas Mensah sat at the front of a very large table in the lecture room 7. His £150 watch resting on a new filofax he had acquired for the occasion. There were fifteen other people present mostly first year students all disinterested, except Susan who had brought Simone. She was bouncing around on her mother's lap playfully.

Thomas looked at his watch, it was 2.05 they were five minutes late. He looked irritated at the small attendance. 'This is the last planning meeting before the big event and the main co-ordinator Brenda is not even here,' he thought, looking at the young faces, 'she's probably painting her nails and trying to look like her cousin Naomi, that is the problem with having a women chair. Fancy this, being upstaged by a woman and a Caribbean one at that, where is her education, her degrees. After all am I not a doctor of history, a past member of Parliament, a distinguished gentleman who has met the queen on more than one occasion and served his majesty's armed forces.' He stood up.

"Good afternoon, ladies and gentleman," Thomas said, looking around the crowd and trying not to get annoyed by the chipping paint work on the doorway. 'This is really a low class institution,' he thought, 'not worthy of my attention.' "This is the Afro-Caribbean society and Black British Club," he said, "I am the President of the Black British Club and Vice president of the Afro-Caribbean Society and Miss Brenda Campbell is President. She has been a little bit delayed, but I'm sure she will be along shortly. Let's start then. I will introduce myself and then each of you must. Tell us which country you are from and what you are studying here."

A young bother with a baseball cap on the back row was tutting to himself throughout the entire speech of Mr Thomas Mensah ex MP of Ghana; at the last statement, he made up his mind to leave. The only thing that stopped him was the entrance of a bodacious black woman a little too well endowed to be wearing what left nothing to the imagination, a tight red mini dress with a slit up the middle, green stockings, blue painted finger nails and yellow dyed blonde hair, with the obligatory extensions. The young brother who had thought a moment ago about leaving sat down with a jolt, "What !" was all he could exclaim. Even Thomas - he had two wives and three mistresses, stopped in mid sentence when he saw her well endowed bouncing frame.

"High everybody," she said, "I'm Brenda, sorry I'm late, I've just been at a photo shoot with Naomi, you know Naomi, she's my cousin." Brenda still bouncing in every direction and still talking, "Naomi's just looking so gorgeous and her boyfriend you know that good looking white man in the films... well he's so handsome and I didn't know before how hard they had to work at these shoots. She works so hard but her hubby is so supportive."

Thomas was going to interject, but he knew when he had been upstaged and sat down in his chair with a thump. "So to get back to business," she said, "oh," getting distracted by the brother in the baseball cap, "you are so handsome, have you ever thought about going into film or TV, your simply gorgeous." The brother smiled rather embarrassed.

Susan who had brought Simone to hear some history about Africa or at least something positive could feel herself losing her temper. 'Brenda's dress should have an eighteen certificate on it,' Susan thought. 'Thomas is as pompous as he is incompetent. The whole thing just reminds me how confused our people have become.'

Brenda was reaching her climax, she was looking for two beautiful Nubians to star in a video for a major production by a leading international singer.

"All you have to do," she said "is take off all your clothes, and roll around in black paint. It's very artistic don't you think, meanwhile they'll be 'videoing' you the whole time. Fun don't you think?" The audience looked at each other confused, the brother in the baseball cap took it off and scratched his head. He reconciled himself with staring at Brenda's breasts.

It was only a second interruption that spoilt Brenda's one woman show.

"Stop that," a masculine voice said. Everyone looked to see where the sound was coming from.

"Stop what," a feminine voice replied. "Do you think I brought you down in here to that dry meeting.. with all those stuck up fools, talking a lot of rubbish which they don't understand, with those women walking around pushing their breasts in your face like little tarts," the feminine voice said. "I brought you here for something else," the voice continued.

Susan laughed out loud and Simone began giggling mainly because her mother was.

"No really," the young man's voice said, "we can't do this."

"What's goin' on here !" Thomas shrieked, from the front of the hall.

"Hey stop a minute, no seriously stop....wait I think they can here us," the young man said. The door of the lecture theatre creaked open and Tayo stuck his head through the gap and peered at the students looking at him. With an embarrassed look on his face he gingerly stepped into the meeting followed by Melanie who had a smile on hers and was in the process of doing up her top.

"Listen I'm sorry," Tayo began, "no disrespect was intended." He caught sight of Susan and felt doubly embarrassed. "How you doing," he said looking at her. The audience turned from him to look at her.

"It's uncle Tayo," Simone called out pointing at Tayo, everybody turned to look back at him like it was a game of Tennis.

Mr. Thomas Mensah could feel his meeting degenerating into, a farce, a comedy. "Listen here," he stood up, 'you don't ......you don't do this, do you understand. We will not have ill mannered West Indians (looking at Tayo's locks and leather pouch) disrupting this meeting."

"You what," Tayo said.

Susan smiled, she had already seen him in action and felt that at last this meeting was going to get exciting.

"It's okay Uncle Tom," Brenda said, "don't allow these lower classes to interrupt this meeting." to Tayo, "Listen Mr Mensah and I will call security, this place is for students of the Poly, not for Rastafarians off the street."

Tayo laughed, a hearty laugh like a much older and wiser man. Melanie folded her arms and Susan waited.

"Uncle Tom," Tayo said, stepping towards the front, "that's an appropriate name. (recognising the surname from his travels of Ghana) You behave just like a tom, an uncle tom."

The audience laughed.

 "Why don't you have a name like Kwabbenah or Kwame like your
first President, those are Good African names not Tom, Thomas. It
reminds me of that cat in those cartoons,' Thomaaaas." The audience laughed again, even Brenda against her better judgment
smirked.

"Kwame, Kwame," Thomas spat out, "Kwame was a fucking communist." The audience gasped, "a dirty Marxist, Russian agent, a
filthy little low class agitator, you don't mention, do you here me,
don't talk about him, you West Indians no nothing."

"Learn some respect," the brother in the baseball cap shouted in a
cockney accent (with no slang), "whatever your views you should-
n't swear in here, you should leave that for outside, they're children here," looking at Simone.

But Tayo was thinking fast. He already made up his mind to
destroy this filthy society and everything it stood for. Thomas and
this semi naked woman next to him represented everything that
was backward about African culture right now, selfish tribalistic,
class orientated and materialistic. Tayo looked down at Thomas and
Brenda like a cat about to go in for the kill.

"A communist," Tayo said, "that is no way to speak about the man
who helped to restore a lot of pride of Africans throughout the
world in Africa. That is no way at all to speak. But your behaviour
does not surprise me. As an elder I want to respect you but I just
can't. You are an ignorant, selfish, self opinionated little man, small
minded and not to mention very, rude (he emphasised the last
word)."

"Listen we don't want any of your juvenile Caribbean ramblings,"
Thomas said.

"No you listen to me," Tayo interjected, "we are one people,
whether we are from the Caribbean or Africa, second, third generation, or first generation black British. We are the same people. Do
you think the police, the skinheads the Klu Klux Klan care where
we are from, they only care who we are." 'I'm not even going to
refute the allegation,' Tayo thought biting his lip, 'about the
Caribbean label, though my parents are from Nigeria. Because that
would give to much legitimacy to your ignorance.'

"Do you think that the BNP who beat up an Asian man two days
ago outside this Poly," Tayo asked, "are goin to stop and ask you,
'excuse me mister black fellow are you from Ghana or Jamaica,' no

there goin to stomp you," Tayo said.

A cry of, "that's right, that's true," went up from the audience.

"I'll tell you this," Tayo continued, unless we come together as one people we are finished. I see crack dealers and prostitutes out on the street, brothers begging for money outside this Poly and we pretending that we don't see it." Susan began to clap followed by the brother in the baseball cap. "I see too many black people have bought this Eurocentric dream, that colour doesn't matter, I see black men with white women and white men with black women."

"Last week," Tayo said, "I even saw a white man arm in arm with a black man, and when I stopped him he said, 'oh (turning to the black man) he's my sex slave'. His sex slave! We only came out of one type of slavery, to put ourselves into another."

Cries echoed around the hall of "shame, shame."

"Yet I hear you want to perpetuate that nonsense with a bare as you dare, striptease something. Don't get me wrong," Tayo said, "I'm no prude, sex is a natural thing and the African form is the most beautiful in the world, it's just that you don't have to show it off for the whole world to see. We have got to many other things to do. As for you sister," he said, staring at Brenda, "you represent the wrong image for this society," echoes of "true, too true," reverberated around the hall.

"We are not here to discuss this, young man," Thomas said irately.

"No I think we are," Tayo said, walking to the front of the hall and staring at the crowd, a little shocked by the fact that his mini coup had attracted a small crowd of students from the canteen, who now stood at the back egging him on.

Tayo took heart. "Do you want me to sit down," he said, there were shouts of, "go on, brother go on."

"Well," Tayo said, "let me rewind and come again."

The brother with the baseball cap shouted, "come again selector" and then looked around embarrassed.

He looked at the audience, "there are brothers and sisters here from Nigeria, Ghana, Jamaica, Barbados, St. Lucia, Sierra Leone, Gambia, The Ivory Coast. There are black people here from North London,

South, West, East. He saw Michael's head poking through the door.
We have black people from Manchester, Northampton,
Birmingham. This is a microcosm of the whole black world. I know
that you want to see changes in this college. You do not want to
see yourselves discriminated upon in your lectures by the colour of
your skin. You don't want to be taught racist and out of date concepts by lecturers who do not have your interests at heart. But what
you have been lacking is leadership," he looked at Thomas and
Brenda who were wishing that they had not entered into his lair.

"Are these your leaders," Tayo said, pointing at them, "an old ignorant man who calls black people derogatory names because they do
not earn as much money as him and a woman who cannot dress
herself in the morning. Go home and get dressed," Tayo joked, the
crowd which was growing, laughed so loud, that Tayo had to wave
them quiet.

"Listen," Tayo said, "leadership is supposed to be elected, you
choose who you want to lead. Do you want them to lead **you**?"

A cry of, "no, we don't," went up from the crowd. Even those who
did not know what any of the issues were about and had never
seen Tayo before were shouting, "No, No."

"Then I move that we have elections immediately for the positions
within the society. Those in favour," Tayo said say, "I."

A resounding, "I" went up from the crowd.

"Your are now compelled," Tayo said, turning to Thomas, "to hold
elections for the leadership of this society."

Tayo sat down back in the audience. Melanie had long since taken
her place to watch the spectacle. She had never seen him in action
before and made up her mind once and for all to have him as her
man, come what may.

Thomas was speechless, there was a moment's pause. "You want
us... to hold elections....is that what you want," he stuttered to the
crowd.

"Yes," came the resounding reply, (fearing a riot).'Most of them are
his lot anyway,' Thomas thought, "Okay," he said, trying to gain
composure, and looking at Brenda, who had an expression of a
mouse that had just been trodden on.

"Okay," he continued, "we need nominations for the post of President."

There was silence, then from the back Susan shouted, "Tayo," the brother in the cap scratched his head, almost as if he was thinking of putting himself forward. But he hesitated, paused, but finally took up the cry until the whole audience was shouting his name.

Tayo blocked out the crescendo of applause.

At last reluctantly he stood and turned to face the crowd, "if you are sure you want to nominate me, then do so, but understand," Tayo said, "I am no sit down armchair revolutionary, if I lead this society I will lead it to action."

"Are there any other nominations for President," Thomas said, there was silence, he did not dare propose himself. "Let us have a show of hands then. Who wants to propose Tayo as President," an army of hands went up.

Tayo looked at the brother in the front row, 'he does not know what he has got his hand up for does he,' he thought, ' he could be voting in Adolf Hitler, but because the crowd is down with it, he's down with it too, 'his brains are in his baseball cap and blue puffer jacket.'

Thomas and Brenda stood up simultaneously as if they knew their time was ended and tried to exit through the doorway, now blocked with people. '

'There is a place for tradition,' Tayo thought, 'respect for elders as a tradition, has its place, but has to be in context. Just because it's a tradition don't make it right. Not all traditions are good. Those that ain't no good don't deserve to be respected. They're not traditions, there superstitions. What are superstitions, they're for superstitious people. What are superstitious people..... but fools! Fools to anyone who will control them. Jamaican fairy tales, Yoruba folk tales, Guyanaese songs, Trinidadian sayings. All very nice, nice, little ditties, but will they lead us to the kind of liberation we need. I mean the kind that will shake the foundations of this unjust world.'

The crowd jeered as Brenda and Thomas jostled there way out of the door, "this is the best thing you've done all year," the brother in the baseball cap snarled, his remark was followed by laughter from the audience.

Tayo stepped on to the stage at the front, a little to confidently, for a man not planning a coup. He looked down at them like a pontificate.

'I need an executive,' he thought, 'one that reflects all the groups at this college.'

"We need to elect an executive," Tayo said, "a deputy chair, treasurer, secretary and library co-ordinator."

"But I'm telling you this," Tayo added, "I'm not the society, get this straight, you are the society, do not expect me to fulfil your fantasies, I can not, will not, must not. You are the fulfilment of your own fantasies. You are realisations of your own dreams. For to long we as African People have sought and waited for a hero to come from the sky and rescue us with a face like Denzel Washington and a body like Mike Tyson, a latter day Jesus. Well Jesus is in all of us, don't wait for him to come to feed your children, or educate your community, don't wait for him to destroy poverty and corruption in our communities because you'll be waiting to the end of time."

"Who will stand for the position of deputy chair," Tayo said, there was a long pause like they had not heard him.

Finally a feminine voice called from the back, "I'll do it," a sister with locks carrying an animated child stood up and made her way to the front. It was Susan.

"Make way for the sister," the brothers called out, as she passed by.

"Good to see you," Tayo said, paternally to her as she stepped over a brother who had stretched out near the stage like he was at the beach, Simone trailing behind her not a little phased or excited by the attention, rather excited to see Tayo. On catching sight of him, she ran, her afro puffs bouncing and her small African face animated, embracing him as if he was her father. "This child really wants me to adopt her as her father," Tayo said, looking rather embarrassingly around the audience at the suspicious faces. 'I'm sure that's his child and wife, I bet their thinking that,' Tayo thought, 'he's probably planned the whole thing and replacing the executive with his family.'

Susan seemed absolutely at peace, her locks trailing behind her serene, majestic, dignified, noble face. Simone standing next to her hands folded behind her back.

"Does anyone else wish to stand?" Tayo said, looking at Susan's peaceful expression.

There was silence. A brother on the first row with a funky hair cut like a peacock scratched his head. Another with a string vest and his stomach and nipples sticking out like a page three girl, a triple chin and acne like a teenager, he looked bemused and elated all at the same time, as if he had never been entertained like this before. 'Entertained,' Tayo thought staring, 'is entertained the right word. Yes I almost believe he's looking for some popcorn and cocoa cola,' as he saw him rummage around inside his bag. But he surfaced with a tissue to wipe his forehead which had become wet with sweat.

A sister, 'she looks,' familiar Tayo thought looking at her, was sitting in the middle attentively, like she was at a lecture. 'She was here two years ago I'm sure,' Tayo thought, 'if I remember correctly she is writing her thesis on Black resistance to racism in the U.K. We'll probably end up as some dissertation.' Tayo thought sarcastically, 'Black nationalist/ racists at a south London Poly, held a meeting were the newly elected President denounced mixed relationships and abused white people.'

'But,' Tayo thought, 'nobody else wants to stand, they're all to busy enjoying the show.'

"Those in favour of Susan," Tayo said, finally, "as President, I mean deputy chair, please raise your hands."

A resounding forest of hands went up.

"Just a minute," Tayo said, "you've just elected someone and you don't know who they are?"

"Yeah but we elected you five minutes before and I don't know who the hell you are," replied the brother in the baseball cap (in a cockney accent). There was a ripple of laughter, the brother just grinned with his arms folded.

"Shall I stand down then," Tayo said, joking.

"Na man ya alright, you're doin' a good job, just don't get big headed," the brother replied.

"I'll try not to," Tayo said and turned to the sister. "Do you feel up to saying a few words," he whispered to her.

"No problem," she replied, "though I don't think they deserve it."

"I want to thank you for voting for me," Susan said, loudly to the crowd, a brother in the back who was trying to get Melanie's attention, took time out from puffing up his chest to watch the proceedings. Tayo watched for the reaction of the crowd. "I would like to echo," she continued, "what Tayo has just said. This is not just a talking shop, or an entertainment centre," looking at the brother in the cap and then at the one stretched out on the floor, who simultaneously straightened himself up. "This society is your voice, I've seen the Sikhs have their society, the Muslims theirs, you know that the whites will have their own. Well this is yours. My task," looking at Tayo, "will be to ensure that all the administration runs smoothly. Posters out on time. Letters to the members, etc." Tayo smiled, there was something very familiar in the smile.

But how had Susan become so calm and determined under pressure.?

Susan

Susan at seventeen had all the aspirations one would expect from a second generation British born African whose parents came from the Caribbean. Her mother was an overweight, pompous woman, who believed that Bible bashing and daily chores would send the devil back to hell and keep your soul as clean and white as God made it. Every week she would go to church and ask for God to, "wash her soul as white as snow." Certainly when she returned home in her Sunday best, white flannel suit, broad brim hat, she was not in the mood to cook and clean, though she felt it was her duty. She treated her children like they were her personal slaves. They stopped attending church from the time that they could sneak out of the house without being caught.

In response Mrs B as she liked to be called, felt it was her God given right to punish them with chores. At 2pm the children would sit shivering in their rooms, as they feared the stomping of their mother's stilettos coming down the street. There would be the characteristic crash of the front door as she stormed in, "where are those heathen children, Mr B (the husband) where are you hiding them. Come out you vile wicked, evil, ones. Pickney face your mother and face your Sunday chores."

Mr B seemed oblivious to the entire matter, as he was to most things, sitting in his rocking chair, creaking back and forth, with the Sunday papers in his hand. He just simply did not care. So long as he had something hot to drink, a chair to sit on and a newspaper to read, the whole world could fall apart around him. Well at least the African world. Mrs B stamped into the front room like an ogre in a fairy story and stared at her husband rocking from side to side in his favourite oak, antique chair.

Mrs. B new better than to ask her husband something twice. If Mr B did not answer the first time, repetition was not likely to produce a response.

"Where are those black heathen," Mrs B shrieked, to herself, "you spawn's of Satan, you black imps, where are you?" Susan was quaking and shaking with fear as she lay concealed under her bed. She always managed to get stuck in the house and get caught. Susan was the youngest and by far the most creative of three children. But she did not feel creative today. "She'll marry a good white man, a lawyer or a doctor," the mother would say, "I've got high hopes for her. "

But Susan was petrified, shivering like a baby deer hiding, as a tiger prowls the forest looking to kill her. She knew well what the stomping of her mother's feet would mean. A sound beating with her leather belt and being chained to the kitchen for four hours cooking the Sunday dinner, roast pork and apple sauce. Her mother's but nobody else's favourite.

"Su....san," came the shriek, as her mother's size nine feet reached the top of the stairs, "you little black heathen, come here so I can clean your soul."

But Susan was tired of doing the cooking for the whole family. She was tired of being shouted out and called a 'little black heathen, all because she refused to go to church.' This day she had made up her mind that she would run away for good, to somewhere, where there was not a fourteen stone mother who had broken her first husband's jaw because he had lost his job and who spent all her money on white Italian shoes.

The door of her room creaked open, her mother with a vice like grip twisting the handle, then with the dexterity and strength of a heavyweight wrestler, she slammed it hard against the wall, it almost came of its' hinges. The white with little blue 'Bunni Rabbit' wallpaper was dented by the impact. Susan had put it up herself, all day on the Saturday, with her mother standing over her, giving her commands and tapping her size eight feet. But now it was quite ruined.

"Where are you little heathen," her mother said, as she came near to her bed, her shadow casting darkness over the room.

Susan could hear the slow thud of her feet, her huge hands clenching and unclenching, the rustle of her new white flannel suit. The steps getting closer and closer, like the scene from some terrible horror film, as the monster approaches.

But this victim wanted to be the hero, well the heroine at least. She could hear her mothers' feet coming ever closer. At last the feet stopped at the side of the bed.

"You naughty little heathen, not only are you trying to hide from me to avoid your daily chores you black demon, but your room is in a terrible mess, look at it," she said, seeing one or two books left on the bed and a couple of pens on the floor. "Don't you know that cleanliness is next to Godliness. Besides you don't need these books, all you need is the Bible, take these foul instruments of

Satan and GET THEE GONE," she screamed, like a insane medieval priest, grabbing the books which happened to be 'African proverbs for children,' 'Africa for beginners' and flung them through the door.

Susan sat shivering with fear, "I know where you are, heathen," her mother's feet were just inches away from her face. Susan could smell her mother's damp deodorant and the pungent smell of her hairspray. She could see her mother's new white stiletto shoes from Ravel made with the finest Italian white leather. So fine and so white you could almost taste and smell the whiteness. So fine and so white that even complete strangers would stop and stare saying, 'aren't they fine white Italian shoes, aren't they absolutely beautiful.'

So Susan could smell her mother's shoes, her hairspray from Loreal and the deodorant from Rochelle channel number 9. The thud of those shoes coming closer and closer.

Finally from the base of her being, Susan stirred up the courage to make a run for it, to get out of her situation, to escape. As a child she had been a tom boy rolling around with boys, somersaulting in the park. She still had the ability even though she was seventeen, she had a waist and build slim enough to squeeze through almost anything. 'Can I do it,' she thought, 'can I really do it, do I dare do it,' she thought. She counted to five, she could almost feel her mother's breath as hot as a dragon's.

"One, two, three.... four... ," she took a deep breath, "five." She sprang out from the bed, between her mother's legs and the white Italian shoes, out of the door. She leapt over the neighbour's cat Tabatha, who had a nasty habit of coming into their house and treating it like her home, down the stairs, just missing dad's favourite oak dressing gown where he kept all his Sunday papers, through the Georgian oak wooden front door only newly varnished by John the eldest son as punishment for not washing the dishes. Susan flew like a bird released from her cage, free at last.

Mrs B. stomped her white Italian shoes and shouted like a mad white missionary in an African village which had decided to go native, despite all his attempts to civilise them.

"You little black heathen, you take after ya father, because ya no 'daa.ughter' of mine, stay out on the streets until you starve," she screamed, her face contorted with rage.

But Susan was already long gone, hitching up her skirt and skipping down the street like a St Trinian in a 1950's British movie and
chewing Bubilicious chewing gum.

Susan walked out on the streets of Brockley like an accident waiting
to happen. With £3 in her pocket and an innocent smile plastered
on her face, there was not a pervert, sex offender who did not walk
past her and think of committing some evil crime. But Susan was
unaware of the white businessman on the way to visit his wife via
the sex shops in Camden town, who saw her standing by a local
bus stop. She did not even notice him, leering at her, looking at
those slim delicate legs and that shy little face with the Afro puffs.

Mr Harris was still thinking about how he was going to do the act
and get away with it, when he saw Susan change her mind and
decide to walk down the road to her friend's house. Mr Harris with
his shiny black shoes, crease down the very centre of his pinstripe
suit, looked every part the model of western society morality.
Public school educated at one of the most prestigious schools. A
professional barrister enrolled at the middle temple. With sixteen
years within the legal profession, he had a pedigree that most in
society would revere. £212, 457 a year, a yacht in the south of
France, a second home in the Bahamas, an avid reader, especially of
ethnic culture, African tribes and the like, who would spend four
days a week keeping fit. One dear son named Matthew Harris and a
beautiful wife.

Was he not the kind of man that most of us in the west were aspir-
ing to be like?

It did not matter that Mr Harris had a one thousand pound collection of the filthiest videos and magazines in the country. His fasci-
nation for sexual excess extended to prostitutes as well. The first
being one paid for by his father on his eighteenth birthday. Harris
would never forget her, his father took him to some address in
Baker street. His father knocked on the door and a mature, some
would say elderly, black woman answered. She looked in her fifties,
wearing an old, worn out, white nightie and a painted smile on her
face, as if this was the first white businessman who had brought his
son to saviour 'ethnic delights.'

Harris remembered looking at Beautiful Black Betty, as her advert
had said and looking at his father like a child in a sweet shop. As if
to say, "father is that all for me." Of course it was all for him, three
hundred years ago he would have taken his son from the big white
house down the track to the slave quarters. There to meet Miss

Louise his favourite belly warmer. It just happened that in the 1960's Mr Harris senior's favourite belly warmer was beautiful Black Betty.

It did not bother Mr Harris or his curious son that Black betty was an unemployed refugee from Namibia who had escaped the hardship that war with South Africa had brought. She had come to this country with her three children. She could have gone to work in the city as a cleaner, get the early train at 5am, work a 30 hour week and take home £90. She could have done that, but she thought to herself, "I have three children to feed and I want them to have the life that I never had." So for the sake of that, she sacrificed her health, her morals and just about everything to sell her body and provide the fantasy, black fantasy for the educated elite of white society.

After his sexual fling with Betty there really was no turning back for Harris. As he went in the evening to the University library, skipping to avoid the puddles in the evening rain, he would visit the local brothel. He spent more time with the prostitutes than he did with his mother. Even some of his school friends would ask, "where does Harris go, he's a smart chap, but what's he doing, always busy and always late for Monday morning lessons."

What was Harris doing ? He was on his back, on his front, in fact in any position he asked for, so long as he paid for it and when your father was a high court Judge, no expense should be spared for his son.

So Mr Harris Q.C. like many men in power shared his desire for control with a lack of control in his own morality. He was later to stand in a position of authority judging other men's actions. But he never judged his own, even when he began picking up younger and younger girls on the street, even some who claimed they were not prostitutes. 'If they weren't prostitutes,' Harris thought, 'what were they doing out on the streets at this time of night, dressed like that. Surely decent girls don't walk around like that. How I was brought up, no woman should be seen out almost naked. They have to be prostitutes. If they weren't, then they should not dress like that.' 'I bet,' he thought, 'even this girl,' following Susan, 'is going to claim she's not on the game, little brown fox, of course she is.'

Susan meanwhile was thinking how lucky she had been to escape her mother and her mother's white Italian shoes. She had felt the wrong end of those shoes far to often on the wrong end of her body, she was not looking for a rewind. It was only when she stopped on the corner of Effra road that she noticed a shadow that was other than her own. A shadow bent double stooping over hers and hovering around, almost imitating every move like a spectre in a pin stripped suit as if his name was Bruce Wayne (you know Batman!).

A streak of fear gripped our young heroine, to have escaped mother was one thing, where the most she would receive was a beating . But this stranger who was following her all the way down Effra road clearly had other intentions. What exactly those other intentions were, she did not know. Her mother had been as effective in sheltering her about the facts of nature, as she had been in terrorising her about attending church. She had done a good job, if asked, "do you know about the birds and bees," she would reply, "I like birds especially robins with their red chests, but I don't like bees so much, but their honey is nice."

At the corner of Brompton Road, Susan became a little worried as she reached the top of the hill that connected it to her friends street.

A thought crossed her mind, 'I'm not going to reach my friend's house am I,' as she heard Harris's quickening steps. She could feel his lecherous hot breath coming closer and closer, the soles of his black shiny shoes clacking on the tarmac path. She stopped at 54 Brompton Road, Mavis her best friend lived at 127.

Mr Harris sensed that he had better act quickly if he was going to get this, 'fine brown fox,' to add to his collection, of successful trophies. Susan felt his shadow darken over hers, the sweat of the armpits he had not washed in two days, the slight odour of Champagne he had consumed that afternoon. Hovering over her like a murdering rapist, like a dog about to go in for the kill in a hunt. Lights flashed in front, so bold, so bright that Harris and Susan stood stunned for a moment. The lights, bright yellow beamed at them, Susan blinking, trying to shut it out, but they penetrated there into her mind, her subconscious.

A Car stopping on the road by the side of them and the lights fading, the driver turning them down.

He wound his windscreen down, "Wha'appen baby," he said, to Susan looking her up and down. He had scars all over his face, "wha' you're, doing " he asked, looking at her confused and startled expression. Mr Harris felt like a dog who had just had his hunt interrupted by the baddest cat on the block.

"I will be going then," Harris mumbled, under his breath, "thank you again, dear for you kind help, it is much appreciated."

The brother interrupted, before he could finish, "Are you dat," pointing out of his car window at the business man.

"I'm sorry," Harris replied, trying to understand what had just been said.

"Are you dat," the brother said, loudly this time to Susan.

She shook her head.

"Gwon," the brother said, waving him away, "you foo foo boy, gwon, 'fore I box you. Batty boy in a suit."

"Now listen here," Harris insisted, "I don't know who you are but..."

The man in the car was already getting out as he spoke and Harris suddenly felt fear running through his veins. The kind of fear a Virginian slave master in the south of America felt when he found out his slaves had revolted and one of the runaways was standing in front of him with a bloody cutlass.

His foot started to shake, followed by the rest of his frame. He stumbled away from Susan and staggered down the road, casting a worried glance over his shoulder as he went. Harris could have protested further, made an attempt to stop this ill mannered and by the sound of him, foreign Negro. 'But here on this street,' he thought, 'nobody can here you scream,' looking at the deserted street, except for the figure of the brother getting out of his car.

"Well I'll be going then my dear," Harris mumbled, staggering backwards and trying to turn the worry on his face into a smile.

It was not that Harris for one moment believed that Susan was not a prostitute, or that he was missing an opportunity to enjoy her. In fact in his white supremacist, distorted mind, he thought, this brother is her pimp and not the accidental passer by he was.

Harris shuffled off and the brother stepped on the road, looking a little too long at her, "ya all right daughter," the brother remarked, looking down at her and rubbing the stubble on his chin. A myriad of thoughts were passing through Susan's mind at the same time. First she thought, 'there is that man, who was here before, that leering creep, goodness knows, what was in his filthy mind, now this guy, whose he, I don't know him. I don't feel well, I wish I could cry, all because I ran away from home. I should listen to my mother in future.' A single tear ran down her cheek and she wiped it with a delicate, youthful, unblemished, untainted, untouched, innocent hand.

The brother looked at her and smiled, his gold and silver false teeth gleaming like a set of traffic lights, lighting up his whole face in the greyness of the evening.

"Don't cry daughter," the brother said, looking down and putting his arm around her, "it'll be alright."

Susan was no fool, but she was young, young to the world and innocent to the deceit that man can show. It was the kind of deceit that drove many sisters to reject all notions of black manhood and look to other men to represent their image of masculinity.

All Susan really cared about was that this man had saved her and she felt comforted and relaxed in his arms, it felt like her father, when he held her after her mother had beaten her.

"My name's Bernhard, Manley" the brother said, "but people call me Busta Manley, or just plain Busta." He adjusted his jacket, doing up his top button, a string vest concealed underneath.

"Yeah call me Busta," Busta said assertively, "it's a 'lickle' cold don't you think," looking at the afternoon changing into night. The sun dying behind the hills and the concrete jungle of the metropolis, the wind picking up from the west, midges and insects beginning to land and search for human **blood** to suck.

"Come on," Busta said, scratching his head, "let me take you home," but Susan would not leave his arms. "Let's at least get in my car," Busta whispered to her. Susan did not want to leave his arms, she felt safe with him, not because Busta was a safe person, but because he had been there at the opportune time. He smiled an artificial smile, his gold and silver teeth shining devilishly and licked his lips with Susan still in his arms. His paws decked in silver and gold rings, seemed to submerge her in his web like a huge spider catching a pretty butterfly.

"So wa ya say, come now," he said, now pointing to his car, black and shining on the road, like his own personal German temple to materialism and greed. There was something about the shiny blackness of it which seemed fake, glossy, unreal, unnatural, foreign. The chrome bumpers and silver metal work polished every morning and cared for as if it was his child. Can one man love a car more than himself? 'Ya nah say this car is boom,' Busta thought, as he led Susan into the front seat to sit on pink fluffy seat covers, with hanging fluffy dice from the ceiling and a swinging map of Jamaica.

Susan sat snuffling in Busta's fake, fluffy, little, pink, world. Pink on the inside, black on the outside. Big tears rolling down her cheeks and dribbling down her face in mini waterfalls. She wiped her face with the back of her hand, smelling the suffocating intoxication of cannabis, alcohol and nicotine. Busta bounced into his seat and the whole car seemed to bounce with him, like a ship riding a huge wave.

"Ya all right daughter," he said, with a sneer, as he flicked his stereo to maximum output. Susan just sat there sniffing and spluttering, the tears rolling down her face whilst the whole car was shaking to the sound of "Za, Za, za za za, zar, za za,- za, zarr za...., zuaz , za za , zig zahya, pom, pom," from the twin speakers.

Susan was oblivious to Busta's attempts at making her feel better. She did not even notice the car shaking like a mini earth quake as Cutty Ranks blurted out another line of Zig zaya. Nor did she see Busta leering at her; like a dirty old man in a peep show. Busta was swaying as if he had put his finger in a light socket, shouting, "pom, pom," at the correct and incorrect places, all the while looking at the delicate butterfly in his car.

The map of Jamaica outlined in gold and made of oak, 'a gift' (so his story went) from one of his 'spars' (now at her majesty's disposal in Wormwood Scrubs), bounced around with the pink fluffy dice, as if they were related and alive all at the same time.

'Ya nah say this gal is fine,' Busta thought, looking at her innocent frame. It was not that he had suddenly gained an appreciation of African beauty. Busta always said, "me nah deal with no colour bar, no colour bar, if the girl fine, she fine. A ting is a ting, Palaney's Palaney.'

Indeed it was true, Busta had every colour under the sun in his bed. Every colour, every shade. He revelled in his, as he called it, 'international bed wok.' His white friends used to call him the, 'original mix and blender.'

"Cooar you ain't got another one have ya," Steve a dealer and friend from the street used to say, "I don't know, you black geezers, are like fucking dogs on heat." Busta used to laugh, because even though he dealt crack and ran prostitutes on most of the streets of South London and had killed fifteen people even before he had set foot in England, he knew how to operate good business and having a white mate like Steve who could sell crack like it was candy especially to little boy's, was good for business. It did not matter that Steve was an unemployable, drug addict, who had been in prison for sexually abusing little boys and selling dirty videos; business was business. Besides Busta had come to this country not to be a priest but to make money. In the six months that he was here he had earned a small fortune, enough to retire on and within a week he had spent it. A thousand on the newest Nike trainers illegally imported from the States, his new car, well that's what he said to everyone, a new 'zig zayah, twenty pounds of crack purely for personal consumption and of course the pink fluffy dice. Busta was a real black man!

"Me a Jamaican, proud to be," Busta could be heard to say, and his definition of pride, was to impregnate every girl he could find with his Jamicaness. He would have impregnated the men too, but he was afraid of being called "batty boy." "I don't de'l with no batty man," he would say. But Steve shafted him more times than his prostitutes got laid on Saturday night.

Steve was a thief by inclination, design and choice. For every thousand pound he made on the street, he gave Busta half. But Busta was happy making his money and he was happy having Steve as his friend. It did not matter that all the fake posing he used to do on the streets of Peckham, black string vest, gold chains like Mr T from the A team, puzzles in his head, the latest brilliant white Nike trainers, gold and silver teeth, he looked about as ridiculous as one man can look without being arrested for insanity.

But Busta was not going to be arrested, though he had already in six months notched up a tally of six dead, nothing said. Busta would never see the inside of a police cell because he paid the local police, 'sshush' far too much money. Besides so long as he kept beating up and maiming only black people, they did not care. It was certain that the death of an average brother on the streets of London was not likely to reach the front page. It happened to often to shock. After all the newspapers want some thing new.

Busta slipped the bouncing BMW into neutral and switched the ignition on. The engine made the car shake even more, if that was possible. Jamaica was shaken up so much that it almost fell down, as for the fluffy dice, well !

"Let's ride," Busta blurted out, placing the car into first gear and pushing down on the accelerator. The car roared down Brompton Road like a jet airplane. The whole world disappeared into a blur of colours. Susan looked up from her tear soaked handkerchief, now sopping wet. She sniffed, peering through the windows as Brockley raced past her.

Meanwhile Mr. Harris who had gone only to the corner of Brompton Road hiding under an old oak tree which had become worn with: age, smoke and graffiti. He stood there under the cover of the leaves, taking down the details of Busta's licence plate. 'I'll teach that ill mannered, foreign, Negro to threaten me,' he thought, scribbling frantically with a note book and pen which he had brought out with him to take down young ladies telephone numbers. The moon gave enough light to see and he was on the last two digits, when Busta started the engines of his beautiful black BMW and roared down the streets like a jet pilot.

"Bloody foreign muck," Harris cursed under his breath, "send them all back home."

Putting his notebook in his coat in a hurried fashion like an albino hamster and shaking his head from side to side like a lunatic, in a straight jacket, who had just been denied his supper. He consoled himself with the realisation that 'the night is young, I may still get lucky, after all there are bound to be other exotic beauties around, just legal, or not, doesn't matter, if it bleeds it needs. Brockley even on a Sunday evening is like Montego Bay, everything's for sale, you've just got to know the price.' He fiddled inside his pocket and produced a crisp fifty pound note. 'With this I can buy just about anything,' he thought and smiled, 'who ever said you can't buy love, doesn't know the power of the cash to turn any woman into a whore, especially these foreign sorts, blacks and the like, you've never seen the like,' he thought, smiling to himself, 'get one of these young ones, flash some coins in front of their face, they'll soon drop their draws, and if they won't, there's another way.'

But Susan was as far away from Harris, his cash, pin strip suits, or his concepts of sex and race. She was 'safe,' in Busta's car. Comforting herself in Busta's pink fluffy seats, sinking her little brown legs in the warmth of the car, though it blurted out and reverberated to the fourth rewind of 'zig zaya.' Through the streets of Brockley, down the back streets of East Dulwich, down East Dulwich Road. The streets were empty, still, deathly still.

The sun was dead. For today at least the moon reigned supreme over the ghetto and it shone it's supremacy over the decaying, crumbling streets of South London. A shrill breeze blowing through the scattered trees that flanked the nearby park blowing brown leaves to and fro over the road, as Busta's car roared through the city like a jet aeroplane, scattering leaves in all directions, sending them up and cascading down.

Busta roared past Kings on the Rye, even now on a Sunday evening rammed back to back with black. Sisters dressed in gold and silver dresses, so tight they looked like they were painted on. Brothers in shiny shoes, chops and gold chains, with white silk shirts and designer bad-boyz frowns.

Busta speeded past them, splashing a nearby sister who obviously had drunk a little to much, by the bleary eyed make up which was running down her face and the awkward gait that she tried and failed to maintain. Stumbling all over the road, holding her stomach which protruded a little to excessively over the front of her dress. No doubt she was making her way to the side of the road to vomit up the fish and chips she had recently brought from Greasy Joe's café round the corner, well known for being the greasiest and dirtiest chip shop in London - perhaps in the world. But did that stop black people stuffing their faces full of fried chips and cod cooked in pig fat.

Even though Mama Africa, the African take away opposite was empty, except for the drunkard who kept asking Mama the owner, for change so he could buy beer.

Mama Africa cooked the best Eba and jollof rice south of the river Thames but with tradition black people on leaving Kings, after sweating and rubbing their lives away, would run like sheep to Greasy Joe's, not Mama Africa.

Joe the owner of Greasy Joe's was a Kurdish refugee who worked every hour that God sends including some she hadn't. He worked until he established his shop. He had done deals and signed contracts with Mad Mike Mclean, where else was he going to get the capital necessary, even if it did mean doing odd jobs for him.

Joe was as greasy as his shop. Rats in the pantry, overcharging the customers, but it did not stop his popularity. "It's good business," he laughed, as he spat and urinated in the frying oil. Not for any particular reason but just to see if he could get away with it. "A bit of flavour never hurt anyone," he chuckled to himself. 'Besides,' he thought, 'would I, a Turkish man go to a West Indian take away to eat my dinner no. No I want good wholesome food cooked by a good round Turkish woman, no foreigner is going to cook my food.'

'Do you see any Turkish people come and eat here,' he thought, as he spat on the floor. 'No they know better than that. But these blacks they'll eat anything. Why not, they live in the muck anyway, even their children. Well, its business. I ain't going to end up on the street. I want money and I don't care how I get it. I wouldn't even bring my dog to eat the muck I cook here. They must be really stupid. Why don't they eat with their own. I don't care anyway, business, is business.'

Joe often spat and urinated in the food and laughed while he did it. 'These lot round here are really stupid,' he thought, as his spit congealed and dried on the tile floor. His urine bubbling in the hot oil and staining it orange, 'sometimes I see those little coloured girls they look so sweet. So nice, I have to just touch them up, in it, why, why not, cause I can do anything I like. They like it any way, dressed like tarts they are, anyway. You see them chuckle now, I give them a free Pepsi if they give it out, why not, if it's there take it. I do as I please, I do what I want, no one tells me what to do. Besides these coloureds don't mind. They don't bother me, don't look at things like other people' and he carried on urinating in the oil.

Busta raced past Greasy Joe's café and the sister who by now was screaming as if she was deranged, waving the shoe she had been wearing at Busta's BMW which had splashed her new frock. Then she realised why she had come outside and decided to add another colour to her dress, the colour of the contents of her stomach, which she vomited unceremoniously over herself. The bits of fried fish and chips were easily discernible, as they dripped down the gold dress, forming a yellow puddle by the side of the road and creating an unfortunate side show for two baggy young brothers with their trousers hanging slung round their waists and puzzles in their head. They bounced and fronted like they were in an original style walking on the opposite side of the road, cracking jokes and stories and laughing like delinquent children. On seeing the sister covered in sweat, water and sick, they stopped everything, to stand and giggle until their bellies hurt, when all the sister really needed was pity.

Busta's BMW ate up the roads of Peckham like a hungry man invited to a feast. Down Peckham high street, Busta's shiny black, but pink inside BMW sped, past the amusement arcades, the liquor stores and betting shops. Past Mr Patel's corner shop still open till late, one of Busta's favourite haunts.

'Ya nah say if that fool (meaning Jamaican Bob) went missin,' he thought, 'me could just sit in that shop and kotch.' As he drove past it.

Busta looked around, hoping to catch a sight of the master Steve at work, hoping to catch him darting to and fro on the streets selling death like he was born to it. But the streets were quiet.

Busta drove past North Peckham Estate which looked in 1983 much like it looked in 1991 and as it will do in 2000, before some white philanthropist gets the idea to modernise it. In other words to move the black people to the suburbs and turn the estate into yuppie flats. But for now it is a concrete manifestation of a ghetto, British style. A concrete jungle, stone hard and cold, boarded up shops, graffiti, dirty promenades and littered courtyards. Looking at London from the air it seemed to rise out of the streets unnaturally, spreading from East Dulwich all the way to Camberwell. Yet despite the crack, prostitutes, drug dealing and crime, there is life, a vibrancy, energy, youth, there are black people. African people from all parts of the world. Pan African Ghettoisation.

But Susan was sinking further into the fluffy pink upholstery of Busta's BMW. She could feel the prickly warmth from the seats invigorating and enlivening her tired worn out legs. The suffocating, intoxicating, aroma of weed, nicotine, blood and yes something else she could not make out (the smell of sex).

Busta leered at Susan's comfort, like a dog watching a small deer feeding on vegetation, before it pounces and consumes it. His gold and silver teeth gleamed unnaturally under the reflection of the blare from the full beam headlights as he beat the lights at the corner of Braemar road and turned down the back street of Denmark Avenue, into his end of North Peckham estate. Why his end you may ask, because he controlled at the behest of the underworld and the establishment represented by the law officials, the entire southern end of the estate as far as Denmark Street. Every illegal form of racketeering, drug dealing, wheeling, dealing happened under the watchful gaze of Busta. But the one crime that he really excelled in was the procuring of prostitutes. He loved prostitution and excelled at the trade, white girls to black men, black girls to white men, the only colour that mattered to him was green.

The ragged, gold teeth bad boy looked Susan up and down, assessing her value and worth, what was he going to do with her next. He backed down the last side street before his flat 35 Quarley Way. 'Ya nah say she's too green,' Busta thought, looking at her innocent eyes. Too innocent for the street, 'she ain't even broke her ducts,' he thought, as he parked the car outside the entrance to Quarley way.

'Daughter we're here,' he tried to say softly, looking at her, as she reclined, her mind drifted off to some far away nice place, certainly not the earth that she inhabited.

Busta was thinking, 'she's boom, green, but me could ride her rhythm all night,' he thought, slowly pushing down the fake chrome handles of his door.

He bounced on to the road surveyed his territory like a predatory dog, 'this manor is too quiet,' he thought, listening to the silence, as a bird squawked over his head. He looked up and kissed his teeth, muttering under his breath, 'them niggers better be out making bread, for me.' He slammed the door shut and strode across the front of the car, not even stopping to lock the doors,(who would dare touch his car).

Susan just sat there, she was oblivious to know what would, or could come next. Busta smiled a fake gold teeth smile and opened her door, "come on d'ughter, can't stay here," he said, beckoning her out of the car, with a dirty little brown finger adorned in fool's gold signet rings with the Queen of England's head on it.

Like a painted devil inviting the victim into hell, he inticed Susan out of the car and she came exchanging the warmth of the car for the warmth of his arms. He banged the door shut, it thudded and shock with the impact as they walked arm in arm down the cul-de-sac that led to 35 Quarley way.

Three years later Susan was a wiser, more bitter person, with a baby girl called Simone born from a father who still thought he was the original yardie. A single parent mother in a council flat in East Dulwich with a child born from a 'man' (in inverted commas) who thought that it was his God given right to propagate every girl that he ever met. There was only one woman that he would ever stay with, that was Beverly a white girl, that he had originally put on the street when she was seventeen. It was not her first time, she had used and been used. Her father and brothers had all taken away her virginity and hope many years ago, even whilst she sought safety in her own bed, some how they found her and violated her.

So she wanted to violate them. It was not that she liked blacks or anything like that, in fact she could be heard to say to her friends, 'I don't really fancy him, his mate Steve is really tasty though. But them black boys are like beasts in beds Girls, get your self one, I'm telling you, you won't regret it. You can put all those vibrators aside," and she would giggle like a mad woman, with her yellow straggly hair jumping about all over the place.

Busta gave up the mother of his child for Beverly, a woman who could not keep her pants on for more than five minutes without a rash forming on the inside of her leg, hell even if she took them off, it was still there, she should have gone to the doctor to check it out, especially as it used to itch and every week she would be guaranteed a yellow discharge. But that did not stop Busta loving her and committing every act in the Karma Sutra with her. Did he not notice the foul smell that originated between her legs, or the fact that every night she went to visit him she had visited Steve only five minutes before. No Busta was in love, or in lust or insane, well Busta was something, or nothing you make up your own mind.

But that did not solve the problem of Susan, every Monday morning as she got Simone ready for the nursery she would dread seeing her ex boyfriend's handy work. That morning was no exception, but some where between the toast that she was preparing for Simone just lightly grilled and the cereal she was reaching for from the cupboard, the thud of the weekly newspaper came.

There was a delay as it landed on her newly hovered porch floor. She knew that some where would be an article displaying his handy work. She flicked through the pages in earnest. There on the fourth page, the article read, "*Black, drug, death, dealing crack addict killed on Peckham front line.*" The article was almost identical every week. But this time there was something particularly nasty about it. She spread the pages on her newly polished dining table. "*A black man was found in Peckham, in what locals have called, the London's Bronx,*!" 'London Bronx what a stupid phase,' Susan thought, scanning through the pages, 'typical tabloid sensationalism, even sadder,' she thought, 'when these local papers are supposed to be above that sought of thing.'

She read on, "*A black man was found early in the hours of 3am hanging from the lamp post at the junction of Denmark road with his throat cut. On taking the victim down he was found to be one Robert Constantine Simms, a known thief and suspected drug dealer. Upon further investigation a man believed to be his father Robert Senior Delroy Constantine Simms was questioned. Robert or 'Jamaican Bob', as he likes to be called by his friends' 'Jamaican Bob,'* Susan paused in thought, 'what a stupid name.' She resumed her reading, "*Jamaican Bob on being questioned was heard to remark ,'yes the bwoy my son, but his mother and me didn't see eye to eye, and he was a bad lot anyway, me always used to say that he would come to a bad end, good riddance to bad rubbish.' On pulling the victim down it was noticed that his throat had been cut from ear to ear.*"

Susan recoiled in shock. She read it again, "*on pulling the victim down it was noticed that his throat had been cut from ear to ear.*" 'They said it so matter of fact like it did not matter and it was insignificant,' Susan thought, 'is that how you say it, a young man has had his youth brutally cut short and do you say it just like that. I tell you what,' Susan thought, screwing up the paper into a ball and throwing it into the bin.

'If he was a dog they would have reported it better. There would be outrage, questions in Parliament and an appeal for the dead dog. But who would raise an appeal for this dead human being. How could society be so caring for dogs and yet so disrespectful of human beings,' she thought, as she walked toward the kitchen.

'I'm tired of it,' Susan thought, 'here I am the father of my child is out there, killing black people, here I am with his child who he does not even want to know. Whilst he's riding that stringy haired devil with V.D. My mother's a devout Christian who is more in love with her white Jesus and her white Italian shoes than she in love with her own black children. What kind of world is this, what has become of black people. My friends, all they want to do is rave, rave, rave like it was a drug they needed to live on,' she thought, taking the toast out of the toaster and putting it on a nearby turquoise coloured plate she had left out for that purpose.

'And this young man is dead and nothing said. Another brother has died and nothing said. There has to be a way to raise the consciousness of the people. I absolutely refuse to believe that black people are finished,' she thought and sighed.

She never forgot the storm of indignation her mother had given her when she came home and told her that she was pregnant. She remembered those shoes flying towards her, the well stitched white leather and hard firm soles as they struck her forehead and cut the skin. That was seven stitches and three year before. But the past shaped her consciousness. 'I am determined,' still thinking about herself, Busta, Simone and that poor youth, 'that one day I'm goin do something better for myself.' She picked up the slice of toast she had so perfectly toasted.

'I'm goin do something better for myself, perhaps even study.' She put her toast down and remembered that she had not checked on Simone. She tightened her dressing gown and walked to the adjacent room pushing open the door gingerly. Simone was scribbling away with her crayons on two huge sheets of white paper. 'It's strange,' she thought, looking at her proud delicate features, brown rosy cheeks and youthful face, that she could be produced from such an Uncle Tom Negro like her father.'

'Well,' she thought, looking at Simone drawing yet another large black circle on paper, 'I'm goin to do something, perhaps even go to college, yes college,' she thought, looking at her daughter, 'why not.'

It had taken her two more years, she had saved every penny she had acquired, worked and studied every hour that the twenty four hours send. Finally she made it, dragged herself from the abyss to some where flat and safe, even if not yet the mountain top.

'Perhaps with Tayo,' she thought, looking at him and remembering where she was, 'they might all get some where high; so long as he can keep his feet on the ground, (looking at his arrogant disposition), long enough to know where he's going.'

The Executive

Tayo looked at the crowd now packing the room, "we need a treasurer, and a secretary," Tayo said, staring at their blank faces. There
was silence, a pregnant silence, like someone had told a bad joke.
Brothers looked at each other, sisters looked at the ground, Tayo
looked at Susan, 'they just want to play around, they've come for
the show, to see me cuss the old man, they don't want to do any
work,' he thought.

"I'm telling you this," Tayo said, looking at Melanie and then in
turn at all of the brothers who now occupied the back row, "we
and this sista are not going to do everything for you. We are not.
Put that thought out of your mind. I mean it." He walked slowly
towards the front row like a predatory cat. "We are not your mothers and your fathers and we do not intend to go down in history as
martyrs, we've had enough of them don't you think?"

Ade (the youth in the baseball cap) was sitting on the back row and
watching Tayo as he slowly moved closer and closer to the front
like he was going to pounce on a little brother who looked scared
to death. The brother was trying to escape into his brown duffel
coat and adjusting his glasses which had become steamed up with
all this forced excitement. Every now and then with a turn of
Tayo's inflection he would pop out like a little mouse from behind
his spectacles, only to disappear again when Tayo happened to
glance his way.

But Ade was smiling like a Cheshire cat on the back row. Adjusting
his baseball cap on his shaved head like a pitcher about to make his
pitch at the Hollywood Bowl. He had sat at the back through the
whole meeting. Watched Tayo perform his act and now he was
expecting an encore.

'It's not that I don't believe in all this,' Ade thought, looking enig-
matically and youthfully at the events. 'But this is just college, the
real world is an unpleasant place. Now I didn't come through all
the stuff I've gone through, just to discover I am black. I know I'm
black. But I'm Ade too and Ade at the end of the day has got to get
paid. No Tayo, no Susan, no African Society is going to stop that. I
didn't come her to get cultured, I came here to get a degree and get
the hell out of this rat hole, make some bucks and start livin' large.'

Ade looked around unzipping his blue puffer jacket scratching his
stomach through his Karl Kani T' shirt. 'Don't get me wrong,' he
thought, 'I'll be around when needed. After all hadn't I cussed that

old man when he disrespected the scene, swearing and all that, he should no better. After all I know your supposed to respect elders. If there was thing about a hard Nigerian, African upbringing you are always taught to respect your elders. I can remember from the age of twelve being given the leather belt so many times by my father that I thought it was a reward for good behaviour.

'I remember,' Ade thought, 'my father, pounding towards me across the living room floor, leather belt in hand like it was attached to him. 'Hop-per tang ' the belt would strike.' Ade anticipated the hard leather serrated edge on his naked legs, he prayed the buckle would not hit him, the tip of the belt would not graze his skin and sting, lightly tearing his flesh and not cutting it deep. He prayed for the deep cut, though it would take longer to heal. He prayed for a wound so deep he would have to take a whole week off school, so he could avoid the embarrassment of all the stares and questions from the class and teacher.

Though Ade was just twelve, it seemed strange to him that such arbitrary punishments could be given for a simple accident of spilling orange juice on the carpet floor. Ade would watch his father as he came home from work via the pub, muttering to himself in Yoruba something incoherent and foolish. His red eyes bleary, his afro all unkempt like he had been grabbed and pulled through a fence by it.

His father a very dark skinned man, who hated his own complexion and married the lightest skinned woman he could find, was not a little bit annoyed to discover that his son was as dark as he was. Through a notion of self hatred, mixed with the affects of the vodka and working on a building site with some of the most racist white people this side of south London. All had their negative affects on the mentality of Mr Adeleke senior, to meet out violence to his young son.

This violent behaviour had given the social services on at least three occasions an excuse to send Ade and his sister to a children's home.

Ade could remember his first weekend in one of those hostels. It was after a particularly bad evening when his dad had almost ripped the bedroom door off in an attempt in his drunken binge to get at the infants sleeping.

He could remember the sound as the door came off it's hinges and his Father's red eyes coming closer. A son should not be afraid of his father; 'but here in the madness that had become the world,' Ade thought, 'everything is turned upside down, boy this world is mad.' Ade remembered thinking, how hard it was to hide the cuts and bruises, covering up to go to school, all the stares and strange looks. This time not for the fact they were one of the few black families in Catford in the 1970's.

It did not take long for the social services to knock on the door demanding that the children be turned over to the custody of the state. The state, the same state that had butchered and murdered so many of our people in mental institutions and prisons.

Ade remembered, vividly being dragged into some strange car with strange people. Two old looking, pasty, social workers bedraggled like they had been resurrected from the dead and only half brought to life who at any moment might keel over and die. In long grey over coats even though it was the height of summer. Big thick grey, moustaches adorning their top lips even the woman. She called it her pride and joy combing it every night.

Dribbles of snot occasionally dropping from the male social workers nose, 'well I think it was the male one,' Ade thought, 'they both look exactly the some, a strange species altogether, that bears no resemblance to human beings as I know them.' As if to corroborate Ade's worse fears was the smell like moth balls and arsenic, just the sought of smell that a zombie should have.

The social workers scurried off with the young Adelekes, like they were personal trophies from a hunting trip. You know the great white hunter goes off into the African bush and comes back with his trophy.

Being bundled into the car and offered foul smelling and sticky sweets did not appease or relieve the tension or fear. Certainly Ade and his sister were more afraid of their new found surrogate parents, than they had ever been of their father. 'After all,' Ade remembered thinking, 'he's still my father.'

The journey lasted for what seemed like a life time across the streets of London, still lined with NF graffiti and skinheads in red jack boots. They peered into the speeding car scratching their bald heads puzzled, why too pure breed Anglo-Saxon's should have two so very black 'coons' in their car. "It ain't right," one of them remarked scratching like an albino Oran-utan as the grey ford trundled past them. "You just don't know what's white, or what's right any more," he said, and spat on the floor very near a young Asian

Asian child who happened to be walking past with her family.

Ade and his sister sat shivering in the back seat and clutching themselves like Hansel and Gretel from the famous story. The only trouble was they had nothing to leave as a trail to find their way home, except perhaps the tears of Bola, Ade's sister. But their hosts seemed oblivious to their two victims torment. They talked through their noses in a language that only they could understand.

"It really is a shame Mary," he said, "what is happening to these ethnic minorities in the ghetto."

"I agree," Mary said, rubbing the glistening mildew which was starting to drip from her nostrils. "It's a shame poor bleeders, there nothing but little wretches," she said, casting a 'paternal' glance in their direction, "I think their father was quite mad, did you see his eyes were red like a wild animal."

"Now then," the man said, turning the steering wheel with the dexterity of a slug, "be careful to remain detached, don't get too attached to them, (like he was talking about to two pet cats) remember you are a professional."

"Yes, yes, you're quite right Tom," she muttered, "I quite forgot myself. It's just that sometimes these bleeden people,.... it makes you wonder why they have children."

"I know what you mean," Tom replied, trying to appear like the liberal, yet sounding more like a closet Fascist, "but this country ....." And he paused for affect, "this country...still believes.. by Jimminie it does (he was getting excited) in free choice and thank God for that."

"Of course, of course," Mary said, "I would never suggest otherwise, but that man in there seemed so wild, so savage!"

"Of course," Tom replied, knowingly, "Franz Fanon always said, it was colonialism that turned blacks into what they were, have you read Wretched of the Earth. What a marvellous piece of fiction." He actually managed to bring some colour to his cheeks in the course of mentioning Fanon, he must have been remembering his revolutionary student days, when he used to wear a black leather jacket like a Black panther and sing we shall overcome in the middle of the road, stopping the traffic.

"Yes I agree," Mary said, "but do you mean to say," adjusting her rain coat and wiping her nose again, "that we are responsible?"

"I feel that......(he paused again for affect), in some way that we are Mary, I feel that we are."

"Well at least." Mary said, smiling sublimely, "these two are out of it, poor little mites."

This liberal platitude, a pastiche like parody of sympathy, affability hiding and masking down right naked racism, went on for what seemed to Ade hours. They talked even as they left the streets of London behind. Ade remembered seeing the trees lining the road side, the moon starting to rise behind the encircling foliage and sleep taking hold of him and then nothing.

The grey dusky evening giving way to the enveloping darkness of night. Waspish clouds flitted to and fro over the evening skies like ghosts of ancestors long dead searching the firmament for a place of rest. The wind whistled through the autumnal trees sending a cascade of leaves through the darkening skies. They fluttered on the breeze, like ballet dancers dancing their last dance.

An owl screeched over the darkening skies, enveloped and silhouetted for a while against the circumference of the moon. It's grey feathers submerged in the all consuming blackness as dusk gave way to night. On they travelled leaving motorways and urban life far behind. On they went down winding roads and back streets, down stony paths and ancient streets. Ade and Bola still seemed oblivious to the world. They did not hear the screech of the owl, or the grey night, as it consumed trees, houses, animals, birds, even the moon itself, in its icy cold. The temperature dropped, but the car kept plodding along. Ade drifting into the subconscious world of his own thoughts.

Ade was dreaming of slaying dragons and climbing mountains. Dreaming of winning, before those who try to control the reality of life would try to turn his subconscious desire to win, into defeat. Can you teach a child to lose, before he has even began to live his life?

Ade held on to his sister even though he had been sleeping now for more than three hours, rocking with Bola side by side as the car chundled along well worn paths, down leafy furrows, fields marked with thorn bushes, patchworks of yellow green and brown farmland. Sleeping cattle huddled together for the warmth, not even stirring as the little car noisily clattered up the road. But Ade and

Bola just slept on. A deep sleep where your spirit travels far to escape the world, if only for a while.

The car screeched to a halt as Tom wrenched the brakes on.

Tom's face contorted suddenly, like he had been grabbed by some fierce spirit. The lines of his face stood out like a diseased prune. Even the blood vessels and nerves on his face - expanded, red and ready to burst. Beads of sweat dribbled down his face and formed droplets on his chin.

"Are you okay, Tom," Mary said, taking hold of his pasty pallid hands, rubbing them between his. But Tom's eyes were round like a raver on eze.

"Tom, Tom, are you okay, Tom, Tom we're here," she said, "Look we're at Churchill's."

Tom partially got a grip, but by now he was gritting his teeth and chattering something indescribable.

"Tom," Mary shrieked, gripping and shaking him by both hands. A long line of saliva had appeared at the corner of his mouth, dribbling down the side of his face, dripping from the right edge of the corner of his chin.

"Tom," Mary screamed again like a lunatic, frantically shaking him, to and fro like a rag doll.

Tom was lost like a swimmer in some great dark pool, floundering around in murky waters. As an adolescent he had developed the handicap. It might had spurred others on to great endeavours to compensate. But Tom's little pasty face and his little pasty life became more vague. Spoilt by a middle class, middle of the road family, with liberal tendencies, who rewarded his every handicap whether genuine or not with little sticky buns. Adolescence gave way to youthful rebellion, the ravenous consumption of Karl Marx and Franz Fanon as if they were the Bible. Sit ins and anti war protest, admiration of the Black Panthers for a brief while, made his handicap subside. He had a vision one day he would be a black panther. One day he would be black.

But youth gave way to the realisation of life, he was what he was, he would never be Huey P Newton or George Jackson. No he could never be them, no matter how many black jackets he put on, no matter how many times he sang we shall overcome, no matter how many times he read Soul on Ice. Besides he did not want to be black. Not really black, not really, not for ever, just when it was fashionable, just when it was cool, just when it was revolutionary,' he thought.

So in the midst of this understanding the realisation drained his strength away, the attacks came more often now and when he least expected it.

Tom woke out of the spasm with a shout, yellow saliva dribbling down his chin, Mary shaking him half to death, Ade and Bola who had been woken by the commotion staring at him. He wiped the saliva from his face and attempted to gain composure. He did not know what had triggered the attack, or how he had managed to park the car. 'Thank God we aren't on the road, I must maintain some control, after all,... I'm the only man here,' he thought.

Ade was thinking as Tom wiped the saliva from his mouth like a baby, 'this man's mad, (very few children can say epilepsy let alone explain it) why has Daddy who is meant to protect us left us with these mad white people.' Bola was wishing that the whole thing was a nightmare and Daddy would come and wake them up. That some how he would be sober, take them home for a dinner of Eba and Stewed fish with ockra, with the garden outside newly mown and smelling of honeysuckle in the summertime.

But that was not the truth. The truth was that were parked outside the children's home, they would spend the next seven years going backwards and forwards from. That they had been driven there by two social workers who cared less for them than they did about the social debt they were paying.

The reality was that Ade and Bola would spend the rest of their lives being moved from their father's house when ever he got drunk, or life got too much for him. They should have been glad to be fed roast pork and apple sauce, surely it was a delicacy. Never mind that the fat ugly care workers stuffed their mouths with too many sweets and their minds with too many foolish ideas. Never mind too that the director of the School, one Sir Michael Mosely ran the place like a concentration camp. Beatings for being late, beatings for not eating your greens, beatings for looking him in the eye, beatings for being too proud, beatings for being too black.

Worst still that the same Sir Michael Mosely OBE, BSC, MBA, MBE of Sir Winston Churchill's Children Home would be arrested and found guilty twelve years later for being a paedophile and commit-

ting indecent sex acts on children. Turning according to the Daily
Liar the children into 'slaves on his own sex plantation.' Ironic and
tragic that many of these same children were of African descent,
either from the Caribbean or Africa. Victims only to be victimised
by the state.

All Ade could think of was how, 'can my father let us stay in this
awful place where this strange man (Sir Michael) walked around
administering his strange punishments, for his even stranger plea-
sures. I thought older people were supposed to be wiser, how was I
to have any respect for older people when they did not have
respect for themselves.' He concluded, young as he was that, 'just
because you are old doesn't make you wise.'

Ade shuddered, coming back to the here and now. Thinking, whilst
staring at Tayo standing like Moses over the Israelites, 'that's why I
couldn't let that damn old fool try and disrespect the scene, like we
are not worthy of respect. No way am I goin' to let anyone disrespect the program because they are older. Nah,' Ade thought, chewing ravenously on his chewing gum. 'People have to earn respect,
after all my own father gave up his responsibilities to get drunk
and beat his children, he should have been taking on the world.
Nah, that ain't correct and it's not righteous, in the future people
will lead by merit, not by age.'

'How strange,' Ade thought, looking down at Tayo, 'that this meeting would make me remember all those painful memories, things
that I had tried to bury or forget.'

Tayo looked up at the crowd but some how he seemed to be just
looking at Ade staring straight at him with those very black eyes.
Ade smiled a nervous, handsome, grin. Perhaps to deflect the pene-
tration.

"So whose going to stand for treasurer," Tayo said, walking from
side to side, like a rabble rouser at a football match stirring up the
crowd.

A small brother at the back, who seemed to be submerged by the
Hillfiger puffer jackets around him raised his hand like he was a
school boy, asking teacher to go to toilet.

"Yes," Tayo said, looking at the outstretched hand which seemed to
rise from beneath a wall of powerfully built brothers.

"I want to stand," said the thin little voice like a girls'.

"You want to what," Tayo asked, looking puzzled, "I can't hear you."

"I want to be the Treasurer," the voice said. Everyone peered in his direction, some of the sisters tittered and whispered to themselves.

"Have some respect," Ade said, "Tayo, get some control of this meeting."

"Na your right," Tayo said, looking at Ade, "brother stand up, I really can't see you."

He did. Some of the crowd broke out into laughter, two sisters who had been staring a little too long at Tayo's eyes took a moment to see where all the attention was now going.

"Nah man, that's not right," Ade said, "at least he's doing what all of you should be doing."

"True," Tayo said, looking at him, but thinking, 'if you care so much why don't you stand, are you really any different.'

"What have you got to say for yourself," Susan said, looking at the small brown skinned brother who emerged from the giant's around him.

"Well I want to stand because I hear a lot of people talking, but not much work being done," he said, in a shaky little voice, "we seem to be good at talking, but handling accounts and paperwork requires consistency and efficiently. I am that man," he said smiling.

There was a ripple of applause from the back which Tayo and Susan added to.

"What's your name," Susan asked, smiling.

"Kwame Ajala," he replied whispisly.

"All right then, Kwame Ajala, does anyone oppose," Susan said, looking at the audience, there was a stunned silence. All the big weight lifting brothers with the puzzles in their head and Karl Kani T shirts who believed they were all so individual but were so much the same, looked at each other dumfounded and confused. Their parents came from all over the African world, they had a diversity which should have led them to be dynamic, but they were speechless. They looked around, some of them fiddling with their phones or pagers like small children playing with their toys.

Tayo looked at them and kissed his teeth, 'what has happened to the spirit of the race, where the young men are so slow to stand up and be counted. What is wrong with us, no really what is wrong with us,' he thought, watching a brother with sunglasses, who was busy looking down the blouse of a well endowed sister in the row in front. 'This brother has not even listened to a damn word we've been saying, all he 's interested in is the size of this woman's breasts.' The brother looked up sensing Tayo's hard stare. Shuffled in his seat like a man under going interrogation in a police cell and knows he is guilty.

He looked side ways and rubbed his chin in a nervous fashion. But all he could feel was Tayo's eyes baring down on him - those black eyes, in a white iris. The eyes staring at him like they were burning a whole into his very soul. 'Was he the kind of brother who would stand for the race,' Tayo thought, looking, 'nah, nah he wasn't, the only thing he's goin' to stand for is this girl.'

Tayo kissed his teeth and then he realised everybody was waiting for him. He put himself back together, "so brother have you got anything else to say," Tayo asked, looking at Kwame doing up his flannel grey jacket, the sharp, tight, short cropped hair. The delicate almost feminine fingers, the child like expression and innocent naïve stance.

'The kind of brother,' Tayo thought, 'who lives under the umbrella, of Daddy's money, Daddy's protection,' he watched him playing with his gold signet ring.(Solid gold mind you, nothing fake, 100% carat straight from the South African mines, worked on by impoverished brothers, for a pittance of pay and a great deal of the punishments. The kind of gold that a brother may kill another brother for, the kind that led Britain to invade the Gold coast (Ghana) and others, the kind that led the Spanish to invade the Inca's civilisation and wipe it out. Gold, for the most part a shiny, but worthless material. That too many people had fought and died over.)

Tayo watched him and waited for Kwame to continue, "I know that most of you are thinking or wondering who I am, but I feel that a lot of times we get together we are hot on the talk, but action is not coming." His voice was a little shaky at first, but their was a slight inflection, not of fear but confidence.

'Why confidence,' Tayo thought, staring, trying to penetrate his soul, 'because his family is wealthy and has power, that's why he's confident' and he sighed.

"I am about sound effective financial management," Kwame said, with a glint in his eye when he said financial. "I know how to organise my finances," (his confidence was building all the time) "and I feel I can organise the society's money well."

Susan was watching him, there was something about the gold ring, and the shine in his eye which made her distrust him. Since Busta every time she saw a brother with anything gold it just reminded her of him, all she could think of is, 'he could have brought a book with the money, instead of trying to look pretty, like a little girl.'

Susan looked at Tayo who was thinking the same thing, 'I want some one else to stand for the position, not because I don't trust Kwame,' 'Okay,' he thought a little deeper and stared at him, 'alright then..... I don't trust him.... so please let someone else stand,' and he twisted his locks with his left hand a little too vainly. He looked at Ade hoping that from his baseball cap would come more than handsome, youthful, reactions, hoping that wisdom was lurking there.

Ade stared back unblinking, 'I don't know why you're looking at me,' he thought, 'I really don't know what's on your case, boss, but I ain't goin' to stand for nothing. I come here to get paid, not political, seriously,' chewing even more avariciously on his chewing gum, 'I want the kris threads, the fly girls, listen to a few tunes of garage music, politics, nah not politics. It's too political.'

"Al'right then," Tayo said, "who will vote for Kwame, those in favour raise their hands."

A few disinterested people put their hands up. 'This is absolutely pathetic,' Susan thought, looking at the few wavering hands, 'I could have taken my daughter to the museum or something, she and I would have learned. They need a serious wake up call. It's obvious they don't want him, but they're to lazy to say anything,' she thought, looking at one brother staring at his huge silver watch for the third time within five minutes, 'oh yeah, and far too selfish.'

"Al'right," Tayo said again, hoping that by repeating himself he may somehow be able to turn back the hand of time. It was not Kwame that was the issue, it was them. 'It's going to take more than this meeting to stir the embers of consciousness in them, it's going to take more than this one small meeting to wake black people up. Because right now,' he thought, watching some now looking bored and disinterested, 'they are asleep. If the Klu Klux Klan came in right now and hung the biggest brother they could find from the roof, I bet most of these others would still be thinking about not getting to their next lesson late. After all they have come here to be the multi-cultural-Negro, to fit in, to succeed, to get paid. They're not here to be revolutionaries.'

"So you've done it," Tayo uttered, beckoning Kwame down to the front with a youthful finger. He turned to the crowd, "this is your executive, for the year. There are other posts which you can stand for later on. But we are here to represent you, for richer, for poorer, in sickness and in health. But do not expect the way to be an easy ride, I know there's going to be conflict with some of you, I swear, especially you," Tayo said, looking at a huge brother playing with his watch like it was a video game, "would you mind not playing with your watch, we will finish in a moment."

The brother gave a scowl and looked down at Tayo thinking, 'who the hell does he think he is, little midget, I can do what I want, who does he think he is, a **superstar?**'

"That's just about it then," Tayo said, ignoring the brother's scowl, or the whispering that followed, "there it is."

The Canteen

It had been a full three hours since the end of the meeting and Tayo was sitting alone in the canteen trying to put the pieces of his mind together. No form of transcendental meditation can prepare an African to take on the world of injustice that confronts us when we decide to commit ourselves to liberation. He should have been wiser, a little less proud, a little more thoughtful than he was. But with the heart more often than not comes the emotion, just because you love it, does not mean you love wisely. After all had not love driven Marcus Garvey to risk his life and everything he had for his people though he died alone at number 2 Beaumont Crescent, West Kensington, London, England.

'Should it be love or hate that moves me,' Tayo thought, tapping his black boots agitatedly like a man about to do some terrible act. 'Hate at the time is more powerful, but love of the race, that endures, or does it? Even with love could I really do any good. After all what qualifications have I got to stand up there, what makes me think that I know anymore than them, how to run things. I don't know.' He began to remember their dumfounded, sullen faces.

'All those biceps, those muscles, puffer jackets and personal stereos, sharp haircuts and slow brains. All an image of blackness, a hollow shallow image, without substance,' Tayo thought, twisting his locks and staring at the empty canteen. He remembered a year ago stepping in there and seeing Tony, Fred and Carl. 'Where are they now,' he contemplated, 'who are their replacements, nothing but fakers and posers. So if they don't know, will they follow? Will they follow me - what makes me think I've got it and even if I did have it, brothers will not follow brothers. Too much ego, but they will follow an idea. But how do you make an African believe in something. You can't force him. You know we must be the must stubborn people on the planet. So can you coax, tease or induce, perhaps, but that's not my style. Why then if I could pay someone, but then I haven't even got the money to buy a pair of shoes. Wealth is one way, but will it create peace, the more I get into this thing the more there is conflict, the more conflict there is, the more enemies of justice intensify their war. Well.'

The red circular tables empty of food or students, strewn here and there an odd coke can. Scrunched in the middle, waiting to be put in the bin by an overworked dinner lady. But none came. They had all gone home, everyone had gone except for him.

He looked down at his leather pouch hanging around his waist and the worn out grey top that he had hastily put on this morning. The black boots with polish rubbed into the worn out edges, 'more than anyone I need to get paid, not stand up in front of a bunch of people, put on a show so that they can go away and applaud or throw stones. What makes some people stand up and some sit down,' Tayo thought. 'Why is it that I do the things I do and they do the things they do. Is it just my background my history, my ancestors. Surely some of them have a similar background, not everyone of their ancestors can be sell-outs. There has to be something else;' in the midst of his thought he noticed a thin line of smoke. It drifted wispishly through the front exterior door. Only to be met with yet another pungent, even stronger cloud of smoke to replace it. It was followed by a circular ring, grey, brown and then yellow.

Then he noticed the rich, sickly, but poisonous smell, 'sensimelia, definitely that addictive herb, a cure for glycomia, but in the long term causes an increase in the amount of female hormones in your body, long term memory loss and eventually insanity. Herb,' Tayo thought, 'I know the smell well. I remember Rastas smoking weed, and getting high, never asking why they're doing this, spending all the money they don't have on a substance that is rotting their brain, but all I get in reply is, 'ya nah say it's just pure levity.' 'No,' Tayo thought, 'it's not pure levity, it's pure foolishness.'

The mist became a hazy smoke that bellowed and ebbed it's way through the corridor, 'anyone within five paces of this place, is going to get arrested for being high,' Tayo thought, looking around. But there was nobody, only the sound of the water tap in the coffee machine, dripping liquid slowly into the basin below.

The smoke wafted towards him, breaking his meditation again. Tayo pinched his nostrils together and wafted the smoke with his left hand, moving his hand from side to side frantically, as if some drunken God had broken wind.

"That's a terrible stink," Tayo said, out loud, staring through the haze, as the sweet smell subsided and the sickly funk took over.

At last through the gathering mists, Tayo heard the bouncing of youthful boots. The rhythmical thud as they came down the adjoining stairs. Through the smoke like a African style Clint Eastwood, Michael emerged, Timberland boots first, brown leather jacket second. A grey Kangol hat in hand his head shaved at the sides and his top locks tied and bouncing on the top of his head. His jeans hanging down around his ankles and an arrogant, self satisfied, but definitely handsome smile, plastered all over his face, with the spliff tucked in to the right corner of his mouth.

He saw Tayo sitting down and bounced right over to him standing over him smoking and smiling, smiling and smoking like a drug crazed Cheshire cat.

"Ya al'right," Michael said, staring down at him and inhaling the smoke, blowing it through his nostrils and shaking his locks.

"I saw you smoking all the way from over there," Tayo said to him looking up.

"Ya not in one of you're lectures now," Michael said, to him staring.

"So ya' goin try and stab me again," Tayo said, sarcastically, "to make your point, well now's a good time to die, **are you prepared to die**."

"Yeah there'll be plenty of time for that," Michael said, stylishly taking the cigarette from his mouth, and flicking the ash. By now a funnel of smoke bellowed around him, "don't push me."

"Don't push me," Tayo said giggling, "you've been watching too many films, isn't that Rambo or something."

"Yeah I think so," Michael replied smirking, "...Anyway I didn't come here," hitching up his baggy jeans and sitting down opposite him, "to fight you, I just came to say that you did alright."

"Al right," Tayo said, "what do you mean all right."

"You know alright," Michael repeated, "that speech and that,.. but don't think that your some big man now." But Michael was thinking, 'I've been looking for this brother all round college since the meeting ended, but I'm not letting him know that.'

"Well that coming from you is praise indeed," Tayo said, ignoring the veiled threat.

"Yeah but it don't change 'anythink'...cause niggers have got to die."

"You what," Tayo said, puzzled, "niggers, I don't know any."

"Y'know what I mean, them niggers in there, there lost, they've got to die, to learn," Michael replied.

"But if there dead," Tayo said, "how can they learn," he started laughing.

Michael trying to hide his own giggles, "listen all this African talk and all that, it doesn't mean anything. I'm not in it, do you understand. What I mean is I don't business..."

"So what then," Tayo asked, "is the situation and what is the solution?"

Michael smiling, "violence," and his whole face lit up.

"Really," Tayo said, leaning back in his chair and rolling his locks with his index fingers, "is it".

"Yeah," Michael blurted out triumphantly, "being almshouse and being able to sustain it."

"Just how almshouse can you get," Tayo said, frowning, "where is your army?"

Michael leisurely flicked the ash form his cigarette like a film star cowboy, "I'm telling you, if you ever see me on the road, fighting, you'll see that I can fight, I don't business."

"Yes," Tayo said, becoming irritated, "I don't think you understand, when I said you, I don't men you singularly, I mean you plural, I mean us."

"Well," Michael said, looking a bit vacant, but disguising it.

"I mean we as a people are in no position to be almshouse with anyone," Tayo said, "we couldn't start anything of that nature and sustain it. What with most of us loving white culture, white people and praying to look like anything other than we are. All those black men with white women are they going to get almshouse, no the only ones they're goin to get almshouse with is you. Most of our people don't even see race, though we're getting busted upside the head every day. We are colour blind. It doesn't matter how many black people end up in prison, or a mental institution, all that matters is so long as there're all right. It's all about their own pleasure, are you like that?"

"What," Michael said, "is that what you think?" A little bit hurt. "I think it's more likely that you are in this for your ego, I saw the way those honeys were looking at you, like you were there saviour or 'somethink."

"Do you ...think that I like standing up there," Tayo asked, rhetorically, "do you think that I don't know that most don't give a damn about the progress of us. I know that, I saw it in their faces, posing, jumping around, they had come for a performance. 'Yah nah what I'm sayin, ya nah what I mean," Tayo putting on an American accent. "It's all foolishness, it's fake about as fake as your Kangol hat," Tayo said, looking at his hat perched with pride of honour on his up stretched knee, "besides why don't I ever see you wear it." Tayo asked inquisitively.

"It won't fit over my locks," Michael said, laughing, this time out loud.

"You poser" Tayo replied, giggling. "But seriously," he continued, "the only way we are going to change it is, is by being different. I know there are those of us who love the race," Tayo continued, "the revolution will not be televised, we are not going to liberate anything with a spliff in one hand and a Kangol hat which you can't even wear in the other, it's goin to take discipline and courage."

"I'm not in it," Michael said, shaking his head, "discipline, like a Muslim."

"I mean discipline like a man," Tayo retorted, "how the hell are you goin to do anything when you can't control your own mouth, when you addicted to cigarettes, when you can't control your penis. How the hell are you goin to achieve anything. You can't, you won't."

Michael shrugged his shoulders and took a long drag on his spliff, "I hear what you're saying', but I'm not given it up for anyone, or my women, like your the saint, I've seen you with that fit looking sister, what's her name....Melanie that's it."

"I see you know all the sisters names, then," Tayo said, changing the subject.

"Well," Michael replied, "you've got to keep your options open."

"I heard them," Michael continued, "after the meeting talking about you, like they want you to go and teach them. I can see you now, my sister, I just got to show you now," pretending to be an American style preacher. They both giggled like school children.

"I guess you want to know what the secret is," Tayo said, "live life right and be correct."

"But seriously, will see if your down," Michael said interrupting, "it seems you like the talk too much, I'm down for the real action. Some day they're goin' to right a book about me, not you, well they might include you in the foot note, but who wants to hear about you, everybody wants to know what I'm doing. I'm the interesting one. No one want's to know about being righteous, they want to be bad. I'm bad and what's more I'm ready to kick arse, still."

"I think you'll find that when it comes down to it, neither of us are really down," Tayo said, "both of us are sell-outs."

Michael inhaled slowly, 'to be honest,' he thought, 'I never heard anyone reason like that before, it's original, yeah original,' he took his Kangol hat from his knee and put it on the table. 'I ve heard people say you need discipline, but never why. But at the end of the day, we're not going to rise like that, row upon row of disciplined soldiers, lining up to get shot down, I'm not in't. To be honest, I'm not goin' to die, just so some other man can come grind my woman. I don't have any faith in brothers, that's honest, I don't believe in anyone but myself.' He articulated his thought, "black people will sell you out."

"They may, but life is not all that anyway," Tayo said, "you never heard 'tis better to live and die for a noble cause, than live all your life a slave.' You never heard that," Tayo said.

"Yeah I know it," Michael said, "the Last Poets, but I prefer there other work like niggers are scared of revolution."

"So you're a scholar then," Tayo replied, nodding in approval, "I thought, you'd like that one, come on we better get out of here, do you know what time it is."

Michael looked at the dial of his Swatch watch, "what ya sayin' it's ten p.m."

"Come on let's get out of here," Tayo said, slipping on his black coat and standing up, "I'm sick and tired of this place. You know this was designed by man that designs prisons. Can you believe, next time go through the walkways and the passages and tell me it's not like a prison, it is." Walking towards the door and doing up his buttons.

"You know it's true," Michael said, flicking the ash between his fingers and the cigarette butt high into the air.

"Do you always do that," Tayo asked, irritated by the gesture.

"Don't start again," Michael replied, "listen one day ya gone realise that I make a very good friend, you'll find that out."

"Yeah," Tayo mumbling, "one day," walking through the door and up the stairs. "But you should still give that up," he said, "I thought it was Clint Eastwood coming down the stairs, you 'know I don't think it's nice you laughing' and all that stuff, you watch all of that don't you," looking at Michael bouncing up the stairs by the side of him, with his Kangol hat in his hand, "I bet he's probably you're hero or something."

"My hero, you mean yours," Michael replied, as they cleared the steps and reached the ground floor, "you know all the lines, next thing you'll be riding a horse into college."

Tayo laughed as he pushed the door of the concourse open, "yeah, yeah, yeah," Tayo muttered, "I'm the lone ranger and you must be Tonto."

"That suits me," Michael said, bouncing over the contents of an over spilling bin which had not been, nor was likely to be emptied, tonight or this week. "Who wants to be the cracker in a white suit, looking like a pansy, anyway," Michael continued giggling.

"That's true enough," Tayo replied, laughing and pushing the exterior door of the concourse open.

They stepped out into the numb air, a shrill wind picked up from the west, scattering leaves across the road and stray litter, old worn out crisp packets, used condoms, leaflets for conscious meetings that nobody attended, handouts for the Celestial Church of God, inviting you to 'save your soul,' before the devil will assume control of your destiny.'

Suffer for your art, go jogging in the Park

The red brick buildings of Elephant and Castle stood out starkly, cold almost menacing in the night air. With their shadows waxing and waning to the sojourn of the moon as it reached its ultimate zenith in the apex of the sky. The grey smog of the city choking the earth, as the city lights tried to filter through. But the brothers kept bouncing their way, laughing and joking, joking and laughing, through the streets of south London. Tayo remembered Gunnislake, how Del had stood their quivering, his great shoulders hunched over in the dark as they stood in the middle of know where, lost, 'I remember,' Tayo thought, 'we were lost and Carl trying to be the righteous one, the perfect leader, all the while wishing that he was back at home with one of his women. Strange how he kept his personal circumstances so secret, yet everyone knew about it, like a skeleton which just would not lie down dead.'

Michael unwrapped his raspberry flavoured 'Bubilicious' chewing gum, he had been hiding it in the bottom of his pocket. Slowly undoing the packet and slipping out the pink sticky material, popping it in his mouth like a toad catching a fly. Tayo watched him as he negotiated the streets, dodging drunkards, dog mess, and broken dustbins, all the while with his Kangol hat, in one hand and yet another spliff between his fore and index finger.' 'These brother's talents are wasted,' Tayo thought, watching him skipping down the street like a model.

"You know you should have been on the catwalk with your swatch watch and your Kangol hat, I bet you wear Calvin Klein underpants don't you," Tayo said.

"You know what," Michael replied, chewing like a cat, "your jealous, you know, I don't have to stand up on a stage coarsing up the sisters to get them, like you, all I have to do is look at them," they turned the corner and disappeared down a subway.

"Yeah, do you think I went up their to get women," Tayo said and laughed out loud, a large booming laugh that rocked his whole body. The kind of laugh, an older more powerful man, would make. "What," he giggled and started laughing again, in fact he laughed so loud he had to stop, under the glare of the subway light and there he stood with a hand on the wall and one on his side, giggling for all he was worth.

"All right, all right," Michael smiling, "you don't do what you do to get women, alright, but it helps though doesn't it."

"There's no rescuing you," Tayo said taking his hand off the wall adorned with a Nazi Swastika and a NF slogan as if they were synonymous, "you're really lost," looking at him inhaling and chewing at the same time, with different parts of his mouth.

"What you need to do," Tayo added, looking at him enjoying the high life, "is suffer for your art, you need to jogging in the park."

"I'm not in it," Michael said, kissing his teeth and stepping past him, "come on let's get out of here," (to Tayo) "you won't catch me in sneakers except to pose, what do you think my name is Linford."

"You wish it was," Tayo said, catching him up, "then you wouldn't have that little scrawny body and hide it under all those puffer jackets."

"I've never heard a woman complain yet," Michael replied, nimbly stepping over a puddle of urine, which by the smell had been newly delivered.

"No not to your face," Tayo said, as they reached the exit of the subway, "they complain to me, (suddenly getting the grasp of Michael's sense of humour) they all say Michael, why can't you be fit like Tayo, he's so beautiful."

"You wish," Michael said, smiling and taking yet another drag on his drug, "the women when I've finished with them are too knackered to say or do anything, it's Michael please stop, I want to sleep."

"Yeah, yeah," Tayo said, feeling the conversation degenerating into the gutter, "but seriously you should do some exercise, that youthful exterior is not going to last for ever, you keep smoking that stuff and eating that muck, you goin' look like a tinted version of a Michelin man."

"You what," Michael said, trying to envisage it and laughing a little too loudly, as he thought about a huge over weight tinted Michelin man with an Afro and a spliff in his mouth.

Just as they were giggling and laughing like two children, Johnny the vic who had eaten yet another vindaloo was walking up the stairs of the subway towards the tube station. Dave his best friend was a little bit under the weather, perhaps it was because of the thirteen lagers he consumed. Toni, had a self satisfied expression on his face.

"You're as happy as a samboy you are," Johnny said, staring at Toni.

"Anyone would have thought you never had a slash, or nothink, cooar if it only takes that to make you happy I'll have a slash over you any day," he laughed.

"Na when you got's to go, you got's to," Toni said, still smiling like a fool. "'Ear' where did you park you're car Dave, I bloody hate this place, too much muck around here," he blubbered, kicking a coke can.

"Listen' what's all that fucking noise," Dave mumbled, staggering up the stairs.

"What are you goin on about you tart," Johnny replied, "what noise."

"Listen," Dave said, wiping a slither of saliva and sick which had begun to dribble out of the crack in his mouth.

Johnny paused for a while, ".... Listen to what," Johnny said, spitting some yellow phlegm he had stored in the back of his throat onto a coke can he passed.

"You've had one to many," Johnny said, picking his nose, and farting loudly, scratching his backside with a gnarly fat hand, 'that's better,' he muttered to himself - as the bad air rifled through the seat of his jeans, spluttering. To Dave, "you're starting to here things you are, a bit do 'lally,' a bit cuckoo." He motioned his finger by the side of his head in a circular motion (to signify craziness).

"Nah wait a minute," Toni said, cocking his head to one side to listen like a cock a spaniel, "I hear something too," he said, after a minute scratching his head.

Michael and Tayo came bouncing up the stairs Michael wondering how he was going to deliver the best punch-line so he could win this round of verbal sparring. Tayo wondering how he could direct the conversation to end on something positive.

As they came up the stairs Tayo did not notice the coke can battered, dented, lying in a pool of Johnny's yellow phlegm, a mixture of the worst chicken vindaloo, Worthington's best bitter and his own general aromatic saliva.

But Tayo did notice the smell of Johnny's fart, a sought of foul pungent stench. So powerful that he could almost taste it on his lips, "what's that smell," Tayo muttered, looking at Michael, it's like somebody just died."

"Yeah man, that's ill," Michael mumbled, rubbing his nose and throwing the spliff that he had put in his mouth down on the ground, "you know what I've lost all interest in smoking this thing now, cause that's just the illest thing I h've ever smelt, it smells like nothink on earth."

"Phew," Tayo muttered, screwing up his face as tight as a brown paper ball, "who... what.. ever, did that, was dead before it was born." They both laughed, but Tayo still had his face set, when they cleared the stairs and bounced on to the pavement.

Johnny the vic stared down from his vantage point at the top of the stairs like a gargoyle perched on a rock face. He could feel the phlegm building up inside his mouth. The mixture of the Indian vindaloo he had just stuffed down his throat, not one, two, but three helpings - no wonder his stomach hung over his trousers like he was pregnant and he stunk like Thamesmead sewer works. The food stains that decorated his T' shirt, (the same one he was wearing last week) were permanent like a pattern. With a sneer all over his flabby arrogant face, beads of sweat and grime on his neck leaving a trail of filth over his collar. A collar which would never be white again so long as he was wearing it. (Ironic isn't it, white nationalist can't get his T-shirt white) Spunk stains on his blue jeans from the black prostitute he had sex with two days ago, Johnny was not going to get an award for being the best dressed Fascist in Bulldog magazine or Screwdriver, but Fascist he was never the less.

He summoned up all the filth from the bottom of the cesspit of his stomach, where the lagers and vindaloo were fermenting together. He could feel the mucus, phlegm, yellow and brown bile from his overactive digestive system being summoned up from his stomach to his throat, he coughed it up. He felt with his tongue the yellow, brown liquid swilling around inside his mouth, with little bits of orange carrot, tickling his tonsils.

Tayo and Michael were clearing the steps two at a time. Michael slide down the zip of his leather jacket as he saw the summit. 'This jacket is just boom, it's freezing out there, but I'm just cool,' he thought and admired the sharpness of his jacket, the smartness of his own appearance, and how fine he looked.

Johnny the vic spat and the spit landed on Michael's arm, the yellow and green texture splattered on impact, sending orange bits of carrot on to his grey Kangol hat.

"What the hell was that," Michael mumbled, sniffing the foul odour which now emanated from the fallen substance, "boy it stinks," he said, looking up towards heaven, expecting to see a pigeon, so he could beat it with a stick for ruining his threads.

Tayo tried to prevent a smirk forming on his mouth as he stared at the mess on Michael's new jacket, the yellow and brown stain, the carrot bits dripping from the grey suede Kangol hat. 'That will teach you to be so vain, buying a Kangol hat just so you can pose in it, indeed,' Tayo thought, looking up, expecting to see a pigeon flying swiftly away from the scene of the crime. But when he looked up, all he saw were three white men looking down.

Tayo stared at Johnny. 'There's something in his face,' Tayo thought, 'it is not that he has a swastika tattooed on his arm, or rights for whites painted on his forehead. No there is none of these obvious signs. But there is something in his spirit, the sneer on the chubby, battered face, the air of superiority. Just because KKK is not tattooed on your face, it's still there in your mind isn't it,' Tayo thought, staring at him.

Michael looked up and kissed his teeth, realising that the source of his new colour coding was not beast, but man, (or was that the other way round). He kissed his teeth again, so hard, his handsome face shock like a man electrified. The little curly hairs on the back of his neck twisted and turned in on themselves, the adrenaline began to run through every inch of his body.

"What the fuck are you looking at, you black bastard ?" Johnny shouted, looking at Tayo. Tayo smiled and hesitated. He looked up at the sky, the clouds grey, darkening into black, the moon hiding and dying behind them, the greyness dimmed by the smug night.

A plane darting across the sky struck dumb by distance, time and place, shooting it's grey trail behind it, staining the blackness of the night. Single solitary stars speckled in the night sky, Orion, the constellation of Alpha sentori. Tayo groaned under the weight of the oppression of the times, the oppression of his place, the oppression of his existence, the spirit kept prisoner, longing to be free from his body. Wanting to be free, free as that plane shuttling across the sky. His spirit yearned to be free. Tayo looked at the ground and kissed his teeth, the graffiti coloured walls, the unnatural blare of the subway light, the urine and filth on the chipped stone pavements. He looked at Johnny and stared, deep into his eyes.

"Who.. and (he paused for affect) I do mean who.... the hell, do you think, you're talking to, cracker!" He asserted.

"You what," Johnny said, turning to Toni who shock his head in disbelief at Tayo's audacity.

"You've got a have him, Jack," Toni said, "he thinks he's in Jamaica or somethink." But Michael had already dropped his hat on the floor and reached in his pocket for his knife, bounding up the stairs two at a time. His timberland boots flying over the steps as if they did not exist.

Tayo could feel the blood running through every part of his body, the sweet feeling of adrenaline rushing, pulsating. He regulated the feeling and started walking up the stairs, not fast, not quick, but as coolly as a boxer stepping into the ring. He could feel each hard, cold, stone pavement. The unnatural plinth and cut of it. The coldness went up from the stone into his boot, into his ankle and the centre of his legs, the joints of his knees. There it tried to hold the muscles of his thighs and freeze them to his sinews. The coldness tried to enter the core of his being, but when it reached his soul, a fire was burning. The kind of fire that would melt the polar ice caps and send the water boiling and cascading over the earth. The kind of fire that burns whole cities and destroys civilisations. The kind of fire that lives on, past civilisations and can not be forgotten by the course of time, because time can not destroy the spirit of a man. A man's spirit is indomitable and unconquerable, it is only man which who can destroy himself, when he betrays his sacred hoop.

"Come on you fucking spade," Johnny was screaming, as Michael hurtled towards them. It was pride driving him on, pride now making him leap like a superman up a flight of stone steps running headlong towards three white men who only a week earlier had beaten an Asian man half to death. Pride. A desire to get even for spitting on his coat and hat, it would not have mattered if the man was black, white or sky blue, Michael had made up his mind, 'to give him more than two lick and broke him up,' he leapt over a nearby railing and kicked Toni who got in his way, full in his head.

His timberland boots landed in Toni's head and his head jerked back like a punch and Judy doll. He tried to gain composure, but the power of Michael's initial onslaught was too overwhelming. The lagers Toni had consumed along with a general lethargy brought about by the 'slap up Indian dinner, the tiredness of the day's general activities of shagging and quarrelling took a toll on his less than healthy frame. He tried to remember, 'I am the master race, a trained member of at least two secret neo-nazi organisations. I am a child of

England, a flower of the sceptered isle; England is the mother of civilisation, it had brought culture to the world. After all, the British Empire was so great that the sun would never set on it, good old Winston and Queen Vicky. Did we not win two world wars. Am I not trained in every form of armed and unarmed combat, by British army veterans and Protestant terrorists as well. Have I not killed, more blacks, spades, monkeys, pakis, spics, micks, coons, then I care to mention,' he thought. But his legs were not listening. They buckled like a boxer who had just been given a knock out punch crumbling backwards against the side of a nearby brick wall, conveniently placed to break his fall, though in doing so he managed to cut the side of his head like a ripe melon and send a cascade of blood down his otherwise coarse, but unblemished pale face.

Michael was already jumping and leaping like a modern day Blade from a Marvel comic. Swinging in upper cuts to Toni who was bent double trying to regain his composure, only to be met by a torrent of further assaults, one ...two ....three, one. The upper cut to the chin, one that was wild and missed his head by feet, another a hook to his head, which sent his jaw shuddering backwards against the same brick wall. His head lurched back and then dropped forward, blood pouring from his nose and mouth, his brown hair dripping beads of sweat and blood. Michael skipped in and kneed him in his head - sending his whole body rocking back against the wall for the third time and putting his jaw out of its socket for good.

"You grey back bastard," Michael shrieked, as he delivered the final uppercut, Toni's frame crashing against the wall for the fourth time.

Johnny the vic had gained his senses enough to figure out that this was not going to be an ordinary day of beating brothers. 'These niggers are crazy,' he thought watching, Michael tearing his best mate to pieces, 'I'm not sticking around here,' he decided to get out of there, though Dave was stooped almost double, half accomatised from his ten lagers.

Tayo was already at the top of the stairs, "where the hell do you think you're going, not so brave now," he said.

"Come on mate," Johnny mumbled, looking for a brick or a bottle to use as a weapon. But Tayo was already within striking distance.

"Listen keep the fuck away from me you...... , you lot are crazy, keep away from me I warn yo..... I mean it.., " Johnny spluttered, reaching inside his pocket and fumbling around as if he had a weapon.

His face was deathly pale and his face shone white, with sweat. His hair clinging wet to him.

"I mean it keep away from me, you lot you're bloody bonkers, you're mad," Johnny blubbered stumbling backwards, "come on Dave," he shrieked, as he clenched his right fist and swung wildly at Tayo who was now only a few feet away.

Tayo skipped to the side and blocked the blow with the palm of his left hand, darting in like a cat, up close to the much bigger but clumsier man. Tayo struck upwards with the ridge of his hand, under his opponents jaw, locking his neck out, wrenching it. Johnny's huge head jerked. Before Johnny could gather his senses, or numb the pain, Tayo hopped in, sweeping both his legs from behind. Johnny's body recoiled backwards, his legs lifting from the ground, unable to maintain balance. His arms flailing in mid air like a man trying to fly. His head hit the ground first. To be more precise the back of his head.

Tayo saw it in slow motion, the falling man, his skull as it hit the very hard, cold, stone pavement, the crack, as it struck the stone and the blood and contents of his head as they spewed out on to the streets of Elephant and Castle.

Tayo stood over the unconscious body and kissed his teeth, "come on," he shouted, "where's your pride, come on, where's your honour, aren't you supposed to have blood and honour, bring on your friends, your uncles, your brothers, bring them out, let me see them, so I can beat them," he breathed and calmed himself, his heart beating slowing, "such hatred and you hardly know me," he continued, almost from the corner of his mouth as the blood swelled around Johnny's unconscious body, and dripped down the cracks of the pavement slabs. "But you know me now," Tayo added nonchalantly and a little too calmly for a man who had put another into intensive care with such ease.

Michael was still swinging at Toni's broken body slumped against the wall, (which was the only thing holding it up, his legs had long since given up the strength to support him). There Toni stood, propped up against the wall like a boxer against the ropes, though the towel should have been thrown in long ago, with Michael swinging for dear life, his opponents head rocking backwards and forwards, like a doll in a rocking chair.

Michael was so absorbed in getting his 'licks' in that he did not even notice a quickly sobering Dave who had slipped around the corner to his car and pulled out a brand new car jack. He had brought it especially for such a job. It had cost him ten new pounds, a discount and a bargain, made of the finest quality British stainless steel. Brought at the knock down price because Mad Mike, famous for Mad Mike's famous car lot had a soft spot for him. Dave remembered the day Mike gave him the jack.

"We've grown up in the same manner, on the same streets, we're like brothers were, we're family,... anything you want mate, a new motor, someone y'want sorting out, a tart I can supply ya," Mike groaned, as he handed him the jack. "This is the least I can do for you mate, honest," he growled, fidgeting with the signet ring on his large, gnarled, bulbous fingers, his huge double chin wabbled in his white shirt collar, and Versace designer Tie.

So Dave came prowling around the corner like a hyena after a fresh kill. His jeans were covered in filth from the sick which he had just vomited from his stomach, he was still woozy and hazy with a hang over. But he was sobering up enough to decide, 'I'm goin to put this car jack into the head of this crazy coon, that's trying to kill my mate.' He wiped the grime from his hand on his blue jean shirt which by the ragged look of its worn out sleeves and faded material had not been cleaned in days. Scampering behind the swinging youth, he lifted the car jack with both hands. He looked at Michael's youthful body darting in and out, his locks flying to and fro like a Rasta in the midst of a dream dance.

Dave looked at the youthful, almost feminine features and resolved to, 'to smash this pretty boy's face for ever.'

He clenched the silver car jack in his hands and swung it towards the energetic brother. There was a pause.

Michael stopped and looked around, as he suddenly realised that there had been somebody behind him. He dropped his guard and turned his handsome if indolent face in the direction of where Dave had been. Only to see a silver saddle flying through the air. Michael peered through his locks, lose from the knot on his head, hanging energetically and strewn around his face. Gripping them in his hands and brushing them back from his head. Staring through the mist and dusk of the evening, even as it turned into night. The silver saddle sailing through the air as it struck Dave not once, twice, but three times.

Dave's body lay poleaxed, pale, his jeans shirt adorned with another colour in addition to the vomit which he had given it. The new colour, the pool of blood which lay around him. There standing

holding the silver saddle as it shined in the night sky like an avenging spirit was a youth. His face emotionless and calm, a wisp of
brown afro hair on his chin and brown dreadlocks down to his waist.
Locks which seemed to dwarf everything else about him. An energetic, youthful, expression and an austere almost serene demeanour.
Blue jeans and CAT boots, brown bomber jacket and a Walkman
around his ears.

"Have you heard this tune," he said to Michael who was just looking
at him. "It's boom you know, police and thieves in the street," he
said.

"I know, by Junior Mervin," Tayo replied, leaping over the body of
Johnny.

"Well you're not entirely Babylonians," the brother said, "so I didn't
lick off his head," gesticulating with his saddle at the body of Dave,
"for no reason. Alright then .. that's cool."

"You know I was watching the whole 'ting', from over there, you
know you're goin' to have to be careful, boxin' bad men on the street
like wha', this place is somethink other than what it is. Me heard
about brae's like you, watcha, goin' around skanking, licking up people," the brother said, wiping the blood stain off his saddle, which
seemed to gleam in response immediately.

"Like your the non violent one," Tayo said walking over to him,
"what's this, instead of flying fist of Buddha, we now having flying
saddle of.. ..what's your name."

"Me deal with that later," the brother said smiling, "it's time to step,
before Babylon reaches, .. but call me Flex," he said, inserting the
saddle in the rucksack, which he had on his back.

"Come now," he said, "this is me yard, but see them bluefoot coming, come now."

The Smalls

They had all been oblivious to the odd flash of car lights passing the scene. It had only taken one call to the police from Mr. Smalls and his wife who were driving back to Brixton from visiting their family after Church at the Apostolic Celestial Church of God in Kennington. They had a beautiful day out celebrating the Wednesday evening in a good Christian way. Roast Pork and sizzling apple sauce, was the main course, followed by raspberry whip ice cream, with treacle. Mr. Smalls relaxed with a pipe of his best cigar as he stood under a beautiful picture of Jesus, blonde hairdo and blue eyed, smiling, pretending not to be Michealangelo's cousin (and failing).

Mr. Smalls looked at his prosperous well to do, middle of the road, middle class family, and smiled a self congratulating, arrogant smile. The sought of smile that reeked of the pomposity that led people to disown their family, for not conforming or generating enough wealth.

Mr. Smalls liked the idea his family was prosperous. After all his daughter was doing well at college, studying accountancy and would no doubt qualify very soon. He was pleased as he looked at her dyed blonde hair and lipstick smeared all over her face. He was proud as he saw her stooping in a dress that looked like it had not been properly finished and revealed too much of her cleavage. He was proud as she kissed her intended husband Richard on the cheek. Proud that her daughter had married a financially secure young man, with all the breeding character and intelligence that Mr. Smalls had come to respect from British society. 'And my,' Mr. Smalls thought, looking at him, 'how handsome he is, blonde haired, blue eyed and skin as white as ... as... dare I say it, our saviour.' He smiled to himself a silly, ridiculous smile.

So it had been a perfect day for the Smalls, they did not expect to have it ruined on their way home. Mr. Smalls, driving in his new Ford Mondeo which Richard had so graciously bought for him, 'my, what a kind and thoughtful son in law he will make,' Smalls thought, as they drove slowly through the streets of south London. Richard kissing his darling fiancee and trying to fondle her as he whispered his next sexual fantasy of, 'tying her up and beating her like a slave.'

They passed by the Poly. Its' red brick work seemed so stark and bland, even with the blandness of Southwark's high rise tower blocks encircling it like a concrete jungle.

Mr. Smalls looked out of the window at the inner city decay, filth and rubbish on the streets, a drunk tramp here and there, 'far to many foreign immigrants,' he thought. As he saw an African lady weighed down with bags and luggage struggling to carry her goods to the nearby train station. Over laid with bags, which seemed heavier than her, with one on her head and another two in each hand - Smalls was undisturbed by the fact that for all of his Black Middle class notions of superiority he could not carry one of them.

He muttered, under his breath, "bloody savages, they come here, can't speak a word of English, giving us all a bad name."

"What are you muttering about dear," Mrs. Smalls nagged, "ya always moaning......oh.(gasping)....., what on earth, look at those louts, look they're beating that poor man." Mr. Smalls turned his head in all directions to see what manner of atrocities were being committed in to quote his phrase,'the lowest part of town.'

Meanwhile all Richard wanted to do was lower, Miss Smalls, dress and give her a good beating. She smiled coyly at him, gripping his wrasping cold clammy hands, kissed his thin jagged lips, still stinking of the roast pork and bottles of whisky he had consumed and grinned.

"Look at those savages," Smalls shrieked, like a child, as he caught sight of the spectacle, "look at those filthy savages, beating that poor man half to death."

Richard looked up, pulled himself from his fiancee's loving embrace, half in disinterest, half just to shut Smalls up, who was bleating like a sheep. "All right all right, Mr. Smalls, what are you goin' on about, I don't see anything ....," he said. He stopped in mid sentence and his mouth dropped open like a frog going to catch a fly as he saw Flex come up behind Dave with his silver saddle. It was as if the whole event was happening in slow motion. Flex's brown locks bouncing in the evening air, the nonchalant bold steps, the brown bomber jacket done up to the neck, the Cat boots carelessly tied to his ankles. Richard watched the puffs of carbon dioxide as Flex moved ever closer, his hot breath almost touching his unaware opponent.

Instinctively, Richard tried to call out to warn him, "look out, look out," fiddling with the door handle like a child, until he realised it had a kiddy lock on it. He shrieked instinctively, all he could see was a black man going to beat a white man, it did not matter that this same 'victim' had beaten and killed people just for the fun of it. It seemed irrelevant, that only last week they had beaten a man half to death, for just beeping his horn at him. It also appeared immaterial that right now he had a car jack in his hand and intended to add to the quota of coloureds he had killed. But most of all the least important thing to him right now was the black woman who was in his arms, whom he spent every night in bed with. But what was important was he was white first, even if he was going to marry Miss Smalls, he would always be white and proud of it.

But to no avail, Mr. Smalls could not stop his car, get out and arrest them on the spot as he wished, a four ton juggernaut was bearing down on him from behind. He slowed the vehicle down to a crawl, slow enough for them to get a clear vision of Flex as he dealt the final blow to Dave's ego, and his head, with his silver saddle. They saw Dave fall, poleaxed, blood flowing from the open wound.

Mr. Smalls moved his foot gingerly to the clutch, lifting the other on to the brake. The car shuddered almost to a halt. All the while the juggernaut rumbled towards them.

"You're not stopping here," Mrs. Smalls shrieked, watching her husband taking his foot off the accelerator, "did you here me Reginald (his first name). Drive on," she screamed shaking with emotion as she heard the beeping horn of the lorry behind them.

"Wha, but..... all right, all right dear," Smalls mumbled like a small child, even though he was the pastor and rector of the Celestial Church she wore the pants in the house. "We'll call the police at the next exit," he asserted looking around for a convenient spot to stop.

"I don't care," Mrs. Smalls informed, "what you do at the next entrance, (her veiled Jamaican accent becoming more pronounced), but get us h'out of this mocka road, do you here me Reginald Smalls."

The daughter Miss Angela Smalls had been quiet the whole journey, not noticing the change of inflection in Richard's voice as he shrieked at Flex, or Father's uncle Tom routine. What she did see were three rather handsome, arrogant black men, 'kick some arse and then walk away as if it was nothing.' She smiled to herself a small reserved smile. The only smile she had ever given to a black man in her whole, entire life. The only time she ever secretly desired, to have such a man by her side. 'Perhaps,' she thought untangling Richard's hand from hers, 'it's for all the wrong reasons, but they look so primitive, handsome, dangerous.'

Strange that she a black woman raised by black people, should have such negative thoughts for three young men defending themselves from violence at the hands of three of the nastiest, bigoted and definitely ugliest men in south London. No Angela, was thinking, 'how can I get one of them, instead of him (looking at Richard and giving him a nasty stare).'

But Tayo, Michael and Flex right now did not care for Angela's obsession or fantasies, nor for the fact that her father had made a phone call to the police the first opportunity he had got. The three brothers were trying to get out as quickly as they could, with Flex leading the way, his brown locks bouncing in the evening air. Down every back street and side alley, round every darkened street corner, until the sound of the police sirens became a blur.

"Where the hell are we?" Michael asked, as they turned a third street, which seemed further and further into the heart of the concrete jungle. The buildings rising up everywhere like tombstones.

"Don't you know your manor," Flex said, (his accent becoming cockney), "we're on Old Kent Road."

"Yeah," Michael asked, puzzled.

"Look," Flex replied, walking down what looked like a dead end. They followed, more curious than trusting - only to be met with the roar of an ambulance, the flashing blue lights of police cars as they stormed in the opposite direction.

"Scene," Michael, responded, "alright, nah, man you've done well. Saved my life and rescued me all in the same day. Nah man that's all right. You're all right," taking his hand and fisting him.

"No problem," Flex said, "now give me you're money."

"You what," Michael replied, puzzled. There was a pregnant pause.

Tayo looked Flex in his eyes and laughed, a bold loud laugh.

"No I'm serious man," Flex said, with a smirk on his face, "Niggers have got to get paid for service like this."

"Not another one," Tayo muttered, under his breath.

"You're a man after my own heart," Michael said smiling, "I was only saying the same to righteous brother over there," pointing at Tayo.

"Yeah well it's true, righteous (looking at Tayo) that's your name, well it's true," Flex said, bouncing up the street.

"And you know there's no freeness," Michael interjected.

Tayo just shock his head as he trailed behind them, with their conversation deteriorating into more, "got to get paid man and did you see me just box him up, did you see his head rock back," Tayo wondering, as he dragged his feet behind them, 'how many beatings does it take for us to realise that we are not niggers or players, but Africans, with an indivisible future, identity, purpose and direction.'

He screwed up his face, only forcing a smile when he realised that Michael's Kangol hat which he had brought to pose with was back there. 'It's probably sitting in a puddle of that cracker's urine, with a decoration of that other one's spit on it,' the thought put a permanent grin on the young brother's face. 'There'll be no more posing with that hat,' Tayo thought, 'I swear I'll never, ever, ever let him forget that as long as he lives, Kangol hat just to pose in. That's pure madness. You see where vanity leads you close to the edge of oblivion,' he thought, as he walked slowly behind the bouncing brothers, looking at the streets of south London going on in there own confused but vibrant way.

Disaster

'The week had come and gone so quickly,' Tayo thought, as he stood at the front of the hall looking at the few expectant faces.' Had he really been at this college for three weeks, it just seemed like yesterday when he stepped through the door hoping to see Tony, or Carl, Del, Fred, David or even Clinton. Now all he saw were film stars, and wannabies.'

Tayo looked at what should have been the triumphant third meeting of the society. 'But instead what,' Tayo thought, twisting his locks and grinding his teeth; 'this place is empty, man this is disgraceful, I mean disgraceful.'

"Where is everybody," Susan said, stepping up to the platform and standing next to him. "Well we've got to tell them something, it's 2.45 we're supposed to start at two. Some of them have been waiting for over forty five minutes."

"I know," Tayo said, "but we can't start with ten people, half of them are the executive." He looked at their expectant faces, Kwame who had come early and now sat adjusting his glasses and rubbing the lens with his handkerchief, which no doubt he had kept handy just for the task. "No Melanie, she's probably getting chatted up in the corridor, no Michael, no Ade, nobody,' Tayo thought, looking at them, 'our people are really in a bad state, it's not like we've asked them to die for us, just come to a meeting that's all.'

"Things are really bad," Susan said, "and I've got to take Simone to the doctor's she was sick all last night, coughing up some yellow thing."

"Oh that's bad," Tayo said, seeming to ignore the expectant faces which were still looking at him. "How come - she usually looks so healthy," he added, looking at her sitting patiently on the back row.

"I don't know, it's probably that child minder, I just don't trust her."

"How you mean," Tayo asked, "she is a black woman and all."

"Yeah well sort of," Susan answered.

"There is no sort of, either she is, or she isn't."

"What I mean," Susan said, "she's as black as us on the outside, but inside, she's like a bounty bar, coconut white and flaky."

"I know what you mean," Tayo said, he had by now totally forgotten about the audience which was drifting away in ones and two's.

"It's like those brothers with big black cars, but when you step inside it's all pink with fluffy dice, and a white woman on the passenger seat," Tayo said, laughing. "You don't know any brother's like that do you," he asked.

"Na," Susan replied lying (and thinking about Busta) all at the same time, "Na I really don't know anyone like that."

"I thought not," Tayo added, "you're far to conscious for that."

"Yeah far too," Susan said, smiling and looking away.

"By the way whose Simone's father," Tayo replied, half reading a hidden thought in her mind.

Susan hesitated, "that's another story," she said finally, adjusting her coat and trying not to look ruffled in case he read her thoughts, "anyway as I was saying before you interrupted me. My child minder I just don't trust her."

"Well what's wrong with her," Tayo said, "has she got two heads or something."

"Na let me say it, I think she's a Christian," Susan replied.

"So was Nat Turner," Tayo answered.

"What I mean to say, if you let me get my words in edge ways," she said. Tayo smiled. "I mean I think her father 's a priest or something, head of a celestial church, or something."

"I know that lot. Praise the lord and pass the money," Tayo replied.

"There is something else, too I don't trust her, I've never seen her man or anything but I know, I just know, he's white."

"How can you be sure," Tayo asked inquisitively.

"I just know," Susan said, "there's just something about her."

"What's her name?" Tayo asked, disinterestedly.

"Why you afraid, she may be one of you past flames," Susan said, smiling and undoing her top button a little bit too suggestively.

"Are you callin' me a cracker, now?" Tayo said, looking hard at her.

"No I didn't mean it like that," she said, "well any way her name is Angela, Angela Smalls."

"That's odd it seems like I should know that name," Tayo said.

"Worse thing of all she was goin' on with some real foolishness, yesterday, about how she saw three brothers beat up a white man."

"What's foolish about that," Tayo replied, remembering their encounter.

"It was just the way that she described it, like she got a sexual thrill out of it, she kept going on, 'they were so slim and fit really gorgeous, primitive like beasts (imitating her voice)."

"Well," Tayo said, contemplating, "that sister does sound sad, more than sick, I feel sorry for her."

"You stay there," Susan said, "you feel sorry for her, you're too soft on sisters..."

"Are you two going to sought this meeting out," Kwame squealed standing up, he was sitting in the front row watching their conversation and slowly losing his temper. He pointed to his gold watch with an effeminate finger. Tayo cast a glance at the clock on the wall it was three pm. They had been talking for fifteen minutes and now were quickly losing their small gathering.

Tayo cast a worried glance over to Kwame and at the declining audience, he stepped up to the front of the small stage. "I'm sorry about all of this, seriously, I know after the first meeting you expect sparks to fly, but as you see they aren't," he said, laconically. The flap of his black leather pouch swung to and fro as he moved backwards and forwards with the emotion of his words. "Really it's bad, I personally spoke to at least thirty people to remind them, you just know they'll be in the concourse, smoking weed, pretending to be rebels. When they should be in here. What - I'm tired of it..... It's like the true spirit of our race is dead. We are black on the outside but the inside is hollow and empty, I have never seen so many foolish and spineless looking brothers as I have seen this year, it's like this country is breeding them. Where the hell is the spirit that gave birth to Marcus Garvey, or Nat Turner. Where the hell is it, down in the canteen, cracking forties and pretending to be Mc Hammer or Ice Cube. Ice Cube what a stupid name, have you ever checked that. They could be in here and learn something about themselves, instead of fronting. Well this is the last time," Tayo said, to a stunned audience, including Susan who was just watching him as he swelled up with emotion.

Tayo looked at the faces, he had not intended to make a speech but there he had. He was thinking on his feet. He walked up to Susan and whispered in her ear. They stood there for a long time whispering and Kwame looked at his watch nervously, genuinely afraid that the few who remained would up and run.

Susan smiled, 'he's got their attention,' she thought, looking at their expectant faces, 'it was not the intellect, or their passions but something else. It is easy enough to stir men's passions, lust or hatred, envy or pride, they are the basest parts of man. One can even stir the minds of men, with fine words and speeches, but to awaken men's souls is another thing altogether. Even more so when those people are African and it's not religion, but common sense that you are bringing. Because African people are stubborn to trust a fellow brother or sister, either through self hatred born from thousands of years of oppression or individual pain brought through trusting and being hurt. It's harder to get an African to trust another African.....well. So Tayo stirs their sprit, he did it before and he was doing it again, not with gimmicks and show, games and nonsense but the truth, if he does nothing else he's worthy of the up most respect, cause I know most of them are listening against their will. Yet because of the diseased state of our minds we take traitors to be our leaders and we treat our friends like enemies,' and she rubbed her eyebrow.

"How should this be," Tayo said, fidgeting with his pouch, "when other people are forgetting their differences and coming together, how could we allow this - go and live our soft comfortable lives, while our race slowly fades into history. So that five hundred years from now a white child asks her mother, "did you ever see an African, I heard they used to really exist." To here the mothers reply, "No they died out long ago, intermixing, black on black violence, corruption, greed, disease, poverty, starvation, it was a shame, I heard they used to be good to have sex with." The audience were watching his every move now.

'There has to be resistance,' Susan thought, as she watched him, 'a culture of resistance, even if 99% of the race sold their soul, their would be 1% who would keep hope alive,' kissing her teeth and smiling at Tayo, caught in the rapture of his revolutionary fervour.

Tayo smiled, stopped in mid sentence, as if he could feel her thought patterns, 'she right now was worth twenty weight lifting brothers in puffer jackets, there was clarity, strength of mind and purpose. A strength of character so lacking in the rest. Not reactionary, emotional excitement, but resolve, determination,' he twisted his locks and then he remembered they were still looking, waiting for him. Kwame with his mouth open. Jennifer at the back sucking a lollipop, her eyes goggle eyed and gaping like a frog, as she sat transfixed. Like she was watching her teen idle perform on stage. 'God he's handsome,' she thought, sucking a little too hard on the sweet in her mouth, so that it broke in her mouth, she giggled like a school girl. Everyone turned to look at her.

If she could have gone a redder shade of brown, she would have, even as the sticky mixture slithered down her throat.

"Sister," Tayo said, looking straight at her, "I'm glad you contributed." She could feel the embarrassment rising inside her like an unbearable heat from the centre of her being, burning and trying to explode.

"Tell us your name, then," Tayo asked smiling at the inquisitive crowd, some of whom strained their necks over the empty seats to see who giggled so loudly.

"Jennifer," she said shyly, twisting her brown kiss curls like a toddler (though she was twenty two).

"Why have you come to this meeting? You know, why did you bother?"

Jennifer gulped and looked nervously around, 'the truth,' she thought guilty, 'is I came - cause this brother's got the best bod' and face in the whole college.' But she said, "I came to find out about my culture, history and that (lying)" and she looked deep into Tayo's eyes and winked.

Tayo winked back, when he should have been content to merely smile and then he realised, as she slowly began to undress him with her eyes, 'she came for me.' He pushed the thought out of his mind.

"So we all came for different reasons," Tayo said, becoming intoxicated once again by the spirit, "but what is important is that we are all here now. Now there are more of us out there, how many black students are there at this college, a thousand. Now even last week when it was ram, there wasn't but one tenth of that here. Hell if we all came, we wouldn't fit in here. Do you know what that means," he twisted his locks in mid sentence, "that means you've got power."

Kwame looked around nervously, fearing that the conversation was getting a little to political. Fidgeting like a small child, until he realised that the little crowd was mesmerised. He allowed a smile to inch on to his face, which started at the corners and then spread, until there was nothing left of the rest of his features, just his smile.

"We have to take the fight to them," Tayo added, "I mean we have to move this society to the centre ground in the politics of this college. Not a single African student can come here and ignore us, not one can front and pretend to be so black, skank in the concourse smoking a spliff and talk about being tough, when right now he should be in here, exercising his mind. Every space of wall in this college on every site of south London where this Poly has a branch is going to have a poster for this society, every morning leaflets will be handed out to every black student informing them of the debates that will take place every week," Tayo was thinking on his feet.

Susan was watching him and frowning, 'what is he going to offer next, heaven and earth. Marcus Garvey reincarnated in person live and direct.'

"There will be a new speaker here every week," Tayo said, Susan gave him a worried look, "even if I have to pull some of you from the audience to do it," her face softened a little from the frown which was forming. "But what we need is help from you, we need you to volunteer your services to help leaflet, to put up the posters. We need you to talk to your friends, to organise, agitate, overcome." There was a pause again, as if their should have been a round of applause or something (but there wasn't).

"All right then," Tayo said, "give your names to Kwame and Susan and the times when you can help out and if you don't mind, your telephone numbers and the courses you attend so we can contact you." They sat there still, stunned, unmoving, like they were waiting to be told to come to the front.

"Come on," Susan inserted, taking from his que, "I know he talks to much, but we want all of your details, especially you Jennifer and your friend," who was hastily packing her books in an attempt to make a swift retreat.

A young slim girl as dark as ebony, elegant, with an African demeanour, powerful yet feminine. Like a princess from some ancient Ausaran tale, skipped down the stairs. Her petite feet not even touching the ground. Her hair natural and platted into a pony tail bouncing behind her. Tayo saw her skipping down the stairs and wondered, ' why have I never seen you before, where did you come from. There is none of that, in your face, yeah I'm sexy look at me, no her beauty is deep, it's like from her spirit,' he thought, as he watched her.

"My name is Appia, I'm doing Art and design here," she said, to Susan who had quickly gathered a notebook and pen. Her voice was like running water, "so I might be helpful with these publicity posters and that."

Susan looked at her, it should have been a look of pure sisterhood, but there was a slight tinge of envy, a touch of jealousy. 'This girl's so beautiful,' Susan thought to herself, looking at her unblemished features, the skin shining like an Onyx. 'Unspoiled, undamaged, unmolested, how she had been before Busta and nine months of pregnancy, and four years...as much as that, of deceit and lies. But truthfully,' she thought sadly, 'I have never been serene, I 've become what I am, but I've never been serene.'

Appia smiled a gentle smile, like an African princess, Susan looked seeing the honesty in the face, the round untarnished African features and dropped her guard. 'She's a good sister after all,' she thought as she scribbled her details hastily in the note book, ' I wonder if they will even be able to read this.'

"Good to have you on board sister, I was getting a bit sick of all these men. About time we had some equilibrium, yes," she continued, looking at the note pad (a little too motherly), "that's fine."

Kwame was watching Appia as she glided effortlessly down the stairs, not seeing Jennifer as she trudged and banged nosily in front of him, sticking her breasts and then her bottom almost in his face, all he was thinking was 'Appia's really great.'

Jennifer was undaunted as she posed her way to the front row, smiling like an underdressed model on a catwalk and brushing her brown hair away from her face. There was a glint of obvious sexual allure. The low cut dress with yellow daffodils embroidered on it, in all the right places and body hugging jeans which left none of her well proportioned body to chance. She shoved her way unceremoniously to the front and stood goggle eyed in front of Tayo, sticking out her breasts and smiling ear to ear.

"Where do you want me to put the address and telephone number Tayo," she said, giggling to her friend. Tayo turned and stared through her, more than at her, reading her mind, "it's okay sister, give it to Susan over there," pointing at her. Jennifer looked at him like a mortal enemy, 'who does he think he is, thinks he's to good for me,' brushing her brown hair back and staring through light brown eyes at his youthful angular frame. 'You know I've had richer man than he begging to sample my stuff, I bet he doesn't even have a car,' she thought, 'But he's still cute,' watching him move. 'He's really cute, little slim, nice body and a nice smile, no... a sexy smile, handsome, but a bit too arrogant, but he's nice.'

She signed her name and address on the paper with two kisses on either side. 'Oh well,' she thought,' I may not get one like him immediately, but sooner or later he's going to weaken, there's no way that a person can resist my good stuff. ' She batted her eyelids in the direction of Tayo who remained oblivious and aloof. "I'd like to be in advertising," she blurted looking down her nose at Susan.

"Naturally," Susan replied looking at her chest. Jennifer gave her a dirty look and then remembered that she was late for her hair cut and rinse. She clumped clumsily up the stairs, her friend confused and bemused following her. But Jennifer was thinking as she ambled, 'this brother, won't play hard to get for long.'

Tayo looked at the small line of sisters and brothers signing their names, 'I don't really have any serious belief that any of them are going to do much,' he thought, looking at them shuffling in the cue, 'except for Appia, their's something righteous about her and of course, there's Jennifer, she's just about vain enough to do anything, she wants everybody to look at her. Oh well that can be used. I just hope that she doesn't have any ideas about me and her, I'm not Star Trek, boldly going where every man has gone before,' and smiled to himself twisting his locks.

The Tube

Michael was taking a long draw on his cigarette as he walked down the subway, almost bumping into Tayo coming the opposite direction.

"What happened to you," Tayo said, "I was expecting you to be there."

"Where," Michael replied, inhaling on the cigarette and flicking the ash out on the street all the while inspecting his blue jeans and marvelling at how smart his Timberland boots looked.

"Where," Tayo replied, "at the meeting of course, where else," becoming irritated very quickly by Michael's smoking habit.

"I'm not...." Michael replied.

"In it," Tayo interjected triumphantly.

"Very good you're starting to learn still. Yeah I'd knew you understand... well make a player out of you in the end.... I swear," Michael asserted.

"No," Tayo said, "we'll make an **African** out of you!"

"Anyway," Michael said, turning around and swivelling his hips like a karate expert about to get into a bout, "you know that brother who saved our skins last week;" changing the subject and finishing the stub of his cigarette which he flicked out of the corner of his mouth falling only as far as his boot, as he kicked it.

"You mean your skin," Tayo said, fiddling with his pouch and adjusting the bag on his back and thinking, 'I swear those names and addresses have made this bag twice as heavy.'

"Yeah whatever," Michael said laconically, "you know he studies at this place. "

"Which place," Tayo interrupted, "the subway, (and he laughed) we seem to spend too much time in subways, I think it must be some of your nasty habits rubbing off on me."

"Don't start that again," Michael uttered, smiling, "I know you've got rubbing on the mind, all those sisters Melanie, Susan, whose that new one - Appia and Jenny."

"How do you know Jennifer and Appia," Tayo questioned, puzzled.

"I get to know them all," Michael replied. (In fact he had bumped into them coming the other way after the meeting had finished, trying to chat them up, all the while smoking a cigarette like a cowboy and posing in his timberland boots. Nobody had taken him seriously except for Jennifer who took a liking to anything that had testicles and gave Michael his dues. He was not the kind of man who was used to being kicked out of bed, well not twice).

"You know Appia's a good sister," Michael said, "calm, respectful."

"Too good for you mate," Tayo replied, "I think Jennifer is more your style," walking past him, "come on I've got to get home, I've hung around Elephant and Castle too long, remember what happened last time, by the way... you were saying about Flex."

"Yeah.... yeah I'd forgotten," Michael said, bouncing up to him and forgetting the veiled insult, his suede timberlands seeming to glide over the ground, "yeah that brother."

"You men your spar," Tayo interrupted.

"He's your brother too," Michael replied, "besides he thinks very highly of you, he goes that brother seemed so righteous and the way he dealt with that, what's the word he used yeah, bluefoot, like a professional, or something."

"Yeah.. yeah," Tayo said, unconvinced as he cleared the first flight of steps.

"I didn't tell him how stush you were. Any way he comes to our place...," Michael continued, "he did an Access course or something, you know he used to be a rude boy skanking and cutting up people like a rudie."

"Lucky for us he still does," Tayo said.

"True," Michael said, thoughtfully remembering the incident only a week ago. "Yeah by the way you haven't seen my hat lying around here," he said, as they cleared the stairs, and stood at the entrance to the tube station.

"No...why," Tayo replied, trying not to giggle.

"Anyway," Michael continued, ignoring the sneer on the brother's face and walking into the tube station. "Yeah he was telling me about all the things he's done and that ya' know he's been prison."

"Really," Tayo said, becoming genuinely interested in the conversation.

"Yeah, I'm telling you he's a good brother," Michael said, as he typed the digits into the brand new ticket machine on the wall.

"I hate using them," Tayo said.

"But there's no choice still," Michael replied, "there's nobody behind the screen," pointing to the old worn out ticket booth with a faded white screen pulled down.

"Yeah exactly," Tayo replied.

"Oh yeah of course," Michael said, putting his money back in his over sized baggy denim pockets, "I must be slipping or something..."

"Yeah, go on.." Tayo reminded him, as they walked through the empty ticket booth decorated unnecessarily by an unsightly pile of used tickets to a myriad of destinations: Marble Arch, Kensington, Ladbroke Grove, Victoria, Kensal Rise, Kilburn, Golders Green, Harrow, all left in a pile. Some torn in half, others looking like they had been chewed by a cat.

Michael looked at the pile and made his selection.

"I'll have this one," Michael said, picking out a £2.50 return to Harlesden and "I'll have this one," Tayo added, finding a £1.20 single to Brixton. 'That will do for my travels for later, I don't think I'm going to need a return,' he thought and smiled.

"Any way, that brother's going to be around he's just been doing some 'think' to make money for his school fees," Michael said, pressing the button for the lift.

"What kind of thing ?" Tayo questioned.

"By what ever means necessary," Michael said.

"Don't mis quote," Tayo replied, "it is by any means necessary and Malcolm was not talking about you selling drugs to get through college."

"Now I never said Flex was selling drugs," Michael replied, "The Government would love to find out about that still, black student sell drugs in ghetto institution, wah, are you dat."

"Yeah...I know one paper would love that, black students - in black college sell drugs on black market scandal." Tayo joked, "they would run it alongside the main story of Busty, Belinda Babcock the one they named as the biggest boobs in Britain, baring her breasts on pages three, five, seven, eleven and twelve," they both laughed.

"To think I see so many black people buying that paper," Michael said, "and claiming they're just looking at the sport section, sport section,...you know they keep page three and throw the rest away and do some serious thwaping (gesticulating with his hands)."

"You know that," Tayo agreed, "by the way, when is this lift coming."

"On a serious point and to change the subject just a little, I remember that paper during the riots - the 1985 riots with the front page, 'catch this Black Bomber and a picture of Winston Silcott.' I remember going to school and the white kids sticking the picture in my face and saying, is that you?" Tayo said, becoming a little irritated by the delay in the lift.

"Yeah, scene, scene, I remember that, you see still how you forget things, just like that," Michael retorted, "you know that's only yesterday and we've forgotten it."

"So Flex, ...then, what else did he tell you," Tayo asked, looking around at the flaky paint work and worn out signs stained brown with filth.

"Well that's about all," Michael said, looking down at his Timberland boots and then suddenly realising that he had not inspected them for at least fifteen minutes. "His address is just around the corner, Kennington or somewhere round there. He said we could we can go and visit him any time we want," he continued.

"You've got the address," Tayo asked.

"Yeah I wrote it on a card in my pocket, ... some.. where ... in here...." he said, rummaging around unsuccessfully in his over sized trousers.

"No wonder you lost them, in those things," Tayo observed seeing him ferreting around. "You would do better to think practical, instead of fashion, remember where you Kangol hat got you and now you've lost the brother's address in these," he said, pointing.

"Yeah, yeah, Marcus Garvey Junior," Michael mumbled, still fidgeting in his trousers like a hamster, "besides I can remember where it is, I went and checked for him after you did you disappearing act that night."

"You men you lot," Tayo corrected, "I looked up and you were gone, you were probably talking about spliff and cigarettes, gal, honeyz, how to be a player and jus' about everthin' else in't."

"How did you know?" Michael said, laughing. "You know you brothers," Tayo replied, "should seriously find something else to do, with the race dying all around you, all you can do is crack forties and kotch."

"Yeah, yeah," Michael answered.

"Seriously though there are better things to do." Tayo added, "Black men, we as black men have got a lot to do. Look, other men have gone to the moon, and we are still comparing the size of our cocks, mine's bigger than yours. We've got to come better."

There was a shudder and a screech and a sound like a car doing a tail spin on a tarmac road.

"What.....?" Michael said, looking around as if a would be attacker was attempting to confront him.

"I think it's the lift.." Tayo said, pointing to the elevator which now stood open in front of them.

"I'd forgotten all about it, you know," Michael said, stepping into it and kicking a nearby coke can which got in his path. The empty tin struck the far end of the lift door and sent the remainder of it's sticky black contents dripping down on to the floor.

"Yeah as you're sayin'," Tayo said, standing in the lift and pressing the over worn button which glowed artificially luminous yellow - indented in the centre from constant use. The walls adorned with vomit and here and there marked with the graffiti of a bygone fun loving criminal.

"This place smells funky," Michael muttered, as the lift doors swung shut and the lift shuddered into action.

"Your damn right!" Tayo replied, kissing his teeth, "this place smells of the same crackers that we battered out there last week, you know the skinhead-jackboot-I hate niggers-I do, variety, you know the ones who think that they have the right to do as they please."

"True," Michael said.

"But the truth is if it only was as simple as that, you and I know that," Tayo replied, "that lot don't hold the real power. The real white supremacists who hold the power on this earth don't walk around Elephant and castle looking for a fight. Know they drive thirty five thousand pound cars and wear thousand pound suits. When they decide to take some people out, it's not a couple of rebellious black students outside a Poly it's a whole village, or a whole town, or a whole nation," he said, twisting his locks. "They talk of justice and equality, freedom and international agreements all the while they develop and create new diseases which obliterate whole civilisations and if you get too many ideas above your station, they just send the B52's to satchel bomb you, and then phew.. (gesticulating with his hands) your gone."

"That's true," Michael replied, as he watched the lift slowly (and I do mean slowly) descending, "but the worst thing is that we, I mean African people, have not even got ourselves to the level where we can start to be viewed as a credible threat. We are still squabbling and bickering amongst ourselves like children, brothers literally looking to kill the next 'brae' just cause he's got somethink' he ain't got, what's that about. So much jealousy. So much envy. So afraid to do somethink for the next bro, in case he rises quicker than you."

"Yeah," Tayo said as the lift ground to a halt, shaking a little from the reverberation like a mini earth quake. "We are literally a joke," Tayo added, as the lift doors swung open and Tayo bounced out, his pouch slapping against his chest.

"So which tube do we need to take to get to Kennington," Tayo asked.

"You want to reach there now," Michael replied smiling, "I thought you didn't like him, too much of a player or somethink."

"Yeah well," Tayo added, "you thought wrong."

"All right then," Michael said, "let's trod."

They bounced down the subway, past the graffiti and urine which decorated the crumbling yellow paint work. The pale red bricks stood out naked, beneath the flaking decor, cold, bland. Over worked handrails, torn out of their joints in the wall. A trail of cement and broken bricks, strange decorations for London Underground, (we're getting there, no they've got there.)

They walked down the stairs, down the adjoining subway and on to the platform. Past a white youth spewing his guts up on the platform. Next to him his friend with blonde hair and blue eyes, his genitals in his hand, urinating against the side of the platform, his urine splashing a couple who seemed oblivious, as they fondled and kissed each other.

A skinhead with jackboots standing and watching the scene like he was an albino genie removed from the real world.

Mr. Harris Q.C on his way back from court, about to go out on the town looking for a new prostitute to spend tonight with. Drunk and debauched, his shirt tail hanging out of his £500 suit like a tramp. Filth on his jacket, his filth, from the time that he failed unsuccessfully to go to toilet. Blurry eyed in a state of automatism, wandering to and fro over the platform.

A stringy haired Oxford graduate, down the end of the platform his green eyes flashing, defecating (shitting) like a dog at the corner of the station.

There amongst the decadence of inner city decay stood Busta and Beverly as if they were not part of the filth and they were. Forced into slumming it, taking the tube since he had crashed his car. Standing under the sign hoarding.

Tayo and Michael bounced in. Tayo looked around, "Jesus Christ," he spluttered, looking around, "what the hell!"

"Scene," Michael said, scanning the platform.

"Look over there," Tayo said, "there's a geezer having a crap!"

"You what," Michael said, screwing up his face into a brown ball and staring, "Jesus this country is completely out of control."

"You smell that," Tayo blurted out, "these streets are like an open sewer," shaking his head.

"You know what," Michael muttered, "I hate this country, the quicker I get out of here the better."

"It's not as simple as that," skipping past the youth who was pissing, "God I wish it was," Tayo continued, "go on a beach, sand between your toes, sun on your back, locks down to the ground, I tried it in Montego Beach. All that: beautiful, sun drenched Black sister, coconut in one hand, a pineapple in the other. Paradise lost. Or Paradise to be achieved. But it does not exist."

Michael rested his foot against the wall. "We have an obligation," Tayo continued, looking at him, "to try and change our people, don't get me wrong, most of our people our lost. They think this lot," pointing to the motley travellers on the platform, "are the **master race**, you know, Alexander the Great, Queen Victoria, and Cecil Rhodes, but look at them, fornicating, urinating, drinking, falling down. They call us racists for just showing them the mirror of the world," Michael started laughing and did not stop laughing until Busta and Beverly walked right up to them.

Busta gave a side ways glance like a dog that had just seen a cat that it intended to hunt to the death. "That bwoy's dissing me," he muttered to Beverly, staring at Tayo.

Tayo was unaware, still trying to rationalise all the confusion. Michael lit another cigarette and played with his leather jacket pocket like a small child. He looked down at his feet doing a kind of pose and looked up in the sky as if he was wishing for a plane too come and take him away to that same Montego beach, Tayo was talking about, where he could lull around in the sun and smoke weed all day. 'That's heaven,' he thought and smiled. Then he glimpsed from the corner of his eye Busta and Beverly. He reached inside his pocket and gently began to unlock his flick knife between his thumb and fore finger, he had done it many times. 'The trick is to release the blade without anyone looking noticing. Ya nah say there's going to be trouble,' he thought, looking at the ignorant expression on Busta's face.

The lights at the tunnel flickered, and from the depths of the entrance came the sound like a mechanical beast, at first in the distance and then closer it roared its' arrival. Speeding down the tracks faster than a man could run. Until it stood where before there had been just space. Old paper cups scattered and litter flut-

tered, as they were displaced by the beast that now occupied its lair.
Tiny, filthy, little rats scuttled to shelter on the edge of the platform, or behind an old Mc Donalds packet, which lay open, con-
cealing a partially digested beef-burger double-pounder, the teeth
marks of it's last victim still visible. The rat decided to add his own,
as he disappeared into the packet to avoid the now resident train.

Busta stared at Tayo and saw his undiluted dignity. The black skin
shining, the lean, mean arrogant demeanour, then he turned to
Beverly, "that bwoy jus' haf to dead, that boy, scene, to feisty, that
bwoy go on like he bad," and other statements.

Beverly nodding and pretending to be interested, she had seen him
cut up and mutilate black men, 'it really is nothing new to me,' she
thought, playing with her blonde straggly hair. At first it had been
a serious sexual turn on to see him killing and maiming at will .
But when she began to realise that he was scared to death of the
police, in fact any members of authority.

She saw him blubber like a baby when the police arrested him for
the murder of Robert Delroy Simms. The police must have shown
him the picture twenty times, stuck it in his face, the cold death
ridden face, the trickle of blood as it dribbled down his cheek, the
eyes lifeless, blank, absent, the pupil turned deathly white through
strangulation. The grey complexion. The mouth opened like a gash,
the teeth blood stained, grey as tombstones, except for the gold
teeth, the tongue lying life less out of the corner of his mouth.

But it was not Robert's deathly cold face, the victim of Busta's
ingrained self hatred, which made the self styled 'ghetto superstar,'
squirm. It was the suggestion by an over eager detective sergeant
that, "they send back little yardies like you, to your own primitive
country, they've still got the death penalty, sunshine. You could be
looking like Robert within a week," he joked, as he smoked on a
cigarette and blew the contents in Busta's face.

Beverly looked through the open window as the wiry little policemen slowly destroyed this so called bad 'gun man.' When he finished Busta looked, 'what's the phrase,' Beverly thought, 'like a little boy, a small frightened little brown boy. '

'But the police did not want Busta off the street, if they wanted
him off, they could've taken him there and then,' she thought,
'nah he must be their boy.' Beverly watched him, 'so violent to his
own lot, but a pussy boy when it came to us,' she thought, as she
watched him now flexing and sizing himself up to Tayo who was

still oblivious.

The doors of the train slid open, "mind the gap, mind the gap," shrieked over the tannoy, Beverly pushed a cursing Busta on to the open train, "man jus ha'f to dead."

"Oh why don't you stop it?" Beverly mumbled.

"Wha', wha'.... " Busta blubbered like a baby.

"If you're go'n do somethink' do it, stop talking abou' it, do it."

'I wonder,' Tayo was thinking, 'what it's go'n to take to get this college together, we've got all these brother's like Flex, Michael, Ade, Kwame and others, they've got skills and abilities, but they don't want to put it to service for the common good. We can't force them, but could I inspire them. I doubt it. Really I do. Well... perhaps if they can believe in something greater than themselves, if they could really believe that the race can win, then they may come along,' Tayo thought, as he stepped into the train, Michael following him and still staring at Busta. Tayo in the midst of his thought, not noticing he was sitting opposite Busta becoming more irate and annoyed, fidgeting in his chair like a child whose mother wouldn't allow him to go to toilet.

Michael firmly undid the blade of his knife and felt the serrated edge with his thumb, he sat next to Tayo.

"Wha', Wha' Wha' ya' sayin' bwoy ya fel say, ya bad bwoy," Busta shouted.

Tayo looked up puzzled.

"Yeh, you bwoy," Busta screamed, like a maniac, standing up and reaching inside his pocket for his zig zaya, but he had left it at home, (he was fronting never the less).

"Come on bwoy, if you fel say ya bad," Busta screamed. Tayo looked him straight in his eyes and then at the stringy haired, diseased looking girl beside him. The red blotchy skin, red and yellow puss flowing from the open sores on her mouth, the dry flaky, complexion and pale washed out demeanour. Then he stared back at Busta, a hard cold stare.

"I will not fight you," Tayo said, calmly standing, "but I will defend myself."

"Wha', ...Wha...," Busta shouted, beside himself with rage.

"I said," Tayo replied, "I will not fight you, but I will defend myself."

Michael stood up slowly behind him. He saw the twitch in Busta's lower lip, the quiver of excitement which ran through the whole of his muscular frame.

"Wha... Wha...." Busta blurted, a little confused by Tayo's remark and the calmness on his face. But Tayo could feel the anger and adrenaline speeding through his veins. His heart pumping faster than a jack rabbits. The beads of perspiration breaking out on the side of his face. He stared at Busta. He had never been afraid of anyone or anything ever in his life. 'Why should I be afraid now of this fool, fumbling about in his pocket for a gun he does not have. With his stringy haired bimbo and his chops and gold chains, he's about as fake as a Negro can be,' he thought.

He slapped Busta. Even before he knew he had done it. He had done it. A good hard slap. The slap that should knock a man down. Tayo saw Busta's head rocking back, his face contorted in rage, self hatred, but most of all surprise. Beverly opened her mouth like a frog. 'I h've never seen one of his lot do anythink like that to him. I've never seen it,' she stood up stunned, not really with an intention of doing anything. But Michael was not taking any chances, he grabbed her and grappled her sinewy arms, even though she bleated like a sheep.

Busta tried to fling out a kick like a temper tantrum baby. Tayo stepped to the side of him and slapped him again even harder than the first time. Busta's head jerked backwards, a thin line of blood emerging from the corner of his mouth. The hours of weight training, beer drinking, smoking and raving, was not the life style to equip him with the skills to match this striking panther in the prime of his youth.

"Wha.... Wha... me fel to jus......" Busta blubbered, rather pathetically, sweating like a drunkard in a strip club.

"You ain't go do nothing," Tayo said, as he saw Busta stumbling backwards down the carriage, as the train shimmed down the tunnel, "you come on this train with ya white girl, shrieking and shouting like a mad man," he screwed up his face.

Busta was backing to the furthest end of the carriage looking for a weapon. But all there was were old coke cans badly crushed and twisted, a crisp packet and chewing gum stuck to a nearby seat.

Beverly was screaming and trying to bite through Michael's leather jacket even though he held her tightly and firmly as the delinquent brat she was, her hair flying all over the place like a demon from the exorcist, her red spotted face almost bursting with anger.

"I bet," Tayo said, "you're one of those brothers jus' come from yard, drives around in a black BMW with I love Jamaica on the window sill and pink fluffy dice. One of those negative brothers that us righteous ones, spend most of our lives having to apologise for, who get a whole string of black women pregnant, but can't stay with any of them, but can stay with this," he said, pointing at Beverly as she screamed obscenities and shouted like a demon from hell, "even though she probably sleeps with your best friend, who you know has to be white."

 "What do you do. What 'doo' you-do," Tayo continued, walking towards him, "sell crack to little African children. Walk around the streets with your chops and your gold chains like you Dan Ronin, or Cutty ranks. But your not. Your just a nasty little two bit hustler; a drug dealing victim, who victimizes us. Just think your self lucky," Tayo said, looking at the train pulling up to the station, "that this is our stop. Or I'd have to seriously kick your ass."

The train ground to a halt at the station, shuddering a little with the motion, as the electric brought the carriage to a stand still. The door slid open a little stiffly, and Tayo bounced on to the platform. He saw Michael flinging Beverly against the carriage wall and leaping after him.

"Kennington," "Welcome to Kennington station," the tannoy announced, "mind the gap, mind the gap."

Busta stood heavy breathing for a while, a trickle of blood dribbling down his chin, sweating like a child who had just received a beating from his mother and now stood waiting to be sent to bed. Tayo stared at him, like nothing had happened, 'I almost feel sorry for him, kicked to the kerb by a youth,' he thought and smiled.

"Mind the gap, mind the gap," "this train is ready to depart, stand clear of the doors please." Busta heard the announcement and made a sudden rush to redeem his reputation, charging forward like a bull elephant - snorting, swinging his arms widely, only to be met by Tayo kicking him in his stomach and sending him back behind the closing doors.

The train shuddered a little on it's rails, as it rocked with Busta's heavy bones flailing backwards, chops, chains, gold teeth, string vest, leather jacket and all, against the exterior carriage wall. The doors closed, the train adjusted and Tayo watched emotionless, as the train departed from the station.

Tayo walked along the platform peering into the carriage, as Busta attempted to gain his composure inside the moving train. He smiled, as he saw Busta shrieking and banging the window, inaudible behind three inches of train glass.

"I can't hear you," Tayo said, walking along the platform, trying to keep a pace with the train and raising his hand up to his ear mocking him. "Ya really go'n to have to talk louder, because I can't hear a word you're sayin'," he said calmly and smiled a wide grin covering his whole face.

The train picked up speed if a little and disappeared jauntily down the tunnel, rocking from side to side, as it changed on to the tunnel tracks.

"What was that all about," Michael asked, inspecting the bite marks on his jacket.

"I don't know," Tayo said.

"You know that woman was crazy," Michael replied, "she tried to bite me, look at this," showing his jacket to an oblivious Tayo.

"You don't seem to be having much luck with your garms. You shouldn't be such a poser, then you wouldn't keep getting trashed," Tayo said, looking for the way out sign.

"Don't start lecturing, again," Michael said, bouncing behind him, "if it wasn't for me you would have been in serious stuk back there."

"Really," Tayo said smiling, "what, who from Mr. T," he kissed his teeth and walked up an adjacent stair way marked in fluorescent yellow, 'Way out.' "Come on," Tayo continued, as he bounced up the stairs, "I don't think he could hurt a fly, not even a dead one," and half laughed to himself as he adjusted his pouch and rubbed Busta's sweat off his hands. "Boy that brother was disgusting," Tayo said.

"I'd gladly swap mine for yours," Michael said laughing.

"No thanks," Tayo replied, giggling, "you can keep yours."

"But seriously," Michael said, as they cleared the first flight of stairs.

"I don't want to hear it," Tayo interjected reading his mind.

"You don't want to hear it," Michael asserted, "but I'm go'n to say it any way, Niggers have got to die."

"But don't you know," Tayo said triumphantly, "that one's already dead."

"True... scene," Michael replied, nodding his head, "you're right."

"You know what," Tayo said, as they cleared the steps and stood at the summit, hardly breaking sweat, and adjusting his bouncing leather pouch, "you know I've only been back in this country for five weeks," he said, turning to Michael, "and do you know how many fights I've had."

"I don't know," Michael replied, bouncing up behind him and pushing past the ticket barrier.

"Seventeen," Tayo answered.

Michael shook his head and counted up his quota which did not amount to seven, including the two this week, 'as if it was a competition,' Michael thought, laconically as he stepped on to the road.

"Seventeen, fights you know," Tayo said, screwing up his face, "and you know I haven't even be trying. It's not like I've been challenging every piece of scum that's looking to prove something, or establish a reputation. Take a look next time your outside, look at the sky and tell me that you don't see a swastika in the sky. Just there between the fluffy whiteness of the clouds, a huge swastika hovering over the earth. Tell me the earth is not torn, cracked. The only thing that's not is this swastika perfectly formed, perfect, floating over our heads casting a giant shadow over the world. You know.... you know, I'm sick and tired of it. I'm not surprised every punk who wants to start something is after me with that thing in the sky."

"Scene," Michael replied, shaking his head, "I know what you mean, but you shouldn't be such a righteous brother."

"What are you talking about," Tayo said.

"I mean you shouldn't be so righteous," Michael replied.

"Explain," Tayo asked, turning away.

"I mean if you weren't pretending to be Marcus Garvey Junior, perhaps you wouldn't attract all these fools."

"Is there any logic to your last statement," Tayo replied, walking on to the pavement, "did you just think of that yourself, or what?"

"I mean," Michael said, "you're always screwing up your face like a bad man, so you've got to expect it."

"Let me tell you something," Tayo answered, bouncing down towards the zebra crossing and adjusting his black pouch, "by the way is this the right way."

Michael scratched his head like a child, and smiled, his perfect white teeth, a little to clean, for a man who spent most of his life smoking spliff and drinking Guinness. "You know wha' I can't even remember," Michael mumbled, "I think it's around here somewhere," looking around and just avoiding a puddle of rain water that seemed to emerge from the crack in the pavement.

"Watch it," Tayo said, seeing Michael's acrobatics.

"Scene," Michael said, on realising his near miss.

"You almost soiled your Karl Kani jeans, that would have been the final straw in't, first your Kangol hat, then your jacket, now your jeans."

Michael giggled, like a schoolboy, realising the playful insult, "besides don't change the subject," he said.

"What is the subject," Tayo replied, "you were getting us lost, in fact you remind me of a brother I used to know called Clinton, always swore blind he knew where he was going, but bwoy he was lost."

"Clinton," Michael said puzzled, "I don't know who the brae is, but, how do I feel like you just major insulted me."

"You should feel it," Tayo said, "I just did."

"Well that's okay then," Michael replied and they both laughed like two small school children at nursery.

"I think that's it, you know," Michael said, pointing at a huge grey monolith of stone and concrete that jutted out from behind a small corpse of decaying trees.

"Is this the place, it looks like North Peckham estate," Tayo muttered, looking at the bland, stark white stone, cemented crudely together like the architect had been a maniac.

The gloom of the tower block cast a shadow over the two intrepid explorers, like a grey tomb, an epitaph to decaying inner city rejuvenation. Here and there marked black, with the filth of the smog, car fumes and pollution. (In fact the filth added the only colour to the otherwise bleached, unnatural appearance).

"You know," Tayo said, genuinely forgetting about the initial conversation about his righteousness, "if animals lived there, these lot here, would kick up a storm of protest, but its' alright for people, it's a damn disgrace, it's a literal disgrace."

"I agree," Michael said, "places like Brixton, or other places where we live aren't exactly the garden of Eden are they."

"True," Tayo replied, looking up at the concrete tomb towering over them.

"Then they'll come knock it down, build some yuppie flats, push the black people out, and move the respectable executives from the suburbs in," Tayo asserted, bouncing towards the building.

"Scene," Michael agreed, "have you seen Brixton recently." Tayo nodded, his little black locks bouncing.

"But don't try and change the subject," Michael said, "we were talking about how your righteousness keeps getting us in trouble, remember."

"No," Tayo said, "that's what you were saying," and smiled arrogantly.

Flex

Flex was flexing in his plush flat in down town Kennington, smoking a huge white spliff. It was twelve inches long, the end charred and brown from burning, a thick brown tunnel of smoke bellowing up and consuming the whole room. Flex stretched out his own feet, on his own table, in his own flat and smiled a comfortable smile.

He looked around, 'this place is alright,' he thought, looking at the shiny ebony, so clear that he could see his locks in it. A huge picture of Bob Marley smoking, like a reflection of him, adorned the opposite wall. His brown locks matted thick and buoyant. A calm serene expression on his face, the mouth slightly turned upwards in a smile.

Flex flicked the ash from the drug dropping out of his mouth and kicked out his feet to the tune of, "Po'lice and thie'ves in the street;... ahhh yeaah, frightening the nation with their... guns and amm'unition." His brown locks reverberated, bouncing to the sound of the beat, each one in turn electrified and enlivened, his head lost amidst the forest of hair.

CAT brown boots, laces undone, strewn by the adjacent doorway, strange bedfellows, for a pair of thigh length high, black leather boots, high heeled and zipped to the top. Cream shag pile carpets, adorned here and there with antique embroidered rugs. Interwoven red and yellow fabrics, speckled with blue and aquamarine. The walls embroidered with paintings of the banks of the river Ganges, rich in gaudiness, as it shed it's silty mud and washed up stream; the mud thick and black, dazzled by the blazing sun, as it lay heaped by the river bank.

Flex like a deadlocked Buddha, in a haze of smoke, high, floating, there in his mind, in the abyss. 'Here, here,' Flex thought, 'there's no me, or Tayo trying to turn back the hands of time, no fascists, corrupt lawyers, no skinheads, beast (police), or secret organisations keeping I and I down, no colour, or race, poverty, hatred or revenge, just pure levity. The whole world's just like the feeling when your sistren and you have a session,' he thought and smiled, as he stretched out like a cat.

A faded picture of Marcus Garvey was blocked for a while by the rising smoke, as it stretched, divided and expanded, doubled, redoubled and replicated, filling and consuming, aborting all intelligent life and reducing it to confusion. A huge cactus plant, it's green stems stained brown with the pollution. Its' spikes wilting under the weight of the consuming smoke, if it had had leaves to shed, it would have. But still it lay sweltering, in never, never land, dream time, Rasta heaven.

Kotching and flexing, Flex, took a slow drag on the noxious substance and exhaled through his nose like a dragon trying to start a fire. He took a glance around his rather too comfortable apartment, sumptuous fluffy red cushions, ordained in gold lace. Velvet curtains hanging ornately, its drapes sweltering in the consuming smoke. Soft pink coloured walls, decorated here and there by a yellow daisy, exquisitely painted, green stem and all. A huge bay window seemingly out of place in such a small apartment, its frames Georgian style, gold encrusted, bustled here and there and capped with ochre. To top it all the central pane, was stained glass, now just a faint reflection of the richness in its myriad of colours. It was dulled by the evening, drawing on to night, the drizzling rain spitting trickles of water against its coloured exterior.

"Bapb, bapb, bapb."

"What, what," Flex mumbled, stirring from his meditation. "What g'won.?" he asked, almost rhetorically.

"Bapb, bapb, bapph...." (knocking at the door) rang out even louder. Flex stirred, like a restless lion, turning the blaring music with a flick of his agile, if lethargic hand. Standing up partially, his shoulders slightly hunched. This time the sound was louder, less hesitant, more demanding, less expectant.

"Chill out, I'm comin'.. you fe'l say me is Carl Lewis, or Linford, or somethink," he mumbled.

But the door which had never been really closed, creaked fully open, Tayo and Michael bouncing in like two great cats.

"What's the matter don't Negroes, knock these days," Flex said, seeing the brothers and half smiling lazily through the haze.

"You know it wasn't shut," Michael blurted, a little embarrassed and looking now at the gaping door.

"Me nah deal with that," Flex said, "I never shut it."

"You what, " Michael said, looking around at the miniature paradise of Flex's flat, "with all these garms and tings, the place looking so kris and all, you leave the door open you must be mad, brother, seriously."

Flex shock his head and waved like a king at his subjects, towards the direction of their muddy shoes. "Take your shoes off and pull the door to, I've got a track, I wan' to play for you, it's boom."

Tayo looked at Flex, through the smoke and coughed, 'what's this about,' he thought, as he reached to undo his shoe laces, and then wondering, 'why I am stepping into a strange person's house. A person I only met a week ago who seems to smoke more money in a week than most people earn in a month. What kind of place is this is,' and he kissed his teeth.

"What you kissing your teeth, for," Michael asked, still bent double stopping from undoing his laces, and looking up at him.

Ignoring Michael, Tayo turned to Flex, "to tell you the truth," he said, he was bending over his laces half undone, "I find the thing a bit odd, I mean you hardly know us and here you are inviting us in, we could be anybody."

"But your not anybody," Flex said, looking at him and smiling. "Your Tayo, and your Michael and you both wannabe righteous brothers, especially you," he said, looking at Tayo.

"How do you know," Tayo interjected, "what, or whom we are."

"Whom, shouldn't that be - who, anyway, I just know," Flex asserted, "besides, if you we're goin' to skank somethink, you'd hardly tell me you were goin' to do it."

"All right, then" Tayo said, "firstly we ain't righteous anything, were just young men, with all the faults of young men, stumbling through life trying to find answers and trying to survive."

"You see what I mean," Flex said triumphantly, "righteous brothers".

"Nah," Tayo replied standing his laces undone, lying all around his size ten black boots, "and what is this about," waving his hands towards the direction of the door, "do you own this whole block, or something, what Don Flex," and he giggled.

"To tell you the truth Sherlock Holmes," Flex said, sitting back in his chair and staring at Tayo, whilst taking a long drag on his spliff like Huggy Bear from a 70's black exploitation flick. "You don't really want to know - do you," Flex replied, his white teeth shinning. His locks vibrating still, to the fading tunes from the huge black stereo. "It might offend your righteous notion of our, what you say, your people."

Tayo looked at him, "nothing you could say, would surprise me."

"All right then Mr. Righteous, take a seat," Flex replied. Michael had already, since he scattered his Timberland boots carelessly by the front door, making for the front room with a keen eye on Flex's pile of weed on the nearby table.

Tayo watching Michael so enamoured of his drug and seeing Flex so eager to tell his story, he sighed a deep sigh, 'I know I'm goin' to regret this, but anything for a good story.' Unlacing his shoes and placing them side by side on the floor, pushing the door shut. He stepped gingerly into Flex's lair. He could feel the carpet on his feet, the warmth, the comfort and he forgot almost for a while the poison smoke which was filling up in his lungs. Flex watched him, as he carefully put his shoes down and smiled, 'far too righteous for his own good,' he thought.

"Hey is this a cactus," Michael said, getting temporarily distracted by the huge upright plant which stood defiant and proud, casting an oblique shadow, "it's maskive,...."

"Yeh I know," Flex boasted, "it's big in'it."

"Seriously I've never seen anything like it in this country, seriously, it's humongous and wha' are you dat," Michael catching sight of the stained glass window, "ya nah say this is a little piece of heaven, this is how I wan't do my place, when I get it."

Tayo bounced into the front room, looking at the elaborate scarlet pillows, the shiny almost gaudy drapes, 'how the hell does he pay for all of this, what is he under, whose house am I in, I could be sitting in here and the door gets busted down by Babylon, locked down for ever, they search through my bags don't find anything, but they look in my shoes, which he's asked me to take off and behold an ounce of cannabis tucked into the leather lining, cunningly hidden, by Flex, who by the smile all over his face knew more about it than I did.'

"Kouch," Flex said, gesticulating with his hand, like a chief in an ancient African village to his underlings. Tayo waved the smoke away from his face in an irritated fashion and sat opposite, staring into Flex's brown eyes. The soft cushions gave way a little and he felt his weight resting comfortably.

"All right," Flex continued, watching Michael crouching down on the floor next to Tayo. "First did you know that I'm at your Poly, did you know that?" The brothers looked at each other, Michael had not really believed him though he had repeated it to Tayo.

Tayo took the surprised look off his face, "did you invite us in just to tell us that," he replied, adjusting the straps of his leather pouch and undoing his coat.

"Chill brother," Flex said, "I'm not your enemy, I'm your guardian angel, (speaking the most perfect English). You see like the other day when I saved your arse, I'm here to protect you."

"Really," Tayo said, coughing slightly as the smoke began to fill up his lungs.

"You don't believe me, I know everything about you, Tayo," Flex asserted, inhaling from what was now a stub between his fingers. His eyes magnified by the light of his rather ornate lamp and the glint of the moon as it trickled through the stained glass.
"You been to Gunnislake, recently," Flex said.

"You what? " Tayo asked puzzled. 'I haven't heard that name spoken for over a year, Gunnislake...... Gunnislake.'

'Gunnislake Cornwall, I've tried to forget that place,' Tayo thought, 'the Dowds, Clinton and his sex magazines, the church, the pub, Aisha, yes even Aisha and every time, I push it to the back of my mind and I happen to look in the mirror and I see the scar and I remember...... I remember why, what happened, I remember what this country is really about, how you can't trust even your own brothers, like Clinton, they'll sell your soul quicker than Mobutu. But I want to know how this brother knows all about this, only seven people in the world, well this part, any way, know that story. You can't trust all our people because they bear the same skin as you, like it or not - and I don't much like it, in fact I don't like it at all.'

Michael cast a concerned glance over to Tayo, "what's this all about then," he said, puzzled, "are you goin' to tell me, or what?"

"There's nothink to say," Flex said, "except there's one question. Is it true for all this right on black power, you were brought up by bluefoots!" (It was said more like a statement than a question).

"Yeah I heard that as well," Michael interjected.

"Well it's no secret," Tayo replied, dismissively, shrugging his shoulders.

"True," Flex continued, "and we sure can't choose are parents. Ya know wha' if I could, I wouldn't choose, the white woman who was my mother, I can tell you that." Tayo and Michael looked at him like he had just dropped a bomb.

"You mean to say your mixed race," Michael said, but thinking, 'will the real black man stand up (and only he was going to stand).'

"Nah not mixed race, brother," Flex replied, becoming a little agitated as he finished the stub, a slight red glare lighting it's tip. "When you look at me do you see the white woman," Flex added, "who gave birth to me, or do you see the black man that was my father. I think you like the whole world sees my father, you see me as a black man. When Babylon comes to arrest me, they don't think or know his mother was white, they say w'ah', let's get the nigger."

"True," Michael said. Tayo just stared .

"Ya' not convinced then, righteous brother," Flex said, looking at Tayo's dead pan expression.

"Well I'll tell you then, ya know that the way you are is not by chance, nor by choice, ya know that." Tayo half nodded. "if you could choose I jus' know you would never have chosen to be brought up in the country with those country bluefoots."

"Well," Tayo said.

"Well anyway I know ya wouldn't, nor would I've chosen to be born by a white woman, it's not me, really, it's jus' not my style. It's like tryin' to be something better, the article, the real one you're not. But then you reach a stage, you must have reached it now, when you realise that you're not the way that you are because who gave birth to you or wha', who ' brung' you. You realise that you are what you are because you are it. People may say are you' dat or this. But ya not, ya either a dan, or ya not."

"Yeah, but," Tayo interrupted, "you tryin' to say that circumstance and environment have no affect upon the way that you are, of course it does."

"I didn't say that," Flex replied, smiling to himself, glad he had finally brought Tayo into the conversation. "But what I'm sayin' is look at dat', you can have a brother brought up by whites in the country and he turns out like Fatima or Frank or somethink, you know them Toms, and you can have another and he grows up like Malcolm or someone. Ya know Malcolm was brought up by whites don't you."

"So," Tayo said.

"You know what," Michael said, interrupting the conversation, "this is all above me, I jus' cam here to relax, not have a lecture in philosophy."

"You see what I mean," Tayo said, smiling at the ignorance of Michael's comment, "if we're supposed to be the righteous ones, then God help the race."

"But we are," Flex retorted, "we are the strongest of the strong, the bravest of the brave," standing and shaking the lethargy out of his legs, "the wisest of the wise, the Bini Dan kana, numero uno, top of the pops, a, number one, head boy, chief scout, the best, tip top, the licks, the Mack, the prophets of hope, in this ungodly age. We are all the race has got. We just don't know it yet. I tell you this, there ain't nobody else." He sat down, a little disappointed there was no round of applause. Michael looking blankly at him, still thinking of Flex's pile of weed.

"Well then if that's the case," Tayo smiling, "then we had better sharpen up are act - you," pointing to Michael who was standing up making his way to the Kitchen to check out Flex's stash, "had better give up cracking forties and smoking blunts and you (pointing to Flex) the smoking Buddha of the Gangees, should cut out trying to escape into the clouds."

"Chill, brother," Flex replied, a little agitated, "I'm telling you there's no point in goin' on bad still, black man's too far gone, finished."

"Now we get the point," Tayo continued, "you've given up on the race, so you figure that you can smoke as much as you want, sex who you want, and talk all this rainbow politics, cause nobody is going to say anything."

"Will ya tell this brother too cool it," Flex answered.

"I keep telling him the same thing," Michael replied, looking enviously at the pile of weed that lay heaped on the mantle piece.

"Yeah and keep your hands off my tings, bro," Flex retorted, leaning back in his chair at Michael.

"Seriously man I'm not a rainbow anything, I mean it," Flex replied. Tayo just stared,"seriously I love black people, well sometimes.. but things don't run like that. I mean most of us are gone. I keep telling you that niggers have got to die. "

"There, you go, on with that foolishness," Tayo said, waving his hand in front of his face like a fan, wafting the descending smoke from his face.

"Your damn right," Michael said, perking up and shouting from the kitchen, "all brothers want to do these days is get paid."

"All I here is you talking about the problem, not the solution." Tayo replied.

"I tell you this," Flex retorted, "that a Negro will sell you out quicker. Brothers will sell their own mother like at-a nothing still. I'm telling you that. They will sell you out and the worst ones are those that say they are fighting for black people, that they're doing all they do, which is front, for liberation, locks today, blonde straight weave the next. All those newspapers who say they go'on with, what they go'on with for us, don't, they do it for themselves still. The politicians who are supposed to stand for man a man, don't. The radio stations which are supposed to be so article black, is what, eh... nah.. man censorship over the air waves, censorship in the books they promote. Even censorship in the films that they lick out. The whole point to make the t'ing look authentic, the article, real thing, but really it's a lie, a damn lie, a **fabrication**, righteous," he said looking at Tayo, "it's fraudulent. Because they're all getting paid. Paid to keep the people darker than blue down. Have, ya not seen the sisters in those thirty thousand pound jobs supposed to be anti racist councillor for Brent or some where, but when a homeless brae on the street asks for some dollars, she crosses to the other side of the road, yet you see her in the newspaper the next day, Black woman of the year, with the caption, 'she's a real achiever, she's really made it. What has she really made. She really made herself a tom, while the whole race falls to pieces around us."

"And what do you do," Tayo asked, "what service are you rendering to the race, how are you serving the cause of the race. What do you achieve stuck here in your luxurious apartment smoking weed and bitching about the world. If all these people are toms and I don't doubt they are, don't get me wrong, they only go on with their foolishness because we allow them to. Most of us spend so much time in church, or on the floor praying to someone, or high on, crack, or something else, (pointing to the weed). Your damn right, those few who do stand up will get the applause, because they stood up, what standing up have you done."

"I'll tell you what," Flex replied, "standing up I have done, but it may well shock your sensibilities about what you think are race is like and the reality."

"Well go'n," Tayo answered, "I haven't heard a good story for a long time. Not since Tav."

"Tav," Flex said, puzzled.

"You either, know it, or you don't," Tayo said, smugly.

"You shouldn't go on like that," Michael interrupted, overhearing the conversation.

"Nah I'm not the story teller anyway," Tayo replied, "Flex go'on man, you've got the floor and he waved his hand towards the centre of the room like an usher, bringing on the next act."

Hard times

"Well," Flex said, "you see me, when I was growing in my mother's womb, she cry screaming 'get this ting out of me - it's trying to kill me.' Imagine that still, your own mother sayin' that 'bout you. Being the second born and youngest, I took my place in line next to an older brother who cut his way to the top. Mother dumped us at our father's house, with a note, *'This is all a mistake, I don't love you, I just can't stand it.'* So much for mixed relationships, the great **melting-pot**, wha' and all that nonsense. Bringing races together.. wha... Beside my mother was from one of those working class families, brothers all vote NF but she would say, 'you know I'm not like them, they're just ignorant," Flex said, in a high pitched voice, imitating her, "but watcha' when she done gone cured herself of the jungle fever, see how she go'on... like the little racist skesser she was. I can say it.. man, if any one can say, I can."

"Still I grew up the 'lickle' bad youth, if not original, bad never the less, cutting and skanking brothers, selling a 'lickle' draw when I could, sex a few sisters,.... in short,... survive."

"Where is all this going?" Tayo asked, adjusting his pouch, and then looking up into his eyes.

"Wait the man," Flex said, laconically.

Tayo half frowned. Michael took his mind off the stash long enough to have a look around the corner and observe Flex's face, but as soon as he heard the word Brixton, he tutted and kissed his teeth, 'that place is mash,.. Brixton, fake Rastas, fake dreadlocks,' he thought, and went back to examining Flex's heap of cannabis.

"Seriously all the so called sensibilities, morality," Flex said, moving the ash tray away from him and across the table, "on the street there missing, in fact just about everyt'ing is missing. You see black men selling black woman to white men and white men selling white women to black men. In fact when I was out there, there waz some geezer, what' was his name, man ... Steve that's it, used to go around with some big fake Negro called Busta, with his fake white girl, fake yard accent and fake foolish face. Fronting and faking all over the place. ..like a clown."

"Get to the point," Tayo interrupted, getting a little irritated.

"All right, righteous," Flex replied calmly, "we used to chuck it from Peckham to New Cross, all the way down Deptford back up to

Atlantic Avenue, Brixton and all that. We used to roll in a crew, link with Wandsworth Massive, Brixton Posse. Thirty to forty man tight. Enugh' man I know now is dead, prison, or strung out on some shit." Flex continued, leaning back in the chair and breathing in deeply like a dragon. "Enough brother' s just wasted, you know, gone, blunted on reality." Flex batted his eyes a little, a glistening film of liquid gleamed over the surface, 'a tear for the lost ones,' he thought, as he pushed the tear back and breathed a heavy sigh.

Tayo stared, 'there's something there,' he thought, 'it's like why should they have gone and I'm still alive.'

"So there I was," Flex continued, "flexing all the while, the world turning. Maxing on reality. Then reality hit me. Now my brae brought us up, vacant father, spent his time blary eyed in the betting shop, or getting drunk on Tenants, playing dominoes, cussing and good-for-nothing. But all we had was ourselves still, man-a-man, used to rely on himself. Tight (raising his voice)."

"Then reality hit like we had all been daydreaming and then suddenly someone woke us up. It was 1985 my brother used to roll with some brothers, doing security at a night club in Brixton what's it name..." Flex said. Tayo shrugged his shoulders. "Any way still, they used to be organised crime, I mean some serious business, well still some of them was definitely into organised crime, you knew white firms, the Mafia even, anyway. News broke that one of them had struck up a deal with that some fool. Ya no Busta and two too's Busta had 'skanked' him. 'Thiefed' the money and go'around Peckham shouting his mouth off with his white friend Steve. Well my brother went hunting this same fool."

"You mean, what's his name Busta or something stupid," Tayo said.

"Nah listen, you've got to listen, righteous," Flex continued, "my brother went to find the brother from Brixton who was his partner ya know the one who used to hold it down at the night club, who owed him the money."

"Well my bro was not the kind to hold it down. So he drove there in his new black BMW and parked outside the club. I heard that he had only been waiting two minutes, when the geezer arrived. My brother walked over calmy, took out a piece he had been carrying in his dash board and boxed him over the head. Then pointed the gun at his head, and said, 'you're not worth killing you know that, but that fool over there in Peckham, he's sorted, do you understand, he's gone get sorted,' he just walked, everyone giv'it the wide stare."

Flex stretched out like a cat, his locks slightly bouncing and yawned. A large copious yawn, his tongue flapping against the roof of his mouth and feeling the dryness of his lips. But he continued, "so there my brother was standing on Brixton high street with a gat in his hands, dripping with the blood of this brother, needless to say Babylon was so hot on his tail that he had to take the back street, just to save his arse. He figured that fool, would be out on the street, or around that Asian's off license on Peckham high street, by the way did you here that he got a lickin, some white boys kicked his arse, just here."

'I wonder if it was that business a few weeks ago,' Tayo thought, leaning back in his chair and flexing his toes on Flex's shag pile carpet.

"Yeah I heard about that," Michael interrupted, sticking his head round the window, "I heard they beat him within an inch of his life and just walked away laughing, you see that, what kind of troubles we're living in."

"Well," Flex said, "that geezer was no angel, some pure foolishness used to g'won, I tell you. There's some big old father who used to be a solider, or something, I've seen him go on dark."

"You mean light," Tayo said.

"Whatever," Flex continued, "I've not even seen an old man in Jam go'on so bad, he's just renk. Even Busta used to jus' hold it down like a bwoy. Anyway Mr Patel."

"Mr Patel," Michael remarked, sniggering like a school boy and catching sight of Flex's overfilled fruit bowl of oranges and bananas. "You mean to say that the Asian guy or owns the shop, he's called Patel. That's just like every stereotype you ever heard."

"But it's true," Flex asserted, "that's his name, and, I'm telling you he sold more than Dragon stout, and Tenants."

"You know that," Michael said (as if he did), I beg you one of those oranges, and a banana," catching sight of the overflowing fruit bowel.

"Feel free," Flex replied, "you wan' some righteous, (looking at Tayo)."

"Nah man," Tayo added, "I'm cool, besides you haven't finished the story."

"Oh yeah where was I," Flex asked.

"You were saying," Tayo replied, "your brother was in his black BMW cruising the streets looking for Busta, that's a really stupid name, he deserves a slap for that alone, a good hard slap in his chops like a bwoy."

"That'll be the day," Flex said, "you should stay out of his manor, he goes packing every where."

"Yeah, yeah," Tayo replied, "a man is just a man."

"Anyway," Flex continued, "my brother was on his way to Patel's shop hoping to find that fool and give him some licks, or send him to the cemetery. My brother had not gone one hour travelling the back streets, when he saw the familiar lights of Babylon in his window. That's about as much of that, that I know. The next time I saw him he was locked down for ten to fifteen years for murder."

"Attempted murder," Tayo said surprised, "I thought...that he just hit the brother."

"That's just the point," Flex continued, "apparently the brother had gone home just after he got his licks ya know to sought himself out and that. Two too's next thing, the police received a tip off, that a man had been seen leaving his flat and waving a gun ."

"Yeah but that does not add up," Tayo replied puzzled, scratching his head, "your brother was still in his Bm'er wagon, how could he be in two places at the same time."

"More than that, you know when they found him, he was hanging, suspended from the ceiling by a rope like he had just been lynched or something," Flex replied.

"Seriously," Tayo said, shocked.

"Yeah and it's known," Flex added, "that Busta's responsible for another murder about a year later, where the brae was found hanging from a lamp-post in Peckham high street. I knew the bro still, he was alright, a bit lary, but alright. Yo know his brother Del," to Tayo.

"What Del," Tayo asked, "the same Delroy Constantine Simms, t'ick (motioning with his hands to signify being big), yeah I know him, from time. Whatever happened to him."

Flex, replied, "he's around, set up his own business, living large making dollars, and that. Trying to forget that his brother was left hanging from a lamppost and this was no white man, a black man did this ya know, you talk abo't white people, but it was a black man, your brother." He stretched again, like an overfed cat. Tayo smiled, realising where Flex had got his information about him.

"Anyway, the whole thing was dodgy, there was somet'ing just odd, I mean it was so quick, he got jumped by the beast, like the whole t'ing had been orchestrated and you know wha' my brother lost everything. Locked him down, they took his flat, seized his garms, his cash everythin', even his car. Two, too's I see that fool Busta, is driving around in his car, he'd stripped the inside, put some fluffy pink ting inside, like a pussy. Driving around like a don, giving it large in my brother's car. Now wha' do ya think abou' that."

"I think," Tayo said, leaning back in his chair, twisting his locks, and watching Michael bouncing nosily into the room with an orange stuffed in his mouth like a prize pig ready to be cooked. "I think, that Busta is in league with the establishment, that the police and him have an unhealthy relationship and he sells drugs on the street with their permission, cause he's their boy, everybody knows that you operate on the street with their permission, if they wanted to they could stop it today."

"Well," Flex said, "I'll tell ya, that fool Busta's driving around in my brother's car like he had just brought it from Mad Mike's car lot,... that fool, .. sometimes... I feel to just cut his clart......." He kissed his teeth so hard his whole mouth reverberated. "Any way my brother's 'respeck' just kept on coming, the powers that be thought wha' this will put an end to his **credibility**," (he said, over emphasising the word to impress them). "The 'respeck' just transferred to me."

"So you're the don," Michael said, smiling like a Cheshire cat, bits of orange in his teeth.

"Not really, but man-a- man just knew it was a set up. Brae's would stop me in the street and say wha' go'on with your bro', like he was their family or something."

'Strange,' Tayo thought, 'we can show so much concern over somethings, but little or none when it really matters, after all this brother was running the street selling this and that, damaging brothers just for the hell of it, we choose the wrong people to be are local heroes, so many of our true martyrs dead and nothing said, so much respect for this brother - no disrespect to Flex, but what had he done to deserve so much attention.'

"Still," Flex continued, "the crew just grew and grew. We used to have a sound and play up and down all over town ya' no. From the time my bra' got locked down we played more gigs than the whole six months we had been around before. It was like people were looking for something to save them, a hero or somethink. There was not a bandy legged youth in the whole of the south side who did not know the coup. That's why righteous," he said looking at Tayo, "I don't need to lock my door, cause anybody who would rob me I know already, and they nah do it cause they knew what's what." Tayo looked at him unimpressed. Michael nodded in recognition, rather than approval of Flex's accent as it drifted from patwa to cockney slang.

"The only one who would trouble me is the beast and no locked door is going to stop Babylon, they're just lick it off, so why give them the pleasure, leave it free and wide still. So there I and I was, the crew multiplying, are sound busting every venue south of the river. Then it all fell to pieces. It was exactly three years, two months and seven days to the day. I was out walking just past Atlantic Avenue going to check a spar I knew, I turned the corner, it was abou' six thirty or so in the evening...." Flex said, scratching his head. "The sun was dead behind the concrete jungles of the Avenue and that renk smell... ya know this smell of cocoa butter, sweat and piss.. that's the only way to describe it. Anyways I turned the street, I just bought some new Bally boot and I was high stepping like a don, my garms were Kris, I had a crease down the centre of my slacks like a solider and boy, I had the lick. Man, brownings would stop me and give me the look like I was the Mack."

"Yeah, yeah," Michael said, looking at Flex's brown locks, he had taken an interest in the conversation, 'besides,' he thought, 'this light skinned boy thinks too highly of his complexion, even if his oranges are boom, he ain't article. There is only room for one Mack and that's me.'

Flex oblivious to Michael's thoughts, "so there I was in my garms, the sun just lighting up the sky red, like blood, and 'mee' high stepping, so I passes not more than thirty meters, it was the usual route I took to visit my brethren. Everyone knew still that was my turf."

"You'll be sayin' you dirty rat soon," Michael said, laughing and leaning against the wall, but his knees were still supporting his weight.

Tayo tittered like a child and covered his face, "that film the Petrified forest is all right though, enough of our people in it, have you seen it," he said, changing the subject and trying to prevent Flex from replying to Michael's challenge to his reputation, they both shook their heads genuinely disinterested.

"Seriously," Flex said, feeling a little upset his guests did not hold him in absolute awe, "so there I and I was going down there, me see it blam, a daughter on the floor trash. Her kit deggy and she was 'maagre' too like Grace Jones. Boy she was gone. And you know what, too bluefoots standing over her, kicking her like a dog, blam, boff, licking her up and laughing, they were going to take her round the back and deal with her like only a bluefoot boy could. So I stepped right up to them still, me nah fear no one. 'What you're dealin' with I says to the big one, cause the smaller one was still kicking her, boff, clapping her round her head and everythink."

"Wait the man,' I says, 'chill out the man,' as he started to hit her even harder. So I stepped over and sought of gripped up his shoulder, this is the little one. He sought of turned round and looked at me like, I never forget the look, his eyes were blue, like a lagoon in the deepest swamp in Barbados. So blue and he looked at me, just kept looking. He sought of adjusted his jacket, he was wearing one of them brown bomber jackets, and blue jeans."

"A street boy," Michael said. "Yeah somethink' like that, no style, not like me, even when I've got jeans on, I still look like a Dan," Flex replied.

"Any way as you were sayin'," Tayo said, becoming impatient at the egomania.

"Yeah so there we are staring at each other, like somethink' goin' go down or somethink' and the big one just comes up behind me and like puts a neck choke on me and other one starts licking me, me thought wha' goin' on, they forget about the daughter, just givin' me licks, and for a lickle' white geezer he could throw some thumps. Meanwhile Arnie behind me is trying to kill me, swearing and everythink,' callin' me nigger and black bastard, all the while strangling me like a chicken. So I got desperate. I used to carry a ratchet in my jacket, it had a twelve inch blade and kind of shone, ya no like my saddle does, silver like."

"So this geezer was lifting me up in one of these wrestling tings and this lickle one just goin' buck wild. Ya no what, brethren I knew from the street since I was a child; brothers, yeah, your brothers, just walked past like nothing happened, and there I was with my legs dangling in the air, like a hanging man, or some-think. So I get vexed and just reach inside my jacket and flex my blade, that's how I got 'me' name still. I just sought of jabbed back-wards in the boy's face cut up him rarse, kick him in his seed and left him their bleeding like Henry cooper against Muhammad Ali, ya'know the second time. The other boy got scared now, start walk-ing back wards, there me is standing their with blood on my hand, blood dripping from the point and me vexed, boy, me just wild, me ready to kill. And two too's the boy starts reaching inside his coat. Me thought he haf to dead now if he reaches for a gun or some-think, then, ya no what' he produces a radio."

"Nah," Michael said.

"Trust me, the bluefoot was blue for real. True blue." He starts talk-ing, "IC3 attempted murder, colleague down, request back up,' or somethink like that, me never really deal with what he goin' on, with some sought of foolishness. So me thought well it's that, if I goin' down me might as well give him some licks too. So I chase the lickle bluefoot down Atlantic road with the blade still in my hand. Man ya should have seen the people come out of their shops like wha' Flex are you dat.' I got as far as Acre lane and it was like a scene from the fugitive or somethink, they had barricaded the street, there was Babylon everywhere, like they had been waiting for days or, somethink. So two too's I start walking back now, when I see the forces of oppression and ya no what, some foolish uncle tom, that I never even scene before with some deggy white girl, she looked like she was on the game or somethin,' gives it, 'he's getting away' and points like a fool to show Babylon where I was. Fool, fool, with a fool's face."

"So two too's, small boy gets brave now and sought of runs after me tackling me in the street. He was tough for a lickle geezer. Tackle me on the street in front of all the crowds. So me just had to discipline him, I whetted him up, when I finished he looked like one of them ripe tomatoes that had been squashed. All the while he's giving it like, you fucking little nigger, and he's little ya know, calling me little,' I'm goin', have you,' but he's not goin' have any one, all he's goin' to have is a mash up face for the rest of his life. I wouldn't have stopped still, if he didn't keep coming, he just kept coming and ya no wha' even though his face was all blooded, he had so much hate in him, he managed to wrestle me to the ground and then it was all over. Man they came from every where, and brothers on the street them just disappeared like, they had not seen any think. When they finished with me I looked like an advert for a lynching ,....you know... after."

Tayo and Michael laughed, "so, what happened," Tayo asked, genuinely, "you don't look old enough to have been in prison for thirty years for attempted murder of a police man."

"Nah wait the man," Flex said, "they took me to some cell, I don't remember cause I was unconscious. They thought that me for dead and make a martyr of me. They got scared like the whole of Brixton would come down there and bus open the cell and release me. But all them man there jus' smokin' a spliff selling rocks and palaney and getting high. **Liberate**, liberate wha', man they couldn't even liberate a fart from their arse. So there I was bleeding to death on the concrete floor in the jailhouse at Brixton."

"The next I remember, I was in hospital chained to a bed," Flex said, Michael shook his head, "nah, seriously, I was chained to a bed, and bandaged up like a mummy like that brae ya know Huey P. Apparently I had spent a week in a coma, they thought me half' to dead for sure. But I lived cause I'm a born survivor. I spent some four weeks in that hospital, ya no they had broken my arm, dislocated both shoulders and cracked my spine, but after the four weeks except for a sling around my arm and a slight limp it looked like me had come away lightly."

"So it went to trial and this is the lick, this is the boom. I'm in there, I had some boy representing me, the case starts and then this black police woman comes in. She comes in like and I'm tryin' to remember where I've seen her, being that she so tight with the bluefoots in blue. Then I remember that she was the one on the floor, the one that they were givin' licks too, and then the whole thing dawns on me, hit me like a thunderbolt, right there as I'm standing in the dock, dressed up like a kipper, I realise that I'm not only dressed up like a kipper, I've been done up like one too! I've been banged to rights. All the while she's smiling at me through the whole thing like yo fool and me jus' shakin' my head like a fool."

"Two' twos' they sentence me and being that I was a junior and supposed to get lighter sentence, ya no first offence and all that, he sentences me to three years in detention, what they call borstal or somethink,' and five years in prison." Tayo looked at Flex from the corner of his eye and right there and then forgave him for his vanity, his smoking weed like a little African Buddha the stupid rug on his floor and the even more stupid stained glass windows, ' all for that,' he thought, 'the brother's been though some things still.'

"So there I was in detention," Flex continued, "all right still, so long as you held you're own, nah body deal with you. Being that I went in for cutting up a pig, I was a bit of a celebrity, even amongst the white boys them, even though they were racist still, nigger and all that. Then I went to Big man's prison, not after three years, but two, cause the Detention centre got overcrowded or somethink', ya no that a lie. I was like one of the youngest there still and y'know them boy go on like (imitating them) 'all right mate how'se it going son, cawh blimey ya alright, apple and pears, up the stairs, alright geezer.. alright mate, howse your bleeden mother, howse your bleedin father, is he alright..' their stomachs hanging over their trousers, white string vest, stinking, with stubble on their faces like bwoy.. they'were some of the worst sought, the ugliest crackers this side of the Caucus. There scene, I've started talking like you righteous. But, them crackers were just plain nasty, kill their mother chop her up and eat her and laugh while their eating her like, at-a-nothink." Tayo and Michael were both laughing.

"Enough batty boy in there, they love fresh black meat I'm telling you, Bwoy the renkness, that go 'on. Them man waxing each other off like, I don't know what. Big brother's on the outside from yard and the street, weight lifting brothers who cut you up for jus' looking at you, all faggot. All faggot. All nancy boys, bending over for white boys." Michael shock his head. "Nah seriously," Flex continued, "white boy pimping them, they're selling their backsides for a few cigarettes or somethink. Ya no that's just about the worst ting still, rapists, killers, man who rape off lickle boys, all squashed in there. Yo' no wah' them white boys' have got that place sorted out, sorted out, you know everybody and everyt'ing, working for them like on the outside. Ya no who controls it from the inside, the Brays."

Michael shock his head dismissively, "that's a tangent, them old men, couldn't control anythink," he asserted, posing as he said it.

"Well that's just where you wrong," Flex said, decisively leaning back on his chair so his locks hovered, suspended in mid air.

"They don't do the business, ya no the killing and tha'. They're the brains, Babylon works with them, sometimes for them, they walk around like Gods. The only ones they don't bother are the IRA men, everybody is scared of them, they just leave them to go on with their business, they have their own block in the prison and everythink.' But the black man. Brothers goin' on like punks. Seriously like bwoy. Big brothers just goin' on like fool and you see them go home to their families like they're real man now cause they did time. When they spent most of it on their back or their front, with some bluefoot boy riding them like a dog."

"And what about you ?" Michael asked, looking at him.

"Yo' what," Flex said, becoming agitated, he managed with great difficulty to calm himself, "tell him righteous he shouldn't half listen, then goin' like he, he's the man. Didn't I just done tell you, I don't do that business. One time some bwoy goin' like I bow and touch up my batty. We was in the dinner que and I had a metal try in my hand with this hot porridge on it. Ya no the brown sticky stuff that burns and sticks how it burns, yah no. Me just put this porridge all over his face and lace him with the tray, wax him so hard, that his head bust open like a ripe melon. No one ever bothered me again, jus' let me get on with my business."

"But seriously them place hard," Flex added, "made to break you, you sloop in, slop out, ya know you have to show them ya business, they inspect ya dodo, to see if you're healthy, sometimes they make you put your hands in it, to make sure you ain't hiding anything in there. Then there's' the strip searches and the solitary confinement. I 've seen man break, big man, but the brothers that survive, are the quiet brothers who just go there try and get a good job in the library or somethink, then you get left alone, push some weights and wait for the time to pass, and true the time does pass. Ya kind of get used to it."

"But you don't forget," Tayo said.

"No you don't forget that nah matter what they're sayin' about' black this and black that, it was a black man who got my brother locked down, and me know it was your sister, righteous, not mine, that got me put away. Black people. I'm telling you me nah deal with that business, me see a man for who he is. Me nah really check for no colour business, me see to much foolishness."

"If that's so," Tayo said, leaning forward earnestly like a politician, "why did you help us out there on the street and why have you invited us into your house, nah, through it all, you still have love for us. You love us. You can't help it, if any of us could help being what we are, we would. But we can't, no matter how much you try and wash yourself colour blind, the world is not, nor will it ever be, and you know it, I know you know it. All these things are part of a system. You have a black policeman in old South Africa who beats a brother to death, it does not stop it being a racist act, he does it on behalf of the state, which is and was a racist state. Racism is not just a simple matter of a white geezer, on a white horse riding across the fields in a white hood with a burning cross. I wish it was, nah they don't come like this any more. Now they leave us to kill us off, and they've got us brainwashed, they don't have to bother coming themselves."

"True," Michael said, "they just leave us alone and we do the job on ourselves."

"Exactly," Tayo, replied, "they just pull the strings and we dance, react, cut and kill each other."

"Nah don't encourage him," Flex said, turning to Michael, "yah nah say he'll get us all in his African thing."

"I'm not sure I want you," Tayo replied, "you're not worthy."

"Not worthy," Flex interrupted, "I heard when you first came to the Poly you thought washing rice meant using soap powder."

"Yeah but look how I've grown now," Tayo said, and they all laughed, even Flex against his will.

International Human Rights

Mr. Thomas senior lecturer and Deputy Vice Principal, smiled a self
satisfied smile as he stared at the first year politics class. He fiddled
with his custom made pockets and began, "all of you are now in
the first year of your politics degree," he pompously looked at the
class. His slip on shiny black shoes from Saville row, shining like
mirrors and his glasses glinting unnaturally under the glare of the
lecture room lights. "As second year students you are expected to
know and understand some basic concepts," he said, "adjusting his
tailored pleats and smiling gregariously like he would, at very
small, disadvantaged, underprivileged stupid children. A young girl
in the front row, playing with her blonde tresses and staring at him
with piercing blue eyes - staring with a little more than admiration
at his shiny black shoes and pleated grey pure wool suit, newly
brought from Geaves at High Street Kensington.

"The international jurisprudence that binds all states together, it's
benchmark, the level as it were of international relations is this,
that the hate crimes against European Jews produced such an outrage in civilised society that it forced the hand of countries to come
to a consensus, an agreement. The agreement was that this should
never happen again. When we look at world affairs there has been
justice and peace in Europe, the standard of human and rational
thought, the reasoned standard of a reasonable society on all matters has been set, that all men should be judged fairly and impar-
tially. The world is certainly a safer place and justice now more
than ever can be said to apply to all men, irrespective of colour,
race, creed or religion," Mr. Thomas said, adjusting his grey suited
waistcoat. He smiled a sarcastic, little smile, it seemed to remain
fixed on his face, like Punch. He fiddled with the top button of his
grey waistcoat with manicured, delicate, almost feminine fingers.

'You know I don't think they've understood a thing I've just said,'
Thomas thought staring at him, 'International human rights, all
they want to do is party and enjoy themselves. It is all very well
having education for all, developing the minds of the young and
all that, what's that, multicultural, and multiracial environments
are all well and good in theory. But I have taught at institutions for
more than ten years and I know that a lot of these minorities can
and do hold back their white counterparts. Don't get me wrong,'
Mr. Thomas thought, looking at their disinterested expressions, 'I
have seen some of these minorities, even some here, go on to do
great things for themselves and their communities, but the entire
standard is just too low,' and for the third time that day he wished
he had ended up at a prestigious institution like Oxford or

Cambridge, or even LSE. Yes even LSE, though it was a little politically correct for him, and definitely socialist orientated, 'there was still that pursuit for excellence. What pursuit was there here,' he thought looking at a young black guy in the front row, playing with his locks and an Asian guy next to him staring blindly at the wall.

'A rather nice little coloured girl,' Mr. Thomas thought, looking at Jennifer absorbed in chewing her mint, triple, banana flavoured Bubulicious chewing gum and adjusting her rather skimpy dress to attract the attention of the young man in the back row. 'She's got a nice little frame,' he thought, looking at her, 'cute, little dimples, reminds me of that other diva I've seen around here, one little perk with the job, these little girls are quite something. What's her name..... Melanie, that's it... Melanie, now she's really something, almost sophisticated. Who is she with again, that's right, I see her with that character,' he looked up at Michael, 'I see her with that radical fringe, the African Society, or something, race hate mongers. They obviously think this is 1960's Mississippi. But it's not, it's.. England,' he thought, adjusting his glasses and peering through the lenses like a mouse.

"Now lets' get a comparative view," Thomas said, "The UN declaration of Human Rights is the natural by product of this international high benchmark in juridicay...."

"Fine words," Michael said, loudly, interrupting him in mid speech, he brushed a biscuit crumb from his starched white Calvin Klien T-shirt and stared at Mr. Thomas. Thomas stopped, stunned like someone had just hit him with something hard. He peered upwards at Michael sitting on the back row, looking arrogantly down at him. "Surely," Michael said, "we are not dealing with theory, ya no stories are we."

Mr. Thomas stared blankly at him, 'don't try and out postulate me, young man,' he thought. "Master Richard's, isn't it, do you have something to say," he said.

"Yes, I do."

The whole class looked at him, Jennifer forgot about playing with her dress, she had been trying to attract his attention anyway.

"The truth is that you are guilty of a crime of omission," Michael said.

"Let's not get biblical," Thomas replied, "I never thought of you as one of those good church going types." There were titters of laughter around the auditorium.

"You don't know what I am," Michael said, staring at Thomas, "the truth is that, you know in your.. speech, well what you're saying, you failed to mention that all this equal rights, the truth is, that black people were still third class citizens in the states by the Constitution until 1964. Ya no that, don't you ! Here is not much better, immigration acts passed, I mean just recently 1971, 1981 which actually took the rights of black people away. So we have a new millennium of righteousness since 1945, do we? Yeah we have international papers supposedly to guarantee rights, but do they. The power and ya know that, rests with big business, the corporations who exploit the southern hemisphere, robbing it of natural resources and international organisations sponsored by the west which start wars in Africa, Asia and South America, wars which just go on forever, no body can remember why it started, or what was the reason, (getting excited, by the classes undivided attention)."

"Peace, peace.. till me if you can since 1945," Michael continued, "why Africa has had more wars than in any other period. Peace, tell that to a child in Mozambique who has had her legs blown off by a mine manufactured in the U.K and shipped over by the tons, making jobs for Britain but butchering the world to do it. Africans and Asians do not manufacture their own guns, y'know where they come from, don't try and fool us! Peace... peace.. . Tell that to the children of Nicaragua, in a war sponsored and instigated by America and Russia on the other side. Peace, yes for Europe.. a certain kind of peace, it's just that war has been exported, like ... like a bad disease to the rest of the world."

There was a pause, almost pregnant. Jennifer looked at Mr. Thomas for his reply, playing with the tresses of her dyed brown hair.

"I know that's what you talk about in your society, radicals trying to over turn the system, is it." Thomas said, irately, doing and undoing the top button of his waist coat, with pink rasping hands. "You are indeed very eloquent," Thomas continued sarcastically. Michael sat unmoved, he was waiting for Thomas' insult to sink in. "You've said it and indeed it is true. When I say peace, I do mean peace in Europe. Now whether you like it, or you like it not, it is better now than it was before," Thomas said.

"Better," Michael blurted out, "better..."

"Yes young man," Thomas said, he was beginning to enjoy the debate, "certainly before 1945 there was no standard, that's how and you of all people should know this, people from your continent, the one you talk about so much, could be brought and sold, to work on plantations in the USA, the Caribbean and here."

"Really," Michael said, sitting forward in his chair and watching the eyes of his colleagues as they looked at his every move, the inflection, the turn of the voice, the gesture, as they hoped he would give up, give in, fail, make a fool of himself so that they could dismiss him and go back to sleep.

"So slavery doesn't happen now?" Michael asked Thomas.

"No not like it did before," Thomas replied, "you're going to talk about economic inequality, aren't you, poverty and all that. But you know there is a difference from the kind of chattel slavery which your people went through, you know it did so much psychological, mental and moral damage to the fabric of African society. Look your names Richards, but that is the name of the slave master that enslaved you, that's not really your name."

"Well let me tell you boss," Michael said sarcastically, he could feel Jennifer's eyes burning into him, he felt her eyes flitting over his face, staring at his chest, his arms, examining the details and contours of his expression, his nose mouth and lips. "Slavery is happening right now, right now. In fact I've got a picture in here......some where.. of the diamond mines in South America, ...look at this.....(he rummaged around inside his bag like a hamster, his voice dropped)."

"We can't here you, Master Richard's," Thomas said.

"You see that," Michael blurted out triumphantly, emerging from beneath his chair like the man who won the Golden Stool. He produced a copy of the National Geographic and held it a loft like a trophy. The overhead lights gleamed on the shiny surface, dated November 3 1990.

"You see I wasn't even going to bring it, look see for yourself, pass it down to the front," handing the magazine to a bespectacled student who duly scanned the open page adjusting his glasses. Recoiling a little at the image of emaciated men and women chained together and covered in filth, hauling huge rocks on their head or dragging baskets though the filth. The mud splattered over their wafer thin limbs, filth hanging dripping over bandaged hands

and feet. Thick wedges and tracks cut into the muddy plateaus by
the dragging of so many tired limbs along the mud covered paths.
Old men women, children, some bandages and a few rags covering
their embarrassment, chained together as if they were a huge monster that had risen from the cesspit of the earth. An overseer with a
modern looking sub machine gun on a white horse, unmarked by
the surrounding filth. The horse's arrogant head lifted up slightly
to exhale the smell of stench. It's grey mane bleached white. The
accumulation of mud heaped up by the side of the road and whelks
of filth dislodged by the movement of the workers, (slaves). The
overseer in a white Del Monte style hat like a rancher from a John
Wayne film. Dressed all in white, with shiny knee length black
boots like a nazi storm trooper.

"Look and see for yourself then, see whose going off on a tangent,"
Michael said, pointing at the magazine as it descended down the
rows to the front, to exclamations of, "shame,"

"Boy."

"If it that was me, I just, pull that boy off his horse," and, "man,
you see that still, young girl looks about ten".

Michael excited by the attention blurted out, "you see this is not a
hundred years ago, it's now, ask those southern Sudanese what's
happening in the Sudan as Arabs from the north go on like devils,
catching children to use them in a brothel, or to work on plantations like this, bwoy, and you know same business go'on in Saudi
Arabia, or South Africa, you just know that."

"You said slavery's gone," Michael said, the magazine had drifted
its way to Mr. Thomas, amidst the tittering and chatter of the
entire auditorium. Thomas fiddled with his glasses again and
adjusted his belt as the magazine was handed to him by a now
indignant female student, who gave him such a hard stare, as is if
to say, 'how dare you suggest there isn't slavery today.'

Mr. Thomas uncomfortably picked up the document and examined
the pages. Like a suspicious insect. "You see," Michael said, he
could feel the students waiting. He felt Jennifer's light brown eyes
transfixed on him, not in admiration, but disdain, another on the
back row with his mouth almost open, the young girl in the front
wrenching her head to stare at him with worried blue eyes, as she
squirmed uncomfortably in her seat. Her grey shirt turned ash with
embarrassment.

"Slavery, is alive and kicking, and that's reality despite any Universal Declaration, the U.N. or all that foolishness and that's the truth you should teach us," Michael said, sitting back triumphantly.

Mr. Thomas mumbled something under his breath, as he scanned the magazine. Pawing over the picture with almost feminine fingers like a puppy dog spaniel. After what seemed like fifteen minutes, but was nearer two, he blurted out, "well thank you Master Richard's for an informed debate, but we really must get back to the matter in hand. As I was saying...." He adjusted his waist coat for the third time and Michael stared blankly at him.

Michael brushed off the remaining grains of biscuit which had lodged themselves in the creases of his shirt, 'so you thought you'd come here and go on like a don, teach all us ghetto youth the truth Mr. Thomas style. But really all you want to do is grand stand, all right, well today,' he thought, resting back as far as he could go, 'you've been told, told by a youth and I ain't even from the Ghetto I'm country. Well let that be a lesson to you.' and he smiled, arrogantly.

'I guess,' Michael thought, 'everybody thinks that, bwoy, I'm part of this black thing, so I guess, I'd better just pass in there and kotch,' putting his feet up on the seat in front, 'next thing they'll be calling me Tayo or somethink,' he thought, he looked around and everyone had gone back to sleep, the brother in front had opened his book and was leaning on his lectern like a drowsy cat. Everyone except for Jennifer. She was looking at him, with confusion, and admiration all at the same time, her bosoms bouncing, hardly imprisoned in her diminishing dress. 'Bwoy,' me feel to just wax that,' he thought, looking at her and abandoning any righteous thought from his mind.

Fame and fortune and everything that goes with it.

Tayo looked at them packed back to back, front to forward, every seat was full, some sitting two or three to a seat. Round faces, slim faces, fat, thin, tall short, bald heads, puzzle heads, side burns, no burns, gold teeth, no teeth. Hillfiger and Versace, Bally boot Calvin Klein and of course Kangol.

'There was no turning back, no asking, to get off the boat, this thing is rolling, over three hundred faces,' Tayo thought, looking at the expectant faces. Michael posing at the back with a smile on his face looking at Jennifer looking at him. Flex with his silver saddle strapped to his back, his locks hanging down over his face like a south London Bob Marley. Ade staring under his baseball cap, a little excited by the turn out. Angela sitting at the back trying to disappear into her chair, hoping that Susan had not told any one about her white fiancee. 'Today I can be whatever I want to be,' she thought, playing with her dyed blonde hair and trying to ignore the stares of a young brother on the third row with brown contact lens in his eyes.

Segun Adegunle, Accountancy student and Kwame's friend stood at the back playing with his short jerry curls like a girl. His Pierre Cardin blue shirt a blur under the lights, looking to and fro at the gathering like a merchant banker looking for a buy, or a sale, smiling every now and then cynically, as Tayo moved backwards and forwards.

Appia sitting on the step peaceful, reserved, watching and absorbing the proceedings, oblivious to the confusion, she had been instrumental in the good turn out. She had put a leaflet in the pigeon hole of every black student she could find and spent her lunch times with Susan leafleting the concourse, even Melanie and Ade had joined in. But if Ade was asked, 'why are you doing this. Is it that you no longer believe that niggers need to get paid,' no doubt he would have replied, 'yeah, I only did it, cause it's a black thing,' perhaps he would have drawn on his past, 'well you know I used to be brought up by white people and all that, I know the coup.' But the truth was that he only helped on that lunch-time because he wanted to impress Melanie.

'She's so fine, she must be the finest girl at this college, boy she's fine,' he thought looking at her under his baseball cap and smiling. The only reason why he was there, now, was because she was there, 'besides,' he thought, 'I don't want to be left out of these tings, this must be half the college' and he looked around, 'but boy she's fine,' he concluded, catching her turning around and her giving him a half smile.

Strange, Ade was there for Melanie, she was there for Tayo, but neither of them were there to start a revolution, or end one. 'In fact,' Susan thought, looking at them as she walked towards the front, most of them don't know how they got here and don't know why they're here, we really have got some work to do, you just know it's fashionable right now, what, the society's fashion, it's a fashion statement. Well look at that, we've became a fashion statement like Karl Kani, or Calvin Klien. The A.S. don't leave home without it,' she laughed to herself. Simone looked at her as if to say, 'Mummy's gone mad now, she's laughing to herself.'

Susan looked at Tayo who seemed in full swing, not even noticing her at the other end of the front of the hall, 'I wonder if he know's why there here, I hope to God that he doesn't think that something has really been achieved, I hope to God. He's got the heart, but there's a naiveté, why,' she thought, 'there's something missing, to much love, not enough reason, he's never really had one of his own hurt him, he does not really know how we can destroy ourselves. He's seen the race at a distance, not the filth and the dirt up front. Ah well, so long as it gets him to wake up some of these fools, that will do some good. I just hope that he does not get hurt, or damaged in the process, a young man like him, not even twenty, with that much fire, can easily self destruct,' and she smiled at him, but he was oblivious.

"Well, this is a beginning," Tayo said, looking at their expectant faces. "It's good to see you," he could feel the blood pulsating through his veins, the drip, drip of adrenaline, as it ebbed through his arteries. His heart pounding like a locomotion train, a thin line of perspiration emerging on his nose and staying there, 'my nose is sweating,' he thought, 'I hope they don't notice my nose is sweating.

Melanie was staring hard at him, but it was not at his nose, 'he gets fitter,' she thought, 'everyday,' adjusting her taught body through her leggings, he's done a good job of avoiding me so far, but that ain't goin' to go on for good. All this African business is fine, but he's going to need some good loving some day and I'll give it to him, believe me when he's ready, I'll give it him' and she smiled though her ample, artificially red lipstick.

Michael looked around at the multitude, 'well there's enough black people still, it's all good, but I don't care, 'niggers have got to die,' you just know that they ain't really down with the coup. If Adolf Hitler came and sat down in here, you just know most of them would just sit here like nothink go'on.'

"You may all be here for many reasons," Tayo said, looking at Flex, who still had his saddle in his hand like it was his gun, in some western film. "I know that some of you have come because, there's a fine girl here that you were looking to check, or because, or because there was a fine brother that took your fancy,' he looked at Jennifer who went the colour of her red blouse. She tried to hide it by putting a set of delicately painted finger nails over her embarrassed face, a face marked with lipstick, rouge and eyeliner like an Egyptian mummy.

"I know very few of you have come for anything like what I would call the right reason," Tayo said, "but then who am I, nobody I guess. But this is not about me, it's about us. The very first day I started at this college, it must have been over a month ago now, there was a line of police cars and an ambulance outside here. Do you know why," his voice raised slightly. He waited for a reply, there was silence.

"An honest God fearing member of British society had mercilessly beaten an Asian man almost to death. Why, cause he beeped his horn at him. This man was just driving his car down the street outside this very college, when this geezer just got it into his head to **finish him** (he said this last word with inflection, so the sound reverberated). Finish him you know like, what, he was some chicken or a fox, that had been hunted, caught and now needed to be killed. Almost killed him in front of his family, wife and everything. Were they brought to justice, no. And the thing is," (his voice became louder, the small vein on the back of his neck pulsating and his heart pounding beneath his chest like it wanted to come out).

"Yet despite all this," he continued, "an off duty police man followed me in here **like I** was a criminal, perhaps to tape our conversations, or arrest some of us, like we haven't been arrested. Some of us know (he looked at Flex) what it means to be locked down, so that can't scare us, but just think of this, he wasn't interested in the crime, only in me and you. Walked past the scene of the crime like nothing, couldn't wait to get in here and mess about with you though."

"There is no joy without pain," Tayo added, "they are inseparable. Just as there is growth, there is regression. Poverty lives side by side with great wealth. Knowledge and ignorance are brothers. The seconds tick and the minutes pass," he paused, rubbed the sweat nose from his nose with a youthful finger and began again, "the present becomes the past in the twinkling of an eye. So it is in the world. Time will not wait for you. You either progress or you regress, if you do not work to build your wealth you will be subject to those who have amassed theirs. In ignorance you will suffer at the hands of those with knowledge. Time will not stop ticking and wait for you to get off your backside black man. Or for you to get off your backside black woman, for you to be the people you ought to be. Time will not wait. You master time, or it master's you."

"Some of you may know this," Tayo added, "that your not the first, or the last to be at this institution. You are not. You are part of a history. When I first came here there were good brothers, Carl, Tony, Fred, David, Del, and sisters like Nzingha, Sonia and before them, there were others. All you are continuing the legacy," he watched their expectant faces.

"All right this year we have an aggressive program. As your servants and we are here to serve you, we intend to provide the means by which we may come to understand this world a little better. Discussions on history, religion, politics, everything. Stay with us, don't go anywhere. We will start a library with black books, the kind that you can't find in the main library. We hope to have a study class, that's our intention anyway. And there's a school near here, a Saturday school and we are looking for volunteers to help with that. We also want to start a savings program, so we can buy things for you, or even donate the money to charity. There will be marches and demonstrations too, against racism, student poverty or just about anything that affects you and we will be asking for your participation and of course there will be the raves, I know some of you just want that. So this is a roller coaster ride, don't get off, you can't get off, there's no where to run to and no where to hide. You are all here for the duration and when we've finished, this will be the largest, smartest, most efficient student society in this God forsaken dump and you will have a voice that you will be proud of."

Flex smiled, a sought of enveloping smile, that started from the centre of his being and pulsated to the rest of his body, 'righteous has done a good job, there's some fine gal here and some coarse brothers, still, there might be somethink to this black organising business, even I might stop skanking and try it for a 'lickle', ya never know I might be good at it still, why should this brae, have all the fun, it might all go to his head,' he thought, looking down at his silver saddle still marked with the dent from him using it on Dave's head. 'It's not goin' stop them Negroes snorting crack up their nose like I don't know what. Or braes waxing bluefoots like it was their first turn around. Sure as hell, it's not goin stop niggers killing each other for being too black, or stepping on each other's shoe, or for looking at each other, or cause one came from the east, or one from the west. Nah, nah ! in reality that's just maxin on reality. But any way it beats sitting around like some maagre bwoy, with a brief case under my arm and pencil case in the other' and he smiled again, brushing his locks from his face like a south London 'rudie'.

Superniggaz

Luke bounced down the stairs two at a time, "you're makin' too much noise, in it." King mumbled irritatingly, "he'll here us before we get there in it."

"So what," Luke said, scratching his short afro, "do you think I'm scared of him," he said, still clanging down the stairs, like a twenty stone man.

"Nah I know that, I know you're not," King said rubbing his chin, pretending to look thoughtful, all the while, brushing his locks away from his face like a girl.

"Well," Luke said, interrupting and stopping to look at him, "so what you're sayin,' do you think I'm stupid."

"You what," King said, raising his voice a little to high for a man.

"You need to just calm down," Luke replied, scratching his short afro with his finger and gripping the coiling red handrail with the other.

"Cause at the end of the day," Luke continued, looking at King, "I don't really check for him, or anyone else that's down with that program."

"Whose program you down with," King blubbered.

Luke ignored him, trying to think whilst not getting irritated at the same time, his short chubby hands gripping the hand rail like a baby his bottle. His baggy blue track suit bottoms bulging with the muscle from bench pressing 200lbs a day. The irony of him standing in a Poly in the middle of South London, 'to do what,' he thought, scratching his head for the second time, 'to deal with this geezer, what, was his name.. .. Tony that's it Tony. Bust him a little, put him in his place. Cause he started his own martial arts, didn't he, started his own class, without the Sensi's permission, like he's a Dan or something. Go'on like he's the man.'

He stopped in mid thought and looked at King wiping his nose with his sleeve. 'This geezer, for an athlete has some bad habits,' Luke thought, staring at him, 'filthy geezer. I just know he's, goin' down on white girls like there was candy up there or somethink, don't get me wrong, I like a white girl, the good looking ones any way, but me nah go down on them, but this one here, boy... he's just renk. '

'Besides,' Luke thought, 'what's all this for anyways,' and he
stopped to think, perhaps it was the first time in his life he had
really stopped to think. 'I'm a black man and all,' he thought, 'but
at the end of the day, man-a-man got to look after himself still, if I
have to lick this big-head boy up, to get a promotion in the club,
then that's all good. Even if I have to do this thing with you,' he
thought, looking at King, 'besides it's all practice and I'm gifted in
the art, the Sensi knows I am. So gifted I don't need this pussy
sucking fool with me,' looking at King dawdling along and waving
his locks around like a blonde model on a catwalk. 'One day I'm
goin kick his arse, stuff those locks down his throat and make him
choke on them. There's only room for one and that's me,' he
thought stupidly smiling, like a clown.

"All right, all right," Luke said, "now let's get this job done, I don't
check for you, you don't check for me but we both want a piece of
him still in't," he said, rubbing the small tuft of hair on his chin.
King gave a toothy grin his gold teeth shined unnaturally, he
brushed his locks vainly from his face, for the third time that
minute, just like Kate Moss.

King was going to say something else, instead he coughed and
cleared his throat, 'too much white powder and white pussy,' Luke
thought and smiled. A little tad of phlegm was still in the back of
King's throat, he coughed it up and felt the yellow liquid slide
around inside his diseased gapping mouth. He spat it out over the
side of the hand rail, it landed with a splat, sending out little flecks
of orange and green phlegm in all directions, the grains of the
inside of his mouth, still visible on the floor below. "Good shot,"
he boasted, smiling .

Luke hung his head sadly, 'you are a dirty git,' he thought, looking
at him, 'I could be with some kris looking honey, a browning with
green eyes, plump batty, big up, or one of those white girls, that
love off black men, but instead I'm with this false Rasta,' he kissed
his teeth.

"Come on we'll be late, (clearing his throat)" King said, "I don't
want to hang around here too long, I hate these places, too many
books and that, gives me a headache. Besides we're south of the
river, I want to be back in Stokey by six."

"All right," Luke said, still clanging down the stairs and blocking
out the instinctive thought he had to grab him by his locks and

hurl him down the stairs and jump on his head like a ripe tomato.
He pushed it to the back of his mind.

Luke cleared the steps with a thud and bounced towards the half
open door. The sign pointing to "Gym."

"It's this way in it," King said, pushing past Luke and bouncing
the door open. His athletic stride bringing him straight into the
glare of the lights of the gym, he blinked slightly, a cascade of
colours bouncing off his retina. King pushing his way unceremoniously past him.

"Have you come to train," A slim powerfully built brother said, his
eyes calm, relaxed, almost serene in their sublime tranquillity, like
an artist or a poet. A thin smile graced his lips, all but concealed by
a masculine goat beard, bristling, slightly.

"You what," King said, regaining his eyesight and staring at the
brother garbed in an all black Gi embezzled with the logo, "Sensi T
Francis."

"We're here looking for some **fool**..(the word was emphasised)
called Tony, thinks he's Bruce Lee or somethink." King looked
around at the class, all looking dumfounded at him like a Martian
had just walked in.

Luke stared at Melanie in her lycra black cat suit and he smiled,
'we'll have an audience as well,' he thought, and, 'she's fit to.' She
was attending Tony's class only for the third time that year. She
was there mainly for the attention that it caused seeing her fine
African physique squeezed into such a tight space. So tight like she
had poured it on.

The class looked at King and Luke puzzled. Appia a regular, his
favourite pupil. Jennifer who had come to watch and Ade who had
come just to watch Melanie. Tyrone posing, in what looked like hot
pants, tight enough for him to audition to be a ballerina in swan
lake, trouble is they weren't auditioning (you would have thought
some one would have told him wouldn't you). Melanie, had been
looking at him for all the wrong reasons, wondering, 'how can a
black man go'on like that, doesn't he know he looks like a fool.'
Mikee with his funky baggies on, looking to get some extra fitness
training in before the football competition. His hair was dyed
brown with silver rings in it, but eclipsed to day by Tyrone's swan
lake and Melaine's funky diva impression. Lastly Kwame on the
end with baggy trousers like they were his father's, a shy retiring

expression on his face - now staring absolutely confused at there unwanted guests. 'I only came,' he thought, 'because all that lot, meaning the brothers from the AS kept going on about it, and now what,' retiring behind Mikee.

A motley crew, but Tony had every expectation of, to quote his phrase, 'turning them into something.' He had taken the decision when he got back from Gunnislake that very day, that he was going to keep his head down, no meetings, demonstrations or anything like that. 'It's not easy,' he thought, 'trying to avoid Tayo, he's every where, if it wasn't him, one of those other brothers, so many new brothers and sisters, let's not forget the sisters,' he thought, gyrating his hips and then looking at King.

"Even if most of the class go to meetings. It's my third year, my last year, I can't afford to be called up to the principal as I was before. Tayo, Carl and all that are my brothers, always will be, always, no matter what, like we were separated at birth, but I'm tryin' to stay out of trouble' and he hyper flexed the muscle in his shoulders like a boxer in the ring. 'Besides where's the old crew,' he contemplated, 'it's like they disappeared. Del with his business, Clinton, where the hell did he go,...... I don't know where, besides I don't care, that brother was lost. Carl into the church, that was the one that got me, the church, you know, can you believe that, after all the things we've seen and done' and he looked up at King.

Tony stood thinking whilst King slowly worked himself into a rage, 'why isn't he looking at me,' he thought, 'what's he thinking about, who does he think he is.' He kicked the floor with the top of his Adidas boots, 'I don't think he's taking me seriously.'

"You're Tony aren't you," King spluttered out of his diseased mouth, staring.

"You're not very smart are you," Tony replied, "who ever sent you must be short of intelligent hoodlums, they have to send the unintelligent ones. Like you !"

"You what," King said, bouncing forward, his locks swaying, he was trying to figure out if he had just been insulted.

Kwame cringed behind Mikee, Melanie felt a slight line of perspiration break on the back of her neck, Appia felt nausea rising inside her stomach.

Tony sized up his adversary instinctively, he felt a sudden surge of adrenaline like a sprinter in his blocks. He leapt up, the blood coarsed through his veins, faster than a locomotive train, he leapt up, his knee rising first, his foot quickly following, powerfully and mightily like a lion, yet swift and graceful. The muscles flexed around his tendons and the tendons around his joints. His will drove them all on, his foot landed on Kings chest, but did not stop there. His might drove his foot on through. Driving downwards into King's chest, past his hastily constructed muscles, into the corrupted, diseased organs beneath. Tony's size ten foot thudded against the very centre of Kings being, past all the martial bravado and into the reality of what he was. King gasped for air, but his lungs were constricted. His locks swung all around him and he doubled backwards in pain, crumpling on to the wooden floor. He felt the world fading away, all he was thinking was, 'this is Tony isn't it, this is Tony I'm sure, I'm going to kick his arse.' That was the last thought, he thought, as he lost consciousness. A thin trail of blood that he had coughed up, adorning the wooden floor.

Tony landed on the floor like Superman finishing a mission.

Luke took a step back on his mighty legs, the thick muscles tensing slightly. 'I got's to try something, this geezer moves fast,' he thought, but fear pulsated through his boy. For the first time in his life, like an injection of poison, it paralysed just for a second his stalwart mighty frame.

Tony saw the heaviness, the second of hesitation, the slight line of perspiration on Luke's forehead.

Tony saw it and faked, turned like he was about to leave, his agile frame partially in circular movement, the sinews which held his joints together partially twisted. Luke saw the movement, 'now I could do it,' but his body was still paralysed, and he just lunged.

Tony detected the movement, telegraphed, as in slow motion and slid his foot between and slightly under the foot of the advancing powerhouse. Connecting with his ankle and sweeping his foot from under him.

Luke buckled, but his powerful frame adjusting itself - more from the muscle around his sinews than because of any skill on his part tottering like a great tower that has been blown up with dynamite but refuses to fall. Tony regaining his stance, spun his hips like a dancer, feinted and struck Luke with the back of his fist to his temple.

Tony's hand spun back with chi like the hand of a reverberating clock. Luke stood stunned for a while, his stocky, mighty shoulders trying to stabilise. But Tony skipped in, hips and elbow in perfect motion, one twisting, the other rising. The elbow struck Luke under his chin, wrenching it back, as if he had been hit by a block of wood. The jaw locked out. The eyes closed, the room went black.

He clenched and gritted his teeth, and released the accumulated chi stored there. The energy came out from the base of his spine and travelled over the circumference of his body, re-animating him like he had just put his finger in a light socket.

The class gasped as Luke recharged himself and stood staring at them as if nothing had happened. Kwame trembled behind Mikee hiding his face.

Tony spun round not hesitating and undaunted, releasing his third blow, "kia," he screamed, as the fist landed on Luke's jaw. Luke's brains reverberated against the inside of his skull, feeling the earth closing in around him, the room going black, deathly black.

"Where's my will," screamed Luke's subconscious, 'where is my will,' but his mind was not listening, it drifted away. His powerful legs buckled and the earth rose to meet him, as his body landed with a thud, almost denting the floor with it's impact. It lay there motionless.

Tony turned to his astonished class. Kwame still cowering behind Mikee, the former with his mouth open resembling a frog trying to catch a fly. Appia shaking her head and Melanie smiling a little too much, 'this guy's a superniggaz,' she thought, looking at Tony standing completely unfazed.

Meanwhile Ade was thinking, 'I think from now on I'll keep coming to the class, there's obviously more for me to learn,' looking at King and Luke's prone bodies.

Tony turned to the class, "you can stop hiding, now," he said to Kwame seeing him try to disappear behind Mikee's quiff. "That was unnecessary and unwarranted," he added. But Melanie had already started clapping, joined in by all the others, except for Kwame who was still too frightened to do anything except hide.

"No really," Tony said, waving his hands, "don't congratulate me for beating up these brothers, they were sick, they need help, I mean seriously they need help," the clapping died down. "Appia you had better go and get one of the sports teachers... Simon or one of them, before these guys die on us." Appia walked, disappeared through the door.

'When is this going to stop,' Tony thought, 'when is it going to stop. I'm sick of this business, somebody's always trying to take my head off, if it's not a skinhead, or a policeman, it's one of your own kind, why, because he's jealous or something, these guys were probably sent by my old club,' he thought, wiping Luke's blood of his hand on his black Gi. 'They are well trained, they probably would have killed me, or something. What for? I am sick of this business, you can't do anything as a black man without somebody trying to take you out.' He looked at the ground. 'What next, they'll put something in my water to poison me and say I died of a heart attack, or something, say I've got a rare disease. What next? What next, this is one messed up world, look what it's made me do to my brothers, look," and he kissed his teeth and shock his head.

Jungle Fever

Tayo smiled at Appia.

"I ve been looking for you."

"Me," Appia replied, innocently. "Why me? " she asked.

"Why not," Tayo said, "is there anything wrong with looking for you?"

"I guess not," Appia replied and smiled sweetly.

Tayo looked at the fine unblemished features, the innocent aquiline feminine demeanour, the healthy expression and felt the relaxed spirit. "I hear your getting really good at training so Tony tells me. You helped him out once, recently, when some one came trying to cause trouble, what was that, a few days ago."

"I hardly helped him," Appia replied, "I just went and got the sports teacher, that's all, but those brothers were crazy, there was something unsavoury about them. But... I didn't know you knew Tony."

"Of course I do, he's a good brother, should come to more meet-ings, but he's alright, no doubt he's got his reasons. But he's alright. Got me out of some situations, I can tell you." Appia looked at him and smiled sweetly for the second time. "Well aren't you goin' to ask me what situations?" he inquired.

"No," Appia said, "if you wanted to tell me you would."

"I like that," Tayo said, standing closer to her, as she pressed against the wall. Her black leather jacket shining like her animated expression. "There's something I've been meaning to ask you?" Appia stood quietly watching him, the firmness of his jaw the slight touch of arrogance in his smile. "You know we are all goin' to see that New Spike lee film, you know Jungle Fever. Well" (he paused) "I want you to come with me."

"How do you mean," Appia asked, "we're all going together."

"No I don't mean that," Tayo said, "I want us to be an item....." he paused. She hesitated, a slight trace of perspiration appearing on her cheek, though she tried to suppress it. "Now don't say why me," Tayo said. Appia smiled, even sweeter than before.

'The smile,' he thought, 'it reminds me of someone....Who? that's it, I remember, how could I forget, why should I forget, had I really been so busy I'd forgotten. Or is it I've chosen to forget her. Aisha. Do I choose not to remember her cute little face and shy confident spirit. Not since Gunnislake,' he thought, fiddling with his pouch, 'not since Gunnislake have I even thought of a woman. Now did I want all that again, those copious letters, sleepless nights, thinking of her, weekends in the country... her move to London. But it was too much of a fairy story to work. It's like we were too close. I would hold her sometimes to my cheek. Feel the brown warmth from her face, the moisture and coolness. The slight hint of perfume (from Body shop). It was like I was holding my sister. You know not once, not even once had we done it. I mean the issue never came up, it was never an issue. It was more than physical. She could read my mind. We would sit for hours just looking at each other. Me getting lost in her eyes like brown pools. Those eyes. How could I forget those eyes,' he thought, rubbing his forehead.

'Marriage, should have been the next step,' Tayo thought, laconically staring down at the whole that was appearing in his boots around the sole. 'I need a new pair, there finished,' he thought, his mind flitting from the subject. 'Yeah marriage should have been the next step, but, you can try hard, too hard, for a thing to work. Trying too hard.........But Aisha didn't need a husband, she needed time to think, to be herself. I needed the time too. It's like my life had been a whirlwind. Time to travel, time, time to... time to... to see something of the world whilst it's still there. So we split. Not like a divorce. But to make ourselves whole. But surely that's not all, what about,.. what about the travelling and all that. New York, Miami, Texas, Holland, Nigeria, Ghana. Sunny beaches, ghettos, foreign tongues, familiar faces, in unfamiliar places. Strange, how far one of those international cards can stretch. Still I'm skint now, can't even afford a new pair of boots. Skint and in this mess. People looking to me for the solution like I know, like I'm an expert. Well all I am is skint.'

'But I ain't,' Tayo thought, playing with his locks and forgetting all about Appia, 'I'm not the expert, I don't know all the answers, I don't. You start to feel like nothing is your own, as if you're public property. I'd even forgotten to ring her, I used to do it every week, haven't called her in a month. See what all this thing makes you do. Some of them think that I did it to grandstand. Say it's my ego or something. What! If I wanted to grandstand there are better ways of running it. I can tell you that. All these brothers sitting back waiting for something to happen. Waiting for...... something.

Then. Man. Nah, this time I want to do something for myself. This time, I want Appia for myself. Why, because I want her. I don't really need any other reason, I just want her. I'd like to take her, to walk, just walk along those places. Those beautiful beaches, Montego bay, without the tourists.'

"Tayo.. Tayo," Appia said softly, more out of concern than anger. He looked at her as though he was a thousand miles away. He was thinking of that hot Montego beach, 'with the sand between his toes, the sun, dying red behind the horizon, the faint smell of sea air mixed with the fresh breeze from the west, a flock of gulls as they sailed effortlessly into the horizon, their white feathers bleached against the evening sky.'

"Are you okay," Appia asked, looking at him and breaking his concentration.

"Yeah sister I'm fine, just day dreaming," Tayo answered, pulling himself back to reality.

"About what?" Appia questioned worried.

"About a **red sun on a green land, with black thoughts**," Tayo said, "but it was just a dream, here's reality."

"Alright, so if you don't mind me asking, if you're okay." She said, Tayo nodded. "I'm going to ask that question anyway, so why me, don't you think that's a good question."

Tayo looked at her agile frame, her back and buttocks pressed so hard the only gap was at the base of her spine. She felt his eyes burning into her, the heat of her emotion mixed with his, the tinge of ecstasy welling up inside her. The beat of her heart becoming quicker, the heat from her womb and the children not born yet bubbling like a cauldron, until it shot out little hot flushes all over her body, spreading to her breasts, her thighs, the nape of her neck. "There are other sisters, good sisters here, why not them," she said, trying to stop the sweat from breaking out on her back.

"Like who ?" Tayo said.

"Well there's Susan, she's a really good sister, strong and conscious."

"Yeah your right," Tayo remarked, "she's a good sister and got some of these rare qualities, you know, strength, determination, organised. Sometimes I don't know where my head is, I get too cross, or day dreaming like to day, or something. But she's there, with the posters done and all that. You've seen that haven't you." Appia nodded. "Your not supposed to agree, you supposed to say I'm always organised (he was smiling). But no, she's efficient, but...but."

"But what," Appia said.

"There's something else, it's not like you should hold someone's past over them and she's a good sister," Tayo replied, "but she'll never be my wife."

"Why do you say that?" Appia asked confused.

"She's done something bad, in her past, I mean really bad," Tayo said, "shack up with some bad brother, I mean Simone's a nice child, beautiful and intelligent, you know how I would want my child to be. But have you ever heard her talk about the father of her child."

"No," Appia said. "That's what I mean," Tayo replied, "I've never heard her, not even once, not even a passing comment you know. That only confirms that he must have been really bad." Appia looked away in thought. "There's something else too, something else.. ," Tayo continued, "like have you noticed sometimes, a sadness comes over her, like a loss of innocence. A loss of purity, being corrupted a long time ago."

"It's funny that you mentioned it," Appia said, "the first time I met her, I mean at the A.S. meeting I saw something."

"What," Tayo said, looking at her.

"It's probably nothing.. but she wants you."

"How do you mean," Tayo replied.

"I mean she want's you," Appia asserted, "more than that I saw something else."

"What," Tayo asked.

"Jealousy," she said.

"Jealousy," Tayo repeated, with a confused expression on his face and he adjusted his pouch over his dashiki.

"Yeah I saw it, I don't like to talk about it, but I saw it like she wanted to be me or something, it was only for a second, but it was there. You know it's strange what women pick up on. Things that men would just miss. Like you know a lot of those sisters who come to meetings, come because your there. The rest come because they want to see Michael or Flex."

"Why," Tayo asked puzzled.

"Now whose the one confused," Appia said. "It's just how women are, they want what they think is the best, and I guess you brothers are the most dominate."

"You seem such an expert, so how do you explain Melanie going out with Ade. You know she's the type of sister who likes to be seen as going out with number one."

"That's simple," Appia replied, "she wanted you and she thought that you wanted her. In fact I'm not so sure that you don't. But any way, she wanted you and made it obvious, you know that's why she joined the society. She didn't have any real interest. You did nothing, after she went to all that bother. She was probably talking to her friends, you know Jennifer and all that. About how she was going to have you. How you would be drinking out of her shoe after only a few days. When she didn't get you now, or did she." Tayo looked at her and smiled. "Well any way because she didn't keep you, it's like she lost face. So she took Ade as a **substitute**."

"Substitute," Tayo said.

"Yes substitute for you," Appia replied.

"You seem to think highly of me," Tayo replied, "every relationship in this college seems to be my fault."

"Well," Appia said, "whether you like it or not, the A.S was the place where most of us met and so you are a major factor, in fact," (noticing the slight smile on his face, and for the first time the scar on his forehead), "I think you like the idea of being a match maker."

"Yeah if it's true, matchmaker for everybody except for myself and I'm looking to remedy that right now," Tayo said, adjusting his pouch for the second time.

"So what you sayin'? Do you want us to be one or not."

Appia smiled as that perspiration began to break out again. This time, everywhere.

"Since you put it that way," Appia said, "next week Friday, for the film, seems like a good time to start."

"All right then," Tayo said, taking her hand and squeezing it a little too much, "until Friday."

Friday

A thin line of smoke trailed above Michael as he sat puffing on his favourite brand of Silk Cut, one foot up against the wall, another placed unceremoniously on the road. His timberland boots undone to the ankles, the laces open and copious like so many little yellow worms. He looked at his watch, 'this man is late still, it's what seven thirty. Film starts at eight, there is no way that I'm missing the beginning, not for any man, still.' He kissed his teeth.

A figure appeared in the distance skipping between two concrete pillars and leaping over a nearby metal fence. His brown locks bouncing and seeming to remain in mid air as if suspended. He bounced right up to Michael, his youthful face enlivened. Michael pretended not to see him, taking long drags on his cigarette until all that was left was a white stub between his delicate hands.

"So you decided to make it," Michael said, turning to Flex, "you know how, he'll go'on."

"Who? " Flex remarked, matter a fact.

"You know who, Tayo," Michael answered.

"Tayo," Flex replied, adjusting his back pack, by tightening the straps, "you mean righteous."

"Yeah, the one who thinks he's Garvey reincarnated .... yeah that one," Michael said.

Flex nodded, "you leave old righteous to me. But you sound like your scared of him, or somethink," Flex said, smiling.

"Scared," Michael replied, "what, of Tayo, (he shock his head and smiled, his white teeth shining) I just don't want him going on like a broken record, or I might have to show him who should be President, what... scared," he started laughing, "you're a joker. Besides, why you making me cuss my brother like that."

"Yeah he's all right in small doses," Flex said, "but he's too right-eous, like he thinks wah, he's a saint or a superstar or something and he ain't, but he goes on like... .. how long has he been President, I think the whole thing has gone to his head. Wha' six months. You'd believe he was president of the U.S. of A or some-think. But .... (reflecting) righteous is okay, too much ego still, but he's okay."

"Like you don't have any," Michael said to him walking towards the tube station, "you go on like your a monk, and you a'int, you ragamuffin. Go' on rudie like, your humble, I've never seen a man stare and skank so much, like you're a don."

"True," Flex said, "but it's just that," and he sighed. They both laughed like naughty school boys. Flex brushing the locks from his face, like a south London rude boy and Michael posing like he was in a John Wayne Western in his camel haired, knee length jacket lined with silk, inside pockets of the finest new Welsh wool from the Cambrian mountains.

'Boy I must look like a don, wha' this is all right still,' Michael thought, still posing, 'I must be a prince, a **Black Prince.**'

The same thought had passed through his mind as he skanked it from Next in Oxford street. He remembered that sense of adrenaline mixed with apprehension, as he stood in the changing room trying to slide the magnetic strip from the jacket. 'Sometimes these things just have to be done,' he thought, finally getting the hang of it and twisting the strip off from the woollen fibres. He pushed the grey curtain of the changing room aside as he bounced out, not stopping to look for inquiring or astonished faces, or even at the attendant who had encouraged him to, "try it on mate, go on don't know until you try do ya, do ya." Michael obliged, although the thought had not come to him before the attendant's suggestion to walk off with a jacket so big, in what was becoming such a crowded shop.

Michael now looked for his blonde, cocky, cockney attendant, but he had since been diverted by a rather curvaceous black woman who had formed an interest in the lingerie section. The attendant had wandered towards her, drawling from his thin lips like a dog and directing the buxom sister, "to try it on love, go on have a go, go on, get in there, go on, get it on, love, don't know until you try, do ya, do ya." He wiped his mouth like a lunatic and stared at her breasts like a rapist. She seemed oblivious, absorbing the attention like a sponge.

'This shop looks like Piccadilly circus, man it's ram, like box up,' Michael thought, bouncing towards the exit, his new coat swinging round him. A female assistant stared at him as he went past her cockney colleague, he tried to ignore her, he was so near the exit. Zig zaging past a family of Japanese tourists who had come to see the latest fashions, all bespectacled, earnest and in haste. They were stooping at every stand with wide eyed curiosity, directed by their father - as if he was an expert in a museum taking a look at the latest things on offer. Camera at the ready, father seemed absorbed by the layout, happily snapping, as he moved around.

At the height of his lectures in Japanese of course. An overweight older man, with a stomach hanging seven inches (certainly no less) over his stomach, bounced into him. The fat man looked at him and brushed the brown hair from his sweating face, adjusting the girth of his belt and staring through ignorant eyes at his Japanese counterpart. But the tourist just bowed and apologised, stepping past him, his family following him. Only when he was out of ear shot - muttering in Japanese, gesticulating with his hands and puffing out his cheeks, at which his family laughed heartily, before continuing there journey.

Michael bounced past them and a group of children stuffing their faces with chocolate and cake, so their white faces were almost obscured by the Cadbury delight.

Michael could feel the spring breeze as it wafted down Oxford street and through the half open doors. The movement of the traffic down the street, a large double Decker bus as it made its way. The waves of window shoppers, posers, fakers, liars, cheats, deceivers, poor and rich, beggars and thieves as they wasted their weekends in the West End.

'Just a little further still,' Michael thought, as he bounced towards the door, feeling the open air on his face, the slight smell of smog, sweat and car fumes.

'This thing is easy still,' he thought. He felt a tap on his shoulder.

He clenched his fists, he could feel his heart beating a thousand times per minute, the adrenaline running faster and faster through his body. 'There is no way that I'm getting locked down for stealing a coat, even if it's a camel haired coat at that.' He turned on his heels, more of a half turn, his fists ready to do some flying. He turned and raised his fists.

There behind him stood the female attendant who had been staring at him.

She took an ungraceful step back on her stilettos, "I didn't mean to surprise you," she said, smiling through thin lips, "I guess you noticed me staring, didn't mean to be rude, but, well, you're really gorgeous, I was wondering if you might go out with me sometime."

Michael stared at her fake eye lashes, the washed out complexion and pale blue eyes, adjusting her bra with green finger nails and sticking out her chest like she expected him to come and feel her up. He lowered his fists, smiled an artificial smile, "give us your number then, and I'll see what I can do alright, not promising." She rifled in her rather too short skirt pocket and pulled out a piece of paper and a pen.

'It's like she's been expecting it or something, wha' see how these white girls getting brave, like their article,' he thought, as he stuffed her hastily scribbled note in his pocket, smiled again, like a clown and disappeared out of the shop, zig zaging through the crowds and down into the tube tunnel of Oxford circus.

'Smiling,' Michael thought, 'I'll smile at a dog, if it means me getting a new camel haired coat, doesn't mean I'll sleep with her though,' and he taw up the girl's number, 'I'm black to the bone, 100% black, undiluted black, not brown tomorrow, yellow the next and white in a weeks' time. No I'm black alright, too black to be messing with dat,' and he grinned, 'far too black.'

Now he stood in his new jacket, a cigarette in his mouth, looking at the tube ticket prices on the wall. 'I'm not paying that,' he thought and he looked around for the ticket collector. A dowdy looking, humongous man, who seemed to fill up the ticket booth, and be half asleep at the same time, did not notice Michael as he bounced past him, or Flex as he followed, his silver saddle glinting on the glass of the booth, even though it was grey with filth. The guard just gripped his mug, with fat chubby grey hands, his double chin wobbling. His blue cap sliding off his greasy pale forehead.

Michael looked back, 'a brother this smart doesn't get caught, wha' your joking, I'm just a dan. I knew it.' His timberland boots did not seem to touch the ground, he was that high. Higher than the weed that he smoked five hours a day. The collector was still sitting as if his flabby buttocks had been glued to the seat. His double chin wobbling like a suckling pig.

Meanwhile outside the Ritzy in Brixton Tayo looked at his watch, like an army commander waiting for the order to go over the top. He tapped his boots nervously on the pavement. Looked at his watch again and then kissed his teeth.

Appia watched him. 'He needs to relax,' she thought, 'getting up tight when there's no need. He knows what they're like.'

'Five past eight, they know the film starts at eight ten, they know,' Tayo thought, twisting his funky dreads, 'Five past eight, you would have thought for once in their lives, they could be on time, instead of playing the game, black man's time and all that, like that's the really cool thing to do. How does that work. How is that. Look at this we're catching hell, we're supposed to be organising something here and they still come drifting in late, how is that, I'm sick of this.' He looked around, 'everybody else could make it on time.'

Susan was standing holding a clip board in her best Dashiki, with a pen in her hand, scribbling frantically the names of everyone present and totalling the money. She walked towards Tayo and asked with a concerned expression, "we're still ten pounds short, do you know that," she frowned, "you would have thought just this once they could have turned up on time. Just this once." She saw the concentration on Tayo's face as if he was waiting for a report from the enemy trenches.

"I know sister, it's just too bad look, I know what your going to say," he studied the firmness of her face, the cool resolution, mixed with a hint of regret. 'Regret,' Tayo thought, 'regret for what.' He looked at the thick blackness of her locks, the strength of her hands, the fixed focus of her stare, he looked to see if he could see further, if he could penetrate into her subconscious, 'what is she hiding,' he thought and then sighed, 'I can go no further. There is a brick wall, a hard forbidden place, secrets, yes and perhaps lies.'

"How's Simone," Tayo asked, resorting to mundane conversation, "you didn't bring her with you, why's that?"

"I think she's a bit young," Susan replied, still looking nervously around for the latecomers, "but thanks for asking about her welfare. You know she thinks a lot about you, she really does."

"Well," Tayo said, hurriedly trying to pass on to another subject.

"No she does, really. Asks for you all the time. I think a lot about you too," she continued, without hesitating.

Tayo felt the sudden rush of embarrassment starting in his face and working to the rest of his body in unequal measure. Appia looked at her watch, pretending not to here the conversation, but hearing every word and smiling knowingly, not even with a hint of jealousy, 'more of I told you so.'

"That's nice," Tayo said, trying to change the subject, "oh...well those brothers are really late." And he looked at his watch again.

"I don't know why your getting all shy," Susan replied, "it's not like I jumped on you or something, I know you've probably got about three women or something, (half looking at Appia) I'm just letting you know that's all. Okay, you know that good brothers are hard to come by."

"Okay," Tayo replied, "well, we uuummh better check on the others," glancing at Kwame and attempting to deflect what had become Appia's concerned expression.

"Sorry, aahh," Tayo said,

"I'd better go" and he wandered towards Kwame.

'So the brother's not that cool after all,' Susan thought, as she sucked her pen, 'it's not like I jumped on him or something.'

Kwame was dusting his glasses and leaning up against the wall like a trainspotter waiting for the seven o'clock from Liverpool at Victoria Station. He squinted as he saw Tayo approach, his nimble fingers rapidly dusting the thick lenses.

"Is that you Tayo," he asked, inquisitively like a hamster, as he saw his shadow. He peered up.

"Yeah it's me, why don't you put your glasses on, then you could see," Tayo said.

"Got to keep them clean, look at this, there' so much dirt in the atmosphere (his Asante accent becoming pronounced on the last word). Do you know how many molecules of dirt lodge inside your lungs just by walking down the street?"

"No," Tayo said, "your the scientist not me."

"Well anyway it has been said to be the root cause of many infectious diseases, and the reduction of the immune system. There's a brother in Uganda his name is Professor Ssali, did a whole lot of research on the immune system and the curing of infectious diseases. Now that's a subject you should bring up at the next meeting, instead of all those other things, you know about mixed relationships and that," he adjusted his waistcoat and put his glasses on. "You just can't change those people's opinion, like that, we have some fruitless discussions, people just talking violence, why are they talking violence." Tayo shrugged his shoulders.

"Violence is the last thing we need to do," Kwame continued, we need to get educated and make a whole lot of money. We should be talking about brilliant men like Professor Ssali not those hot heads like Malcom X and all that."

"I don't agree," Tayo said, looking at Kwame in his grey silk waistcoat, "I think we need to talk about all our people, who want to, or have done something for our people, it's not either or, I think it's and, do you know what I mean."

"Well," Kwame said, ignoring the comment and looking at Tayo's funki dreds, "I think the first thing is, we need to start dressing properly, you know **nicely**, sharp suit, ties and that, there's no reason why we should be all scruffy." He looked, at Tayo's, black boots and the leather pouch fastened to his chest like a Mexican bandit, "as a President you should set an example."

"I think your right, I should set an example," Tayo replied, "but I don't think that's the kind of example I should set. But..."

"Any way," Kwame interrupted, "what are we waiting for, is it those hoodlum friends of yours again, their going to get the society in to so much trouble one day, mark my words, seriously."

"Well," Tayo said, "I hear what you're sayin." And he smiled to himself at Kwame's confidence. He remembered the first time he had seen him, his little voice squeaking like a mouse.

"Well anyway .." Kwame continued, adjusting his glasses, "it's just like that, I guess you feel obligated or something."

"Well I wouldn't say that," Tayo said, adjusting his pouch and noticing Jennifer, Melanie, and Michelle all about to cross to the other side of the street. "Listen brother we'll have to continue this conversation another time okay." Kwame shrugged his shoulders and went back to studying the program.

Tayo bounced over to the moving trio to remind them about the time, Jennifer wearing a pink skirt so tight it looked like she had painted it on, Melanie in an all in one black cat suit, with a waist length jacket just covering the vital areas, 'don't they feel naked or something,' Tayo thought, as they wobbled across the road. "Don't get lost now," Tayo hollered, but they seemed to ignore him and kept walking, he gave up trying to catch them and stopped, he could feel his socks poking through the whole in his boots. 'I need to earn some money,' he thought, 'not waste my time trying to convert the unconvertable.'

He looked at his watch agitated, "at the rate we're going we ain't going to get in there at all," he said himself, turning his back. He started making his way back to the cinema, not really caring whether they had heard him or not. He felt a squeeze, a sensation like someone grabbing his backside.

He turned around to see Melanie standing behind him, "sorry," she said, smiling like a cheeky school girl, "I couldn't resist it, I saw you turn round, your little cute bottom and thought wah' let me just rush back here and give it a good squeeze."

Michelle and Jennifer were on the other side of the road giggling and watching like school children.

"I don't know," Tayo said, feeling more than a little violated, "why you keep doing things like that. You're going out with Ade now aren't you."

"So," Melanie said. "He's not you."

"I really don't know," Tayo said, trying not to look into her beautiful opal shaped eyes and those ample red lips. "What's wrong with you, first it was because your man wasn't down with the program, now what's the reason. He's only just over there, see him," pointing to the edge of the cinema, where Ade was sitting by a huge red brick wall, listening to music with Funki Mikee doing some toasting or something, swinging his hips and spinning around, in his blue flared jeans like a kite on acid. Tyrone just tapping his feet to the beat and posing in a silk shirt and Pepi Jeans like he was on the streets of South Central L.A.

"Look he's just over there," Tayo said.

"So," Melanie said, "he's not you, that's all that counts. I hear your going out with Appia now."

"My news travels fast," Tayo said, looking away from her, as she stuck her chest out and pouted.

"So why can't' you look at me Tayo Akinjo, why can't you look at me, what are you afraid of. Afraid of not being so righteous, afraid of wanting to have sex with me, or **every sista** (she over emphasised deliberately) in this college. You know your not so righteous. I know you want me. You do. You like my face, my body and you want it. You like the way I move, I see you staring at me, examining what I've got and I've got a lot," she was posing now, "I'm nice. You want to sex me but your sacred, your scared."

"I'm not scared," Tayo answered, "but your in a relationship and so am I, as you so rightly pointed out and that's the end of that," and he turned to walk away.

"Well that's not the end of that," Melanie hollered after him, "mark my words, you can't turn your back on your emotions like that."

But Tayo was not listening he was trying to block out the memory of her face, her body, the smell of her perfume, 'Poison,' it was still in his nostrils, though he rubbed them, it just would not go away, 'why wont it go,' he thought, as he walked back towards the Cinema.

'You know Appia was right,' Tayo thought, 'she was damn right about her. I mean Melanie, perhaps about me to, well, well, I've got to get my head straight.' Tayo bit his lip forcing himself to think of something else, to block Melanie out, 'these brothers better come soon, there's thirty five people waiting, I can't keep them waiting, but through it all, that Melanie, she's...., I've got to stop thinking about it, I refuse to think about it, or her, even if I wanted to I wont' and he bit his lip.

Peter stood nervously looking in through the glass of the cinema at the moving crowd of students from the society who were now lining up. He stood in his over sized jeans and irregular afro, uncomfortable in his Dr Martin flat soled black shoes.

He finally saw the distraction he needed from Melanie and wandered towards him.

"Are they going in then," Tayo asked, managing to block her out of his mind.

"Yeah they've had last shout, or something," Peter said, faintly, like a door-mouse, as Kwame disappeared into the cinema entrance, not even turning to look back at Tayo.

"Are you okay," Tayo asked, looking into Peter's murky lenses.

"Yeah.. yeah," he said vaguely.

"You always seem so worried. Like your carrying the world on your shoulder or something, your names not Atlas or something?" Tayo asked.

"No I'm Hades," Peter said, nervously smiling.

"Hades," Tayo said, "keeper of the dead, you mean like the Egyptian Anubis. Why choose him?" He looked at the crowds disappearing into the seating hall. "Your always looking deep into things," Tayo continued, "from day one you saw them BNP boys beat that Indian guy almost to death."

Peter nodded, "you see Hades sees the underworld," he said.

"Well still," Tayo replied, looking at him from the corner of his eye, "all most of us were thinking about was our own future, degree and all that, all the while death is so close and we don't even know it."

"True, see what I mean about the underworld, walking with the ancestors," Peter replied.

"Yeah well, if you want to see this film I think you should get in there now," Tayo said, noticing the declining line of students, the empty space that had appeared around the ticket booth and Susan like a good School teacher keeping up the rear.

"Yeah I think your right," Peter said, "you'll be alright," turning back to him.

"Yeah man go and enjoy it, I'm waiting for the others they've gone into that shop down there or something. Yeah, yeah I'm cool (seeing him hesitate) go on enjoy yourself."

"Oh yeah there is just one thing, one thing," Peter said, turning back, his little frame only half way through the door.

"What's that ?" Tayo asked, almost irritated.

"You know that thing I mentioned," Peter said, looking at the line of agitation that had appeared on Tayo's face. Tayo looked at him puzzled.

"You know Tayo, the Student Union, you know remember, now do you," Peter said leaning against the door frame.

"Oh yeah, that thing" Tayo said, looking around for Michael and the others.

"Look at my boots," Tayo said, pulling up his trousers to reveal the worn out leather with holes and the polish worked in. "Look at my face," Tayo added, rubbing his bald head and twisting his baby locks with his thumb and forefinger. "Look I'm a quarrelsome, loud mouthed, youth, do I look like the kind of person who is respectable enough to become a President of an institution, do I. There's never been a black President and I don't see why I should break the tradition," Tayo said, watching the expression of dejection slowly emerge on Peter's face. "Anyway you're really going to miss this film, we'll talk about it some other time, really we will alright," Tayo continued.

"Okay," Peter said, a little heartened, "we will have to, there's nobody else" and he shuffled through the door allowing Susan to direct him into the seating hall.

'I've never seen a brother looking more like an accident about to happen,' Tayo thought, 'but still he's got some insight, even if he's off on his own trip, but Student Union, what, he must be crazy.'

Tayo tapped his foot to relieve the agitation welling up inside him. 'Appia is some where inside there, I could be inside there, with her, instead of outside here like a fool, trying to chaperone these delinquent children. What responsibility. Melanie was right too, I am tired, sick and tried of being righteous, all these sisters seem to have got me figured out, but have I figured them out...... No,' he thought.

Tayo looked out at the streets of Brixton, a drunk tramp here and there, scattered like so many leaves, with their stench wafting occasionally as far as his nose with the change of wind. A tree out of place, it's bark black with filth, leaves dropping dead on the cracked pavement, soiled here and there with dog (or human) excrement. The grey concrete jungle rising into the night sky silhouetted against the horizon. The blur of the concrete pavements, darkened by the towers of cement as they absorbed the light and spat darkness out. In obscurity, shadows lengthening, waxing and waning, the red brick work of the cinema oblique, as the sun spilled its guts across the sky like a sacrificial lamb brought to the altar for slaughter.

Tayo looked out across the city streets and kicked the pavement again, with his Magnum boots. Distracted for a while by the blur of the lights of vehicles, as they sped through the city. At last arm in arm he saw them, their shadows lengthening longer than persons, at first in the distance, the bouncing frame of the brothers hindered a little by the women they had arm in arm. Michael's familiar smile visible from a thousand meters. There they came. Jennifer and Michelle on either end with Melaine in the centre flanked by the two bouncing brothers, like they had just caught three ripe fish.

"Look at the gal we found, **righteous**, hiding they were in that shop down there, goin on like wha,' " Flex said, grinning like a mad man.

"Two for me and one for him," Michael said.

"No.." Melanie, interrupted, "have some respeck," and faked a punch into Michael's stomach. He pretended to double in pain.

"Oh'h' see how she loves it rough," he said. Tayo just stared. "Any way are you lot coming in, or what," Tayo said calmly, like he had not seen any of the behaviour.

As if stunned by the lack of attention, no lectures, no chastisements, they trooped in, heads hung a little lower than they had been before, like naughty children outside the headmaster's office after he had given them a sound hard thrashing with his best whip. Even Melanie's effervescent bubbliness was remarkably flat, almost dulled. Tayo smiled as they went past him. 'Well there's nothing left to deal with, everyone's in there now, I probably missed half the film any way,' he thought, as he pushed the door open, not like a youth, but weary like an old man.

He walked towards the hall and there Appia stood, calmly waiting. "I was worried, couldn't sit in there without you, trying to enjoy the film, I couldn't. Are you sure, your okay?"

"I'm sure now," Tayo said, taking her hand in his, "I'm sure now," as they walked into the cinema to shouts from thirty African students throwing popcorn at each other, cussing and otherwise behaving as if the world was their own. 'Had nobody told them this is England,' Tayo thought, as they walked in, 'what will they say,' and he sat down in the midst of the crowd still holding Appia's hand.

Leopards in the temple

"Last night was kris," Michael said, stretching out his legs on the chair. "Boy I never had that before you know, so many Africans, at a cinema, it's just the lick."

"The best one," Flex said, leaning his head on his hands as if he had a hangover, "the best was when that bluefoot with a sister got up, you know."

"Yeah, yeah," Michael said. "You remember righteous."

"Yeah I remember that," Tayo said.

"It was just that point, you know when the old papa was give'n it the big un, remember," Flex continued. Tayo nodded. "What was that, you know about white gal being the symbol, ya no like she's a queen or something, being denied and wanting her more cause it was like forbidden fruit. It was just kris."

"Yeah," Michael said, stretching himself out even further if that was possible, "that was just wicked, and remember the whole crowd, all of us getting up still and most of the Africans in the place, giving a round of applause, standing up you know and giving a round of applause like a standing ovation."

"I've never seen that before, it's true," Tayo said smiling, "I never even heard of that before."

"It was then that the bluefoot got all vexed," Flex said. They started laughing.

"Yeah remember and he stood up with that foolish black woman, I guess she was his item or something. He stood up ......" Tayo was giggling and, "he goes... What did he say? Some foolishness, what was it."

"He goes ... " Michael was trying to stop himself from crying with tears, "and he goes, he's standing up you know and the cinema packed with us and he's givin' it the big un, we've all sat down now and he's standing up, and he goes, 'I really appreciate."

'Yeah," Flex said, "that's it, really appreciate it."

"Yeah," Michael added, "I would really appreciate it; if those ill mannered louts at the back would be quiet."

They all laughed incessantly. "Ill mannered louts, you know," Tayo said, "like we're some dirt beneath his shoes. What, ill mannered louts, you know. He might just have called us nigger or something."

"You know, he had a black women still," Michael said, "and he's goin' on so dark," Michael said.

"You mean so light," Tayo interjected.

"Yeah true," Michael said, "he's goin on so light, like he's the Don, like he's Don Corleone or something."

"And then," Tayo said, "you just saw all this popcorn boxes, bottles, coke cans, bits of food and everything just coming his way, boy he got hammered."

"He looked like a Christmas tree without the lights," Flex said, they all broke out into uncontrollable laughter like delinquent children. Michael almost falling off his chair, Tayo slapping the table with his hand, to relieve the pressure the laughing had caused.

Flex managed to mumble out of his giggling mouth, "and his black thing looked like the fairy on top." This time Michael fell off his chair and lay on the floor rolling in agony, all he could mutter was, "they got hammered,..... really hammered." .

"And did you see them leave," Tayo said, standing up and miming, his head bowed and walking on tip toe. "Just humbled," Tayo added, and they fell about again, rolling on the floor, slapping the table and screaming in joy like lunatics from the asylum.

It was at least fifteen minutes before any of them were able to establish any order or reason over their senses. Fifteen minutes of continuous and uninterrupted giggling.

"Seriously though," Michael said, trying to change the subject, "I had a dream."

"No don't start again," Tayo said, "I think I'm going to die if I laugh any more, your killing me."

"No seriously," Michael said, "I had a dream." Flex looked at him like he was waiting for the punchline, but it did not come. "No the dream was bad, a hard dream, you know what they call a waking vision."

"So your a saint now," Tayo smiling.

"No I feel like you," Michael replied.

"The next thing," Flex said, "you'll be speaking in tongues and foaming at the mouth."

Tayo smiled, "no go on tell us then if you want, about your dream."

"Nah forget it, it's a tangent," Michael said.

"Why did you bother to start something you weren't going to finish," Tayo said, sitting up and adjusting his pouch, around his middle, "what's that about, finish it now."

"Come now," Flex said, "you've got us all on the move, scene, want to know if you tell stories like you tell jokes."

"Alright," Michael replied, brushing his shirt down and collecting his thoughts, "its really strange, I mean really strange. I don't even know if I can talk about it still, it's like odd."

"Come on the man," Flex becoming agitated. Tayo just looked at him expectant.

"Well," Michael said, "it started like this, I don't know, it's odd, but it goes like this, any way. There was like this temple, a huge white thing, made of marble or something, like one of those Roman coliseums. You know the ones with the marble towers. But this temple was huge, like fat and wide, you couldn't see where it began or ended. Now in this temple were tapestries like the ones you might find in a castle or something. Those huge ones that stretch up to the ceiling and back down again. Then the most striking thing, there was an altar, a huge gold altar and on the altar, is a painting, a painting of a man, I can't make out his face, but his face was white, definitely white, with blue eyes, but I can't quite make him out. Like I'm seeing his face though a cloudy mirror so it's distorted. Distorted and disfigured, I can't make out the features. It's kind of scary still."

Tayo and Flex listened intently, the latter even forgetting to brush the single brown lock that had flopped down over his face. "So there," Michael continued, "into this temple walks a leopard. Just by itself, like the temple is part of his territory. This thing just walks straight in you know and then like two others follow it. So there's like three of them prowling, you know how those cats walk. You can see all it's sinews and that, the muscles on the back of it's leg, and there, agile to, like fit and slim. They've all got this bad ass look on their faces like Wha' they're go' do something, radicks. They're all strutting into this temple, you know looking around it and I can see the tapestries now, embroidered ya' know in red, white and blue, with gold leaf. Tapestries ya' know with pictures of battles and kings and all that, but these cats have got this bad ass faces, I'll never forget there faces, like nothing's going to phase them. And they're like so strong and what's that word 'lithe'. That's the word Tayo isn't it."

"Yeah I think so," Tayo said, "yeah, lithe."

"Yeah these cats are lithe, and they givin' it. And then like the one that walked in their first cause he's got the most arrogant face of all, this one you know he's really calm one minute and then he like gets vexed. And you know like this picture, the one I said is like obscured, he leaps towards it, smashes it, glass flies everywhere and he bounces back like nothing happened and then all hell breaks loose. These cats go buck wild, mad, start ripping the tapestries down and everythink, tearing it and ripping it with teeth, ripping the fabric with their claws. There's like bits of material everywhere, and these cats are just leaping you know, really high, like they're on acid or something. Then do you know what, they start tearing into the walls themselves, ripping out the stone, biting the marble with their jaws and tearing out huge lumps. I've never scene anythink' like it."

"You know what. When they've trashed the place when there's nothing left, when everythink' is mashed you know what. These cats start roaring. Now Leopards don't roar do they. But these ones start roaring. I've never heard anything like it, as if they were huge great lions or somethink,' roaring and you know what, this whole temple starts crumbling, I mean from the foundation, the thing starts falling to pieces, cracks start appearing and the thing starts rocking from side to side and these cats just keep roaring. Then I wake up and you know the sheets are soaked in sweat and I feel like I've just ran a mile or something. And I don't sweat at all." He leaned back on his chair exhausted and stared at Tayo and Flex almost bewildered. Tayo looked back firmly into his eyes.

"But the strange thing is," Tayo said, "I understand your dream, and you know what it means too don't you."

"I'm trying not to, it's a tangent," Michael replied.

"It's not a tangent," Tayo asserted, "those leopards are us, and that temple....that's this place and white supremacy, in fact everything that these lot stand for, and you know what we have to do don't you, it's the same as those cats. You know it, you've been told now, you've been told, now heed the warning" and he stared at him.

"What warning is that," Michael asked, sarcastically, "prophet, teach."

"I don't need to teach," Tayo replied, adjusting his pouch and sitting up, "but I will say this though, that this country is dread and it's going to get dreader."

"I'm down with that," Flex said, "that's why me' gone."

"Gone," Tayo said, "gone where, there's no where to go still, there is no paradise on earth, no paradise to be found, only one to be made." Flex looked and played with his locks. "Look at this, still," Tayo added, "you know how long black people been in this country. Do you know how long?"

"Know tell us righteous," Flex asked, coldly.

"Since time, Igantius Sancho, Francis Barber, Oladah Equinano, Ira Aldridge, all black men living here in England in the eighteenth century. If you go back further, there are more still, more black people still, and further back you go, you find more and more. It's like this country has got so many secrets. But they tell you like, that Windrush was where it started. They tell you that Windrush was how it started. They tell you that because they don't want to tell you, they don't want you to know what happened to them. They don't want you to know how they almost wiped you out. Just how we are wiping are self out right now. They don't want you to know what they did to them and what we did to ourselves."

"Alright righteous," Flex said, "all very interesting, but what has dat, all of dat go to do with me."

"Nah," Michael muttered thoughtfully, "I see (sitting up and playing with his top button) where he's going still, but he's taking a long time reaching. You mean Sierra Leone, Liberia and the Creoles of West Africa, don't you."

"That's what I mean. I mean exactly," Tayo added, "the black people enough of them who were here got shipped back to Africa, to Sierra Leone, or Liberia. During Oladah Equaino's time, gave them money and everything and told them they could go. Most of them ended up dying, and do you the nasty thing about that story."

"I know what you're going to say still," Michael said, interrupting, "about the prostitutes."

"The prostitutes," Flex said, becoming genuinely interested, "wah prostitutes!"

"Well tell him," Michael replied, looking at Tayo. But Tayo shook his head and folded his arms.

"Nah I'm not saying a word," Tayo said, "cause he'll say I'm makin it up, to win the argument."

"True," Flex replied, "I would say it."

"Alright then," Michael said, "since everyone is playing games I'll say. They rounded up all the prostitutes."

"Who's they?" Flex asked.

"They," Michael replied, "is the Government."

"No weight the man," Flex said, screwing up his brown face in confusion, "you just said that all these 'braes' (brothers) were in this country and you mean they got all them bluefoot prostitutes to walk with them, nah, wah, that's dread."

"You know what, still something," Michael said, leaning back on his plastic chair, "they don't tell you that the biggest killer of them apart from starvation and all that was syphilis. The same syphilis that these white girls were carrying who were put on the ship with them."

"Alright," Flex said, "that was an interesting story still, me fel glad you told me. But what has that got to do with Michael's dream, or me waxing out of this hell hole as quickly as me can reach."

"Well it's like this," Tayo replied, "we have to fight in this country, because every time we allow ourselves to get mixed, cheated, or killed out of this country, it gives these lot here the license to go and butcher more of our people. Look carefully at history. You see every time they kick the blacks here and finish them, they come looking for some more. Like we've got to get some more to kick, I mean they must say to themselves that was so easy, let's get some more, I need some fun," he smiled- "but we are princes, yes black princes without kingdoms, Ronin - Samurai warriors without swords. That's what we are - its are duty to fight against the evils of this world, like some B movie western, you know, the good sheriff in the bad town."

Flex brushed a brown lock from his face. Michael rubbed his chin thinking.

"So the dream, is telling us," Tayo said, enthusiastically, "we've got to fight for what's right. We've got to fight, right now, and right here, cause right here is where we are and that's the truth of it. So what do you think now rude boy."

"Well," Flex said, triumphantly, "but niggers have got to die first."

"True," Michael added knowingly.

Tayo shock his head, kissed his teeth and thought, 'have they not listened to a damn thing I just said, what does it take, what does it take, no really what does it take, I might as well be talking to myself, I'd get a better, quicker and more intelligent response. What does it take, to make a black man listen.'

"What's the matter, with you," Michael asked (almost through his teeth) looking at Tayo's screwed up face.

"Nothing," Tayo replied, "I'm trying to die, so that then, you'll listen" and he adjusted his pouch, and gritted his teeth like a vexed leopard.

Mad Mike Mclean

A huge heavy weight, beer barrel of a man waddled down Elephant and Castle towards the tube station. His skin deathly pale and hanging around his frame like an old sack. Pants sticking to him from the faeces he had discharged an hour earlier, but had been too lazy to wipe from his backside. Sweat dripping from his humongous body, as if he was a suspect being interrogated in Tottenham police station, his grey T-shirt sticking to his sagging hide like a swimmer.

Mad Mike McLean, of Mad Mike's famous car lot sat in the back of his Silver Shadow: a huge Rolls Royce with chrome bumpers, tinted windscreen, paint polished as shiny as a mirror. His car rumbled past, like a jet aeroplane, discharging filth through its exhaust on to the enormous man as he dawdled down the street.

"Ca....ow that's a f..at, filthy, Chubby, Checker," Mike rumbled (just like his car) looking out of his window at the sweating man. Mike's huge chin wobbled, "look at the belt buckle on that geezer, what a Robbie Tusin belch boy, should ne'er have been born, cooar bloody hell. Don't see none of that in the Islands."

"The Islands," Alf said, puzzled in a cockney accent, as he sat uncomfortably on the front seat - fiddling with the gold chain he had just stolen, at last putting it in his pocket.

"Ye...ah," Mike said, his huge coarse face emotionless, "just came back from Jam...aica." Mike had a way of speaking without really opening his mouth. His voice groaned like an ogre at the bottom of a cave.

"Jamaica," Steve said, now also puzzled, he was sitting next to Mike.

"Yeah, bloody Jam...aica," Mike replied, "bloody al...right. It was al..right, Jam..aica. The local tots are al...right. They're al...right you know. Paid 15 knicker for one. Just fifteen, hardly legal. Bit worried mind you, she had a little'in, a little tot of a thing it was, but kept makin' so much bloody noise. Had to put it outside, when we're doing the business. She's working for me now. But Jam...aica is al....right, got the local boys on the payroll. You know them **yardies**, bloody good at their jobs," Mike folded and unfolded his huge gnarled white hands like a Germanic chief.

"People are laid back," Mike continued, "as long as you pay the lingua, their kushtie mate." He rubbed his chin jutting out like a mountain face, with short broken teeth in a slash of a mouth. Clean shaven, almost to the bone, the skin tough and tight, the eyes inset, the hair balding, the rest in short back and sides from Luigi's barbers shop in Romford. A £1,000 pound designer pin-strip suit, made to measure (of course), but still bursting around his beer barrel chest and enormous arms. 'At six foot four,' he could be heard to say, 'at six foot four, weighing nineteen stone, I don't have to apologise to anyone, for anythink.'

"My mate though," Mike added, "he's in Kenya. Kenya ya no. Bloody Africa. Got a beach house, got them out there bloody working for him like slaves. Personal friend of the local chief, could have something to do with the fact he gives him 10,000 a year. It's cheap, cause once you've paid, that's it, the police out there don't bother you, no one says or does anythink. I'm telling you to get out there, especially you Steve, with your talents in the women business. You Alf can give up all your low life pals like black Charlie and that stupid stall of yours. Can't go wrong. Six months here, six months there, you'll have your nest feathered for life."

"Yeah I might just do that," Steve replied, with Alf nodding. Mike adjusted his white and blue tie around his huge round head, there was no neck at all - just a head resting on two great shoulders like a great ape.

"Here did you here," Alf said, changing the subject and finally managing to tuck the chain into the bottom part of his pocket, "what happened to Jack and Toni, got a good lickin', just around here somewhere," he looked out of the window at the concrete infested streets.

"Yeah I heard," Mike said, "bloody liberty still. Went to visit Dave my mate, he needed seventeen stitches in his head he did. If I ever catch those ge...ezers, they'll wish they'd never been born, I can tell ya. But I've told Jack, what's that name he goes under, Johnny the vic, in it, standing for victorious or something, well he wasn't victorious four months ago was he," he chuckled to himself. "Needs a ventilator just to breath. Well - I've told him loads of times to give up all that busi....ness he's into and come and make some **money** with me. He's got the aptitude for it. Still the way we've got these streets work...ing for us, all that kind of unruly behaviour will be history." Mike's chops and silver chain shone brightly under the evening glare, as he clenched and unclenched his bulbous fists.

"Oh take the next turn left and step on it," Mike murmured - then raising his voice to Joe the driver, "you're not in your bloody kebab shop now."

Joe, of Greasy Joe's café gave a side ways glance, as if he was going to protest, but he finally swung the wheel to the right. 'I know,' he thought, 'I shouldn't have signed that deal without reading the small print about being his chauffeur at weekends, sometime I goin' to make a deal with the Turkish Mafia and kick his cockney arse to the curb. I didn't come to this country to be anybody's slave.'

"You two," Mike said, looking at Alf and then Steve, and switching his manner completely, "get out he..re and start making me some money, or you're both be back in sing sing, do you he....ar. Ye...ah and if you see your mate. What's he called, that loud mouth git whose doing some business for me in Peckham, what's his name....... Busta, in it, that's it."

"He's not my mate," Steve said, "it's a working relationship". 'I don't have any black mates,' Steve thought, 'it's just business,' he adjusted his white T-shirt and tried not to look ruffled, brushing his blonde hair away from his face and smiling like the pimp (he was).

People may have wondered how a man like Steve who had such racist tendencies could do business on Peckham front line. Steve laughed under his breath as he dealt death to little black children. He laughed at Busta, as he boasted and showed off his silver chain. The silver chain which he knew very well 'Black Charlie' had stolen a week before. In fact Steve spent most of his day just laughing. As for respect, respect Busta. He respected his pet Bulldog, more than he respected Busta.

"Anyway," Mike replied, "that bloke if you see him, when you're doing, whatever you're doing with the natives," he grinned, "tell him, he owes me a grand for that shooter I gave him last week and I want paying.. now."

"Alright," Steve replied, twitching a little, he had a habit of doing that when Mike spoke to him. 'Perhaps,' Steve thought, 'it's Mike's eight inch fists and the Middle weight boxing championship belts that decorate his walls, which make me uneasy. Or perhaps, it's the night clubs in London, Birmingham, Manchester and the Caribbean that he owns.'

'It was probably the boxing gyms,' Steve thought, 'that he finances though his underworld connections and associates in the

Metropolitan police. I know I'm not meant to know this, but I know he's got the Chief Inspector of police in his pocket. Even though according to my reckoning he's killed, or had killed at least sixty people over the last ten years, in London alone. Not been to jail once. Not once you know.'

'Or perhaps,' Steve contemplated,' because he's such a mad son of a bitch. Anyway, I'd rather be working for him, than running away from him.'

Mike adjusted his designer tie with his gnarled fists and looked at Alf fidgeting in his pockets for the chain that he had now misplaced. 'It's lucky,' Mike thought, staring at their dirty T-shirts and unwashed hands, 'I don't rely on this lot for my income, they're so clumsy. With the five pubs that I own, the real estate companies, housing associations, six houses, including one in the south of France, Ibiza and Jam...aica. Six amusement arcades in Bournemouth, Brighton, Clapton on Sea, the Seychelles, Montego bay and Antigua. Within five years, I'll be totally... legitimate. I'll move in with the big boys - scum like this won't be sitting in my car. Any way nothink better than having friends in high places, Reginald in the police, Harris Q.C. in the law, that's who should be in my car, not these scum' and he stared at Steve, who did not dare look back.

So Reginald and Mad Mike drank at the same club, had the same taste in women, on occasion had shared the same one at the same time. Where else was Reginald a chief Inspector of Police going to get a different women every night he wanted one. Especially to perform sado-masochism on his pale, white, huge, sweating diseased body.

Mike remembered only last night at the (member's only) club the conversation, "After all," Reginald blubbered, staring down his nose at Mike pompously, as he sat drinking a tipple at the club, "I've bloody earned it haven't I, it's my little bloody tipple, my quirk, but I've bloody earned it, haven't I." And Reginald thought, as he poured himself another glass of claret, 'morals, that's for the bobby on the street - or on a job, what's the point of having a position if you can't abuse it.'

Hate lessons

Mr. Thomas sat in **his** favourite chair in **his** office, rocking backwards and forwards and staring at Tayo.

"When I look at you, I think of how great your ancestors must have been. I mean your so noble looking," Mr. Thomas said, adjusting his waist coat. "There is really nobility in you. I mean this college, it's full of some of the dregs of society, but you're different. I wish I had some of what you have, look at me, an old cynical, intellectual."

"I tell you how," Tayo scowled, "have your baby ripped from his mother's womb and stomped to death in the front of your face. Be abused, ridiculed, for 5,000 years and spend 500 years under the yoke of tyranny by Europeans: shackled, castrated, raped, raped, raped again, so you don't even know who your own mother is. Stolen from you, your history, your name, your achievements. Scattered to the four winds of the earth, to islands where the islanders don't even want you. Starvation and ridicule in your own land. Brought back to the imperial pit that once enslaved you. Back to build after their war. Back to build it to the stage it once was and there where you thought to hide, to be squashed, trapped, mashed, your face a face of dishonour, your place a place of dishonour. The lowest of the low, the filth of filth, the slime rotting in the heart of a decaying carcass. So filthy that a fly wouldn't even lay his maggots in you..... When you can go through all this and still shine, shine like a candle in the cold dark winter's night, then you can be me. Until then, you're just fronting" and he adjusted his pouch and stared at Thomas. Tayo hesitated, "the romantic notions," he added, looking at the smug expression on Thomas face, "you have of being me, are not born out by the reality of my existence, I'm not different, I am not different," leaning back in the leather upholstered chair and adjusting his pouch.

"I mean that in a good way," Thomas said, smiling through his thick glasses at the eloquence of Tayo's words. The creases in his forehead ironed out by false affability.

"I think you'll find if you think about it, I'm just the same. We are all what we are, you know a leopard can't change it's spots. You know that don't you," Tayo said, twisting a lock with his thumb and index finger.

"Indeed young man," Thomas said, sitting down behind a huge ebony table so highly polished that it shone like a mirror. Tayo watched him settling back in his chair, the softness of his smart, casual, colours oblique to the clean, smart almost ostentatious appearance of his office. 'His clothes sense has improved anyway,' Tayo thought, 'how different from that first day. He's like another man, a new man. Well, he's learned something any way, I hope not from me," he looked across at him. 'The forced softness of the face, the glasses thick as a windscreen, a barrier to hide what was inside. What was the saying, the eyes are the gateway to the soul,' Tayo thought.

Tayo scanned Thomas' office, he looked at the book collection. It seemed to span the entire length of the opposite wall, from end to end. Coded alphabetically and according to subject like a mini library.

"I see you looking at my books," Thomas said, "do you read much?"

"A little," Tayo replied (lying) and smiling, "you've got a real collection, though." He peered forward at the masses of brown and coloured spines filed neatly against the mahogany case. I see some rare books there still," Tayo said.

Thomas stared at him inquisitively as one would at an endangered animal. "You mean over there," Thomas replied naively.

"Yeah, you got some real good ones," Tayo continued, straining his eyes, "yeah you've got *Macritche, Britons Ancient and Modern, Destruction of Black Civilisation* by *Chancellor Williams, Ancient Egypt light of the World by* ... is that Churchward, yes *Albert Chruchward.* That book is not even in print. *Frederick Douglas narrative of a slave life*, that one's quite common. But this one *Ignatius Sancho*, his diaries isn't it." Thomas raised one eyebrow. "That's rare, and this one here *Othello's' children,'* is so rare, that, that one you've got there, is the only one I've ever seen, I mean I've never seen it before. Is it an original!" he said, excitedly.

"Yes it is, young man," Thomas said, "indeed I was lucky to get it" and he smiled, self satisfied like a snake that had just swallowed a live baby cow and was now sleeping it off. He fiddled with his waist coat.

"I've got something else in here too," Thomas said, like a dirty old man trying to entice a school child. "It's a book, well more like a diary, it's the diary of Marcus Garvey." Tayo looked at him. "You've heard of Marcus Garvey then," Thomas asked. Tayo nodded, matter a fact to avoid further discussion on what he knew, or didn't. "Well," Thomas said, reaching to the side of his table and opening the draw, "this is the last diary he wrote, you know on his death bed, the stuff in its' never been published, in fact this is the only copy."

Tayo looked at him as if he wasn't interested, "really," he replied.

Thomas put the book on the table and smiled, fingering the pages like it was his mistress. His almost feminine fingers caressing the faded brown leather cover, the yellow inner pages, the initials woven on the exterior M.G. "There's really some good things in here (repeating himself)."

'Why should it be that this man should have something so precious, if he thinks it's so important,' Tayo thought, 'why doesn't he publish it, or may be he wants to keep the information just for himself, why tell me, just so he can show off, make out like he knows everything, what.... Anyway, why, what am I doing here? What has he invited me here for, so he can do further study on me, like a vet on an animal.'

"You know how I came across, this," Thomas said, "one of my great aunts, (he chuckled to himself) well she, you'll never going to believe it, she used to be his house wife when he lived in west London. Apparently they had quite a thing going on." He giggled and looked at Tayo for a reaction.

"Well I'm sure," Tayo said, "you didn't invite me here to listen to old wives gossip," and he fiddled with his pouch irritated and adjusted his dashiki.

"True young man," Thomas said, his pale face slightly flushed, "indeed, indeed, not for that, for something else?"

"Well..." Tayo answered, looking at the huge silver mirror on the side of the wall where he could see his own reflection and next to it a huge picture of John F Kennedy standing on a pulpit.

"I'll get straight to the point then," Thomas said, "I hear your running for the Student Union Presidency. I hear you standing this year."

"How do you mean," Tayo answered, genuinely puzzled.

"You are standing aren't you," Thomas asked, concerned.

Tayo frowned and then remembered, 'that's the stuff that Peter had been talking about last week, elections and all that. Hustings, voting's. What... what I don't know, is how this bloke knows so much about it, when he only mentioned it to me a week ago and I certainly haven't told any one what I'm going to do." He shuffled uncomfortably in his seat. 'You can't trust anyone or anything here, besides why should it matter to him who runs, why should he want to endorse me,' he thought. He looked at the picture of Kennedy again and then at the books, 'trying to play the liberal of liberals, is he, well will see.'

"I haven't decided, yet," Tayo said, hiding his thoughts.

"Well if you decide," Thomas said, fingering his old Eaton school tie like it was his penis, "I would like to say that I'll give you as much help as I can."

Tayo frowned and rocked back on his chair, the back legs dug in deep into the underlay of the carpet he sighed, 'there's a bribe in there some where,' he thought, 'if only I could figure out where and how.'

"Thanks for the offer, but..." Tayo said.

"No I mean it," Thomas interrupted, his white shirt gleamed like his perfectly straight, capped white teeth, "I remember you even from the first day. How you came in and took control, you're a natural leader..(he hesitated) you do know that don't you." Tayo raised one eyebrow.

"Well for what it's worth, as I told you before," Thomas added, "well I think I told you, I'm the vice Principal here. Very few things go on here which I don't know about."

"Yes," Tayo said insolently.

"Yes," Thomas continued, "I mean I'm aware of your friends, don't forget Michael that little ruffian's is in my class. Lots of your fire, but not the same eloquence. An interesting young man, though, he's probably going to end up on the wrong side of the law."

Tayo looked at the antique clock its brass second hand incessantly ticking, and the white humidity regulator as the florescent red numbers flashed annoyingly.

'Everything seems regulated, ordered,' Tayo thought, 'like it all has its number and place, but I don't.'

"Thanks for the offer," Tayo said, "I'll bear it in mind, but I don't know what I'm going to do yet. After all it's my second year."

"Don't worry about that," Thomas.

"How do you mean?" Tayo replied and frowned confused.

"I mean it is rare for a President of the Student Union to fail his course," Thomas said and he leaned back on his chair like Al Capone. His glasses, the teeth, the white shirt, the mirror, the ebony table, in fact everything in the whole office seemed to shine all at once and unnaturally. Even his small shrew like face seemed animated.

"Well," Tayo said, and he sighed, feeling the blood suddenly rushing all at once to the centre of his brain as a thousand thoughts entered it.

"No really," Thomas interrupted, "think carefully about what I said."

"Thanks, a lot," Tayo replied hastily, "I'll, be off now, if that's all," and he stood.

"Just a second young man," Thomas replied, "there's something else that I need to say to you." Tayo looked down at Thomas, as he saw the faint line of sweat emerging on his forehead, a slight irritate movement of the hands as he shuffled Marcus Garvey's diaries from one end of his table to the other.

"Sit down," Thomas said, shrilly like a spoilt child. Tayo looked at him. Thomas managed a half smile, "I mean please sit down Mr. Akinjo, do, please...there is something else."

A trail of perspiration broke out on Thomas' bottom lip, his cheeks were red and flushed, "al right," Tayo said, after a moment's pause and sat slowly, watching him from the corner of his eye.

"What I mean to say," Thomas said, staring at him, "is that you need to be careful. Very careful indeed."

"Careful," Tayo replied and smiled, "careful about what?"

"How can I put this," Thomas said, "you've got some good qualities, but you shouldn't waste them." Tayo looked at him blankly. "I mean you should be bringing the students together, not separating them. You could do much good in the union, even help to dispel the rumours, you know about you and you're friends being racists."

"I didn't know there were any rumours," Tayo answered and yawned, his white teeth shining.

"So I'm boring you now Mr. Akinjo," Thomas said.

"Actually you are," Tayo retorted, "cause I know what you're going to say and I know how you're going to say it."

"Really," Thomas replied, intrigued, "well tell me then."

"Well it's like this you're going to give me an offer I can't refuse, stop talking all this black stuff, or you and you're friends are going to get into some trouble. You know scratch every liberal and you find a racist underneath."

"What did you say," Thomas said.

"You heard," Tayo answered.

"I'll have you know," Thomas said, "that I've been campaigning for equality.."

"Don't give me any more of your liberal speeches," Tayo interrupted, "I'll tell you this, don't think that black people are stupid, that the only kind of racist we can recognise is the jackboot, skin head kind. You think that if you read enough Nietsche and Karl Marx that, that you can blot out what you're doing. Some of us know what you're doing. "

Tayo shuffled in his seat, "I watched you as you looked down your nose at us, and passed little sarcastic comments. I watched you - rather be teaching at some prestigious institution like Oxford or Cambridge." Thomas blushed. "You've let down the family have you, well the path to hell is paved with good intentions. You view us, especially me as one of your cultural experiments. You mess about with people's lives and expect us to submit."

"Really," Thomas said, "and am I to be blamed for every bad thing that is happening in your community. For the spread of aids in Africa, drug pushers and prostitution, black on black violence, the fact that your men and women can't form functioning relationships, don't try and blame me, you did all those things to yourself, you have no one to blame but yourselves."

"No," Tayo said, sitting forward in his chair and clenching his fists, "you must have been listening to some of our meetings. I don't have the time or the inclination to convince you of anything. All I'm saying is leave me alone. Let me do my own thing and don't try..."

"Are you trying to threaten me," Thomas replied, slightly amused.

"Take it any way you like," Tayo irritated, "but if you really think that I'm in a position to threaten you." (He paused.) "That's so typical. One black man speaks his mind and people feel threatened. It's like a brother gets beaten up by the police and he gets charged with assault. The victim becomes the criminal" and he adjusted his pouch again.

"Don't you think you're becoming a little paranoid," Thomas interrupted.

"Paranoid," Tayo said, "interesting choice of words, look at this, you invite me in here, basically tell me that big brother is watching me, so I had better be careful, but if I do the things you tell me I'll be alright."

"I didn't say that," Thomas interrupted, (he over emphasised the last word).

"Well any way," Tayo retorted, "and then you say, that I'm paranoid, paranoid indeed."

"Calm down, young man," Thomas said, feeling perspiration break out all over his pasty round face, "or I shall have to ask you to leave."

"No it's okay," Tayo said, "you don't have to ask me, cause I'm leaving any way," and he stood up. "Oh yeah, and since you lecture in law you should be very careful before you start offering gratuitous benefits as rewards for behaviour. There is such a thing as ethics, yeah and something else too, while I remember it, it is not up to you, to decide who or what people should stand for at elections in this college. It is for the students to decide. You may read all those books, but it doesn't make you right, it just makes you... well, better at lying" and he bounced out and slammed the door. The huge silver mirror encrusted with ornate decorations reverberated against the wall.

"Well thank God," Thomas gasped, rubbing his glasses with his favourite handkerchief, "there aren't too many of them sought of firebrands here." Thomas undid the draw and put Marcus Garvey's diary gently in it. 'At least,' Thomas thought, 'most of the students black or white, just want to party and have fun. He's going to be disappointed too if he thinks he's going to turn black students into revolutionaries. He'll get burnt out and give up. I've seen it so many times before. It won't last. Even if it does, he's just a lone voice in the wilderness,..... besides the tide of time is against him. The way his people are integrating, mixing out, a new culture is being created in the ghettos. He says he represents it, but its' not what he thinks it is. It's certainly not that African identity. No way. It won't happen.' Thomas lent back in his French polished chair, 'besides, he's not from the ghetto anyway, I really don't know why he claims he is, it could never produce the kind of mind he has. But still, he.. he's a hot head and an idealist,' Thomas thought, looking at the framed picture of Kennedy,' and you know what happens to them, it's regrettable, but true, I'm afraid' and he smiled.

Appia

Appia lay alone in her comfortable spacious room in her father's four bedroom house in Camberwell. The walls starched white and clean, an ornate Adinkra symbol for Unity framed and placed on the wall like a guardian - it's glass frame smelling of beeswax polish. Appia was sifting through the thoughts of her mind. She sighed a little and adjusted her position to lay on her left side. Her thoughts began to drift from her, though she could not sleep. 'I think I am in love with him,' she thought. 'I've been trying to deny it for as long as the first time that I met him. But I cannot. I love him.' She sighed.

'What kind of love is it,' she thought, opening her eyes to look at the decoration that her wallpaper made on the wall. 'People say love all the time, when what they really mean is lust,' she thought. 'Do I lust after him, I know I care for him, do I lust after him, I can't deny that, that it's there, I would be lying to myself, deceiving myself and him, if I say that, that wasn't there, sometimes when I think of his body, the way he moves, his eyes looking at me, looking into me, feeling every part of me I get lost in it, I feel like I'm losing myself in him, its like I can't see myself, only him. Is that lust, or is that real love.'

'Maybe it's just infatuation, or obsession, am I obsessed by him, you know.....I'm sure I am, so what if I am, better to be obsessed about a brother fighting for the race than some young white pop star. There are worst things that I could be obsessed with. But it's not like I'm a stupid person, I respect him, I respect myself, I'm no fool. But I trust him.'

'How do I trust him,' she thought, laying on her back, 'does he like other women, I'm sure he does, perhaps Susan, Melanie definitely, well who wouldn't, isn't she the image of what most brothers want, not to black, slim, flirtatious and available. Though I don't wish her any harm. How would I feel if I found out that he had been with her, or if instead of organising meetings he was there in her arms tonight, holding her, kissing her. How should I feel. If I was insecure wouldn't my fear drive me to disrespect him, where there was no reason to and create a predicament that didn't exist before. But it's stupid of me to be naïve, to think he's perfect.'

'But I know he's not perfect,' Appia thought, slightly bending her knees and feeling the softness of newly washed sheets. 'He doesn't need to be perfect,' she thought, 'or even nice, just try to be good. I don't need a another father. I have a father, a good one, decent, even though I know he drinks to much, a strong Asante man, raised three daughters didn't he, even after mother died, now that's a real man, I don't need Tayo to be another father, I've got one. Tayo's a man in his own right.'

'I've seen it before,' she contemplated, 'so many times before, so many sisters with a good man, but expecting him to be perfect, so they can convince themselves. Then what, they try to change the men they've got. Why do they do it? To make them into what they feel is a good man. Why? So we can play God. The changes are small, small, small. You know it's like why don't you do you hair **nicely**, or try this on for a change, or wear this shirt instead, you look so handsome in this, we say. We do it, after a year, two years, perhaps three if he's strong, he end's up being completely different. It's little things becoming big things and ends up as **everything**. Then when they've changed him around it's, oh I don't love him anymore, he's not the man I married. Get the hypocrisy of that. Not the man I first met, how do we justify that as women. I don't know.'

'All the while we are destroying the relationship we should be building. They would do better by growing to understand the man they are with, rather than trying to re invent some artificial entity. Worse still, ' she thought, brushing a hair that had come loose from her hair grip, 'when they can't find this superhuman black man, they accuse all black men of being dogs and beasts. Don't get me wrong some are, in fact too many are, but some are not. I think we've got to understand why men do the things they do. Most men are scared. They are scared to be real men. I mean black men are scared of being real men. They knew real black men don't live long. They know it subconsciously, even if they can't articulate it consciously.'

'We are not as sisters,' she thought, 'going to help brothers over-come their fears and be the men they ought to be, by giving them a whole new set of fears and insecurities.' She looked up at the huge ornate bedroom curtains tied at the top with gold braid. She peered though the gap and saw the morning drizzle trickling down the window pain. She looked around her bookshelves stocked with books, Encyclopaedias, Dictionaries, History and politics. A huge book marked the *Life and Times of Kwame Nkrumah* stood out from the rest. A tattered flag of Ghana adorning the adjacent wall, framed, her father had been an Nkrumah man and kept the momento from the day he kicked the British out.' A copy of '*Acts of Faith*,' lay open on the bedside table, before it became fashionable and a glass of Evian water partially consumed, waiting for the ancestor who watched over her to drink the rest.

'Then the worst thing,' she thought, 'when there are some brothers like Tayo, Michael, Flex, even Ade has his days, who aren't afraid, its like all the women want them. They all jump on them at once, its like there's a good black man and I want him. Then when one gets him now, it's like he's all mine, do you hear,' she smiled thinking, 'all mine, like he belongs to them and all of you can't have him, that's what they think.'

'Even,' she contemplated, 'when we do get a strong one, it's like I've got to tame him now. I've got to make him into what I want. So we start all that business, you know, why can't you be more sensitive, more caring, why don't you take me out anymore. What is that all about, nothing but selfishness. It's just selfishness. What are other women getting their men to do, other women force their men to be courageous not cowardly. During the last World War in this country, I've read the newspapers, if you weren't in the armed services you couldn't get a date, you wouldn't get a woman. Because women understood it was a struggle for the survival of the nation and therefore any man who was not doing something for the country was not worthy of respect. Right now are people are engaged in a war for at least 500 hundred years for the survival of our nation, our culture. Any man of our race who is not fighting for our liberation is not worthy of respect, he's not going to get it from me, I don't care how big his car or his bank account is. I don't care..... If more of us thought like this wouldn't we be in a better condition. Wouldn't we...... we shouldn't be keeping our men from the front line, we should be pushing them to it and supporting them the whole way - that's the only way we are going to get out of this condition.'

'Worst still, if that was just the end of it,' Appia contemplated, 'a lot of us out there are even worse. Their top prize is not the brother with the most honour, or the most courage, it's the one with the biggest car, or the biggest bank account. I knew a sister who said she married her husband because he told her on their first date if he won a million he would give it all to her. What kind of foolishness is that,' Appia laughed to herself. 'But you know,' she thought, 'as soon as one's like Jennifer leaves this place that's what they're going to become, or perhaps even worst...... Well perhaps not. Let's hope for the best.'

'But how is that a way to run a relationship,' she reflected, 'money is important, but whatever happened to working together to make something happen. You know the more I think about it, the more I know that this materialism is a white thing been put in our minds, especially us. I know it is, since most brothers aren't earning bank, but sisters want it, eventually the sisters are going to get frustrated and start looking for bank some where else, and we know who owns all the banks,' she thought, and sighed.

'So if I love Tayo, and I'm not going to deny any more that I do. If I do, I'm glad that I found a brother out there who has so many qualities that I can respect. He's even got some that my father hasn't, though I shouldn't be comparing him with my father, I guess it's inevitable. But he has. If he's a little arrogant perhaps he needs to be. But sometimes I wish he would open up and just talk to me. There's some pain in there, there was a girl once..... Aisha, wasn't that her name, he doesn't talk about her much, but she's got part of his heart, I can live with that......... just. But I don't think the pain makes him do the things he does. I think he does those things because he believes he was born to do them, not because he has some space in his soul, I could be wrong. But I don't think so.....uummmmmh.'

'But that other sensation is there, it's just hit me again,' she thought, feeling a warm feeling beginning in her womb and spreading to the rest of her body, her back perspiring and a sweet sensation of ecstasy, though she tried to stop it reaching certain parts of her body, she could not. The sensation was there and getting stronger and warmer. 'I'd better stop thinking about this,' Appia reflected, 'I've got lectures early in the morning and I don't want to be up all night like a love sick child. So Tayo, until tomorrow.'

We've been watching you

William Lynch sat drooled over his seat, he had only had three pints of beer in the student bar, but they had gone straight to his head. He had sang, 'show me the way to go home,' so many times his voice was hoarse, he felt just a little bit sick. The oxygen was leaving his brain, 'perhaps the lack of sleep the night before has got something to do with it,' he thought, as he stretched out over the plastic man made table. 'Reports, reports, anybody would have thought I was a pen pusher, a bloody secretary, not a police officer, just keep an eye they said, just look out they said, I mean you're studying there, so just have a look, it can't hurt can it. How was I supposed to know that there was going to be so much stuff. Every corner there's another one of these fanatics, Muslim, Sikh, or one of those black ones, I surprised any of this lot do any studying, they spend all there time shouting about what whitey has done. Whitey this, whitey that, I failed my course because I spent my whole time partying, it must be a conspiracy from whitey, it's raining to day, oh that's got to be because of whitey. It's real nonsense. If they don't like us so much why don't they piss off out of it and leave the country to proper Englishmen,' he thought and frowned.

William played with the half filled cup of coffee, stabbing at the centre of the hot sticky mixture with his plastic spoon. The paper cup hardly withstanding the pressure. He prodded and prodded as if he was searching for something inside and frowned so hard, that the lines upon his face seemed to become a permanent facial feature. At last he relaxed his fingers and shuffled a little in his seat, his rain coat rustling against the plastic exterior. He rubbed the stubble on his pasty chin and breathed out, smelling the stench of his own breath and recoiling a little. 'I stink like a dirty fishmonger,' he thought and put his head under his arm to smell his armpit like an Oran-utan. 'Cooar, what would they say now at the station if they saw me, call me a real student they would. Probably chuck me out of the locker room.'

He looked around, 'seven pm on a Thursday evening,' he contemplated, 'sometimes this place is like so alive, so high, people jumping every where, it's like one of those American talent shows. I'll say this for them, they're lively. You know sometimes when I go to visit my family in Wiltshire, out there in the country. I think if they saw a black man they'd have a heart attack. Out there, you know it's so quiet. Perhaps a little too quiet. That's what I'll say about them, every where they go, they've brought it to life. Everywhere. I'll say that for them, just a shame that all the other stuff goes along with them. Some of there women too, cooar....(he hesitated as a sudden rush of excitement came over him) there built, like, their built... well like nothing I've ever seen.'

Like a train spotter looking for his last train, he looked over at the fruit machines in the corner, the occasional light of its' internal mechanism flashing. A coffee machine literally covered in filth, a huge cobweb decorating its exterior. The words Maxi Coffee flashed within the top of its huge bulky structure, like the eyes in a seven foot monster. Beneath the flashing words were some inappropriately drawn pictures, as if they had been scribbled by a child. Inside, was a huge silver tube with a nozzle incessantly dripping hot water. William looked at the machine, discerning a spider's cobweb labyrinth visible even from where he was sitting.

He thought to himself, 'I must be crazy to have chanced it, even a hang over from Webster's best bitter is better than death by coffee poisoning, I bet that coffee machine has not been cleaned in months.' All the while he sulked, like a sullen school boy and resorted to poking his coffee cup with his plastic spoon. Not even the momentary glance of a female student as she passed by the glass door on the far side of the room was sufficient to erase the lines on his face. He did up the last button on his jacket and wrapping himself like a tramp for the night, rested his head on his hands and partially closed his eyes. The light faded as his lids fluttered, everything flickered, the electric overhead bulb, the maxi coffee machine, the distant blur of a few faces passing by. 'Passing by,' William thought, 'I can't even be bothered, let me just sleep here, I swear that's the last time that I do reports all night, then go on a drinking binge the day after, I swear.'

Tayo was bouncing down the stairs two at a time, clearing them with the dexterity of a triple jumper. Almost knocking into a courting couple coming up who seemed oblivious to the whole world. As if for that moment all that mattered was their soft brown eyes, 'I hope that in five years, they are not looking at blue ones,' he thought, scanning their vacant expressions, fake Karl Kani jeans and sprayed on shiny hairstyles. Tayo looked at them as they passed him, watching their air of superiority, the brother with his nose in the air, so high, obviously looking for something to fall from the sky.

She passed Tayo and glanced at him smirking through plastered on lipstick. 'I don't know why she's smiling at me,' Tayo thought, as he passed them and cleared the last flight of steps, 'she's got a man and she's smiling at me, like I wont to go over and do something, or perhaps...' Then Tayo stopped.

A woman coming towards him from the far side of the canteen. Her pale, sanguwine expression lacking life or vitality. Lipstick and rouge at least an inch thick on her cheeks, a stupid pouting expression on her face and straggly brown hair hanging down over her face. A skirt short to show off all the backside she did not have and a skin tight top with silicone implants jiggling about. A ring through her belly button and red painted finger nails. Tayo saw her through the glass door of the canteen walking down the aisle like a prostitute on her patch, swinging her hips and posing.

'What does she think she is,' Tayo thought, as he bounced through the door of the canteen, forgetting all about the amorous couple, or the sister's look of love.

'What does she think she is,' Tayo thought again, so loudly he almost said it, 'is this the epitome of beauty, the goddess of the earth, is this what most of the women of the world emulate to be, is this what brothers would throw their wife, mother, daughter, sister out to be with, a fake pre-fabricated, manufactured thing.' Tayo stared at her as she jiggled towards him, pouting more as she caught sight of him.

The woman waved her hair like a lap-top, table dancer and grinned at Tayo, 'he's a bit of all right,' she thought, 'fancy that, nice muscles, cute little face too, look at that, I've been at this place for over a year and I have never had one of them, fancy that, fancy that, not even once.'

Tayo scowled at her, like he was looking at a dog that had just shit on his shoe. 'What do you think you're looking at,' Tayo thought, 'you dirty little skeeser, look at something else, I'm not into jungle fever, what, with a woman with more attachments than Frakenstein's monster. You must be joking, what,' he was getting angry the more he thought about it, 'what makes her think that she can entertain such a thought, what is going on.' She jiggled passed him swaying from side to side and wafting her pungent perfume as she went, thinking all the while, 'I'm the most beautiful woman in the world.' But all Tayo was thinking about was, 'she looks just like Susan Thompson a.k.a. the dog, the pasty faced girl from school, who got her melons out on the way to Ironbridge, waving her huge great pink monstrosities at me like I was expected to consume them. But I didn't want them then and I don't want them now.' She looked at him and smiled again, as she bounced right up to him.

"Do you know where the canteen is," she asked, in a high pitched voice like Marilyn Monroe. "I'm really lost," she added, batting her eyelids and flicking her hair like a porn star in the middle of her sex act, she stank like a French brothel.

Tayo stared into her eyes, 'why has she stopped me, what is she doing here, what is this about?' He scanned the canteen, 'it's deserted, but for,' he thought and looked closer, 'isn't that the stupid policeman from the first day of college, what's he doing here, at this time, what, is going on.. what's it all about. Is it a.... ' he rubbed his chin. 'I could be getting a little paranoid, after all even if I do worry when I hear the sound of strange voices on my telephone like there's somebody listening to me. Or people watching me as I cross the street, or go to meetings, people that I've never known coming up to me and asking me questions, I don't know them, why are they asking me questions, why should they ask me, who the hell am I that I should have all the answers, I don't have them, I don't even have some of them, I'm just trying to muddle my way through.'

'Besides she knows this is the canteen. So why should she ask me. With Pc Plod in that stupid raincoat sitting over there, and Miss Frankenstein standing with her mouth open, that's too many coincidences. Besides white woman don't come up to me, they just don't,' he looked back at her. She was standing waiting, tapping her left toe slightly on the ground, a slight line of tautness and tension in the face, mixed with irritation, 'why hasn't he answered yet, is he stupid, I thought he was smart,' she thought.

"No," Tayo said and bounced off.

"No," she muttered under her breath, puzzled, "No," she repeated and looked back to see if he had even cast a passing glance, he hadn't. She bit her lip with vexation and walked slowly to the far end of the canteen, pretending to look at an interesting, if some what dust covered reproduction of Salvador Dali hanging on the wall. She made a less than energetic exit out of the canteen, through the double doors and up the stairs.

'What are they going to say,' she thought, 'not even established contact, well. They'll be other times, the youthful exuberance will soon die down,' and she disappeared.

Tayo bounced passed the now awake William Lynch, the young man's head in the air like a triumphant leopard.

"So what's wrong with her," William hollered at him, half standing to make the sound clear, so it reverberated around the empty canteen. "Too white for you, is she," he said, looking at Tayo who did not seem to have any intention of stopping.

Tayo turned swiftly, adjusting his pouch and stared, "you words not mine," Tayo replied. "You really shouldn't put your own women down, but it's just not my cup of tea, old boy, (putting on an accent) just not my cup of tea, any way good bye, Plod."

"You cocky little man, who do you think you are, don't you know this is England, don't you know that," William said, almost to Tayo's back as he walked passed him.

Tayo turned, "oh I know what this place is," he said, "I know alright, I was born here, lived here nearly all my life, I know what this place is. Don't give me a lecture about we are watching you, or other crap, because not only do I not want to know, I don't care either." He screwed his face up, "and don't presume to tell me about my people and how come the year 2000 they'll be **finished**. What are you going to tell me that half are going to be white women, or white men and the rest so strung out on crack, cocaine, and self hatred that they'll be no use, don't bother."

"All right then Mr. smarty-pants," William said, "don't think I haven't forgotten you from the first day, I remember you with those other boys, rejects from some American music video, and you walking around like you own the place. Well you'll soon find out the world is not what you think it is. I'm telling you, your people don't give a shit about what you're talking about. They don't care. They are a primitive people, (he lost control of himself a little).. I mean they're different. They'll not ever think the way you want them to think, it may seem hard to you, but they just want to live, you know, just be happy, it's even in your music."

Tayo smiled, "I'm not going to stand here and discuss the finer points of revolution with you, I'm not. The police have enough information on me, oh yeah, (seeing William's expression as he shuffled in his mack) I know you're a policeman. (He paused).... so if you don't think we're such a problem, if you figure I'm going to run off with a white girl perhaps that one you just sent, you're dreaming. By the way, do answer me this question. If you don't think we here are a problem, why is it that you're spending so much time and have such an interest in me, why do you take it so seriously."

William looked at him, his mouth was tightly shut, with the bottom lip slightly quivering, like a spoilt child denied chocolate candy by his mother.

"Nothing to say William," Tayo said. William gawked puzzled, "oh you didn't know I knew, well William, still trying to live up to your name, well you're doing a good job. Slave owner wasn't he? Used to burn brothers like me at the stake didn't he. Well come on then, why don't you have a go, come on, let's have you!"

William sat rooted to the spot.

"Not so keen," Tayo added calmer, "alright, take care then," he turned to go, "and oh yes, the next time you send a woman, make sure she's a woman, a real woman, I mean a woman from A..f..r..i..c..a, (he put on an accent) do you know what I'm sayin. Not Frakenstein's monster." He bounced out, smiling a little too much just like he had won a great debate.

"Alright," William said, under his breath, "so it's going to be like that, so be it" and he sat down in his rain coat, adjusting his worn out old T-shirt, besmirched with alcohol and sticking to his unwashed armpits.'

"There'll have to be another way," he muttered, "another way altogether."

Tayo and the wasps

"You don't have to go at all," Michael said, leaning up against the wall, then getting temporarily distracted by Jennifer's breasts as she bounced, obliviously down a nearby corridor.

"True," Flex added, "you know man-a-man don't respect a loser, still, they like the don, the don Gordan, the Mandingo." They all laughed.

"There's some truth in that," Tayo replied, "but I want to go, if I'm going to do this thing and I don't know if I am, but if I do. Well it's good to see what they have to say, you know check them out."

"Do you want us to come with you," Michael asked.

"Nah," you've both got lectures, anyway haven't you."

"So," Flex said, "when did that make any difference."

Tayo smiled, "yeah well it's better that I go alone."

"Yeah well don't be righteous," Flex said, "every one loves number one."

"True," Tayo said, turning to leave, "I know that for sure."

"He thinks he's John Wayne for sure," Flex whispered to Michael, "walking off into the sunset, the good sheriff in the bad town , going off to meet the outlaws," and he laughed.

"Yeah," Michael said, "but I love him like a brother still, if anythink happens to him with them crackers, I'll bust their sledge, even though he's an arrogant son of a bitch. There's good things that's been done here still, that I thought, wah that can't even go'on."

"I here that," Flex said, looking down the corridor, "I'll be with you, I just wish he didn't have his ego dripping from him."

"Like you don't," Michael said.

"I think we," Flex replied, interrupting, "have had this conversation before."

"Well let's wheel and come again," Michael said laughing. Flex stared at him.

Tayo skipped through the double doors and across the street even so the afternoon drew in the evening and a slight breeze blowing from the east. Bouncing towards the Student Union. Through the double doors chipped from the outside and marked with graffiti. The glass marked with filth. He cleared the first flight of stairs three steps at a time. Bouncing through the smoke and the overpowering stench of alcohol wafting through the open doors and into the corridor.

'Strange it is," Tayo said, to himself, "I've been at this college for two years and I've never set foot in the student union bars. Two years and not even once.' He surveyed the red painted walls, chipped and broken, crumbling here and there with loose cement, or a whole kicked into it from a fight on Saturday night. Cigarette butts scattered here and there, an empty coke can, a broken glass, the smell of sweat and filth, the slight touch of tension in the air. Tayo felt it like a slight humming noise in the back of his head, a faint ringing that would not go away though you tried to squeeze it out.

He cleared the steps and stood on the landing to the first floor bar,' two o'clock, they said, well it's that now,' he thought, looking at his watch. He bit his lip feeling his heart beating a little faster than before, 'I can hear the sound of them re-living their pagan rites, drinking to some Norse God or something.' Tayo thought, 'do I really need to do this, what for. What I need to do is link up with my people, that's what I need to do. Well I'll do it, .. though I don't want to.. I'll do it, even if it's just to keep Peter happy I'll do it. But I don't like it.'

Tayo adjusted his pouch over his black top and straightened himself up, taking a deep breath, inhaling smoke, the smell of alcohol and, 'something else that I can't make up my mind what it is' and he pushed the double doors open - only to be met by someone shoving the doors the other way, pushing his way past him and into the corridor. A young man in his twenties, blue jeans, white T-shirt, with his hand over his dis-coloured face. He stopped just at the entrance to the corridor, bent over, released his hands from his face and vomited what must have been the contents of three days meals on to any unsuspecting person walking up the stairs. Bits of red carrots, yellow celery, lumps of roast beef only partially digested, and some green peas, all coated in yellow and green slime. The spurious substance spewed out of his gapping, pale, face with the speed and ferocity of a demoniac possession. His white cheeks scarlet for a while with exertion. Tayo looked away and stepped through the doors, 'now I know why I don't come here,' he thought and kissed his teeth, 'I swore since Gunnislake that I would never walk into one of these places again and here I'm doing it.'

The stench of alcohol, nicotine and sweat seemed to rise from the oak paneled decor, the red fitted carpets and the students drunk and getting drunk, scattered everywhere.

Tayo peered into the gloom, a tall young man with a swarthy complexion stood hunched over the counter, taking long drags from his cigarette. Blue jeans, drainpipe style and sporting running trainers, a blue Hillfiger jacket undone carelessly like it did not cost him three hundred pounds. Slim legs, but an angular, muscular torso which seemed to swivel around independently of the rest of his body, as he smoked and drank.

"Give us another drink mate," the young man said, to what looked like a barman, "my throat is as dry as a tarts tit."

"All right," Rory (the bar man) replied, in an Irish accent fumbling around behind the counter like a hamster looking for his winter store.

"You know you better sought your life out, Mick," the young man said, "or will pass a motion, get your ass kicked out and put some good old English rose behind here, with tits like watermelons and an ass like one of those black bitches on .. what is it MTV."

Tayo watched the glances as he bounced across the bar, through the smoke, bigotry, assumed expectations, which seemed to fly in all directions - as the students murmured, and whispered behind their pints of Tenants and Tetley's best bitters. Over on the far side, a young man staring blindly at him in the shadows, the blueness of his iris silhouetted under the luminous beam of light, the face obscured slightly under shadows, so the eyes seemed to shine alone in the darkness.

A young couple who had seen him from the beginning, pretending not to notice as they smoked and stared at each other - but watching as he bounced over to the bar from the corner of their eyes, like a prey they intend to kill. A couple of rowdy what looked like rugby players, just back from a game, sat joking and laughing, spilling beer on their open neck sporty, stripy shirts and slapping the hair on their chests. There faces flushed and pasty, the whiteness stark in the dimness of the shadows, as they giggled and fell around their table swearing and telling rude jokes.

They did not notice Tayo as he bounced up to the bar, he could here the incessant whirl of the fan and the murmuring of the rugby players like a swarm of wasps, "did you here the one about the coon who crossed the traffic lights. Now you see me, now you don't," one of them mumbled, with a drunken slur.

"Shut the fuck up," the tall youth said, turning to them, "my mother was black." Their was a pause and silence as they looked back at him. Silence.

"No offence Jeremy, we weren't talking to you," they said to the youth. Jeremy turned back as if he was speaking to the bar "that's all right then, I let you off," he muttered.

Tayo went up to the bar and lent over motioning Rory to him with his finger. Rory shuffled clumsily like an old tramp, rather than the young man he was.

"Is there a Harris here," Tayo said, looking at the worried looking bar man who stood in front of him. Rory opened his mouth as if he was going to say something.

"Who wants to know," a voice said. Tayo turned, he had been trying to avoid eye contact, or any conversation with him at all, from the time he walked in.

"I'm talking to you," the voice repeated. Tayo swung around like a ballerina, effortlessly and stared at Jeremy.

"I do," Tayo said, emphatically.

Jeremy smiled, "are you that bloke from over the road, the one that keeps talking about all that black shit," he mumbled, more like a statement than a question. Tayo looked at him speechless.

"So," Jeremy continued, leaning on the counter, his brown straight hair highlighted under the bar light. His pale brown eyes accusing. "Can I come into one of your meetings, how do I fit in," Jeremy said, "my mother was black, just as I was telling my mates here." Tayo looked around at the joking rugby players who had stopped laughing and the couple over at the corner who had stopped looking into each others eyes and were now looking at him. Jeremy's Gautier watch and white trainers shining in the shadows.

Tayo, stared, 'where is the African blood in you,' he thought. 'Perhaps there's a tightness in the curls of his hair.' But the hair hung limply in a quiff. 'Perhaps the nose,' he thought, but it pointed sharply like a beak. 'The lips then,' but they were thin and pursed, like a petulant aristocrat. 'So where is his mother in him, he may be lying, but that's not the sought of thing you would lie about, not in here anyway, so where is the blood.'

"I don't know," Tayo said, staring and feeling a slight surge of adrenaline, "where do you want to fit in,... here," and he smiled arrogantly.

"Well I'll tell you," Jeremy replied, still looking at the counter, "all your notions of race, and all that, it's bollocks, it's real bollocks, you know that. It's really crap (the word seemed to reverberate in his mouth) I mean really crap. My mother was black, what you would probably call, what, a half caste, or mixed race, my dad is white. They both loved each other, so what are you going to do about that?"

"I don't want to do anything about it, that's your problem, not mine," Tayo said, looking around the bar for Harris. Jeremy turned his whole powerful frame so he faced him.

"No I asked you, what does that make me," Jeremy said. Tayo shrugged his shoulders dismissively.

"Well I'll tell you," Jeremy said, "it makes me white, and proud to be it."

"Well good for you," Tayo said to Jeremy, but looking at corner of the bar and the eyes in the shadow which seemed to be getting closer and closer as the figure stepped out from behind his table and came towards them.

"Shall I tell you why," Jeremy said, staggering towards Tayo, the later could feel his breath, "because you're lot are finished, your **scum**, I can say it, I can say what I like I can, I can say what I like, I've got you're blood in me and I'm telling you, your scum, drug dealers, prostitutes, your filth."

"Really," Tayo said, nonchalantly, "well one things' for sure, ...you really are white" and he turned his back to him.

"Yo," Tayo called out to the bar man, ignoring Jeremy as he slowly began to work himself into a frenzy. Rory turned to look at him.

Meanwhile, the eyes came out from the shadows as the youth who owned them stepped towards the bar. His blue Pepe jeans hanging limply around his ankles, not more than five-foot seven. 'That's the bloke from the first day, I remember with no manners, who walked into me and went on as if he was Adolf's illegitimate son,' Tayo thought, as he watched him. Tayo turned back to Rory the bar man, who looked increasingly worried at the movement around his bar.

"So, Rory, that's your name isn't it," Tayo said, to him, "do you know where Harris is, Mathew Harris?"

The bar man opened his mouth again like a frightened lemming, as if he was going to say something.

"Put that bloody glass down," a voice said, "you're a fucking hooligan, you're not on the rugby pitch now."

Tayo spun around to see Jeremy putting his glass on the table and resort to kicking the carpet with his trainers, 'why do I feel that glass was intended for my head,' Tayo thought, looking at Jeremy scowling at him.

"Simon, go and get, Mr. Akinjo a drink, and you," to Jeremy, "you lanky streak of piss, go and clear a table over there so we can talk," the voice continued.

The youth who had been in the shadows went over to the bar, pushing past Tayo and then turned suddenly like a ferret, "what do you want then," he said.

"Nothing," Tayo replied, 'but thinking this must be Simon then.' Simon still at the bar made a face with his mouth and propped himself up, almost where Jeremy had been before. By now Jeremy had bounced over to the far table, cleared the couple away from it, like a waiter in a professional West End restaurant. Tayo peered over to put a face with this voice that was shouting so many orders.

'And how does everybody know my name,' Tayo thought, as a young man walked up to him with his hand out stretched and a fake smile on his face. 'This is getting stranger than one of those films, where everything that happens is deja vue,' he thought, recognising him as the one who had pushed through the doors and been sick down the stairs, 'perhaps, he's been watching us the whole time. Just listening until he could make his entrance.

It doesn't take that long to be sick.'

Tayo stretched his hand out and shock his, "you're Harris then, Mathew Harris," Tayo said.

"Yeah," Harris said, sizing him up, "you're a big fellah," he looked at him, "how tall are you, what six foot?"

Tayo looked at the faded white T-shirt and starched white trainers, 'what is it with white trainers and jeans, like they all can't afford any thing else, I know they can, I bet Daddy's Prime Minister or something, head of ICI or MI6 and he's just slumming it.'

Then Tayo remembered the question, 'he's really taking the piss, I mean really taking the piss, I come all the way over here to face grilling from his personal slave over there, Jeremy, or whatever his bloody name is, I walk into this place, so he can ask me how tall I am.'

"Surely," Tayo said, "you didn't invite me here just to ask me about my height did you?"

"Don't get touchy, phew... boy you've got a chip on your shoulder," Harris said coldly. "Don't worry, well get down to business soon enough," he continued.

Tayo said nothing, but thought, 'I'll let that last comment ride, because I want to find out what this is all about and why Peter made me come here, but,..(and he looked at the slight frame of Harris) you ever give me cause, I'll kick your ass and show you how big my chip is. You little sawn off runt, giving out orders like Napoleon, and you a'int.'

"Alright then," Harris said, "come with me," and he walked over to the far side table. And sat down. Tayo bounced behind him, wafting the smoke from his face as he went and kicking an old coke can out of his way. Tayo sat down on the furthest chair, feeling the soft velvet seats, remembering how tired he was. He adjusted himself on his seat and watched, as Simon sat on the far side with Jeremy, like a waiting servant standing behind. "You've got to excuse Jeremy, not only is his dad one of the richest men in the country, his mother's a fucking babe, but he's the captain of the rugby team and you know how all that rugby messes up your head. Tackles, scrums and all that shit they do in the showers, what is it towelling and rubbing down, they're weird, I mean really weird, strange geezers, I don't trust them. It's just that he's a third down black belt in Karate and he's useful to have a round. So long as you can stop him from talking, he's alright. So Mr Akinjo, what can we do you for?"

Tayo looked at them and bit his lip, the adrenaline which had started to flow was now driving its' way through his body like a locomotive train. He felt the passion, the rage, all the while mixed with a tinge of recklessness. 'I feel to just kick all of their racist asses, this cocky little midget his side kick who likes hanging around in shadows, and lurch at the back there,' he thought.

"Well," Tayo said, calmly, "I thought, it was the other way round. Peter told me to come and find you here, something about..... what is it now, the Student Union."

"Yeah," Harris said, rubbing his chin, "well it's like this, well, even before I do that, sometimes I'm so rude, I didn't even introduce everybody. Jeremy you know, this is Simon, I think he studies the same course as you, but you'll hardly see him, he's a boffin don't you know, lucky bastard doesn't need to study, some guys have all the luck, still he's not as handsome as me. Oh yeah, my name is Mathew Harris. The only son of one Mr. Harris Q.C. wealthy and influential barrister, whose likely this year to get his promotion to judge. Selfish bastard though, wouldn't pull any strings to get me out of the shit last year when I got caught with half a pound of speed in my rucksack. You know what father's are like, always want you to struggle."

"Well," Tayo said, unimpressed, adjusting his pouch.

"Well," Harris replied, "you are direct aren't you. One question I wanted to ask, what have you got in that pouch, a gun or something, you're going to shoot me are you...." and he laughed rather guiltily.

"No don't do it, I'm too young to die, what's your name John Wayne is it, you know, he looks like John Wayne don't you think Simon," Harris said.

"No," Simon replied coldly.

"Well I think he does, he's got the height for it, anyway," Harris mumbled.

"So," Tayo said, feeling his ability to control his anger reaching its' limit as he agitatedly clenched his fists under the table, and a line of perspiration broke out on his forehead. 'I can feel my ability to maintain control drifting from me,' he thought, as his left leg began to shake involuntarily. He breathed deeply.

"So," Harris said, annoyingly, "you all right. Are you okay, are you?" He saw the lines of concern on Tayo's face watching his erratic movements. "What's the matter," he said, "listen, were not prejudiced like you. We don't have any prejudice, I can sit down here and talk to you. The fact your a different colour to me, has got nothing to do with anything. Well that's what I feel. I don't know how you feel." Tayo stared blankly at him.

"No I'm not prejudiced, but I know you lot are. What do you call mixed relationships. What jungle fever," he laughed. Jeremy frowned, the corners of his face turned inwards. Simon just kept staring, his blue eyes like pools of clear water in a swamp.

"Jungle fever, indeed," Harris chuckled, smiling, "where do you lot get off with that term. That's horrible. This country is about free choice, don't you know that. Never heard of love. Ever heard the term love has no colour. You should remember that. What do you call us crackers, bluefoots," he laughed out loud, "crackers, like Jacob Creams, but I like mine with chocolate on. What does that tell you about me."

Tayo bit his lip, he could feel his brain about to explode.

"Listen," Harris continued, "hah, hah (laughing) you lot are crazy. Any way (trying to gain composure). Well it's like this I ain't prejudiced. I'm not, I couldn't be. My father, apart from anything, didn't raise me that way. He's a tight fisted old git, but he taught me how to respect other colours. I remember I couldn't be more than fifteen. Yeah I was about fifteen, he picked me up. Didn't say where he was going you know. Didn't tell me a damn thing. You know what dad's are like."

"Yeah," Jeremy replied.

"Well he picked me up, drove down into the West End," Harris continued, "in those days we used to live in Brockley, you know those massive houses out there, past the estates. Well." Tayo adjusted his pouch and twisted the foremost lock on his head between his thumb and forefinger.

"Anyway," Harris said, "it was near Baker Street some where like that. I remember we went pass Madame Tussauds. Yeah it had to be

Baker street. So," Harris said, leaning back on his chair, "there we were in Baker street. Got out of dad's new car. It was some huge house. White brick stone, just stained here and there with the smog from pollution. Now I don't know where I'm going, I really don't know, just following my father. How am I supposed to know. So he takes me to the top, knocks on the door. Knocks really loud. It was a huge great white door. It was ornate with a huge brass door knob and handle. Now listen I was only fifteen, but I kept thinking, what is my father doing bringing me to this place at 10 pm at night. There I am waiting. You know at this door. You know the story don't you," Harris asked, turning to Jeremy.

"Yeah," Jeremy muttered, under his breath.

Harris shuffled in his seat like a pervert at a sex show, "well," Harris blurted out triumphantly, "you never guess what. The door opened, really slowly. It sought of creaked. It remained like that for a while and then I looked in, do you know what was in there. You'll never believe it. It was a black woman. She was like frowsy and frumpy. Old enough to be your mother Akinjo."

Tayo stood up, "what did you say about my mother," and stared at him, 'this cracker has said enough for me to kill him and chop his body into pieces,' he thought clenching his fists.

"All right, all right, boy you are touchy, really touchy," Harris said, he looked him up and down, "I said old enough to be your mother, I didn't say your mother, calm down." Jeremy sized him up and Simon put his hands in his pockets like a gangster in a 1920's film.

'I could have 'em all,' Tayo thought, looking at them, but I've got business to deal with.' Tayo sat down still clenching and unclenching his fists, blood pounding through his arteries like a bullet down the barrel of a gun.

"Anyway," Harris said, obviously not learning from the first time. "Do you know what she was," he asserted. He looked at Tayo like he expected him to give an answer. "Do you know what she was? " Harris said, looking at everybody. "She was a pro," Harris said, triumphantly, like a man who had been storing up the answer, "an old pro, an old pro you know. A tart, a whore," Jeremy laughed so loud, he almost forget he was supposed to be tough.

"It was my best and first shag," Harris said, "she was from some place like Quadagogo, Bongo-Bongo land or something, I don't know and I don't really care. Course she gave good head, good back, in fact good everything."

"Dirty slag," Simon muttered, under his breath.

"Have some respect," Harris replied, turning to Simon, "but she was a filthy slapper and I do mean slapper. Dad gave her £200 and she was up for anything. It was like it was my initiation into manhood or something. Family tradition, my grandfather had taken my father I think in the sixties or something, apparently his father had taken him before that. So it was like tradition." Harris smiled like a demon in the centre of hell.

"So what do you think of that Mr Akinjo," Harris continued, "how does that conform to your notions of Black Nationalism. How does that feel. No I want to hear?"

Tayo looked at Harris' peevish little face, almost pubescent in its' child like wickedness. His fifteen pound haircut and his white T-shirt splattered with traces of his own vomit. ' One day I'm goin' to finish you, so that your own mother won't recognise you I swear it,' Tayo thought. He tried to clear his mind, "I didn't come here Harris to discuss Black nationalism," he said, "or White nationalism for that matter, or the finer points of your 'initiation' (he made the word sound like an insult). I heard you had something to say, so come on and say it, or I'm out of here."

Harris smiled like a rat, "alright, but has nobody ever told you that patience is a virtue, discretion is the better part of valour, Shakespeare, I think. Has nobody. Well all right then (he paused) it's like this, you're head of the biggest Black society, are you not. I mean I personally feel that you've stretched free speech to it's limit, but that's not the point. You've got three hundred members. In any election that's three hundred votes. But the trouble is Mr. Akinjo that even with all those votes and say the seven hundred other blacks (he made the word sound like a 'cus', like an Afrikaaner in South Africa saying Kaffir). Even with them, but right now, they don't give a damn. But even if they all were to vote for you, you would have a thousand votes. Max."

"But that's as many as you're getting. Cause, the Asian society have got three candidates, this splits the ethnic vote in half and besides, even if you all voted together and you wont, you are still a minority. Because if you didn't know and I know some of you over there forget, this is England. Yeah it's England and in this college there are ten thousand students. Eight thousand look like me. Do you understand what I'm saying. I'm saying that," And he stretched his

arms out at this point like a reclining Caesar at a Roman festival.
Like a Caesar who had just put a bet down and won on the chariot
race.

There was silence and a pause, pregnant and expectant. Even the
fruit machine in the far corner playing the 'star spangled banner'
electronically was perfectly audible.

Tayo looked up smiling, "well you don't need me," he replied. "If I
do run and I haven't even decided I will, as you've said, we don't
stand a chance. So why bother. I mean what's the point in losing?"

"Well," Harris said, "I've kind of over simplified, I know personally
that I will win the Presidency, because I will bully and quarrel, to
get my people to vote for me. But my candidates are not standing
for all the positions. There's some (his eyes twinkled like an insane
mad scientist) minor positions that some of these communists are
standing for."

"Communists," Tayo said, puzzled.

"Yeah," Harris said, "pinko left wing communist, red flag waving
ruskies. Ruskies (he giggled to himself) huh.. huh.. sounds like a
sought of animal you should go and hunt, Simon doesn't it." He
nudged him, but Simon was still staring at Tayo blindly, like a mad
man.

 "Well," Tayo said, still puzzled.

"Well," Harris replied, "I thought you were supposed to be smart.
It's like this, blacks are all right, I mean when you're with the boys
you may crack some jokes and that, but you're all right. It's these
Ruskies, man. I hate them, they are unpatriotic. Look what ever
you say about Mrs T she's a strong leader, she's made this country
great again. I hate them."

"I hate them too," Simon said, looking at Tayo.

"Shut up," Harris interrupted, turning to him like a psychotic mass
murderer, "nobody asked you to speak, just shut your mouth
alright. (He turned back to Tayo). So there's some of that lot standing. You know I don't know there names, workers revolutionary
and left radical something, I don't know. Anyway, this is the idea."

Tayo watched Harris, 'his little pasty face is really animated with
his master plan, he looks like he's on drugs or something,' Tayo

thought, as he watched his cunning mind at work.

"You lot, you're lot, you know all of you lot over there, you stand for the minor posts, you know Maps faculty, things like that, women's officer and a few others. You can even go for Communications officer, if you want. But the lesser positions anyway. That way we'll keep the reds out. So what do you say, I've talked enough (he leaned back in his seat, his blonde hair lit up by the luminous overhead electric light) what do you say (his whole face seemed like one white glow)."

"Do you know what," Tayo replied, standing, "thanks for the hospitality, I really appreciate it, and I will consider your proposal, I think it's a very fair one, almost too fair bearing in mind you are obviously in the stronger position. But thank you anyway." He turned to go.

Harris looked at him like he was waiting for something else, "well," he asked, his mouth half open waiting for a reply. But Tayo had already turned and stepped past the table.

"Well," Tayo replied, "I let you know and once again thank you." He bounced past a puzzled looking Jeremy who scratched his head with confusion and Simon who looked at Harris as if he was going to provide some clarity.

But Simon was looking down at the table in front, 'what colour is his (Tayo's) blood,' he thought, 'Black, red, certainly not royal blue like mine, I want to find out.'

Harris tapped his foot thinking, 'this bar is really plush, the oak panels look good, a little tacky, but alright, and if this black bastard doesn't take my offer, I'll give him the biggest hiding of his life, no matter how tall he thinks he is" and he scowled, resting his chin on his chest and picking his nose all at the same time.

Hustings

Tayo stood on the stage, his heart pounding out of his chest, the beats racing faster and faster, until the veins on his forehead stood out like a man being strangled on a rope. The scar on his forehead shining and glistening with a film of perspiration extending from the top of his head to the tip of his nose. He steadied his position adjusted his pouch for the last time, gripped the podium for security more than to read the notes that he had hastily assembled, and now lay strewn on it.

"I was going to give the kind of speech, well..." he said, and then stopped.

"Go on Tayo," Susan shouted from the front row.

"I was going to give the kind of official speech, you know the kind, the official one, that this lot gave," he pointed to the other candidates on the stage. They looked nervously over in his direction, except Harris who stared blindly into the audience like a dictator at a Nuremberg rally, his blonde hair gleaming unnaturally and his eyes shinning like two small, fake pearls.

"I could come up here and say all the rubbish that they've just said," Tayo said, "but I'm not going to insult your intelligence, I believe that you're smart enough to know what's the truth, even if you don't like it."

Pete head of the Workers revolutionary Movement, looked down at his shoes. 'I'm the out going President,' he thought, 'but I know there's not a chance in hell of me being re-elected. Too many factions, too many movements, but even so. Even as the last President, I still stood for what I believed in, rather than this lot, Harris over there is just a fascist, plain and simple. Khalil, he's got the Asian vote anyway and Andrew well he's just into raving. He hung his head even lower, as for this Tayo, who does he think he is, Martin Luther King or something. Not that I've got anything against black militancy, but it's not enough to mean anything. He'll never win. Even if he's a bit colourful. I mean that in the best possible taste, I'm a Marxist.'

Tayo scanned the audience, 'this is the make or break time,' he thought, 'all the opposition are here, all the weeks of campaigning, it'll mean nothing, if I mess this up now.' He looked at Susan and Appia with their expectant faces, 'expecting what,' then he realised perplexed, 'even if I win, I can't give them what they want, I can't do it. They all want so many things, so many people. Look Ade sitting there, what does he want, or Flex, Michael or Jennifer what does she want, the world to be more beautiful, more raves, the world to be a nice little place with red roses and green summer meadows it's not. It's a nasty place, a very bad place.'

He adjusted his position again and gripped the podium tighter, 'what do they want,' he thought, 'what does Melanie want,.... me, I can't even give her me. Or Mikee, or Peter, what does he want peace, we all want so many different things, we are all are so different. Are other people's so different. Are all people's different, so. Why try, why talk about this black thing, why not talk about justice. Why not talk about healing people's wounds.' He looked out at the smoke filled room, the crowds of people packing the hall from end to end and he remembered what he was trying to forget. 'For more than five hundred years we've been at the bottom of every barrel, every where in this world. We've been shackled, chained, raped, castrated, left to die, our continent has been taken and controlled, our people dispersed. To build, not to build so that we can reap the benefits, but for others profit. Even taking away the history, what have I seen, on the first day here, what are we treated like, by the police, the courts, even the education system, all the while someone can murder, or beat one of us and go free. I read the reports of Rolan Adams trial, suspended sentences, what! I know they'll be more murders. The reality is that this country is a fundamentally racist country that had better reform it's practices. Why should I stop. I won't, I can't, until it does. I don't care if my career is finished, what career? Or even if some nutter takes my life, at least it will be a life given for a right reason,' he adjusted his pouch.

"So," Tayo said, trying to relax, "this college is part of the world. It's not separate. It's part of it. Every person, citizen of this world, has an obligation to stand up for what is right. We have a duty to do the right thing. It's not a thing where we can choose, but something we are obliged to do as human beings. Right now in this college, in this country whether you like it, or not, racism is endemic, it's a filthy disease which afflicts the very foundation of peoples thought, speech and action. You have an obligation to stand against it. You have a duty to fight it. Whether you're black or white. But don't presume cause you're white to be lecturing us about it as if you're the expert. You're not and could never be. (There was a round of applause, with cries of true, true). But the system and the people that say they represent you, perpetrate it. Since I have been at this college, when I said I wanted to run, people have attempted to bribe me, (there were boos and cries of shame)" Tayo looked at Mr. Thomas who was sitting at the back of the hall, his head in the air like a slave master on a plantation. At Tayo's words his face went scarlet with embarrassment.

"They have attempted to threaten me, offer me a lower position, just so I don't get an opportunity to speak to you, what are they afraid of, what do they think I'm going to say. Even for this meeting, they weren't going to tell me about it. They weren't, I had to find out about it from my sister there, pointing to Susan, she's been like a rock. You know we men can stand up here shouting, but it's the women which keep a thing going, through hard times and there have been some hard times. I can tell you."

"I tell you this you have a choice," Tayo continued, "it's not a hard one, its simple. Whatever pain you have gone through, or whatever you understand about the world, it is about doing right or wrong. Some of you may be single parent mothers, have been though the pain of rejection, overcome immense obstacles just to be here, or you could have been adopted, given to somebody else to look after, even left for dead, you could be from the ghetto in and out of prison, but you still made it here, or you could have been born with everything, silver spoon in your mouth, thinking about why you are here with all of these defective people when your so perfect. Firstly your not so perfect. He looked at the audience, nobody is perfect (there was shouts of true, true.) But we can all be better, by trying to be right (there was a ripple of applause). I am determined to be right, are you, I am determined to fight for the truth, are you....... then do it."

Adetunji Rotimi stared transfixed, as Tayo turned and twisted his words like a rapper on a mike. He watched him moving, thinking, talking all at the same time whilst he read the emotion of the crowd. ' He's Oso, (one that speaks well) I'll have to find out,' Adetunji thought, 'where he comes from and what he's going to do. Politics should be for them who have the right, who are born to it. Not for ragamuffins off the street.' He looked Tayo up and down, his boots and twists in his hair, the leather pouch around his chest and he shock his head. Adetunji's solid gold Rolex watch glinted under the glare of the stage lights, his Karl Kani shirt looking like it had been bleached, it was so white, like the false, capped teeth in his austere, youthful, mouth.

Tayo looked at the audience, his trousers were stuck to his legs with sweat. His whole body shaking, vibrant, alive, like a boxer after nine rounds. There was a pause, Harris hung his head - in fact all the candidates hesitated, even Khalil's bristling moustache drooped.

Mr. Thomas stared wildly at Tayo, biting his lip, his glasses steamed up with agitation. Susan and Appia smiled. Susan watched him, as he moved away from the pulpit and almost instinctively began to clap, Appia joined in and soon all of them were clapping. It spread until the whole audience resounded with applause.

Tayo looked at the ground, 'don't clap me,' he thought, 'because even as you cheer for me now, people are fickle, to raise a person and then later to destroy them,' he pushed that thought out of his mind. Sitting down, feeling every bone, sinew and blood vessel. He bowed his head refusing to look up, to accept the applause, even with the shouts from the audience of, "Tayo, Tayo, Tayo," echoing throughout the auditorium at a deafening volume.

Ade

Ade was sitting almost cross legged on the full length chair. He had been trying to think about something over the last few days except for 'doing right.' It was six p.m. in the evening, there was only Susan there and him. She seemed utterly absorbed in her papers. Surrounded by her administration, strewn everywhere.

'Such dedication,' Ade thought, 'why can't I have the same dedication. I never really cared for anything really but myself and my sister. Why.... perhaps just because of my experiences, not being loved, not feeling my parent's love. Well. That's too easy. Did Tayo not go through the same experience. And there are others as well. No that's not enough. There has to be another reason. I can't blame all black people, all of my own people for a crime, if it was a crime, .. oh yeah and it was a crime, it shouldn't have happened. But I can't keep blaming myself for there mistake.' He looked around at the peeling paintwork, the posters everywhere advertising the campaign, 'vote for Pete keep the Tories out,' 'vote for Mathew Harris for free beer,' embezzled with a effigy of a semi-naked woman. 'Was I really going to sit by and allow people like that,' Ade thought, 'to win this election after almost a year at the society, hearing all those things about our history and that, some of us are standing up for something, that we believe in and what am I doing. What am I doing, nothink!'

"I'm goin' to stand for a position," Ade blurted out.

"You," Susan replied, startled and surprised looking up from her papers, "I thought all you were really into was Tommy Hillfiger and Melanie of course."

"No Melanie is not among the things I want, Hillfiger maybe, but not her," Ade said.

"So what's wrong with Melanie these days," Susan asked.

"Nuthing," Ade replied, "it's not me she wants, its' someone else, like all the time she was with me, she was thinking about and wanting another, it was odd like she went out with me just to get her own back," he reclined back on his seat, "as if she needed something to validate her self worth. Can you understand what I mean?"

"Oh I understand," Susan said, "more than you know. It's like Angela, I told you about her before."

"Oh yeah," Ade said, "I remember wasn't she the one who came to a few meetings with you."

"Yeah," Susan replied, brushing one of the locks from her face and looking around as if the information she was going to give was top secret. "She saw some brothers beating up on some white boys, she was like a changed woman, now she's left him."

"Left who," Ade said.

"The white boy, but now, its like she's hitting on every brother she can find, trying to find one like them... Any way you said you were standing, well tell me more," she said expectant, "is it Tayo?"

"Everyone always thinks it's Tayo," Ade said, "is it that no other brother can have a righteous thought."

"No," Susan replied, defensively, "its not even that, it's just that after his speech you seemed to be moved, I mean moved to action."

"It was a good speech, but it wasn't that, it was something else," Ade said, fiddling with the zip of his jacket like a child being told off by teacher. Susan looked at him patiently, like a mother watching her child take his first walk. Smiling, if a little bemused by his cockney accent without slang.

"Well it's like this," Ade said, "it's not a long story, but about a week ago, yeah it was last week, just after we had that discussion on Genocide. You know I hadn't been swung by the whole thing, you know conspiracies and all that. I've seen us do too many things to ourselves, if you know what I mean, to believe that somebody is planning it. It's just too hard to believe. Anyway I'm just sitting there on the tube in garms and there Kris. I mean I look kris, really kris, any way. We just got past Kennington, I was going out to visit a friend."

"What Melanie, who you said you didn't like," Susan said.

"No," Ade replied, rather guilty.

"Anyway," he continued, "I'm just sitting there, you know thinking and really like disregarding all those ideas about the destruction of our race and then I notice opposite. It was really odd, I mean really strange. The strange thing is nobody else thought it was strange, but I knew it was like, what's the word 'poignant,' that's it. There was a woman, a black woman, well she was mixed you know well she..."

"I get the picture," Susan said, "she was of mixed parentage."

"Yes, that's it," Ade said. "Well she was sitting there, I mean I wouldn't have noticed it, but I did and sitting next to her was her daughter. Now what does that make her daughter."

"What does what," Susan asked.

"I mean this woman had, had her daughter with a white man, he must have been really white too because, the child had blonde hair and blue eyes. And you know like with most of those people, even though they try to deny it, you can tell they've got some black in them, you know that singer from Wales with the curly hair, I can't remember his name, Tom or something... .any way." He adjusted himself on his seat.

"Any way with this child, you couldn't see any colour at all, I mean no colour, there was nuthing there, nuthing at all. Not a drop, not in the hair, or the complexion, not in the face, the nose or the lips, nothing. The child had blue eyes. You just know that when she grows up into an adult, she'll say that she ain't black, you know that. Well.... I'm not going to say anyway again, it's a bad habit."

"Your doing fine," Susan said, encouragingly.

"Well," Ade said, "the thing that was most striking is that the child had two dolls. I mean, two dolls. One was white, you know with blonde hair and white skin, and I don't know if the mother felt guilty or something, but there was a black one as well. And you know what the child was doing, for at least fifteen minutes I swear, I'm not exaggerating, for at least fifteen minutes the child looked at the two dolls.   nean she couldn't have been more than three years old. But she was looking from one to the other. Then do you know what she did, she put the white doll to one side and started smashing the black one. No I mean, it was really strange like she had become possessed or something, she just started smashing this doll against the arm rest. It was so odd. The mother started getting embarrassed, wondering what was going on, took the doll from her and started whispering. You know all that baby talk, 'don't you like baby then.'(imitating the talk). Here what, the child shock her head. You know when the mother asked her a question, the girl shock her head, I thought what. What's goin' on."

"So the mother thought lets' try again, gave her the doll again. You know what the child did, she just grabbed the dolls head, pulled it off and threw her body half way down the carriage. At this, most of the carriage broke out in spontaneous laughter, they were all white anyway, I just kept looking. Here what she did now, she took the blonde one, you know the doll, with blonde hair and started hugging it." Ade lifted his head visibly exhausted by the story, "I thought what's going on and then I realised that's the future of our race, if we don't watch it, that's how we'll all end up like that. And you know the mother looked at me, the whole carriage with all them, what do you call them.... 'crackers,'.... all laughing. But me just staring. She looked at me and she knew, she just knew that I knew it." Ade shock his head and kissed his teeth, "I've never seen anything like it, so white you know, like that's what's going to happen to us all."

"Well that's that's up to us," Susan said, "the first thing is we've got to get all of you elected, there's a lot of work to do, are you up to it!"

"I shall have to be," Ade said, "but I'll never forget it, she just threw the doll across the carriage you know. No way after seeing that could you just pass it off."

"Well," Susan replied, "the important thing is you decided to stand up for what you believe in and that's a stage a lot of us don't reach," she looked around, "we suffer in silence, slowly going insane or something. Look at this place, so many black people. Do you think they're interested in all this stuff, they're not, I'm telling you they're not. Even with the society, when it comes to putting up the posters, you know most of them are watless and I mean the executive here. It's only Appia really, she's a good sister, she's alright, but the others, nah, like even your friend Melanie, just posers, really they are. So everyone of us, like you who stands up is one less zombie caught up in the confusion of the world. For other races it's natural but for us its such a strain, it's so painful. Well if we don't wake up. That child you saw destroying us, that's the future, our future, I'm telling you."

The Nigerians

"Wah, so your goin' reach, righteous," Flex asked, inquisitively, as Tayo bounced down the corridor. He had just finished his lecture on, "the Hausa-Fulani ruling elite and their control of alternative dispute resolutions in the Niger Delta." Tayo remembered, sitting at the back of the lecture theatre, slowly falling asleep, as Mrs Lawson muttered incomprehensible statements about the creative legal entities evolving in the Niger delta and the Amazon valley. 'It is only the third lecture,' he thought, twisting his locks with his fingers, 'I have gone to this week and now I realise why I don't bother, I'll learn more at an A.S. meeting.' So absorbed in thought, he forgot all about Flex's question.

"Yawa," Flex said, as Tayo began to drift off again.

"Yeah, yeah," Tayo said, coming back to reality, "I heard the first time. Yeah I think we should and before you say it, this time I'll take your advice, you can come, if you really want, see what my so called countrymen are really like."

Flex flicked his locks away from his face and half smiled, looking at Tayo's expression, 'there's something else in that still, he go'on like wha, he's alright, but there's some bitterness.... bitterness for what. Rage for what. It's true I've never seen him go'on like some of them, speaking Yoruba, I should say shouting Yoruba. It's true still, there's some difference. Me nah no why? He does the things he does, perhaps he ain't so secure as all that. Living with bluefoots. For all of them skills he must have..... there must be something missing still.'

"Where's Michael then," Tayo asked, almost from the corner of his mouth as they bounced out of the Elephant and Castle site and towards Denmark street.

"You know him still," Flex said, watching Tayo's expression and the slight line of perspiration breaking out on his top lip, "he done reach already, kotching and smoking blunts, he couldn't wait still."

The air was cool even as the sun filtered though the trees, speckling the littered streets with green and yellow light. The smell of alcohol from the nearby pub grew stronger and stronger as they crossed Southwark street and walked towards where it joined Denmark street. The stench rose from the city like mustard gas.

The pub's gaudy sign swung to and fro in the wind as the evening

descended on the streets of South London. A prostitute way off in
the distance plied her trade outside the concrete tower blocks.
Hitching up her skirt to reveal pale white legs imprisoned in black
fish net stockings. Her short dress soiled by her last customer and a
weather beaten old black leather jacket, metal studs sown into the
worn out leather. Her hair straggly and unkempt, tied at the back
in a red ribbon, lipstick smeared over the pale washed out face. A
huge black Volvo pulled up outside her block and a large brown
arm protruded, beckoning her over, she skipped like a child
towards him. Tayo and Flex just kept on walking.

A pigeon flew across the greying sky, nestling in a nearby tree and
discharging it's filth onto an unsuspecting pavement. The white
and brown liquid dropped unceremoniously on to the leaves and
dripped. The brothers walked, Flex's locks bounced all around him,
the heel of his boots not even touching the ground. The brown
bomber jacket open - to reveal the Timberland shirt beneath. His
mind relaxed.

Tayo contemplated, 'I don't know if this is a good idea. I know
there Kwame's friends and all, but something's not right. I've seen a
few of them at meetings, it's like their just their gathering information. Information, information for whom, like the powers that be,
need them in there so obvious. Anyway there's just something I
don't like about it. The way they come dressed in designer shirts
and gold chains, four hundred dollar crocodile shoes. Their glasses,
smelling of the beeswax their slave has used to clean them - I don't
like it. All that bravado, what do they say oku`to` (well done), well
done, well done for everything you know. I know my father comes
from that stock, my whole family, but doesn't mean I have to like
it.'

'I remember.... though I try not to remember, its painful - my memories as a child. I remember no more than one years old, barely
able to stand, holding my mother's hand for the last time. I
remember them talking Yoruba, dressed in the finest ten robes - but
didn't stop them doing what they were going to do. My father
walking across the side of the road, my mother following. There I
was trying to go after them and being shouted at, I was just one
years old, being shouted at to stand still, to stand still, just like
that. Not wait here, but, 'stand still' shouted at me, like a command. The tears falling, dribbling down my little brown cheeks.
Until my face was soaked, Sobbing until I felt I was going to die,
dressed in my best white shirt and brown sandals and red blazer,
but all I could do was cry. My father shouting from across the road,
'take him, take him now.' Two strange, long haired whites grabbing

me and shoving me in the car, though I screamed and fought them.

Driven to some foreign country place to be beaten for staring back, dished up roast beef and Yorkshire pudding. Even though the 'man of the house,' was an alcoholic and his wife a kleptomaniac, until the police arrested her and sent her to jail for three years. Sent on again by social services to another house where the man there thought it was his right to sexually abuse every child in his care. He tried it on me, until I hit him over the head with a frying pan and cracked his skull. Now what did the idiot say to his wife, 'I fell down the stairs. Really,' Tayo thought, 'no, everything I am I have had to fight for, every piece of consciousness or identity,'

Tayo kicked a nearby pebble across the road. Flex stared at him, 'what's up with him then,' he thought.

'Most black people don't even know there black,' Tayo thought, not even noticing Flex's eyes examining him, 'they don't, it's only when it's taken away from them, do they realise how important it is. I've have had to fight, just to find out who gave birth to me. As a child you don't know right from wrong and you blame yourself, you do, you think you've done something wrong, that your parents are leaving you there, that's what you think. How can people do that. It's not like it's an isolated incident or something. What..... there are thousands of Yoruba and others sold into exile, to be beaten and abused, ridiculed in all white schools.. how can this be. Then people will come tell me this and tell me that, like Yorubas have the monopoly on being African, as if they are the only Africans, they are not.' Tayo suddenly became irritated with his own thought, 'don't let anyone come tell me this, or that, don come tell me anything. I don't want to know,' he fiddled with his pouch, 'until you have been through what I have been through, you have no right to tell me anything.'

'Now,' Tayo thought, as he twisted his locks, 'when I found them. I do mean found them, did the research on my name and tracked them down, it was like I shouldn't have bothered. I mean it wasn't that they didn't 'kill the fatted calf' and bring all the extended family over to rejoice. But it was all a sham. It was empty, meaningless. They were strangers to me, and the behaviour even stranger. All that rejoicing and shouting for what. All that so called culture, but you give children to foreigners to look after. All that history, but you fail to recognise your part in slavery past, or present. Nigeria has a responsibility as the largest populated country of black people in the world, does it live up to it, no.'

'So,' Tayo thought, as he bounced down the street, his pouch slapping against his chest like a metal breastplate, 'I drifted away, it was not like it was deliberate, it just happened. A few phone calls every now and then, besides that's all they wanted anyway, so they could go to their friends, my son's studying law you know, he's doing well, 'okuto'. They don't want me there, staring at their fake hair styles, fake nails and fake lives. Relatives posing in ten robes of white cloth, but cleaning toilets for a living. Whilst others, multi-millionaires driving in BMW's and Mercedes Benz's and never thinking of giving a cent to help the rest of the family, though they embrace and hug each other, they would rather take a contract out on each other's life. Nigeria.'

'It's even worse when your there,' Tayo thought, as he bounced along the pavement, 'it's worse, you know when your family is so close to the centre of power and you know that power is, thoroughly corrupt and wicked, you feel yourself getting seduced into it. You see yourself doing things and saying things, you acquire slaves, you call them servants, but there slaves, house-boys and house-girls, some of them are even your poorer relatives. It's just wrong. That may be my western mind, perhaps, then again... perhaps not, but the longer I stayed there the more I was likely to become just like them, designer clothes, Versace tie and Pierre Cardin shirt. Nah man, that's not for me.'

Michael was standing next to a red brick building, one foot on the wall, a cigarette in his mouth like an advert for a famous cigarette company. His grey coat hanging down to his knees, smiling so that even from a distance you could see his straight white handsome teeth.

"There in there you know," Michael said, when he saw Tayo and Flex approaching.

"Go-on," Flex said, "don't you greet us now."

"Yeah, yeah," Michael replied apologetically, "my mistake, I was just trying to listen to them" - he fisted them. "I was getting jealous, y'know," he continued, "I can here them all the way out here, lots of words, sounds, can't make out the word, sounds like Oy..booo or something."

"Oyibo," Tayo said, "it means white-man."

"You mean you can speak the language?" Michael asked, "wha go'on."

"Not really," Tayo said, "it's just that it's the first word you learn, when you there, if your not from there. You learn it because people shout it at you, all the time. You think people take you as a brother or sister, nah, they'd' be more ready to take a whiteman I tell you, rather than you. I mean it."

"Really," Michael said, "I heard people say, that going back to Africa was like going back home."

"Yeah me to," Flex said, "like it's just paradise."

"It's not true, there's no, or very little colour consciousness, I can tell you, people give you certain props because your bringing foreign currency, so they say, 'ohh my brother,' (putting on an accent) to anyone, even a Chinese man from Peking. Even that respect is there only so long as your visiting and you can pay the dollars. When your like permanent and the money starts running out, see how people **switch** now. See them."

"Scene," Flex said, "I remember as a youth still when some of them braes, would come straight from the mother land, some of them would just go on stink, you know. Just renk y'know and bad like their royalty, y'know," thinking, 'I've got to stop saying y'know it's a bad habit.'

"Yeah well," Tayo said, "we're going to get more of that." He walked towards the concrete steps and Michael and Flex followed. The latter looking around warily as they cleared the first flight and proceeded up to the second. Tayo bounced the door open and strode into the corridor. A sign above read, 'Denmark Street Site,' underneath in black lettering, 'Accountancy and Finance courses Room 279 and 276.'

The three brothers sauntered into the corridor, half lit by the strobe light. They bounced past room 274, 275, 276. They stopped.

"Do you wannna do the honours," Tayo said, to Michael.

"Alright," Michael replied, Bapb, Bapb (knocking the door).

The latch of the door swung too and it creaked open, a trail of dust cascaded into the gap.

Tayo, Michael and Flex stood at the entrance and peered in.

Adetunji Rotimi stared back though his Gold rimmed spectacles.

His slim athletic face tainted by an arrogant jaw, fixed, resolute, austere. A pencil thin moustache over capped white teeth. A designer haircut and pale brown eyes staring through the gloom like two jewels, in a white jelly. Five others flanked him: Ogun, his father was a general in the Nigerian army, rubbing the calluses on his knuckles like a boxer, small scars all over his face as if a cat had scratched him. Segun playing with his short jerry curls like a girl, his father was a merchant banker. David cleaning his glasses, with his handkerchief like a senior civil servant making notes. Ebi playing with the strap on his bag and Leke with a smirk all over his face like the delinquent he was. All decked in designer shirts, and flannel suits, smelling of Paco Rabane, Obsession and Hugo Boss. The place stinking of French after-shave like a brothel.

Tayo looked around - the tables were stacked carelessly at the far end of the room, the paint chipped from their metal legs. A blackboard, with dry chalk smugged on it. Chairs some turned upwards, others piled as if they had been drunk on palm wine and fallen on top of each other. The carpet grey with filth and worn here and there to the underlay. He looked back at Adetunji.

"`Ob`ure,`wa," (unfortunate person) Segun said, when he saw Flex's shoddy jeans, big boots and locks.

"Oyinb`o," Ogun said, staring at Tayo, followed by David echoing him and then laughing like two children, leaning up against the nearby window though it was grey with filth.

Tayo stared at them as they insulted and giggled - trying to stop the adrenaline that was flowing through his veins.

Adetunji walked towards them, "Bawon,nkan, yeah and congrats, that was a good speech," he said, to Tayo, stretching out his hand for him to shake it - he had a way of speaking broken English which was pompous, yet precise.

"Kobade, (not bad)" Tayo replied.

"Oh well," Adetunji replied, "I know you don't speak Yourba well," listening to his accent and sighing, staring at Tayo and then looking Michael up and down saying, "huh, hah." Michael frowned.

"Do you know who I am," Adetunji said, his mood suddenly changing, "me a OSO (one that speaks well) me a Oni`ja` jagun, jagun (fighter), no worry me, me a cutter, catcher, I will fuck you up."

"Ok`uto," (Well done) Segun said, grinning like an idiot who had just come out of St Anne's (mental institution). His jerry curls glistening, even under the fading light of the classroom.

"Really," Tayo replied, "but that's alright, I don't want violence, I'm going through a transition phase right now," he folded his arms.

Flex laughed, and relaxed his shoulders, the adrenaline beginning to flow through his youthful muscles. He watched Ogun, rubbing his knuckles and staring wildly at them like a boxer weighting for the bell, looked at David as he fiddled in his pockets like he was searching for a weapon.

Michael had already undone the latch on his blade and held the white, engraved, ivory handle firmly in his hand, it rested concealed in his pocket.

"On ko Nigberaga, (he is arrogant)," David said, looking at Tayo's expression.

"Oyibo," Segun said again, and his friends all laughed, yet again. This time Michael turned and looked at him and Flex kissed his teeth so hard - he could feel them chattering together.

"If you call me," Tayo said, to Segun, "or one of these brothers a whiteman one more time, I swear I'm going to put your head through that glass window," pointing to the classroom window, "and see if your blood is the same as ours."

Ogun stood upright, clenching his fists and walking towards him.

"Cool down," Adetunji proclaimed looking around at everyone, walking to the middle of the room, waving his hands in all directions like a teacher getting school children to class, "or I'll beat you all up!"

Tayo smiled, adjusting his pouch again and staring at Ogun, still sizing him up, his fists tightly closed, his eyebrow vibrating with nervous tension.

David watched Flex as he raised and lowered himself on his heels - kissing his teeth for the second time, Flex's back soaking in sweat, 'me, feel,' he thought, adjusting his position, 'to lick off all them man's head, scene, just for there uppity renkness.'

David thinking, watching him, 'this little `obu`ure,`wa, light skinned boy, me, will kick his arse.'

"We want to start our own thing," Adetunji continued, "you don't represent us, that's what we're saying. We want a club for Nigerians. For us, for the families of those who have it," rubbing his fingers together in front of Tayo's face as if he had a thousand pounds right there. "We don't want your kind of, Jamo,'(worthless), what do you call them, 'riff raff,' in our thing"- he slapped his chest with his hand like a Senator making a speech. "Insecure people," he added, "who where locks like dada, you're not dada, you're jamoo, you're oyibo. Who told you, you could where locks. You don't know African culture, you don't, what do you know about it."

Tayo looked nonchalantly at him, watching Segun fidgeting with his jerry curls and still thinking about cracking his head open.

"You haven't got what it takes, you Jam`o, you haven't." Adetunji said, "now why should we follow you. You can't speak your language. Look.. A..k..i..n..j..o (spelling out the letters), that's your name, a good Yoruba name, but you don't know anything about Nigeria. You haven't even been. I heard you lived with white man all your life. Ahh white man, are not bad, it's we who are the problem. You need to find out about your culture before you start lecturing us about Africa. I am a real African, you're not, your a white man." The cries of "oyibo" and "Jamoo" echoed around the classroom.

"Yeah," Tayo uttered, calmly through the uproar as Leke giggled like a girl, "as for my own shortcomings. Indeed I have many. Am I a white man, I looked in the mirror and I was black this morning."

Michael was already on his tip toes thinking, 'I don't business, I'll fight anyone, I don't business.'

"Since you brought it up," Tayo continued, "when people are looking to discredit the truth, always looking for something personal. I have many faults. What they say I'm arrogant, egotistical - who do I think I am, a superstar, they ask. I'm not perfect. It's true I can't speak Yoruba fluently, but then I can't speak Fante, or Twe, or any other Akan language either, I don't know Wallof, and my Swahili's a bit rustie. But it's strange that you don't question me about them."

"Ahhh," Adetunji said, interrupting, "Swahili, Wallof, that's nothing to do with me, I'm a Nigerian man, a Yoruba man from Ogun

state. I am an African man, I don't need to know all that, you
know nothing of Africa. You can't tell me anything. Who is your
grandfather, what is his name, who is your grandmother, what is
her name, where are they from, you talk about white people all the
time, but you don't know who you are (his accent was pronounced). Who gave you the right to lead anything, what makes
you think that you know anything, who the hell do you think you
are. Who do you think you are, you're an Oyibo," with this last
comment he raised his youthful hand and attempted to push past
Tayo as one would an irritating fly.

Tayo stepped to the side gripping Adetunji's fingers with both
hands and twisting them. Adetunji's bones twisted, the index finger
snapping under the pressure, he could not adjust his agile frame.
Tayo gripped him around the neck strangling him - pushing his
thumb into his windpipe, whilst Adetunji's aroma of coca-butter
masked by the sickly funk of Obsession (after shave) filled the air.

"If your friends," Tayo said, watching them advancing and Ogun
picking up a chair, "come any closer I'll kill you, this strangle hold
is very good, it only takes fifteen seconds, now this I did learn from
a white man, but it works."

Adetunji waved them away, his face more and more discoloured,
his eyes bloodshot and his index finger hanging limply. Ogun put
down the chair, the others stood motionless like robots turned off
at the mains - but Michael kept his hands in his pocket and around
his Ivory handled knife. Flex had already unbuckled his saddle and
stood grasping it tightly.

"Now," Tayo declared calmly, "it's one thing to say or accuse me of
being something other than what I am, but when you start to lay
hands on me like a bwoy. That can't run, do you here. I know
you're used to having slaves, what, your father's a diplomat," (looking down at Adetunji) "the ambassador no less, well, well," he was
still strangling him, "you're used to having your own way, well it's
like this, I was going to just walk out of here and let you go your
own way, I was. But now that can't run. That's not goin' to happen.
Listen you have only got eighty votes maximum in this college."
Tayo's heart was beating as fast as sprinting leopard, "it's not going
to make that much difference either way. But now it's the principle
of the thing. You'll all vote for me and support your fellow brothers
and sisters in these elections, because we are doing this for you. I
don't want to stand, but circumstances have dictated that I must.
Now we are consolidating the black vote and you are black and you
are African, as all black people are African. You do not have the

monopoly on being African. You have no right to deny nine hundred million people the right to be Africans simply because they're not Nigerians."

Tayo feeling Adetunji passing out, gently relaxing his grip around his throat, his adversary falling to the floor choking, muttering, "e`s,u, enia burburu, o`ris,a` (you devil)," blood dribbling from his mouth. The marks from Tayo's finger still in his youthful arrogant neck.

"Listen," Tayo continued, backing towards the door, with Michael and Flex by his side, "we are your brothers, whether you like it, or not, don't think you can come here play about a bit, then go back to Nigeria live life rich, carry on exploiting our people. I know your the sons of Millionaires and entrepreneurs, generals and the like, have dinner with the President do you. Well when I become the President I may invite you to have dinner with me. Then again I might not. So you have no choice now, you vote for us, or we're going to have to come back and sought this another way. Oh yeah," he said, opening the door, Michael and Flex darting through it, "my grandfather used to say, do not despise the reptile for not having horns, who is to say that it will not become a dragon, oddbo, (goodbye)" and he stepped out calmly, shutting the door - as a chair thrown from inside landed against its wooden frame, its metal legs buckling on impact and ripping into the wood - splinters flying everywhere.

They turned to walk down the corridor, but Michael twisted on his heels, even before Flex who had reached out a youthful hand could stop him, opening the door and sticking his head through it, Michael looked at their startled faces, gathered round the gasping Adetunji.

"By the way," Michael said, as they looked up astonished at him, "I ain't no Jamoo, I'm an African and I'd be speaking Yoruba better than you, if your lot hadn't sold me." He banged the door shut, the brass latch coming off in his hands, he threw it on the ground, its now used nails sticking in the carpet and he skipped after the others. Tayo and Flex stood concerned at the end of the corridor, hardly lit, their three shadows elongated.

"What did you say in there," Tayo asked, worried.

"Nuthing," Michael said, "but I don't think they liked it much, come on I think we'd better get out of here."

"Yeah," Flex said, as they cleared the building, skipping down the stairs and on to the road, he turned to Tayo as they went, "why do you keep making speeches all the time, when man a man, should be busting head."

"Why don't you ask, Michael that," Tayo said, smiling.

"No," Flex said, as they turned the corner and walked down towards Denmark street, "I'm asking you."

"Well," Tayo replied, becoming a little agitated, "don't you get the point?"

"What point," Flex asked, stopping under a nearby street lamp, his face contorted for a while by the unnatural light.

"The point," Tayo said.

"I don't see any point at all," Flex interrupted, his face animated by the artificial light, "it's just self grandisement, scene. Why do you wax lyrical, when you should be doing somet'ing still. "

"Yeah," Michael said, agreeing and fiddling about inside his huge grey pockets for a cigarette, "you went on a bit didn't ya."

"Is that the most you two could say, you're lost, I need to get myself some other brothers, some new ones," Tayo said, twisting his locks.

"Watcha," Flex replied, "we ain't lost, just know when to fight and when to talk, that's all, unlike you."

"Well if I could have got out of there without a fight, I would have," Tayo said, looking at the metal decoration on the lamp-post as it wound upwards to the greying sky darkened by clouds.

Flex frowned, brushing the locks from his face and thinking, 'he got away too easy, me sure he just likes flapping his gums, there's no reason for it.' He placed his saddle back in his back-pack with the dexterity of a Samurai and looked at the sky over the decaying streets of Britain, 'I swear that's a swastika up there,' he thought, looking at the shape of the clouds, 'well that's appropriate still.'

"There is no way," Michael said, smiling and locating his cigarette, which he duly popped in his mouth and proceeding to talk out of the corner like a 1940's detective, "we were going to get out of there without some blood, some licks, I'm just glad still it wasn't me - some of them brothers were tick, (motioning with his hands, for big). You would have seen my funeral still, a whole string of girls now, all crying and threatening to kill themselves, cause they can't live without me still. You see the newspapers now, Don Michael Richards, the mackiest, Mack daddy of them all was killed brutally yesterday, this country is now in national mourning." Flex and Tayo stared at him and shock their heads simultaneously, forgetting all about their initial disagreement.

The drink, the toilet and the screwdriver

Mathew Harris' glass was full to the brim with Tetley's best bitter, the white froth on the surface of the brown contents, bubbles rising and falling in sequence. Harris' slim, almost feminine hands, grasping the glass like it was his own penis on a Friday night. Bitten fingers to the cuticle, a sneer and a frown (if that's possible) all over his face.

"Give us another and put some skates on," Harris blurted out, "you move as fast as a snail." Rory the bar tender shuffled around trying to gather his wits, but failing; he resorted to scratching his head.

"I tell you what, if you don't get your arse over here, I'll kick you from here to fucking Elephant and Castle, I swear, do you understand, you lazy stupid mick bastard," he screamed, pushing the chair away with his heel.

Simon sauntered over to Harris, still a little bit under the weather from the drinks he had consumed all afternoon. His eyes, bloodshot, stained red, the pallor of his cheeks flushed and tinged. His slim frame wrapped in a baggy white T-shirt, not noticeable but for the creases and crumples in it. Harris was still ranting, as Simon whispered in his ear (like his lover) gently caressing his neck. Harris stopped in mid syllable as his young friend put his lips to his ear and muttered. Harris smiled a sadistic reptilian smile, like a snake who had coiled its enemy. Within a second the smile had turned into a frown, a deep dark frown that stayed on his face like it had been painted on by a cynical artist.

"You what," Harris said, through his teeth, "and what're you looking at, Paddy," to Rory.

"You what," he muttered again, almost to himself, "you fucking what, you mean that lot won, they won, how... I mean how do you mean.....?"

Simon turned and looked at the floor, "yeah its real, its really real, honestly," he replied.

"But niggers don't win," Harris continued, "they don't win, they lose everywhere, I've never seen them win anything, even if it's just raise a family, they lose. Why the hell should they start winning now. Not in England, not here, not bloody here, what's going on." He kicked the bar stool with his white trainers, so hard that part of the oak panelling came off leaving a crack in the varnished surface.

"Come on mate, its not all that bad, this place is full of them anyway," Simon said, looking around at an Asian student with his arm around his blonde girlfriend, who seemed a little bit big for the small T-shirt she was wearing.

"No listen," Harris said, "we're the majority, they're the minority, we are. Us, not them, ya'know some of our people must have voted for them, bloody liberals, namby - pamby-do-gooders." Harris turned to look at the Asian student, "I'm sick of this shit, if this fucker keeps giving me the evil, I'm goin' to put this glass in his head just to see the colour of his blood," he spat.

"I tell you what," Harris added, "I'm not standing for it, I'm not having it, do you understand," looking at Simon, "I'm not goin' to stand for it, do you understand ... I'm not bloody having it...." his face was scarlet with rage.

"Be cool," Simon said, "we gave one of them a good hiding, we'll get them, just not right now, that's all." Harris stood, his feet astride, the blood vessels on his neck bursting, as the blood pumped faster and faster to his brain. Like a river that had reached its zenith and now bubbled and seethed before it tumbled down a huge waterfall. His waspish hands bleached white in rage, his cheeks flushed and fleshing.

"Where's Jeremy then," Harris asked, with an almost far away glance, managing to calm himself down a little, "you can never find him when you need him." Simon looked around, "he's probably in the bathroom washing his hands, he really went to town on that little geezer, I mean he went wild. It was like it was personal, or something. There was blood everywhere, he couldn't come out like that, he'd be arrested."

"Well," Harris said, "good for him, he's probably got the savage stuff in his blood."

Harris gritted his teeth thinking, 'I've got to think straight, lose a battle, to win the war. But I ain't lost yet. I refuse to believe I could lose to a nigger. A spade you know, a coon, wog, spearchucking slave, I refuse to believe it.'

Tayo stood in the concourse. It was ten p.m. 'The result must be out now,' he thought, 'perhaps I shouldn't have left Peter up there in the Union by himself, but if I'd stay there any longer I think I'd go insane.' He looked at Flex and Michael, 'they're both trying to pretend they aren't here to wait for me and the count,' he looked at them. Michael in his grey coat and timberland boots posing in the nearby mirror. Flex with a personal stereo in his ears jigging up and down, 'a little bit to smooth for ten p.m. on a Friday,' Tayo thought. 'Well it's better than being with all those pen pushers, besides, where are they anyway, you know the likes of Kwame, he's been scarce these last few days. Perhaps the whole thing has got to hot, too close, it might harm his future prospects of being President of Ghana,' he thought, and kissed his teeth, 'I thought he was changing, going forward not backwards. Well.'

Flex's locks were spinning around almost in tandem to the music, each one seemingly suspended to the beat. 'Ghetto heaven,' Flex thought, 'is just about the only track, that's come in the last year that's all right still, man its got somethink' that's sweet still,' he thought, as it blasted out the second chorus, "Kind of like my baby.... especially each..... she leaves it by the radio and listens to it every week, every week, Ghetto heaven, it's time to make some ghetto heaven,......" He switched the volume to maxim, with the dexterity of a DJ mixer putting in his last mix, totally ignoring Michael by his side.

Michael had his head in the air, thinking, 'should I, or shouldn't I, smoke a spliff or a cigarette, spliff or a cigarette, which one,' when Tayo walked up.

"I've been meaning to ask you," Tayo said, then seeing Michael's mind so absorbed, "what you're thinking about?"

"Nothink," Michael replied.

"Any way I was going to ask you, you know those girls I saw you with on that first day of term, what happened to them, where are they?" Tayo asked.

"Which girls," Michael replied, he's was trying to remember from all the girls he had ever been with, which ones Tayo was talking about.

"You know," Tayo said, "those girls, the ones who were with you in the classroom, you know." Michael shock his head. "You know," Tayo added, "there was a big girl, and another one half asleep."

"Oh yeah, now I remember," Michael said, "the big one, you mean mampie, ... well that's a long story anyway."

"How do you mean long," Tayo puzzled, adjusting his pouch and leaning up against the wall smattered in posters for the election.

"They don't come here, you know," Michael replied, "they're from country like me."

"What's that place," Tayo asked.

"Northampton," Michael answered.

"Yeah that's right!" Tayo exclaimed, as if he had just thought of it himself.

"They just reached for me," Michael added, "you saw them kotching like they were native, but they were just on a bligh."

"You mean to tell me," added Tayo, "you were sitting in that classroom spliffing with those girls and they weren't even from here, what, you smuggled them in?"

"Its' got to be done," Michael continued, and laughed and Tayo tried not to.

"What go'on, what you dealin' with," Flex said, rather too loudly as Ghetto heaven was still blasting in his ears.

"Nothink," Michael said, smirking like a delinquent child.

"Nuthink," Tayo said, "why don't you speak properly, the word is nothing."

"So you goin' teach me," Michael exclaimed, "how to work the Queen's lingua' are you, wha' me nah for dat'. I remember when I first met you how you used to talk all proper, pronounce every word and dat. Now look at you, like ya from Trench town, wah."

Tayo half smiled.

"I tell ya though," Michael continued, looking around, "if you want someone to speak like they've a pearl in their mouth," (looking at Ade running towards them down the end of the corridor), "here's dat man."

Tayo watched Ade as he got closer and closer. Sweat rolling in beads down his face, his Karl Kani T shirt open almost to the chest. His slim, dark, handsome features agitated. Flex took his ear plugs out, but Tayo was half way down the corridor. Ade stood like a school boy waiting outside the headmaster's office, his hands clasped behind his back.

"What's up," Tayo rumbled, "what's going on?"

Ade stood silently numb, "come on brother," Tayo said. A line of sweat dripped down Ade's forehead, stopped for a moment at the bridge of his nose, it held itself finally at the tip, as if gravity would force it down. But it just stood there.

Ade wiped the sweat from his face with his hand. "Okay," he said, still breathing heavily, "Peter, it's Peter, someone just broke him..." before Ade could finish Tayo was half way down the concourse. Even as Ade shouted after him, "there's something else too.. you've.." But Tayo was through the double doors and striding across the road towards the Union bar.

The blood was rushing to every corner of his brain and body, pumping faster and faster, until they almost burst through his blood vessels. Anger, bubbling like a cauldron on an open fire. Still he bounced towards the Union, his fists clenched automatically.

Tayo felt the spring air on his face, the slight breeze from the east. The wind wiping up the leaves and scattering them all around him like confetti at a wedding (but he wasn't going to one). He bounced, kicking the leaves aside as he went - undaunted by the growing stench of alcohol and nicotine. It tried to block his thoughts for a moment, compassion, regret, fear, disappeared, only vengeance. He bit his lip and kissed his teeth, as he bounced over the broken concrete steps like a cat. 'Violence,' Tayo thought, as bounded along the pavement, 'how can you meet violence with singing and holding hands, we tried and failed, it may have worked for Gandhi, but he had numbers and world opinion, what have we got. Martin Luther King - lost his life just like that, but the system's just as bad. As for us, nah. So what is the way....well, I ain't going to do no singing and no praying.' He clenched his teeth and bit his lip, his conscience drip, dripping away - like a mask made of ice, in the blazing summer-time. All that was left was revenge.

Even his clothes hung on him irritatingly, he adjusted his pouch, it swung to slightly, bouncing against his chest like a bullet proof jacket. He swerved past an over spilling dustbin, coke cans and filth littering the city streets.

Swung the glass door open, it swung to and shuddered against the exterior wall. Tayo bounced in and up the stairs, three at a time, not even stopping for breath, 'I know what and how I'm goin' to do what needs to be done. I just hope he's there, my God I hope it.'

Tayo kicked the door of the student union bar open, he did not notice the empty seats, but he saw Rory staring bleary eyed at him. Tayo put his finger to his mouth, 'be quiet now,' he thought, to himself, as he stared at Rory. Rory just looked on bewildered. Tayo was across the bar before the larger that Harris was drinking had slide down his throat. He should have felt the cat's presence, as he loomed towards him, his sixth sense almost failing him until at last, to late, he turned and there Tayo stood over him. Harris with the glass still in his hand, still partially filled and he was alone. Tayo scowled and clenched his teeth. He transferred his weight to his toes, his heels partially off the ground. His hips were turned obliquely, the move was effortless, even when accompanied by his knee as it rose followed by his leg as he kicked. Striking Harris' hand and the partially filled glass. Harris squealed like a pig, panicked, the sharp throbbing pain of the kick resounding through his whole body.

He dropped the glass. Its' sticky contents splashed all over what was left of the oak panels, the glass shattering. Tayo bounded in, skipping and striking simultaneously, the front jab struck Harris' face in the jaw. Tayo was gliding and darting around his adversary, a second blow hit Harris in the temple and the third, a hook, delivered so smoothly that the sound reverberated in the air. Harris' head jerked back, like a punch and Judy doll, blood dripping from his nose and mouth. His brain rattling against his skull as it was knocked backwards and forwards. His body turned limp, as darkness and ignorance took over. Tayo gripped Harris' collar with his hands, lifting him almost off the ground. Gripped him so tight, he could feel his own heart beat through his fingers.

Tayo looked at the mouse like face battered and bruised, the blonde hair now matted with blood and sweat. Blood congealed on the lower lip. The skin cut and broken around his jaw like a red and white mosaic. Blood dripping from the broken nose. The pale eyes closed within their lids. The shocked expression ingrained on his face.

"Aren't you supposed to be," Tayo said, lifting his face up to stare at it, "the good man. Aren't you supposed to win? Aren't you the hero, what business have I got busting your head. Look at you. Look at the state your in, punk, your bleeding all over your shirt like a pig. I should put you out of you misery, but I'll not go to prison for killing you, think yourself lucky."

He released his grip and Harris slid down the bar, like a pile of faeces down a toilet. His own bar stool breaking his fall. Tayo spun around like a dancer and looked at the faces, who stood there stunned, shocked, the Asian guy with his white girlfriend in silence. Rory trying to hide a smile.

"Any one else want a go," Tayo said, "anyone, you," pointing to a student on the far side, who had come over to see what all the trouble was.

"**Master race**," Tayo said, calmly, "master race, whatcha,' you've just been **mastered**." He bounced out, smiling, kicking a nearby bar stool that got in his way half way across the bar. The scar on his forehead glistened with sweat, shining, his heart beating faster than a leopard though he tried to control it.

Michael was walking towards the Technology block. Ade had told him, 'there's one of them called Simon, whose always with them, he's a nasty bit of work, I know that he's part of it, I think he walks that way to go empty his locker, he's got some racist literature that he puts up in the locker room, I know cause I've got one in there. That's where you'll catch him if he had anything to do with that attack on Peter.'

'Well,' Michael thought, as he bounced towards the grey concrete building, 'let me see, if I can get lucky.' He had not walked more than fifty meters when a small white youth, bounced into him, stopping in the middle of the street, and instead of apologising, put out his small, pale looking hands and tried to shove him aside. Michael looked at him, "why are you putting your hands on my coat, cracker," he said calmly.

"Fuck off you black bastard," Simon shrieked, recoiling backwards, with the futility of his previous action.

He reached inside his pocket and pulled out a plastic handled knife. The blade glinted in the evening air.

"Wha," Michael said, laughing, "your name wouldn't be Simon would it."

"What's it too you coon," Simon said.

"No reason," Michael said, calmly pulling out his ivory handled knife and flicking out the blade. "I just like to know when I cut out someone's heart whose it is, scene," a thin line of perspiration broke out on his forehead, (though he would always deny it).

Simon stopped and looked at Michael as he bounced towards him, 'that's a real knife and I think this thug looks crazy enough to use it, look at his hair (looking at his locks), I bet he's just taken some drugs or something. He looks crazy,' he thought, his heart missing a beat.

"Al right," Simon said, stepping back. "I don't want any trouble, all right, (like he was talking down to a child)." He flung the knife to the side, it landed in a nearby ditch, blade first, the plastic handle sticking up in the air, "if you want to fight, lets fight fair," he said. But he had already reached in his pocket for his screwdriver.

Michael came towards him, "let's not," he replied. But Simon lashed out swiftly with his weapon like a snake, slashing wildly and cutting Michael's coat wide open at the front, a wide gaping whole now yawned.

"Wha' wah' you doing," Michael shrieked, and kissed his teeth, "I didn't steal this thing, for you to come and broke it up."

Simon stepped back, "I'll kill you, I will, you black bastard, (strange language for a potential MP wasn't it).

Michael watching him shuffling his way back against the railing. His blue eyes flashing in the evening air. But he scuffed his heels like a schoolboy clumsily. Michael read it before he could adjust, he advanced. Bouncing on his toes, Michael struck, kicking the screw driver out of Simon's hand, spinning around, and elbowing him in his face, his head seeming to swing in motion. (All those expectations, a keen future in politics and he was out brawling on the street.)

Michael hopped in close to him, he could smell his bio, the stench from his un-washed mouth and kneed him in his head, with the ease of a dancer performing Swan Lake. Simon's head swung back, but Michael gripped him around the neck, though it was by now slimy with his sweat like a snake - he held his knife to Simon's face. though the latter struggled in vain.

"What were you going to do with that screwdriver, something like this," Michael said. He pushed the blade towards his face. The shiny edge coming ever closer. Simon tried to wriggle out, but the knife had already reached his face, slicing his cheek like a surgeon. Red blood oozed out like wine from a rotten grape, sticky, wet and stinking. Simon blubbered like a child, "be quiet," Michael said, looking at him, as the blood streamed down and stained his coat like dye.

"If I wanted to kill you," Michael asserted, "I would. In your life there are many lessons, learn this, if you keep pushing people, sometime there goin' to push you back." He turned and left, Simon still clutching the rail, his weak hands, rasping and pale, squealing like a baby and embracing his blood soaked face, though the blood trickled through his fingers, stamping his left foot on the pavement, like a temper, tantrum baby and blubbering.

Flex was near to the toilets with Ade as Jeremy was coming out.

"There's one of them," Ade muttered, under his breath as they passed him.

"Wha' now you say," Flex replied, as they passed him.

"Why do you think I took you this way," Ade replied scratching his head.

"I thought you wanted to go ease yourself, or somethink, wait here," Flex said. He turned and bounced after him.

"Yawa," Flex hollered as he went down the corridor. Jeremy turned on his heels, every muscle and sinew flexing.

"You talking to me," Jeremy answered.

"Me feel to just teach you some manners still," Flex pronounced, "don't you know when 'mana'-man talks to bwoy, bwoy not's supposed to talk back, till he's told."

"What," Jeremy said, "I don't understand a word you just said, talk English, this is England."

"Yeah," Flex replied, looking at the glint in his eye and a certain agileness in his movement, "but you don't look so English to me."

"Well," Jeremy said, "you don't look so black to me, (looking at his brown locks)" and he chuckled to himself and turned to leave.

"Black enough," Flex answered, "Black enough to know, I going to b..e..a..t you. To teach you to respeck your eldeis still (he was only twenty), bluefoot bwoy."

Jeremy turned around for the second time and smiled, "do you know what I was doing in there," he said. Flex looked at him "I was washing the blood of one of your kind off my hands, do you know why, cause we just beat him up, upstairs, outside the count-ing room, they had to call an ambulance. But do you know why I did it. It's not like I had to, I wanted to. I really wanted to. Do you know my mother looks like you (he adjusted his position). I mean she does. What you're mixed race in it (looking at his brown locks). Well, she looks like you. Do you know what, I've always hated my mother. I always wanted to be like my father, to be all white, but she just kept reminding me, I wasn't. But do you know, every time I kick one of your asses, on the rugby pitch, in training, or in the gym, I feel whiter, can you understand that half caste," he said.

Flex stared at him, "bwoy you talk to much, you goin' fight or what, your mouth is fat and you keep flapping your gums, come now," he replied.

"Now you don't want to fight me," Jeremy said, "listen you don't, I'm a black belt in Karate third down, I'll break everything, every bone in your body," and he took up a Karate stance, bringing his fists back and clenching them, shouting, "K..i...a." so loudly the small blood vessel on the back of his neck pulsated.

Flex stared at him resting on his heels, and smiled. His teeth should have been stained yellow with nicotine, but they shone white as if they had been bleached. Jeremy saw the teeth gleaming brightly, the slight turn of his body and the movement as Flex twisted, but he saw it too slow. Flex had already wrenched his saddle out from the strap on his back and struck Jeremy before he could alter his position. Jeremy stood dazed for awhile, his brain still trying to regain the composure of his body, but Flex spun around and struck him again, his saddle shining, dazzling and bright, under the elec-tric lights.

Jeremy tried to gain control, but failed, his world turned black, and he fell. The dent in his head glared and blood trickled from the open wound in his skull, he fell and landed on the corridor floor, prone. Flex stood over him, his saddle stained with blood, like a knight who had just slain a dragon.

"Being black is not somethink you where bwoy," he said, "ya nah say you can't put it on and take it off like a mask, nah, it's an obligation and a responsibility still, but bwoy, ya too white to understand that, so you suffer" and he stepped over his lying body and down the corridor. Ade hearing all the commotion running to meet him.

Tayo strode across the road, as it greyed into absolute darkness. The dimness only foreshadowed by the beam of the overhead street lights. Clouds of filth blocking the faded beams of the moon. The sky pocked with stars blighted and obscured by the grey concrete towers of despair, choking the air, thought, life.

Tayo skipped down the streets, his pouch bouncing against his chest nonchalantly. 'Black people will think I'm strong, one day, they'll say what you did was extreme, it was strong, that's what they'll say,' he thought, as he blinked under the headlights of the passing vehicles, 'they think I'm **strong**, but they're wrong, they're oh so wrong, they're just **weak**. All I really want to do, is go and wrap myself in Appia's arms, that's all I really want to do, to hell with all this foolishness,' and he looked at the bruises on his knuckles.

'So much fronting,' Tayo thought, scowling, 'black people, do so much fronting, puffer jackets, Karl Kani, Calvin Klien and Kickers, Paco Rabbane, Timberland, they're like badges of ownership. Ownership of what.....' he rubbed his bare chin, 'our souls. They own our souls. Front teeth, gold teeth, back teeth, no teeth, short dress, long dress, no dress, all fronting. Look at that: ravers, rude-boys, raggamuffins, recidivists, rascals, but where were they today. A brother get's put in hospital, but where were they today. Out here, out there, out somewhere, but, they're not right here, where ever it is, they're fronting, **fools**.'

"Yawa," Tayo heard and he peered through the dimness of the night. Michael came bouncing towards him smiling, like the cat with the cream. "What are you smiling at," Tayo demanded, seeing the smile on his face, as he bounded up to him, his Timberlands not even touching the ground, "what have you been up to and where's Flex and Ade."
"Beats me, dunno," Michael said, trying to strike a pose - even though his jacket was falling to pieces around him. "Yeah," he

added, changing the subject from himself, "where you going to so fast."

"No where," Tayo said, "so, what's up!"

"Well if you'd stop long enough," Michael replied, "for me to tell you, it's like your trying to run a marathon or somethink. Listen."

But Tayo just kept walking.

"I'm not running after you," Michael continued, "I'm not goin' to run after you, do you here. Listen you talk about all this black stuff. You're the one who talks it not me. You can't fight this thing by yourself. You need a family. Right now, cigarette smoking, pot taking, coat stealing brother that I am, I'm your family and so are all them others, Melanie, yes even Melaine, Susan, Ade, Appia, all of them still. We are family. This ain't lone ranger, where the cracker rides off into the sunset on a white horse. You ain't no cracker and there ain't no horse, especially a white one."

"Alright then," Tayo said, stopping and sighing, "what's up?".

"You know what," Michael said, "I don't even know if I should tell you. Sort out your face," he said, still posing and attempting in vain to adjust his torn coat.

"What happened to your coat," Tayo asked, looking at him under the rising moon as he grappled with the torn pieces of material.

"What happened to your fists," Michael replied, looking under the faded moonlight at Tayo's blood stained knuckles.

"Nothing," Tayo said, trying to hide them behind his back.

"Well there's a whole lot of nothink happening to night," Michael added, "I wonder if Flex is up to nothink, knowing him, probably he is, or Ade, what's he up to, nothink, well."

"Well," Tayo said, watching Michael's frustrated attempts to look cool with his jacket disintegrating around him, "before I start laughing at the fact that all your, to quote you, your kris garms keep getting finished, tell me what's up."

"Al right," Michael replied, shuddering a little at the cool evening breeze, "first you know, I guess you know about Peter."

"Yeah, something should happen to the perpetrators," Tayo said, smiling.

"I agree," Michael answered, grinning.

"What you grinning teeth for," Tayo asked.

"Nothink," Michael replied.

"Let's not start that again," Tayo added, looking away, "alright so we're going to visit Peter. In fact I'm going to find out which hospital he's at and call them tonight. I know it's got to be done, and I agree, but you didn't come all this way just to tell me that did you."

"I'll tell you, just to shut you up," Michael muttered, under his breath.

"What," Tayo asked, confused.

"You won," Michael said.

"Won what?" Tayo puzzled, and playing with his baby locks.

"You won the election," Michael said, "what did you think I was talking about."

"You're joking," Tayo said.

"Do I look like I'm joking - no I'm serious," Michael replied.

Tayo sighed and looked around the grey buildings of south London, concrete monstrosities disfiguring the landscape. The stench of the streets rising even as the night enveloped itself across the metropolis. A stray dog with his tail between his legs, limping across the tawdry streets he had been fighting with a cat. The faint red and yellow blur of the traffic speeding down the back alleys.

Tayo adjusted his pouch and sighed again, shaking his head, 'I never thought I would actually win, I never thought it really.'

"So what are you going to do now then," Michael asked, staring at him and finally deciding to disregard his jacket altogether, tearing off what was now strips of grey material and leaving it in a clump on the pavement. 'I spent all that time to thief it, get chatted up by some flusie, now look at it,' he thought and kissed his teeth, 'too much pain for too little gain.'

"You know what," Tayo said, twisting his baby locks with his thumb and forefinger, "I don't know, you know what I mean,..... I really don't know" and he laughed.

"Yeah something else," Tayo added, turning to Michael, "you once said that someday they're going to write a book about us."

"Not us," Michael said, "me, cause I'm a Dan."

"Well whatever," Tayo replied, grinning at the reply, "but your wrong, even if someone could be bothered to write it, do you think anyone would want to read it. Nah all people want to read about is slackness batty rider, pom, pom, and foolishness, do you really think anyone could be bothered. They don't want to know the truth."

"Well," Michael said, smiling and shivering in just his Timberland shirt, "somebody will read it."

"Perhaps," Tayo replied, "and if it was written and if it was read, which I don't believe will ever happen, let's hope that this some-body understands it. I'd commission the work, just to get some of these armchair brothers and sisters off their backsides."

"I hear that," Michael said, "but now your the don, can't you do anything?"

"We'll have to see about that," Tayo answered, smiling, only then remembering the youth all those months ago who he had given his last pound to and his promise, 'I wonder,' he contemplated, 'if there's some truth to it, look at the things I've done....well......' and he sighed, 'but y'know what they say, old men dream dreams, but young men live them.'

Read Read if you want to stay alive:

This book is dedicated to :

A strong fighter for truth and justice:

Read **Waiting to Explode**: by Onyeka

Recommended Books

Destruction of Black Civilisation Chancellor Williams
Two Thousand Seasons Ayi Kwe Armah
The Healers Ayi kwe Armah
The Isis Papers Dr Francis Cress Wilson
African Holistic Health Lila B. Africa
Enemies a Clash Of Races Haki Madhubuti
Black Man of the Nile and his Family Dr Ben Johacanon
The Culture Bandits I and II Del Jones
The Art of Leadership Dr. Oba T Shaka
Black Power the Blueprint for Survival Dr. Amos Wilson
Soledad Brother George Jackson
Travels Oladah Equaino
Britons Ancient and Modern Macritche
The United Independent Compensatory Code System/ Text book
Neely Fuller Jr.
Spirited Woman Olayinka
Waiting to Explode Onyeka

website www.onyeka.co.uk